The
ISCARIOT
SANCTION

Also by Mark A. Latham and available from Titan Books

The Lazarus Gate

The
ISCARIOT
SANCTION

MARK A. LATHAM

TITAN BOOKS

The Iscariot Sanction
Print edition ISBN: 9781783296828
E-book edition ISBN: 9781783296835

Published by Titan Books
A division of Titan Publishing Group Ltd
144 Southwark Street, London SE1 0UP

First edition: September 2016
10 9 8 7 6 5 4 3 2 1

A CIP catalogue record for this title is available from the British Library.

Printed in the USA.

Did you enjoy this book? We love to hear from our readers.
Please email us at readerfeedback@titanemail.com or write to us at Reader
Feedback at the above address.

To receive advance information, news, competitions, and exclusive offers
online, please sign up for the Titan newsletter on our website:
www.titanbooks.com

PART 1

Hark! death is calling
While I speak to ye,
The jaw is falling,
The red cheek paling,
The strong limbs failing;
Ice with the warm blood mixing,
The eyeballs fixing.
Nine times goes the passing bell:
Ye merry souls, farewell.

ALFRED, LORD TENNYSON

ONE

The whore giggled as Lord de Montfort stroked her cheek. He had missed London of late. His visits were all too infrequent, and it was good to be back. There was nothing as important as family, after all. That did not mean, however, that he could not find some entertainment whilst fulfilling his duties in the capital, and there was no place where entertainment could be bought so readily as on the Ratcliff Highway.

Lord de Montfort helped the girl down from the hansom cab. At his signal the driver flicked the reins and departed, leaving his passengers standing on the cobbles. The hour was late and the weather inclement; no one was about, and even if they had been, no one would care.

'Are we going somewhere fancy, m'lord?' Her voice grated on de Montfort's nerves a little, but he let it pass.

'Of a sort. I have a place set aside for… special liaisons.'

She giggled again, an annoying snort preceding a rolling, childish laugh. De Montfort remembered how she had behaved when he'd first approached her—hard-faced and unobliging. His coin had done some of the work; his unique talents, and a few glasses of gin, had done the rest. Lord de Montfort was not a man for fumbling around with girls in a filthy East End alley, and so he had brought her here, to a quiet street in Seven Dials. As they walked arm-in-arm, the bang-tail's head leaned on his shoulder as she sighed drunkenly.

De Montfort looked up at the sky. There were hardly any stars visible any more as the deep crimson fire rippled overhead like liquid. He remembered the day that the sky had started to burn: it had been in 1872, the day of the Awakening; the day that de Montfort had torn free of the estimable shadow of his forebears and become something more than he'd ever dared hope. The great minds of the time had since been fixated on healing the world, of closing the Rift and ending the madness that swept the globe; but not he. De Montfort turned his eyes back to the street and smiled. He liked the fire in the sky—it felt like an eternal dawn, and it filled him with the same hope that a new day's light might bring to lesser men.

Just hours earlier, de Montfort had found himself in another vile area of the forsaken city. Deep within the Isle of Dogs, in a stinking slum, he had stridden into the House of Zhengming— the most iniquitous den of vice in the Empire. Lord de Montfort had not been there as a patron, to partake of the opium pipe, for such earthly pleasures were far beneath him these days. No, he had been there on business, to talk with a man whose tangled web of intrigue had made him indispensable to the plans of arch-criminal and law-bringer alike; to every tyrant and politician in the realm. Tsun Pen, 'the Artist'—a man who had earned a reputation as a self-effacing, loathsome master of lies and broker of intelligence. How de Montfort hated the Artist, but how he needed him…

De Montfort had steeled himself before entering the Artist's lair, for one never seemed to leave the House of Zhengming with a full hand, regardless of how well one played the game.

On this night, de Montfort had disembarked his carriage and entered the Artist's domain with far less than a full hand. His power, wealth and talents were of no use in this matter. Of all the Majestics created at the Awakening, only Tsun Pen had the infallible gift of foresight. If de Montfort's people were to stake their claim to the Empire, to wage a secret war against the rulers of Britain, they had to be certain their gamble would pay off. Only Tsun Pen could tell them that.

De Montfort followed Tsun Pen's guards into the opium den, stepping over the dreamers who lolled on cushions on the floor as they chased the dragon in the smoke. At the end of the room, Tsun Pen sat languidly on an ornate throne, set atop a raised dais. Where the low stage would once have sited a piano and bawdily dressed songstress, Tsun Pen now sat like an emperor of old, surveying his kingdom of darkness and depravity. The Artist ever had a feel for the dramatic. He dressed in the finest silks, and his black hair flowed long around his shoulders. His eyes were quick and cunning, observing everything and revealing nothing, while a sickly, sardonic smile seemed rarely to leave his features.

Lord de Montfort took an envelope from his breast pocket and held it out. At the merest nod of Tsun Pen's head, a servant took the envelope and began to count the money inside. The Artist was always surrounded by servants and burly henchmen— de Montfort mused that a man as hated as this wretch could not afford to take chances. For every fortune Tsun Pen helped to make, there were those whose lives he would destroy. Only the highest bidder could rely on Tsun Pen's assistance, or his integrity.

'Your predecessor asked me a question, and I have striven to answer it,' said the Artist, the vestiges of his Chinese accent softened to an almost aristocratic purr. 'Yet you must have eyes to see. Look there, and tell me if you are pleased with the result.' Tsun Pen waved a slender hand at the large rectangular object to his right—a canvas, some six feet high, covered by a dust sheet.

De Montfort stepped towards it. The Artist was notorious

for his cryptic messages, delivered through the medium of his paintings. Sometimes the glimpses of the future were vague and abstract; other times they were clear as day. De Montfort sought certainty on behalf of his people—of his master, though he hesitated to admit such—and he would brook no tricks this night. He pulled the sheet away and studied the painting, illuminated by the flickering Chinese lanterns that hung all around. De Montfort gasped.

He had his answer, it was clear. Victory, it seemed, was at hand. But there was something more; something less easily interpreted, which filled him with dread. He gazed at the canvas, searching for clues, for there was clearly a danger ahead—the Artist had laced this painted prophecy with a dire warning, a price for triumph that perhaps even de Montfort was not ready to pay. And there was an implication for his own part in the future—an implication that would surely not be lost on his master.

He turned on his heel and glared at the Artist. 'A simple "yes" would have sufficed,' he snapped.

'"For I dipt into the future, far as human eye could see, saw the Vision of the world, and all the wonder that would be,"' Tsun Pen said. 'Tennyson. Do you care for poetry?' De Montfort's glare gave its own answer, and the Artist sighed. 'The future is sometimes made clear to me; but I can assure you, "Lord" de Montfort, the path that takes us there is never simple. Your people asked a question, the answer is clear, is it not?' Tsun Pen's voice was soft, almost musical, but his mocking tone tested de Montfort's patience, as always.

'But this... what does it mean? How can this outcome be avoided?'

Tsun Pen looked to the servant who had finished counting the notes at last. The little celestial nodded to his master, answering an unspoken question. The Artist turned back to his customer and sighed lazily.

'In my line of business, speculation is a dangerous pastime; more dangerous, even, than handing out free advice. If you wish me to undertake more work, to commune with the fates once more on your behalf, then you know the fee.'

De Montfort allowed rage to well up inside him, revealing for an instant his true nature. He took two paces forward, fists clenched, and was met in an instant by three blades, held at his throat by Tsun Pen's guards. The Artist's smile broadened, and de Montfort checked himself.

'You understand, Tsun Pen, who I am? And whom I represent? You understand that these men of yours risk their pitiful lives by threatening me?'

'My lord, it appears that you have taken offence at my terms of business,' the Artist said, still smiling. 'I shall forgive the transgression, though, for I know how vexing it can be when all that you hold dear depends upon a wild throw of the dice. You have your answer, and if you persist upon the course that you have set, the outcome is clear. If you wish to commission further works, I will be waiting.'

I will be waiting. Was it de Montfort's imagination, or were those last words delivered with a devilish gleam in the eyes? He could scarce believe the Artist's audacity. De Montfort would have gladly torn apart all in the room if he thought it would uncover the answers he sought; but there was something unsettling about the Artist's certainty. Some trick, perhaps… this time, discretion would win out. But one day the Artist would get his just deserts— de Montfort was no soothsayer, but he saw that part of the future plain enough. Satisfied by these thoughts, he relaxed, and the guards lowered their wicked knives, visibly relieved.

At least they are terrified, de Montfort thought. *Good. They should be.*

'I… apologise for my quick temper. I will take the painting and complete our transaction. If there is more work to be done, I shall contact you presently. Rest assured, I always know where to find you.'

* * *

The whore giggled again. Sally, was that her name? Or was it Molly? De Montfort could not recall, and at this stage in their relationship, it mattered not.

He pressed her up against the rough brick wall of the cellar. She smelled of corruption, fitting right into the dark, dank chamber. He brushed his lips across her throat; squeezed her thigh just above her garter. He could feel the gooseflesh of her skin, the thrumming of the blood in her veins. His nerves jangled for a moment... he had to stay in control. She was his no longer.

'You're so cold, guv,' she squealed as his hand slipped beneath her bustle. 'I bet I can warm you up.'

'I'm afraid not,' said de Montfort, his voice as cold as his flesh. He withdrew half a step from the bang-tail. Her silly laugh repulsed him. He was drawn to the warmth of her body, but he was beyond carnal desire. He had his orders.

''Ere, what do you mean? Come on, lover, don't go shy on me now. I mean, I know you're a gent and all, but I can't be your first...'

The words died on her lips, along with her smile. De Montfort had removed his tinted spectacles, and allowed her to gaze into his eyes for the first time. The glasses must have seemed at first an affectation, but now the girl saw that they hid something peculiar. His eyes gleamed in the half-light, the way that torchlight shines off a fox's eyes. Like all de Montfort's kind, his shone violet.

'Oh, I don't mean to be coy,' he said. 'It's just that you aren't mine. You're for my friends—my cousins, actually.'

The wench suppressed a sob. De Montfort relaxed his hypnotic hold over her a fraction, allowing her to become abruptly aware of her precarious situation. She blinked and looked around, seeing the cellar as if for the first time, snagging her tousled hair on the rough mortar of the wall behind her.

'I want to leave now,' she said. 'This ain't what you paid for.'

As she made to move past de Montfort, he put a hand to her chest and pushed her back towards the wall, gently but firmly. Her eyes darted around, panicked.

De Montfort leaned in to her. 'My dear, if it is remuneration you desire, I am sure I can give you more than you bargained for; do not worry on that score.'

He reached past her with his free hand, and her eyes followed, widening as she noticed at last the heavy, studded door behind them. De Montfort unlatched it, opening it to reveal utter blackness beyond. A draught blew through the doorway, carrying with it the rank smell of damp earth and a strong, metallic tang that de Montfort could taste on the air, like carcasses in a butcher's market.

The girl's eyes grew wild. This was the kind of thing her friends whispered of in the doss-houses; the kind of thing that always happened to someone else, never to them. Only it was happening now, to her. There came from the dark void the sound of clinking chains, and a low, rumbling growl. Panic grew in the girl. She lashed out, but de Montfort was immovable as stone. She clawed at him, and managed to dig a nail into his face, where a lump of his pale white flesh peeled away beneath her fingernail, yet no blood spilled from the wound. He slammed her against the wall before turning his violet eyes upon her once again.

'Please...' she sobbed. Her shoulders sank. The best she could hope for was that his 'friends' would take their pleasure and turn her out onto the streets. But she must have known in her heart that this was not the game they were playing. De Montfort savoured the moment—the confused mess of defeat and resignation to a dark fate, coupled as always with the glimmer of hope that all men and women carried with them to the very end.

'Shh... enough of that. I would like nothing more than to ease your suffering. I am ashamed to say it is in my power to do so; but my kin are not like me. They need your fear.' He leaned close again, letting her smell the grave-scent that lay beneath his fine cologne and shirt-starch. He looked her in the eyes one last time. 'Fear... sweetens the meat.'

He flung the girl bodily through the door with a mighty sweep of his arm. Her scream echoed around the subterranean tunnels beyond, and was joined by bestial snarls. De Montfort shut the door against the noise, latching and barring it quickly. He put his back to the door and mopped his brow with a handkerchief.

'Degenerates...' he whispered, with distaste. 'But perhaps there is hope for them yet.'

He turned, calmness returning as the frenzied sounds subsided. De Montfort touched a hand to the aged wood, running his fingers over the iron studs. He recalled the words of the Artist, and smiled as he recited under his breath:

'Thou shalt hear the "Never, never," whisper'd by the phantom years; And a song from out the distance in the ringing of thine ears; And an eye shall vex thee, looking ancient kindness on thy pain. Turn thee, turn thee on thy pillow; get thee to thy rest again.'

De Montfort smiled thinly. Yes, one should never show Tsun Pen one's full hand.

EXTRACT FROM *THE NEW YORK TIMES*

16TH AUGUST 1858—The Fox family consisted of the mother and three sisters, one of whom, Mrs. Fish, was a widow. The rapping performances of the two youngest sisters, Catherine and Margaret Fox, gifted mediums, it seemed, commenced at Hydesville, an obscure village in Wayne County, New York, within a few miles of the spot where the Mormon apostle Joseph Smith found the Golden Plates. For some time their art was the wonder of that neighbourhood, and crowds were wont to collect, chiefly on Sundays, to witness its exercise. But somehow the miracle grew unpopular, and the family removed to Rochester, where their peculiar gift soon began to attract attention. Strange stories were told of secrets revealed, and fates foretold. Each of the sisters was a medium, through whose agency the spirits of the dead conveyed information by alphabetic raps on the floor and upon tables. Committees of leading citizens were appointed, who reported that they heard sounds, but could not tell whence they came. To be sure, there were not lacking statements of fraud discovered and exposed, but the public ear was never open to this side of the question. It craved miracles, and got them in abundance.

The extent to which table-rapping has been carried, not only in this country but in Europe, is one of the greatest marvels of the century; and the phenomena which were first discovered by this family are still a puzzle to philosophers.

TWO

'Everything is ready as you requested, sir,' said Mrs. Bailey. She sounded weary. She had been working all day to dress the drawing room for Sir Arthur Furnival's latest soirée. Velvet drapes ran floor to ceiling, gathered double like something from the Lyceum stage, while long tables were adorned with black cloths and silver candlesticks were dotted about the room, supporting a hundred candles.

'Splendid!' Sir Arthur replied. 'That will be all for now, Mrs. Bailey. My thanks again for working so hard at such short notice.'

The middle-aged woman made a small curtsey and left the room. Sir Arthur continued fiddling with his cravat, when finally he saw in the mirror his valet enter the room.

'Ah, Jenkins, there you are. Be a good fellow and help with this cravat. It really is proving quite irksome today.'

Jenkins looked grave, and strode forward with a letter in his hand. 'I'm terribly sorry, sir,' he said, 'but I think preparations might have to wait. This just came for you.'

Sir Arthur took the letter, and knew instantly what it was.

The wax seal on the envelope was imprinted with a cameo of Apollo, and that could mean only one thing. He tore it open while Jenkins adjusted the cravat. Within moments he looked quite dapper again, but his spirits were somewhat deflated.

'I think you had better send apologies to my guests, Jenkins,' said Sir Arthur. 'I simply can't conduct a séance the day before an assignment.'

'Of course, sir. It does so take it out of you at the best of times, if you don't mind me saying.'

'Oh, don't fuss, Jenkins,' Sir Arthur chided. But his valet was right. Sir Arthur's powers as a medium were celebrated amongst London's intelligentsia, but it was a dangerous path that he trod. And a lonely one at that—beyond the séances and club meetings, he was shunned by society, as were all his kind. And normal folk were right to do so, for since the Awakening the path of the psychic had proven to be fraught with danger. How he longed for those days when he'd simply been the awkward boy with 'unusual' talents. It had been frightening at the time, but at least then the world had been ordinary. Who would not crave a little of the ordinary in these troubled times? But what was done was done. He tried to push such thoughts aside, and focus on the here and now. 'By the way, Jenkins,' he said at last, 'did you enquire as to who my assistant might be this time?' Over the years, Jenkins had almost become as much a member of Apollo Lycea as Sir Arthur himself, and his inside track with the club's messengers and servants proved most useful.

'Yes sir,' and again Jenkins looked most serious. 'It is Miss Hardwick, sir.'

Sir Arthur sighed, and sat down in his favourite armchair to read the letter more carefully. 'After the last time, I'm surprised the old goat lets his daughter anywhere near me. Although it was she who damn near got me killed.'

'And saved your life, sir,' Jenkins reminded his master, helpfully.

'Yes, that too,' Sir Arthur muttered. He looked up at his valet, a sense of foreboding creeping over him. 'I need to prepare myself.

Send word to the guests first; tell Mrs. Bailey she is excused for the evening, and give her my apologies. In fact, best not mention that the séance is cancelled; the poor woman has worked very hard today. And then prepare my case.'

'Very good, sir. You'll be needing etherium, I take it? How much shall I pack?'

Sir Arthur's eyes blazed for an instant before he replied, coolly, 'If they're sending me out with Lillian Hardwick, you'd best pack it all.'

SOUTH KENSINGTON, LONDON

The twenty-one candles atop Lillian Hardwick's cake had barely stopped smouldering when the telegram arrived. Silence had descended upon the little dining room, broken only by the occasional clattering of plates as the servants cleared the table.

Whilst the party guests sat uncomfortably next door in awkward silence, Dora stood at the foot of the stairs in the hallway that now seemed too large and empty for her, wringing her hands with worry for her only daughter. She had urged Lillian not to go; not right away at least. But her pleas had fallen on deaf ears. Lillian was her father's daughter, and duty always came before... before anything, really.

Lillian finally emerged onto the landing. She wore a severe black uniform, which replaced the crimson party gown she had been so reluctant to wear. Dora hated the way her daughter dressed for her work—hated the fact that she had to do such work at all—but there was no point in arguing the point again. Instead she steeled herself for the goodbyes, and watched resignedly as her beautiful girl descended the stairs. Dora pretended not to notice that Lillian scarcely looked her in the eye. When she stepped into the hall, Dora instinctively fussed over her daughter's hair, trying to push a loose, dark brown ringlet back beneath her hat. Lillian, just as instinctively, leaned away. Dora wondered, as she often did, when exactly Lillian had stopped being her carefree little girl. Looking at the agent before her, bedecked in a fitted black dress and stern coatee, Mrs. Hardwick wondered if her daughter had ever been the way she remembered at all.

'Will you not at least say a proper goodbye to our guests?' Dora asked, trying once more to delay her daughter's departure, on this day of all days. 'Savill has come all the way from Kedleston, after all.'

'Mama,' replied Lillian, firmly, 'there is not one of our guests who would approve of my occupation, nor even of my attire. I will ask you to say my goodbyes for me, and to apologise for me if you desire. And as for Savill, if we were ever to be a match, do you think it would really work? Could he be husband to an agent of the Crown?'

'Perhaps he would not have to be, dearest, if…'

'If I settled down, had his children, and gave up this foolishness?' Lillian's hazel eyes flashed for an instant. Dora knew that Lillian found her match-making and fussing tiresome, but what else could she do when her only daughter seemed intent on following her father and brother into danger? 'We've had this conversation before, Mother,' Lillian said, somewhat more gently, 'and we both know how it ends. Now, I have received a summons that I cannot ignore—won't you wish me luck?'

Dora Hardwick's shoulders sagged, once more defeated by her daughter's stubbornness. 'Of course. Lillian, I do worry so… please be careful.'

'I will, Mama,' Lillian replied, stooping to kiss her mother's cheek. As she did so, Dora whispered one last request into her daughter's ear:

'Do not follow Sir Arthur blindly. Please… he is a dangerous man.'

Lillian straightened. A confident smile played upon her lips, accompanied by the almost haughty expression that she had used since childhood to shield herself from the judgement of others. Yet to her mother, the façade was betrayed by the sad look in her eyes.

'I'm a dangerous woman, Mama,' she replied.

Lieutenant John Hardwick skirted the edge of the gloomy factory floor with practised grace. The noise of smelting, grinding and hammering was infernal. Sparks rained down onto gigantic conveyor belts, providing intermittent illumination. Chains rattled overhead as they slackened from enormous pulleys; coal furnaces belched fumes as they powered huge, static steam engines, and burly workmen toiled relentlessly. John could barely hear himself think, though he was glad that the noise and grimy darkness covered his infiltration.

The munitions factory was supposed to be inoperative. For over a month, no shipments had reached the War Office stores from this, their biggest supplier in Cheshire. Letters of bankruptcy had been filed from the factory's owners, Messrs. Hopkirk and Myerscough. The closure of the plant should have been little more than an administrative footnote in the quartermasters' ledgers. Until last week, when Corporal Moreton of the Hyde Yeomanry had been sent to deliver papers to the owners, and was never heard from again. Now the Order of Apollo was involved, and the evidence was overwhelming. Freight trains to and from Hyde had been loaded and unloaded at the factory every day this past month; so where were the products of all this toil?

John watched from the gloom as dozens of sweating, soot-blackened workers filled moulds with molten lead. Artillery shells, cast by the hundred, heading to the black market. John scowled. As if the world wasn't in enough trouble from the Riftborn, that warmongers and crooks should also conspire to weaken the Empire and strengthen its enemies.

John kept to the shadows as best he could, treading lightly past gigantic stacks of crates and sacks. He stopped occasionally to peek into an open crate or peer under a loose tarpaulin upon a wagon, only to confirm matters. Every cart was laden with shrapnel shells, cases of bullets or kegs of powder.

He crept towards a black iron staircase that rose up into the even blacker heights of the building. John bounded silently up the first few stairs. Almost too late, he realised he had allowed his mind to stray with feelings of righteous indignation, and had been inattentive. The flare of a lucifer had registered only as John cleared the first few steps. In the hollow behind the staircase, a soot-faced factory worker had been loitering, sparking up a cigarette, and he stared at John from between the gaps of the metal treads.

The labourer stepped out of the shadows. John froze instinctively.

'Now then, sir,' the man said, in an abrasive Mancunian twang, 'I don't think the boss is in. What can we do you for?' His question was fair, but his tone was adversarial.

John straightened and turned around, taking a few steps down towards the man. 'Well, my good man...' he began, but did not finish. Instead, he pounced forward and struck the man in the windpipe, before slipping around behind him and wrapping his arm around the labourer's throat. He squeezed until the man passed out, blue-faced.

That was like something Lillian would do, he mused. John was not usually one for violent confrontation, though he fancied himself a more than capable fighter. His sister, however, was a noted wildcat, and deuced formidable with it.

Now, John scanned the vicinity until he was certain no one else had seen or heard any commotion, and dragged the unconscious man to the nearest pile of crates, covering him with a tarpaulin before continuing on his way.

John carried on up the stairs, more cautiously this time, circling around the edge of the sweltering factory floor to a dizzying height. At the top of the stairway was a long, thin catwalk, with a full view of the manufacturing operation on one side. From this vantage point he watched the employees scurrying like worker ants, illuminated by the flickering red light of the furnaces, then turned his attention to the row of doors ahead.

He walked past the first door, marked 'Foreman', and stopped at the second, marked 'General Office'. Once he was certain there was no one about, he opened the door and slipped into the darkened room.

THREE

'Same to you n' all, you stuck-up cow!'

The dolly-mop took her leave of Lillian Hardwick, still chuntering in a gin-slurred cant as she pushed through a group of bemused Jack-tars and back into the smoky embrace of the Jolly Sailor public house.

Sir Arthur braced himself as Lillian, face hard and eyes ablaze, strode back to him, trying her best to ignore the taunts and unsavoury jeers of the sailors and dockers.

'So this is all I am worth?' Lillian snapped. 'I was assigned to help you because a woman's touch might persuade these... these bang-tails... to be more free with their information? Perhaps you would have more luck extracting information if you came back later and paid the going rate.'

'Don't be vulgar, Lillian,' Arthur chided. But in a way, she was right. She'd been waiting a long time for her father to send her on a more taxing assignment, but this one was ill thought-out. The prostitutes of the Ratcliff Highway would not freely speak with those in authority, and certainly not in the open, beneath the watchful gaze of their cash-carriers, who loitered in the shaded alleyways nearby.

'We're no better at interviewing these wretches than the police.' Lillian nodded towards the two constables sent to escort them through the arterial narrows that branched from the notorious highway.

'This investigation is out of the hands of the police now, and into ours. Where the police have failed to find this mysterious killer, Apollo Lycea hope a Majestic will succeed.'

'I do not wish to cast aspersions upon your psychical prowess, Arthur, but this is the last resort. You've dragged me to every place of ill repute for miles about, and for what? A fine way to spend a birthday.'

'Birthday? Oh, damn it, Lillian, I forgot—'

'I was not trying to make you feel guilty. I just meant that… well, suddenly tea in the company of gentlefolk doesn't seem so terrible.'

Arthur turned away, trying not to smirk at that. He could imagine that for Lillian Hardwick even trawling these low alleys was preferable to 'tea with gentlefolk'. Nonetheless, he resolved to send Jenkins out later to buy Lillian a present.

He looked up at the sky. They had seen the worst of London's gin-palaces and bawdy-houses that afternoon, from the notorious White Swan to the doss-houses of Shadwell, and now it was getting late—these days it was never truly dark in London, which was not as reassuring as it sounded, especially to a Majestic. One could only tell that night was falling when the sun's wan light slowly transformed into the crimson glow that permeated the darkness, and the devilish fire that licked at the clouds became more prominent. Arthur felt the fearful gnawing at the back of his mind growing more insistent as the hour drew later and the burning sky grew hotter. Other thoughts and other voices fought to enter his mind. He kept those doors locked.

'There are other means of finding what we need,' he said, keeping his esoteric worries to himself. 'But without some physical link to the missing girl, I'm afraid my skills are limited.'

They had spent hours trawling the pubs known to have been frequented by one Molly Goodheart. The unfortunate had gone missing almost two months before, but no one had seen fit to report it until a spate of similar disappearances had made the newspapers. Why these acts—not uncommon in the East End— had drawn the attention of Apollo Lycea was anyone's guess. Arthur had learned not to question the leaders of the Order on such matters. On the streets, however, uncertainty over the culprits' identity brought fear of reprisals for common folk, and no one would admit to even knowing the girl.

Lillian looked thoughtful. Arthur frowned—with that look usually came trouble.

She turned abruptly, staring into the nearest alley where a group of four men spoke in hushed tones, spitting plugs of tobacco onto the already filthy pavement. Then she was off, striding purposefully towards the men, who saw her coming and looked around skittishly. Arthur hurried after her.

''Allo, missy,' said one of the men, a grin of bravado on his flat features.

'Lookin' for a change o' career, are ye?' said another. 'Know just the fella who can 'elp you with that.' A round of guffaws rippled through the group.

Lillian hadn't broken stride. Arthur had hoped Lillian would keep a cool head in such environs. He should have known better.

'That's not all I can help you with, love,' sneered another man, his grin revealing an uneven row of sparse yellow-and-black teeth.

The fourth man had said nothing. He stood further back, tall hat shading his features, quick eyes shining in the light from the reddening sky. He had menace about him—a ringleader. Lillian headed straight for him.

Laughs died on the lips of the three hangers-on as Lillian stepped through their circle and drove a fist into the nose of the quiet man, who staggered backwards yelping. The thug with the bad teeth put a hand on Lillian, and almost lost it as she twisted him around so violently everyone nearby heard his wrist crack. She spun him about, slamming his face into the brick wall, before turning her back on the others and marching straight to the leader once more. Arthur knew she was trusting him to protect her back. He drew his pistol, and stepped between Lillian and the three thugs, who froze and eyed him warily. Behind them, Arthur saw that Lillian's antics had caused quite a stir in the street, and the two policemen were already struggling to maintain order. He glanced over his shoulder to see how Lillian fared.

The ringleader growled, 'I'll kill you, you filthy—'

Lillian kicked the man's crotch so viciously that he could not complete his insult. He dropped to one knee, but Lillian dragged him up by his throat and pushed him to the wall, before drawing a long, silver pin from her hat, and placing its gleaming point to the man's eye.

'You... you can't...'

'Can't what? Torture you? Beat you? Tell me, is that because I'm the law, or because I'm a woman?' The needle pricked at the sagging flesh beneath the man's left eye, and he took on an aspect of panic, swallowing hard. 'I assure you, you are wrong on both counts.'

'Whatever you're doing, Lillian, do it quickly,' Arthur warned. He was standing beside her now, and the three men at the end of the alley were reluctant to leave their boss. Arthur doubted very much that they were unarmed.

'Molly Goodheart,' Lillian said. 'One of yours?'

'Never 'eard of her,' the man said.

Quick as a flash, Lillian pulled the sharpened hairpin away from the man's eye, and pushed it through his earlobe, yanking him away from the wall, leading him at a stoop almost like a farmer leading a prize bull.

'Molly Goodheart,' she said again. 'Who knew her? Who was her cash-carrier? Speak up, or the next time your friends see you, you shall be missing a few vital parts.'

The man screamed with pain and impotent rage. One of his accomplices moved forwards, but Sir Arthur waved the gun at him and he backed away again.

'All right, all right. I swear it weren't me. But I saw her. I saw her the night she went missin'; saw her get into a cab with a gent.'

'Who?'

'I dunno, some nob.'

With each question, Lillian tugged up and down on the hairpin. Arthur winced at the man's shrill cries.

'The cabbie, then. Local man?' Lillian asked.

'Dresden,' the man gasped. 'Jeremiah Dresden, off Butcher Row. That's all I know, woman—leave me be!'

Lillian withdrew the pin and pushed the man away. 'There, that wasn't so difficult, was it? Sir Arthur, would you mind awfully checking if this man is telling the truth.'

She stepped forward and took the gun from Arthur, keeping an eye on the shifty trio. Arthur cracked his fingers and stepped towards the cowed leader, one hand outstretched, the other held to his temple.

The thug backed away as a look of dim comprehension crossed his features. Arthur feigned a look of intense concentration, half-closed his eyes, and moved forward slowly, until his hand almost touched the man's forehead.

'Mercy, no!' he shouted. 'You're one o' them! I swear I'm tellin' the truth. I swear! Ain't no need to scramble me brains.'

Arthur opened his eyes. 'No?' His skills at telepathy were almost non-existent, but the thugs were not to know that.

The man shook his head and sunk to his knees. 'You already made me a grass; don't go doin' that ungodly stuff to me.'

'Very well,' said Arthur, haughtily. 'But I have your measure now, sir. I could find you anywhere, blindfold in the dark. And I'll be sure to bring her with me.' He jerked his head towards Lillian.

The man nodded fearfully, and Arthur left him kneeling in the dirt. Police whistles sounded in the distance as more officers arrived to break up the scuffles outside the Jolly Sailor. Sir Arthur and Lillian pushed past the three underlings, who parted warily, as if seeing Sir Arthur in a whole new light.

'You played your part wonderfully, Sir Arthur,' said Lillian, when they were out of earshot. She handed him back his pistol.

'Well, I am a Majestic,' Sir Arthur said. 'I know the role well.'

'Yes, well, there's no point taking any unnecessary risks. Although he didn't have to know that.'

'Unnecessary...' Arthur said, flabbergasted, waving a hand to indicate the fighting still erupting in the street.

Lillian began walking up the street, ignoring the trouble she had incited.

'And where are you off to now?' Arthur called after her.

'To catch a cab,' she replied, looking back over her shoulder at him with a wicked grin.

Sir Arthur Furnival raised his hands in resignation and followed her, as he always did.

John opened the shutter of his dark-lantern as much as he dared, casting a narrow beam of light around the windowless room. The office was ill kept and dirty, the desk scattered with papers. John looked through the only set of drawers in the room, finding them stuffed to bursting with accounts books and bills of lading and ledgers, seemingly without order.

He rifled through the papers, scouring them for some clue. There were copies of receipts for steel from factories in Sheffield, and coal from as far afield as Newcastle, which John folded neatly and slipped into his pocket. A docket for the delivery of five hundred howitzer shells to a dockyard in Hull was likewise secreted away. He scowled when he found a similar dispatch note, and saw that the recipient was a private individual in Austria. The desk drawers contained several demands from the War Office for unfulfilled orders. Finally, he found a delivery note, positioned beneath a mould-filled teacup, and gave a smile of satisfaction.

'Thursday, 16th October. A delivery of twenty-one carts of guncotton, three carts of gunpowder, and two carts of "sundries",' he read aloud.

These were supplies delivered to the factory for the

manufacturing process. John had no idea what the 'sundries' were, but he intended to find out. He scanned the right-hand column of the note marked 'delivery area'. All of the powder had been dropped off at the warehouse adjacent to the factory. All except for the mysterious extra two carts, which had been taken to the cellars.

John shuttered the lantern completely and slipped out of the office. He was about to head back to the stairs, but froze as a pair of shadows slid along the far wall, warped silhouettes thrown against the brick by blood-red light from the smelters.

A moment later, John saw the unmistakeable forms of two men. John moved away as quickly as he dared to the door at the end of the catwalk. He guessed from the chill draught emanating from it that it led outside, but he did not know for sure. There was no other option.

The cold air hit him, a merciful change from the smoke and heat of the factory behind. John stood on a platform atop a spindly iron fire escape, which clung tenaciously to the side of the massive building like ancient ivy. Left and right, huge chimney-stacks belched thick, black smoke into the chill air. So far from the chaos of the city, the skies did not burn with dreadful ethereal fire, and yet the rare treat was spoiled by the smoke from the forges, which blotted out the stars and moon. Beyond the iron stair, the roofs of a dozen huge storage sheds and warehouses stretched out for half a mile or more, before meeting a thick line of black trees.

John knew he should make his way to ground level—he had what he needed, for now, at least. He should return to London at the earliest opportunity. But he felt that the owners of this factory had committed a great wrong; his indignation and curiosity got the better of him.

He stooped at the door, pressing his eye to the keyhole. At first there was nothing to be seen—it was dark inside and out of the factory—but when his eyes adjusted, he saw two figures moving around outside the office door. One of the figures stepped out of view, and a brighter light soon illuminated the other man. His companion must have lit a lamp inside the office.

The man who waited outside the office was impatient. He checked his pocket-watch, then turned around to face the factory floor. John made a mental note of his features; he was a pale young man of noble bearing, with thin black moustaches and a rather affected little beard. The second man—a shorter, older fellow—stepped out of the office, and the two began to exchange words. The taller man became agitated, gesticulating pointedly, before turning to stare out below him, hawk-like.

They've discovered the dockets are missing.

John had no sooner thought it than the tall man spun on his heel and fixed the outer door with such a penetrating gaze that John held his breath. The man took a step forward, and craned his neck like some predatory creature, staring at the door intently, until the smaller man seemed compelled to cease his agitated chatter and focus on the door also. John had the most irrational, creeping sense that the tall man was not only looking towards the door, but at the keyhole; *through* the keyhole, right at him. There was only one explanation...

Majestic.

John moved quickly and noiselessly from the door, and stole down the stairs. He reached a lower platform, but did not have time to descend the next flight before the door above opened, accompanied by the thrumming of machinery from within, and followed by a footfall on the iron decking above John's head.

'My lord,' came a nervous voice from above, 'I think you are being paranoid. I must have misplaced the dockets, that is all.'

'Like you misplaced my caskets?' came another voice, cold and assured. 'Your office is as untidy as your mind, Hopkirk, and I will take no more chances.'

Footsteps rang softly on the iron stairs as someone began the descent to John's hiding place. John saw a pair of shiny black shoes through the gaps in the treads, and a pair of mud-splattered gaiters protruding beneath black trousers.

'I told you, my lord,' said Hopkirk, 'no one could have got in. I've only been gone half an hour; most like I simply mislaid the dockets. As you said, I am a man of untidy habits, and—'

'Stop your babbling!'

Hopkirk was silent at once, and advanced no further.

John held his breath, but he knew he could not evade discovery. He didn't like working with Majestics, but now he rather wished Sir Arthur Furnival was present, to mask him from the uncanny senses of the man on the stairs. John set down the lantern as quietly as he could, and pulled his gun from the holster at his breast. At this stage, he'd be glad of anyone to watch his back. Even Lillian, if their father would ever allow her to stand in harm's way.

The tall man took a few more steps before stopping, straining to hear his prey, or perhaps to divine the presence of intruders in some other, less natural manner.

'I know you're there,' he said, his voice crisp and aristocratic. He took two slow, deliberate steps. 'Who is... Lillian?'

John almost cursed out loud at his own carelessness. He focused hard, trying to mask his thoughts from the Majestic's probing.

'Why don't you come out of the shadows and face me like a man?' the tall man goaded.

'A fine idea.' John stepped from behind the stair rail, gun cocked and aimed at his adversary. Hopkirk, standing at the top of the stairs, gave a high-pitched whine.

The tall man merely smiled, and glowered at John through tinted spectacles. 'You have taken something from me,' he said. 'They are perhaps of little import, but it's the principle of the thing, you understand. Hand them over, and you may leave.'

'Returning to London with evidence of a crime is one thing,' John said, 'but apprehending the culprit is quite another. It's the principle of the thing, Lord...?'

'De Montfort,' the man said flatly. His grin broadened.

'Enough talking. I think it better that you come with me, one way or another.'

In a trice, de Montfort was no longer on the step in front of him, but beside him, striking a blow that sent John staggering backwards towards the railings. John squeezed the trigger as he flailed back, and heard Hopkirk scream. John dimly comprehended the fat little man hopping on one leg upon the top landing before crumpling to the walkway, out of sight.

A vice-like hand in a black leather glove gripped John's wrist; another hand tightened around his throat. De Montfort hoisted John from his feet and pressed him back over the railing. His strength was devilish. John's head tipped back, and he saw a darkened alley some four storeys below.

There was no time to lose. John wrapped his right foot around the crook of de Montfort's knee, and let go of the rail. The sensation that they might both fall caused de Montfort's grip to slacken, just a fraction. Just enough.

John brought his hand up between them, the uppercut cracking into the man's jaw. It felt like hitting a brick wall. The aristocrat barely flinched. John kicked his heel into the back of de Montfort's left knee. The tall man twisted back a little, giving John an inch to push off the railing. They hurtled away from the precipice, crashing into a metal stair post.

De Montfort twisted John's arm so hard that he dropped the revolver. John replied by thrusting an elbow into de Montfort's nose, and driving a knee into his midriff. The tall man finally relinquished his hold on John's throat, and John took a gasp of air, which was quickly expelled again as de Montfort dealt him a hooking blow to the gut.

John struggled to stay upright, but spied his gun upon the platform and dived for it. As his fingertips touched the cold steel, de Montfort gave him a hard shove, sending him hurtling down a flight of stairs to the next level, while the gun spun over the edge of the gantry and down into the shadows below.

John hit the floor hard, pain shooting through his legs. Head spinning, he pushed himself upright, summoning all of his strength, remembering his training. Never allow yourself to be put on the back foot. Always get up; always attack.

He spun to face his opponent, who wasn't there.

A brutal jab came from nowhere, crunching into John's ribs. De Montfort had somehow cleared the flight of stairs and was already on the offensive. John raised a forearm to block another strike, and winced as pain flared though his bruised arm. He hoped it wasn't broken.

'You could have walked away from this,' snarled the aristocrat.

'So could you.'

With a flick of his wrist, a knife flashed from up his sleeve, and John punched it into de Montfort's shoulder, withdrew it, and slashed out, cutting the tall man's porcelain-white face.

De Montfort staggered back two paces. No blood issued from the wounds. John frowned in disbelief.

At that hesitation, de Montfort surged forward, shoving John hard in the chest and sending him toppling over the railing. John reached out desperately, catching the edge of the platform with his left hand, his right useless with the spring-loaded knife in the way. He looked up at de Montfort, who had stooped down to pick up a few scattered items that had fallen from John's pockets. In his hand, de Montfort now held a small, ivory card.

'Lieutenant John Hardwick, The Apollonian Club.' De Montfort smirked. 'I wondered how long it would take the Order to come calling. Oh, I do hope you're a relative of Lord Hardwick—that will make this all the more personal, don't you think? I hear he's quite masterful when he's angry.'

John grunted with pain, and tried to shake the knife loose so he could get a grip on the metal ledge. He was dimly aware of a shrieking voice from somewhere overhead wailing: 'He shot me; I am shot, sir!' And then de Montfort trod on John's hand, twisting a boot-heel into his fingers.

John gritted his teeth against the pain, and looked about desperately for some escape. There was none. De Montfort stamped again, and this time John's fingers betrayed him. He let go, and plummeted to the ground.

John called upon his training once more, letting his body go limp as the wind whistled past his ears. When he hit the ground, it gave beneath him, enough to absorb some of the impact, and bounce him momentarily upwards before he crunched to a halt. His head spun. He believed he could make out de Montfort's face, gleaming in the darkness above. Then he heard an ominous cracking and creaking, like the timbers of a wooden ship taking water, and he realised he was atop a pair of huge cellar doors. Half-rotten, wooden cellar doors.

They gave way beneath him. Cold, damp air that tasted of iron and old earth filled his lungs, before he hit a hard, wet floor, and consciousness was knocked from him.

FOUR

The cabman's wife cuffed her husband once more about the head. Lillian disguised a smirk at the man's discomfort. Mrs. Dresden, it seemed, was a formidable woman, broad of features, blunt of opinion, and possessed of a strength earned from working the mangle all day long. Jeremiah Dresden, by contrast, was the sort of fellow who stayed quiet whatever the situation, keeping his own counsel whether it was wise to do so, or foolish.

'You tell this lady an' her fine gen'leman what you were doing carting a hussy about at all hours,' Mrs. Dresden barked. 'And tell me while you're about it. I didn't see no extra shilling for the private hire, and I wouldn'a wanted it, neither, had it come about by some disrep'uble means.' The woman gave an awkward curtsey towards Lillian and her fine gentleman, seeking their approbation.

'It's why I didn't tell you 'bout it, woman,' said Dresden, sheepishly. 'I knew how you'd carry on if'n you knew. But we needed the money.'

'And where is the money, Jeremiah Dresden?' his wife glowered. 'I see no coin, and now we have fine folk knockin' on our door, askin' us about missing harlots. Why, I curse the day we married!' She reddened, perhaps fearing she had said more than she could rescind, once this trouble was done with and life returned to normal. Dresden merely stared at his feet.

'Please, madam,' Lillian said, 'I'm sure I speak for both Sir Arthur and myself when I say that we make no judgement on your husband or upon your household. What a man must do to earn a living in these difficult times is his own business. No one is saying that Mr. Dresden was cavorting with ladies of disrepute, nor that he had any hand in the... murder... of this unfortunate young girl, barely more than a child, God rest her.' Lillian emphasised the words 'disrepute', 'murder', and 'child', which had the effect of turning Mr. Dresden quite pale. His wife's sharp eyes darted towards him so fixedly that, had she been a Majestic, her husband would have been stricken senseless where he stood.

'Murder...' he said, dumbly.

'Oh indeed,' Lillian continued. 'It is almost certainly murder. Perhaps many would not have noticed the loss of another such lowly soul, but this one has been noticed, and has come to the attention of our agency.'

'Agency?' asked Dresden, tremulously.

'A very special agency,' Arthur interjected. 'We report to Lord Hardwick himself; perhaps you have heard of him.' Now it was Mrs. Dresden's turn to pale—everyone had heard of Marcus Hardwick. The former head of the War Office, a man who had been given his title by Gladstone, on the Queen's orders, and tasked with restoring order after the devastating effects of the Awakening. The man who, it was whispered, had ordered a thousand tortured souls to vanish without a trace for the 'greater good', and who fought every day to destroy the Riftborn that preyed on the innocents of the Empire. At mention of his name, Mr. Dresden gulped.

'I don't want no trouble,' he stammered. 'I took the job, I don't deny it, because the gent paid cash up front. I drove him around for a couple o' hours, and I turned a blind eye to his doings, as is the cabman's code. Everyone does it, from time to time, when pickings is slim.'

'Did the gentleman give a name?' Lillian grew impatient. It

seemed that Dresden was stalling for time, perhaps so that his dull mind could come up with some cock-and-bull story.

'No, but they never does.'

'So you have done this more than once?' she said. 'It is, of course, against the law to engage a hansom on these terms. A fine is the usual punishment, but given the seriousness of the crime...'

'Please, there's no need for that. I'll help as best I can, but I can't really remember... it's been a long while, you see, and—'

'Calm yourself, Mr. Dresden,' Sir Arthur said. 'My companion, Agent Hardwick, is simply very eager to get to the bottom of this affair, by whatever means necessary.'

Dresden looked from Sir Arthur to Lillian. 'Hardwick?' he croaked.

'My father would not come all the way out here in person,' said Lillian, masking her annoyance at the name-dropping. 'But we do have the power to summon a constable, and take you to him. If we do that, Mr. Dresden, he will have his Majestics help you remember. It would be a great help if you were to comply with them, but it is not without... risks.'

'Mercy!' Mrs. Dresden whispered, and sat down at once on a kitchen chair.

'Wait... wait,' Dresden said. 'I think it's coming back to me. When I picked 'im up, the lamplighters had just done their rounds. I think I did catch sight of his face in the light, just the once.'

'And?' Lillian prompted.

'Tall chap. Thin, too. Little black beard and skin pale as you like. Funny spectacles, he wore.'

'Funny how?'

'Coloured glass, like. Red... or maybe purple. The kind you sometimes see blind folks wearin'. But he weren't blind.'

'And you're sure he was a gentleman?' Arthur asked.

'Aye, sure as I can be. He spoke all proper, like yourself, sir, only more so, if you take my meaning. And the girl...' He paused.

'What about her?' Lillian snapped.

'She... she called him "my lord".'

Lillian looked to Sir Arthur, who frowned. It could have been an affectation, a term of flattery between a bang-tail and her fare; but if not... it was a clue.

'Where you last saw this man, and the girl he was with?' Lillian said pointedly.

Dresden paused. His wife prodded him sharply in the ribs.

'Seven Dials,' he said at last, sullenly. 'I dropped 'em at Little Earl Street, and they headed up the alley behind the chandler's shop.'

'Is there anything else you can tell us?'

'No, miss. I swear that's all I know. I came straight home, and that was that.'

'You did not take the man anywhere else, except between the Ratcliff Highway and Seven Dials?'

Dresden froze for a moment. Lillian saw something in his eyes—fear, she thought. 'No miss.'

'You are quite sure?'

'Yes miss.'

Sir Arthur handed his card to the cabbie. 'Mr. Dresden, you have been most helpful. If you remember anything else that may be of use—any detail, no matter how small—please do send a message to my club. If we have further questions... well, you'll hear from us, in due course.'

Dresden twitched at that. As he took the card, his fingertips brushed against Sir Arthur's. Lillian noticed that Arthur had removed his gloves, which he rarely did. Dresden flinched as he took the card, as though some electrical charge had passed between the two men. He looked momentarily frantic, eyes skittish.

Arthur turned, and looked towards the back of the room, at an open door through which Lillian could see a poky hall.

'Arthur?'

Arthur said nothing, but marched through the door immediately. By the time Dresden and his wife mustered a protest, Arthur's footsteps could be heard on the stairs. Dresden rushed after him, Lillian close behind, the man's wife hesitantly bringing up the rear.

Lillian followed Dresden into a small bedroom. The man had stopped, half-blocking the doorway, and so Lillian pushed past him, and saw that he was gawping at Arthur, dumbfounded.

Arthur held a large box. By his feet, a rug had been thrown back, and two loose boards removed. Sir Arthur Furnival was like a one-man divining rod at times.

'Now, what do we have here?' Arthur said, opening the tin and rifling through the contents. 'Calling cards, gentleman's gloves, a silver watch, and... this.' He held up a small handkerchief, and then winced as some premonition came over him.

'How did you—' Dresden started.

'I warned you about my father's Majestics,' Lillian said. 'Now, what's all this?'

'Nothing... much,' he gulped. 'A few keepsakes, s'all. Dropped in the cab, like, and never claimed.'

'And what does the cabman's code say about lost items, Mr. Dresden?'

'I... um...' Dresden was defeated. Even if his crimes were small, he had become embroiled in a bad business, and now crumbled beneath the hard stares of two agents of the Crown, not to mention his formidable wife.

'Lillian,' Arthur said. 'This was hers. And the man she was with that night... he is not a man to be trifled with. I can feel it.'

'Well, he was lying when he said he took the gentleman nowhere else,' Arthur said, as he and Lillian walked along Butcher Row, attracting nervous and curious glances from the impoverished denizens.

'Really, Arthur, I don't require your powers to see that. The real question is, why? I'd wager he was paid more than a few extra shillings for his silence.'

'No,' said Arthur. 'I don't believe it was out of loyalty to a paymaster; he was frightened.'

'Our man threatened him, then.'

'Perhaps, though I sense it was something more. Maybe we'll

find our answers in Seven Dials. Or maybe we'll have to follow through on your threat and bring Dresden in.'

Lillian winced inwardly. She would betray no weakness to Arthur, but she did not relish the thought of condemning Dresden to the attentions of the Nightwatch. The Order's cabal of pet Majestics were different from Arthur; they would take a man like Jeremiah Dresden apart, piece by piece, until his secrets—his soul—were laid bare. Whether they would successfully put him back together again was another matter entirely.

'I'd rather you didn't mention my father during these interviews,' Lillian said at last. 'It was unnecessary.'

'My apologies. It seemed the more expedient method.'

'It was, but I'd rather you didn't, all the same.' She thought of her brother. John lived in their illustrious father's shadow just as she did, but he had managed to forge a reputation in his own right, despite his youth. John would never use the Hardwick name to further his own ends. He wouldn't have to.

Sir Arthur softened, and held out his arm. Lillian smiled, and took it.

'I am yours to command, dear lady,' he said.

'Very good. Then hail us a cab, and we shall away to the Dials.'

John felt himself falling before he even knew that his legs had been taken from under him. He hit the wooden floor of the gymnasium hard, forcing the air from his lungs. The familiar, single clap of hard hands punctuated his dismay.

'No, no. Again!'

John turned his head with a groan, to see Mrs. Ito staring disapprovingly at him. The diminutive Japanese woman was a curiosity and a terror in equal parts, and John was only thankful that she was not his sparring partner today.

He sat up with no small effort, and pushed himself back to his feet to watch Lillian, just nineteen years old, a head shorter than him and considerably lighter, skipping away on bare feet, looking jolly pleased with herself. He was meant to be teaching her to fight, not the other way around.

'No laughing!' Mrs. Ito snapped at Lillian, her harsh accent cutting the air of what she called her 'dojo'. Lillian straightened her face at once. The other agents sitting around the perimeter of the chalk circle fared less well. Agents Smythe and Hanlocke soon stopped their private joke when Mrs. Ito's bundle of bamboo canes rapped down hard at their feet, causing them to jump back in shock.

'Hurry up. Again!' Mrs. Ito commanded.

They said Mrs. Ito was a hundred years old. They said she had been smuggled out of Japan by Lord Elgin after she had saved the diplomat's life from a government-sanctioned assassination attempt. They said she had killed three samurai that day with nothing more than a walking stick. But then again, John mused, they said many foolish things at the academy.

He bowed to Lillian, who returned the gesture, never taking her eyes off him. He had got the better of her in all their previous matches, but those defeats had awoken a determination in his little sister that he could barely understand. She trained relentlessly, spending many hours alone. She had no confidant in the academy, so far as John knew, and no one whom she trusted enough to form a sincere partnership with during field tests. However, in just three short months she had gone from timid girl to the best fighter in the class. Smythe had almost had his shoulder dislocated the last time he had sparred with her. She practised the oriental arts of fighting day and night, when she was not improving her marksmanship, that was. But John was no slouch—he had been one of the best before Lillian had become Mrs. Ito's favourite, and he intended to reclaim his status, beginning today.

The Japanese woman signalled for the round to begin. Lillian struck quickly, as she always did—she knew no restraint, only attack. John parried three swift punches, and knew she would follow with her favoured front-kick, doubtless expecting him to dodge aside into her feint. He did not.

He caught her leg as she kicked, twisting her around and over into a submission hold, but released her at once. In his eagerness to win the round and use his strength, he had been clumsy, and Lillian's face hit the floor with a thud, causing her to cry out in pain. John released her and stooped to check on her at once. She held a hand to her mouth; her hair had come loose and covered her face.

'My God, Lillian, I am sorry,' he said, softly so that others would not overhear and think him weak. 'Dear sis, I didn't mean to hurt you. But you are too reckless, and rely too much on aggression. Remember, even if you are the best fighter in England, you're never alone in the field. The day will come when even you cannot stand alone. But on that day, I shall stand with you. Count on that.'

He smiled at her warmly, and squeezed her shoulder. She looked up at him through strands of tousled hair. He had said that to her many times before; a pet piece of brotherly advice that she had at first loved, but now he thought she sometimes resented.

'Thank you for that, brother, but today is not that day,' she whispered. 'And this round is not over.'

She stood quickly, taking John's hands away from her and spinning her brother around so fast he did not altogether understand how he came to be upright and looking in the wrong direction. His confusion did not last long.

Lillian kicked John's legs from beneath him for a second time that afternoon. The last thing he saw before his head cracked upon the boards once more was Mrs. Ito's look of utmost disapproval…

John groaned, and touched his fingers to the back of his head, wincing at the sticky fluid he felt there. It was cool—he hoped the bleeding had stopped.

He forced himself upright, stifling a cry as pain flashed through his body. In his groggy state he swore he could still feel where Lillian had kicked the back of his legs; but he dismissed the fancy almost at once and realised his present injuries were all too real. But he moved; his limbs responded, and he slowly dragged himself to his feet. He hadn't broken an arm or leg, he was sure, though the pain in his ribs made him certain he hadn't entirely escaped fractures.

His primary concern now, however, was the darkness. The hatch through which he had fallen was gone, covered over or closed. In any case, John could see no light, not even the reddish glow of the sky, and that was a worry. Had he been moved somewhere else while unconscious? Or had he been sealed in here? The former was the lesser of two evils. John had escaped worse scrapes, he was sure. But if he had been locked in... why would anyone do that? Leaving an agent of Apollo Lycea to his own devices, even if half dead, was a mistake more than one villain had found costly in the past.

John cleared his thoughts, focusing past the stabbing pain and throbbing of his head. He could smell damp earth and mould, and the faintest whiff of coal-smoke from the smelters. In fact, now he concentrated, he could hear the distant reverberation of machinery. He reached out until he touched a wall—rough stone, cold and slick from slime and calcium deposits. He was sure he was underground. He searched himself—the spring-loaded concertina device that held his knife was still flapping about his wrist, broken, but the knife was gone. He unhooked it and cast it aside. He still had his wallet, a few of the papers he had taken from the office—though some had been dropped during the fight—a concealed derringer and four bullets, his lockpicks and, mercifully, his matches.

There was no way he would have been captured and not searched. So they had left him where he had fallen, and sealed him in. To confirm this suspicion, he struck a match. Squinting in its sudden flare, he saw a rough-hewn passage stretching into gloom in both directions, and the splintered wooden hatch above him, now covered with something black and solid-looking. Metal brackets were embedded in the wall beneath it, suggesting that a ladder had once led into the tunnels from the hatch above, in the manner of a tavern cellar; but there was no ladder there now.

John saw that there were lights set into the vaulted ceiling of the long corridor—many of them covered in cracked and dirty glass, and each connected by lengths of thick cabling. Electric? If this was a delivery tunnel for the warehouse, then it wouldn't be unheard of, yet he could see no switch.

As the match began to die down, John saw its light glint off something metallic nearby, and stooped quickly to snatch up his knife. As he did so, the match went out.

The returning darkness heralded something altogether more worrying. A distant screech echoed through the corridor, carried on the foul breeze. John's blood ran cold. He lit another match, and in its yellow flare he saw a grey-painted box on the wall nearby, with a wooden handle jutting from it. He limped to the box, and threw the lever, giving no heed to caution. Better to know the danger, and to face it head on, than to be attacked in the dark.

The junction box fizzed and hummed. There were a few loud pops and a faint smell of burning, which John guessed were fuses overloading, but whatever circuits survived buzzed to life. Along the corridor, which John now realised was far longer than he'd thought, at least half of the lights that adorned the vaulted ceiling flickered with a dull yellow glow. Some grew brighter, while others flickered intermittently, throwing sections of the passage into brief illumination and then into pitch dark. One grew painfully bright for a few seconds, until finally it went out with a loud bang, showering the corridor briefly in orange sparks. John shielded his eyes.

The great dream of the Intuitionists...

He started.

Something moved in the distance. Concealed by the cascade of sparks—or perhaps startled by it—a pale form scurried away, spider-like, into the shadows at the far end of the corridor. The scratching sound came again, this time from the other direction. John wheeled to meet it. There was nothing there but a hundred yards of tunnel.

He wheeled again as a bestial hiss echoed from the opposite direction. This time a long, gangrel shadow slipped across the far wall momentarily, before melding into the embrace of a dark tunnel and vanishing altogether. More clicks, snarls and hisses ebbed and flowed from all around, at first jarringly near, and then more distant.

Yes, the only reason any villain would leave an agent of Apollo Lycea down here was if there were something even worse waiting in the darkness.

'This is not a place to linger at night,' Arthur said.

The Dials were alive with colourful characters and more colourful language, and the stench of beer was strong in the air. Sir Arthur and Lillian attracted more than the odd queer look as they squeezed through the press of bodies congregating outside taverns and doss-houses.

'We're not lingering,' said Lillian. 'We're here with purpose— and no man may hinder agents of the Crown.'

'Tell them that,' muttered Arthur, trying his best not to make eye contact with three burly ne'er-do-wells as he sidestepped between them and the two brawling women who they were jeering at. He hurried after Lillian, thankful that the sharp exchange of hard slaps between gin-addled wenches provided more entertainment than a toff in a fine suit, for now at least. As a rule, he knew, the lower orders would not accost a gentleman, nor a lady so long as she was chaperoned. But with each passing hour such conventions were less assured. As surety against inconveniences such as pickpockets and hawkers, Arthur formed an idea deep in his mind, focusing on it until it became a talisman, projecting outwards until its influence took hold of the folk who scurried back and forth on their low business.

I am no one. I am invisible.

It was a charm, a simple one. It was enough to allow Arthur and Lillian to pass by the dullest of wits without drawing too much attention, and to allow them to vanish into the crowds before a light-fingered urchin could attempt to dip into their pockets. It was not enough, however, to attract the other kind of attention that Majestics often inspired; the predations of the things beyond the veil. Or, at least, Arthur hoped it was not.

Lillian led the way confidently, as though the seven indistinguishable roads of the Dials, with their spider-web of passages and side-streets, were as familiar as her home in Kensington. Sir Arthur did not wish to know how; rumours persisted that Lillian trained for her missions ceaselessly, risking life and limb alone on dangerous streets, often in disguise, to keep her reflexes and awareness sharp. She would stop at nothing to prove herself the equal of her more celebrated brother, and even her father.

They hurried past boarded-up shops with signs proudly proclaiming 'rag and bone', 'first-rate ironmongery', 'fine kitchen wares' and 'live birds and rabbits for sale', outside which haggard old sots lifted their skirts for passing strangers while wiry louts brawled on the cobbles. The air was ripe with the sour stench of urine; of days-old silted gutters; a dog's corpse so far lost to the rot that even the snipes hadn't touched it.

Finally, thankfully, they came upon the chandler's shop, closed for the night. Under the gaily painted candle-shaped sign, in the doorway, a pair of shameless souls fumbled about beneath a tattered overcoat. Lillian did not stop to pass judgement, instead making her way up the narrow alleyway to the left of the shop. A sallow-faced drunk, urinating while whistling 'Sally in my Alley', was quickly moved on by Lillian's best withering glare, the tune dying on his lips.

In the twisting narrows of Seven Dials, Sir Arthur could not trust to his powers alone; he felt more at ease once he placed a hand on his revolver, transferring it from the holster at his breast to his jacket pocket.

Unlike the streets they had left behind, the alleyway was dead quiet, almost unnaturally so. Ahead, it twisted and turned several times before reaching the next street of the great confluence of the Dials, while overhead a wood-panelled bridge adjoined the flats above the chandler's shop and the next-door chophouse; or perhaps it supported the two structures, for they leaned into each other like companionable drunkards. A small window overlooked the alley from the bridge, and judging by the foul-smelling slime that ran over the alley's flagstones, it was used mainly for ejecting the contents of chamber-pots from the meagre dwellings above. Lillian pointed to the window, and Arthur nodded; someone may have seen something, though finding that someone and persuading them to talk would not be easy.

Along the alley, narrow doorways peeked from brick walls—cellar entrances and back doors, and some that must have led to sheltered yards. All were padlocked, or had iron gates fastened across them to keep away opportunistic burglars.

'They may not have stopped here,' Lillian said. 'They could have cut across to the next street.'

'There's one way to be sure,' Arthur replied. Lillian nodded, and delved into her clutch bag, withdrawing a small, greying handkerchief that smelt faintly of rosewater.

Arthur removed his gloves and took the cloth, his other hand outstretched to the darkness, his eyes closed. It had belonged to the girl, and if the unfortunate had ended up the same way as some of the other wretches who had been stolen from the streets of late, the physical link to her would at least lead Arthur to the body.

He could feel Lillian watching him, and blocked out the distraction as best he could. He channelled his thoughts and feelings inward, through his arm, into the cheap handkerchief and back, drawing the very essence of the girl into himself. Arthur took a deep breath, filling every fibre of his being with the etheric vibrations left behind by the girl.

She is dead.

Arthur opened his eyes and looked about. Time had frozen; the alleyway was utterly still. Motes of red dust, which went almost unnoticed in the day-to-day, hung in the air, stationary, glowing like tiny embers. They came from the fire in the sky, and Sir Arthur Furnival had learned some of their mysteries; these particles connected all things, living and dead, and through the use of etherium—what some naively called 'Crookes' Nectar', after its discoverer—he could find anyone or anything by following their trail.

Ahead of him, Lillian Hardwick stood stock-still, a statue of a woman with the colour drained from her, as it was from everything. Everything, that is, except the crimson sky overhead and the glowing particles that fell from it like red snow. The fire in the sky was the only thing that moved, and in this half-life it was more vibrant than ever, clouds of liquid flame billowing and mixing with the firmament like blazing oil atop a lake.

The vividness of the vision came from the etherium. Arthur had known he would be called upon; it was why he was sent. He had injected himself with a single, tiny phial of the stuff in the cab en route to the Dials, despite Lillian's protests. He had his own orders.

Arthur looked down at himself, at his hands through which the glowing red fire pulsated as the etherium coursed through his veins. It linked him to the energy all around, to the power that was now manifest across the globe, but most tellingly in London. With a great, concentrated effort, he harnessed that power, pulling himself from the faded, frozen tableaux, and stepping from his own body like a moth emerging from its cocoon. He turned back to his own physical form, still and grey, arm outstretched, fist clenched tight around the handkerchief.

Behind his body stood Molly Goodheart.

The apparition wore a simple pale dress and worsted shawl. Her eyes were black orbs, cold and dead. She did not really stand there, but floated inches from the ground, feet hidden by the orange mist that covered the flagstones. Arthur looked down at his own feet rather dumbly, and saw the same. He was as incorporeal now as she.

The ghost of the prostitute drifted past Arthur, passing through his body, through Lillian and onwards along the dark alleyway. It was longer, more twisted, and yet more claustrophobic now than it had been moments earlier. The brick walls seemed to bend inwards, creaking like trees in a forest, forming warped tunnels that branched away in all directions. This was an illusion. Sir Arthur focused again, and the alleyway restored itself to some semblance of normality, albeit a cold, darkened one in this twilight world between worlds. Molly Goodheart's ghost drifted onwards, shimmering silver in the gloom, twitching and jerking occasionally, no doubt as she struggled to remember that she was no longer flesh and blood.

Arthur followed the spirit along the narrow passage. He would have to be quick, he knew; too long spent away from his body would dull his senses, and leave him open to attack by the Other. He strained his ears to listen for danger. In this realm, the sounds of lost souls reverberated through every stone, were carried on ice-cold breezes, and were felt in the bones. They sounded like muffled cries travelling through water, indistinct and rumbling. But there were other things, too, in the dark realm that Majestics called the 'Eternal Night'. Chittering, clawing things, native to the void, that were drawn to intruders as to a candle in the darkness. The Other. When these things came, the wise Majestic must flee back to his body, for no amount of etherium could defeat them. To face the Other was to court disaster; to allow gibbering entities ingress to the real world, where only blood would sate their hellish appetites. And so Arthur stayed alert, his mind concentrated on the mission, and his senses stretched outwards, sensitive to the merest danger.

Time flowed differently in the Eternal Night, if indeed it flowed at all. No matter how hard he focused, Sir Arthur could not tell how long he had spent following the spirit. The alleyway seemed to stretch into for ever, and though his feet did not really tread the stones, Arthur began to feel exhausted, as though he had drifted on the orange mist for a lifetime. At last, when he had almost forgotten why he had come to the other realm, the spirit stopped. Arthur saw with growing dread that she was changed; her dress was covered in blood, her arms and face dripping with it. She was barely recognisable.

The spirit stood beside an iron door, and looked towards it with her glassy black eyes. She had showed him the way to the place where she had met her end.

Arthur was about to say something, some parting word to the ghost of Molly Goodheart, but he was interrupted. A jarring, scraping noise rang through the alleyway, coming from all directions. This was not a muffled wave of sound, a deep resonance somewhere on the fringe of Arthur's senses; this was something close and sharp and threatening. Long fingernails scratching rough brick, teeth gnawing at bone, night creatures calling each other to the hunt.

A boot scraped on stone from somewhere ahead. A figure, dark and unreal, many-armed and many-eyed, began to form itself from the orange mist. Arthur backed away. He turned to address the spirit that had led him here, but she was already gone, now little more than motes of pale dust swirling up to a blood-red sky. Molly Goodheart had returned to the realm of the dead, for she knew what came for them in the Eternal Night.

Come to us, Arthur Furnival.

The voice of the Other scraped at his mind with probing fingers. He fought it, refused to let it in. Arthur began to count backwards from ten, trying to breathe—his body's breaths—to restore himself to the real world. He could sense, rather than see, the horned thing, the hooved thing, sliding through the shadows ahead.

Ten—nine—eight—

Run along, little human. Little blood-sack. We shall snip-crack your bones and bite-suck the marrow.

Seven—six—

We shall emblazon your world with living fire.

Five—four—

We shall skin-flay you alive and make maggot-palaces of your flesh.

Three—two—

We shall take your woman and claw-gouge her eyes. We shall...

One.

Sir Arthur gulped in the air until he almost choked. Lillian came to him at once, taking his arm in a firm grip.

'Arthur... that was remarkably quick. Did you find it?' Her expression was grave.

'Quick?' Arthur said. His heart pounded in his chest; his knees almost buckled beneath him.

'A few seconds at most. Did you see it... the Other?'

Arthur nodded. He could feel the sweat upon his brow, and resisted the temptation to dab it away with the dead girl's handkerchief. 'A damn near thing,' he muttered.

'It finds you more quickly each time,' Lillian said, adopting a softer tone. 'We had best take extra care.'

The feeling of nausea and weakness passed quickly, and Arthur straightened himself. He took two more deep breaths for luck, fiddled with his cravat that he was still certain was tied incorrectly, and led the way up the alley, where he knew he would find an iron door and, somewhere behind it, the body of Molly Goodheart.

FIVE

The passageways seemed endless. John's lungs burned; the sounds of his own footsteps on slick flagstones rang in his ears. That sound was a comfort, for each time he stopped running he heard the beasts that pursued him calling to each other in the dark.

Logically, John knew there would be another way out of the tunnels; they would not be so long and winding unless they ultimately fed into other parts of the factory site. But whatever was down here with him was stalking his every move, herding him relentlessly into smaller, unlit passages and storerooms. He had heard their scratching steps, their strange chittering calls. Once or twice he fancied he had seen their shadows cast on the walls far behind him. When he had become so angry as to double back and confront his pursuers, there had been nothing there. It had crossed his mind that the Riftborn, those entities that Majestics called 'the Other', may have found some way into reality down in these depths. He could not believe that. Even if the Majestic he had confronted earlier were of extraordinary power, the presence of Riftborn would amount to more than just strange sounds in the darkness.

John cleared his mind, trying to push aside thoughts of demons, and of the burning pain that he felt in his ribs. He had to find a way out.

A screech sounded again, so close that he thought something was about to pounce upon his back. He did not even look about, but took flight again, taking a turn into a dark tunnel that he hoped would lead to an exit. He had studied the plans of the factory site back at the safe-house—an inn a few miles south—and knew he should head south-east, to the main yard where surely the tunnels would surface. However, he had been turned about too often, railroaded by the hounds, or demons, or whatever they were. He had no compass, and was purely guessing at the path he should take.

The hateful sounds eventually subsided, and John stopped, doubling over as a stitch and his cracked ribs conspired to cripple him. He straightened to get his bearings, and found that he stood at the mouth of a passage that extended some twelve feet before terminating at a planked door. He cursed; the way back was dangerous, the way ahead uncertain.

He pushed his shoulder hard against the door to move it from its jamb. The damp in the cellar, which seemed worse here, had engorged the old wood, and it put up a struggle before finally relenting with a loud scrape. John struck a precious match and peered into the room.

Steps led down, some distance, too, by the look of them. John would have abandoned the idea of descending as folly had he not seen more electrical cabling protruding from the brick near his head, and trailing off down the stairs. If there were another junction box, he could investigate further. The match was burning low—he had no time to ruminate. John hurried down the steps, and breathed a sigh of relief when he found another lever jutting from the wall. He threw it, and a lonely lightbulb sparked to life, casting the room below in a woefully inadequate yellow glow.

John left the stairs and looked about. It seemed to him that it must be a storeroom for the factory workers' food, though it had certainly not been put to much use recently. Only one half-empty barrel sat in what was surely the beer store, and the large larder looked as though it had been hastily cleared out. A few mouldy loaves were scattered across the floor, food for the rats.

'Thank the Lord,' John muttered. His eyes had alighted on a simple object set down beside a rotting bench, which now offered him more comfort than all the tea in China.

A lantern.

He checked its oil and, finding it sufficient, used the last of his matches to light it.

Beyond the large cellar, John could see another corridor leading off. He moved cautiously along it, wary of the slippery blue-brick floor that sloped gradually downwards as he progressed, until finally the passageway terminated at a large iron gate. As he neared the portal a noisome smell assailed him. John held his handkerchief to his mouth, feeling it wholly inadequate for the task.

On the other side of the gate was a circular chamber, with further passages leading off left and right. Why such a labyrinth would have been built was beyond him, but it seemed old. Wooden detritus lay scattered about, the remains of large packing crates. The cargo, which John could only assume were the mysterious shipments from the paperwork he had found, were revealed, and filled him with a growing dread.

Coffins. When the Majestic upstairs had remonstrated with Hopkirk about his missing caskets, John had not taken him literally. Whatever the strange pair were keeping down here, it was not munitions. And if they had been brought down here, they surely would not have followed the same route as John, for the way was too winding and laborious. John's spirits brightened, just a little: one of those other passages must lead out.

The lock was stiff, but it was old, and John picked it with relative ease. The gate swung open with a heavy groan. He had no idea if the lock was there to keep intruders out, or to keep something far worse in, but he stepped into the chamber regardless, fighting the rising tide of bile in his throat from the terrible stench.

'In for a penny, in for a pound,' John muttered to himself.

Water dripped steadily from the high arched ceiling, echoing around the cold cellar. And where it dripped, it mingled with blood and rot, and the slime of decay. The coffins had been wrenched open with force, spilling their contents onto the stone floor. There were no corpses, but the signs—and stench—of their recent occupation was evident. Ragged clothes were scattered about the floor of the chamber with abandon.

From the amount of water running towards an iron grate in the centre of the room, John guessed this would once have been an ice-house.

It occurred to John that perhaps he could find the means to identify the deceased, wherever they might be. The ragged clothes did not look like typical burial suits—murder victims, perhaps? Spies? John could think of little reason to have corpses shipped to a munitions factory in Cheshire. Removing the evidence of a crime? That made some sense; but why not just bury them or, better still, throw them in the huge furnaces next door? And if these poor souls were murdered by the Majestic or his lackeys, when and where had the crimes occurred?

John stooped to pick up what looked like a torn blazer; the War Office crest was unmistakeable over the breast pocket. But once he had taken it up, he instantly recoiled.

In the sleeve of the blazer was part of a human arm, which dropped to the floor with a horrid squelch. John threw the garment back into the pile of filth and wiped his hand hastily on his trousers. When he had recovered his wits, he knelt to inspect the arm. A forearm, severed at the wrist and elbow. It had been torn and gouged, the protruding bone scored with teeth-marks.

'Think, man...' John chided himself. Dogs, perhaps. Feral hounds, or even wolves, roaming the tunnels to stop intruders using the maze-like passages to infiltrate the factory; or to dispose of bodies... but he was sure the figure he'd seen earlier had been human, though he had to confess the shadows were playing tricks with his mind. Better to believe it was a pack of dogs than the alternative. No agent had ever faced the Riftborn directly and lived. To this day, even the Order did not know the demons' true form, except for descriptions gleaned from the ravings of a few half-mad Majestics who had seen 'the Other' in their visions. Rather, if the infernal creatures grew strong enough to manifest themselves, they appeared in myriad ways, depending upon the mental state of the onlooker, and usually with terrible results. If the Riftborn had manifested themselves down here...

No, he couldn't think about it. Even thinking about them gave them power.

It was unusual for John to be indecisive, and he felt increasingly annoyed with himself. His teachers at the Order's academy had always taught him that 'action trumps inaction'. He did not take that mantra quite so literally as his sister, but still...

The thought of Lillian, the notion that he might never see her again should he die down here in the shadows, helped him make a decision. He considered what he had already learned: that these corpses suggested an addition to the already considerable crime of arms smuggling. That powder and lead were being shipped to the factory on a regular basis, and that the factory was fully operational under the watchful gaze of a Majestic. The traitors who might well be selling munitions to foreign powers under the table were also involved in bodysnatching and probably murder.

John's duty was to report these findings, and not to risk his life. He had been foolish coming here alone. John looked to the two new passages, trying to get a sense of which way would lead to salvation.

A scuff, a scrape, and an ominous, reptilian hiss echoed from the right-hand tunnel.

John breathed a deep sigh, and ran down the left-hand passage as fast as he could.

He rarely found himself without a plan of sorts. Now, his choices were being made for him.

* * *

The squalid slum had been derelict for some time, that much was clear. Lillian scanned the room for any signs of life, but other than a few piles of rags indicative of vagrants, there was nothing.

'We should take care,' Arthur warned. 'This building could be part of a rookery; we do not want any unpleasant surprises.'

Lillian poked her head into what she presumed was once a kitchen. Now, like all the other rooms of the poky tenement, it was stripped bare, the plaster fallen from the walls like rotted flesh, revealing the rough brick behind, and covering the floorboards in rubble.

'Here,' Lillian said. Sir Arthur stood at her side and looked where she pointed.

'Most unusual for a slum, wouldn't you say?' he mused.

Before them was a heavy door, ironbound and studded like the door to a vault. Its frame was similarly reinforced, and the door was secured by a large lock and two substantial draw-bolts.

Sir Arthur reached out and touched the cold metal panelling, closing his eyes. After a moment he turned to Lillian.

'She's down there,' he said.

Lillian reached to her hairpins, and knelt by the door, working the lock expertly. She had practised her craft on every type of lock imaginable. John had taught her; he had even given her a chest full of locks for her to practise on for her last birthday, much to their mother's chagrin. Lillian liked to think she had surpassed her brother in the art, however. Locks were the only things for which she had any patience. She appreciated the craft; loved the idea that she was pitting her skills against another artisan, listening for the tumblers to click perfectly into place. The greater the precision of the locksmith, the more difficult the task.

She smiled as the lock clicked open. It was a good one, expensive. Too expensive for a slum.

She stood and dusted herself down while Arthur withdrew the bolts and opened the door. She at once wished he hadn't.

The stench that assailed them was unbearable. Lillian's

investigations had taken her to more than one dead-room, but this was something else entirely. It was the iron-tinged scent of blood in a Spitalfields slaughterhouse; the smell of disease and corruption in a poor hospital; the filth of the worst jail cell. Lillian retched, moving as gracefully as she could to the corner of the room before evacuating her stomach. She was ashamed—Sir Arthur Furnival did not react at all, other than to pull his muffler up around his nose and mouth. He was not known for his physical fortitude—their pairing was often thought an odd one, because Sir Arthur was not a fighter. How then, could he hope to protect the Order's first female agent? In fact, it was the other way around. Sir Arthur Furnival was a Majestic, and one of the very best they had—she was assigned to protect him in the field, for no one would ever suspect a slip of a girl to be a deadly assassin, burglar, and spy.

Or so she liked to think. She had had few opportunities to test herself so far—her father had seen to that.

She straightened herself as Arthur's hand gripped her arm, nodded to assuage his concerned expression, and returned to the door, this time braced for the assault on her senses.

Behind the door was a steep flight of stairs, stretching down into pitch darkness. Sir Arthur shone his lantern into the cellar, its beam barely illuminating the floor at the foot of the stairs. Lillian would have steeled herself with a deep breath, but did not trust herself not to be sick again, and so she held a scented handkerchief to her mouth and led the way down the stairs.

'Lord preserve us,' Arthur gasped.

Lillian said nothing. She followed the beam of the shuttered lantern as it shone along the walls and across the floor, bringing into stark focus thick, congealed blood smears and piles of gnawed remains. Human remains, mostly, flung into piles with the rotted bodies of rats, cats and dogs. Lillian spotted the tattered remnants of clothing in the corner of the cellar, and as she went to investigate she cried out despite herself. Sir Arthur shone the light upon her at once, and Lillian staggered away from the thing that had alarmed her, that had touched her.

A human torso hung from the ceiling, suspended upon a butcher's meat hook. It was mostly stripped to the bone, but some muscle and flesh still glistened upon it, enough to reveal the sex of the victim. The right arm was almost intact, slender and pale, terminating in a small, feminine hand with grubby fingernails.

'Is… is it her?' Lillian asked, feeling the strength sapping from her as her nausea grew once more.

Arthur barely needed to concentrate his energies before he nodded. 'It is.'

'Who would do this?' Lillian felt it was a stupid question, but she had to say something to allay the shock.

'Perhaps the question should be *what* would do this?' Arthur said, shining the beam of the lantern to where three sets of rusting, heavy manacles were affixed to the bloodstained wall, all but one hanging empty. In this was a pale hand, its severed wrist still oozing blood onto the cellar floor.

'Oh…' Lillian moved towards the manacles. 'Is this even human? It looks strange—some kind of ape, perhaps. I've heard of worse things kept in captivity in London.'

'I'd like to think so, but I doubt it.'

Arthur stepped closer and shone the light at the grotesque object, and Lillian knew at once she was mistaken. The hand was large, with unusually long, bony fingers ending at thick, talon-like nails, but it was human nonetheless.

'It's been bitten off,' Lillian said. 'Another victim then.'

Arthur shook his head solemnly. 'I doubt that also. I think that the wretch who chewed through his own hand to escape these shackles was also the killer of these poor souls. Or at least, was employed by the killer to do the deed—nothing chained up down here could entice a victim to the cellar, after all. And look at the walls.'

The chains were long; whatever had been held by them would have had the run of half the cellar. Lillian estimated that, with the exception of arterial spray, the blood upon the walls was smeared within reach of the chains. She tried to dismiss the notion that there were human handprints within the blood, but once she had thought it she could not see it as anything else. Arthur was right.

Her thoughts were abruptly shattered by a distant but unsettling noise like falling masonry, followed by a strange, low, staccato growl, definitely made by some kind of creature. Lillian fair jumped out of her skin, and felt deeply embarrassed yet again. If Arthur had noticed her fright, he said nothing. Instead, he unshuttered the lantern completely, bathing the cellar in light.

'The time for stealth is past,' he said gravely.

Both agents looked beyond the half-gnawed cadavers, and to the far corner of the cellar from where the noise had emanated. Beyond a pile of bricks and timbers was a large hole in the cellar wall, which led to a rough tunnel.

Lillian drew her pistol and moved stealthily to the man-sized aperture, glad of something to take her mind off the horrific stench and her jangling nerves. Arthur followed, lantern held high, and his own revolver readied. In the eerie cast of light, a pale form was revealed lying on the earthen floor of the tunnel, bloodied and half-eaten as if by some monstrous beast. The cadaver itself was not recognisably human—not in any normal sense—but was long-limbed and white as alabaster, with hideous lumpen deformities to its head and body. Its legs had been devoured, all but a foot that lay discarded further along the shaft, while its rib cage had been prized open, presumably so that its assailant could reach the organs within.

It smelled even worse than the other bodies. It smelled like the grave.

'Good lord...' Arthur muttered.

At the far end of the narrow tunnel—more a burrow, Lillian could not help but think—something moved. Swift and pale, one second an indistinct, ghost-like shape, and the next gone, melded into the very shadows.

And in that second, Lillian was after it.

Arthur's protests fell on deaf ears. His cautious nature would not catch this killer—this monster—and so Lillian moved as fast as she could, crouching as the tunnel grew smaller, soil falling upon her, the heat of the earth stifling, hanging roots whipping at her face. It also sloped downwards, steeply in places, and that worried her more than anything else.

Sir Arthur had followed, but the light of the lantern faded regardless as the passage narrowed such that Lillian, despite her slender frame, almost filled it. She realised she was rushing headlong into pitch darkness, and fought her impulse to stop and wait for her fellow agent. Hesitation would not win the day. *Action always trumps inaction.*

She emerged at last. She hadn't expected to, but was instantly grateful for the rush of cooler air that greeted her, and the reassuring ring of hard stone beneath her heels. And yet, she was not in a cellar, but in a larger cavern. It was dark, although her eyes quickly became accustomed to a dim glow from shafts set in the ceiling periodically, along a large, arched tunnel.

The light from Arthur's lantern drew closer, dancing on the floor by her feet, dully illuminating the narrow platform, the ballast beyond, and the rails.

Lillian was about to turn back to the tunnel, to urge Arthur to hurry, when she felt something move towards her from the shadows; an almost imperceptible rush of air, the feeling of imminent danger causing her skin to tingle. She barely had time to meet the threat, her pistol aimed and readied by instinct before she had fully registered what was happening.

Looming from the darkness, too fast to counter, a hideous face, luminescent, was just inches from her own. It came and went so fast that Lillian's mind could picture only large, yellowed fangs, an upturned, porcine nose, a bestial snarl on a marble-white face, and those eyes. Bright, violet eyes like amethysts twinkling in lamplight. It was there, next to her, a high-pitched shriek tearing from its ghastly maw like the wail of the banshee, and then it was gone.

But the pain remained.

Lillian's shoulder felt as though it had exploded as the claws had raked it, ripping through her jacket like it were crepe-paper. She felt her own blood against her skin as she wheeled around and fell to the ground, the wind knocked from her. She was vaguely aware of Sir Arthur arriving, shouting something, stooping to her. Her vision swam, but she caught sight of something pale and lithe racing along the tunnel, leaping up at the ceiling and crawling along it like a monstrous bat.

She squeezed off three shots into the shadows, the noise deafening her. And yet she still heard the darkness reply. A scream of hate and rage; and then nothing. The creature had escaped her.

As Arthur tried to staunch the bleeding from her shoulder, Lillian struggled against an overwhelming desire to faint. As her vision swam and her head throbbed, all she could think was:

What will my father say?

They had been briefed for this assignment by Sir Toby Fitzwilliam, commander of the Order of Apollo, with Marcus Hardwick in attendance. Lillian loathed such briefings, in which she was always reminded of her junior status in the Order, and made to feel like a schoolchild before the withering gaze of her father. Afterwards, Lillian had sent Sir Arthur ahead to make the preparations for their mission, whilst she herself loitered outside the famous library of the Apollonian Club, waiting to catch her father before he departed. Several grey-haired old clubmen passed her as they went about their academic business, and some stole disapproving glances at Lillian. It had been three years since Apollo Lycea had changed its rules to allow women into the Order, whose headquarters formed the heart of the grand gentleman's club, and still Lillian was not accepted by most of the members. They frowned upon her sex having any sort of career or opinion; they frowned upon her unconventional attire, for all its practicality. But most of all, they frowned upon her intrusion into their traditional retreat. Three years—and yet in that time only three women had risen to any sort of prominence in the militant arm of the Apollonian, and Lillian was by far the youngest of them.

Perhaps it's not the intrusion that they resent, mused Lillian, *but the fact that I'm* his *daughter…*

Almost as if he had heard her thoughts, Lord Hardwick appeared at the top of the stairs. He paused when he saw her, a flicker of annoyance crossing his features for a moment, before he marched down to the landing.

'My business is not over yet,' he said, dismissively. 'I have an appointment with the police commissioner about the latest Rift breaches.' Marcus Hardwick's responsibilities had increased tenfold since the first breach. Now he was the Minister for Defence, a relatively new position that had elevated the old soldier to one of the most powerful men in the Empire, changing his relationship with the Order for ever. And with such responsibility came a long list of commitments, upon which his family, it seemed to Lillian, sat very near the bottom.

'I'm sure you can spare a few minutes for me… Father.' Lillian held his gaze confidently, and he sighed.

'Very well, but only a few minutes.'

They made their way down to the great marble lobby and through to the members' bar, where they secured a private booth.

'How was Alaska?' Lillian asked.

'Cold,' her father replied.

'You look tired.'

'It was an arduous voyage.'

'Had it not been for the summons to the briefing, I would not have known you had returned.'

'What is it, Lillian?' Marcus Hardwick sighed again. 'Were your orders not clear enough?'

'Perfectly. In fact, Sir Arthur is down in the armoury right now, no doubt haggling with Lord Cherleten's secretary over exactly how many forms he must sign for our supplies this time.'

At the merest mention of Arthur's name, Lord Hardwick let out a disapproving snort. 'Father, please,' Lillian chided.

'What? Must I be happy that a daughter of mine is off gallivanting around the country with that... that...'

'He's a good man, and a good agent. Would that I had his experience, so I could serve my country half as well.'

'So it's true?' He raised an eyebrow.

'What is?'

'You and him?'

'I shouldn't have to dignify that with a response. Am I not a lady still?'

'I don't know, my girl, are you? I certainly raised you as one; and yet the rumours suggest that you have had "relations" with a... a... Majestic.'

Lillian felt embarrassment and anger in equal measure redden her cheeks. 'I thought I could bear the callous remarks and tittle-tattle of the so-called "gentlemen" of this club, but to learn that my own father listens to such hearsay is hurtful indeed. As it happens, it was my mother—if you even remember you have a devoted wife—who raised me as a lady. What you raised was a killer. And now, when I am finally given the chance to serve my country as you did, you join the gossiping old men of society in slandering me?'

'Hold your tongue, girl. Your privilege as my daughter carries you only so far.'

Lillian rose. 'Sir Toby has been more of a father to me than you have these past years, and I barely see him. I do not feel especially privileged to be your daughter.' As she stepped around the table to leave, her father grasped her wrist firmly.

'Wait. I...' He took a breath, and tried his best to soften his tone. 'Don't be upset, child. What was it you wanted to say?'

'I was hoping you would wish me a happy birthday,' Lillian said, coolly, 'before I go off "gallivanting" with Sir Arthur Furnival.' She pulled her arm from her father's grasp, and without another word walked briskly from the room, leaving him silent in her wake, as the sage old clubmen pretended not to pay any heed.

John rushed into another room, throwing shut a large door behind him, and slamming his back against it.

But for his lantern's pale glow the room was dark; no electric light shone in here. The air was distinctly musty and foul, carrying the scent of soil and age upon the gentlest of breezes. He could hear scratching and tapping ringing in the corridor behind the door, accompanied by a muffled sound as of deep, guttural voices, or perhaps pig-like grunts. The tiny derringer in his hand suddenly looked most inadequate.

The tunnels were impossibly vast and labyrinthine—they could not have been put here by the builders of a factory. More likely, John guessed, they were catacombs from some ruined abbey, now pressed into service as stores. He felt like he had run for miles.

John cast the lantern about, praying for a way out. The meagre light fell upon a set of stone stairs up ahead, and John's heart lifted, just for a moment.

Even as he stepped forward, the door behind him burst open, and something—several somethings—scrabbled into the room. He saw shadows move and felt hot breath upon his neck.

John leapt forward even as something grabbed at him. He felt his trouser leg tear and almost fell flat on his face.

There was movement to his left and a pale shape leapt through the air. John saw it from the corner of his eye, as though time itself was slowed, but it was too late to react. The snarling thing crashed into him, and the two of them rolled across the stone floor before smashing into a pile of crates.

The lantern rolled away, casting ghastly shadows dancing on the walls, and illuminating just briefly a writhing mass of grotesque creatures, pale of skin and bright of eye, scurrying about the shadows.

John's arm was pinned to the ground in the creature's vice-like grip; he could not bring the derringer to bear. He kicked at his attacker as hard as he could, but it was strong, and did not withdraw. Instead, it turned an ugly, bestial face towards him, and let out such a low, keening moan that it chilled him to the bone. Its large eyes sparkled violet for a moment. Its features were unmistakeably human, though hideously deformed and pale. John yanked his knife from his jacket pocket and pushed it into the monster's throat. He kicked at the brutish creature again, and this time it staggered backwards, clutching at the wound.

John sprang to his feet and snatched up the lantern, turning about in all directions wildly, pointing his derringer at the shadows that even now leapt about in an amorphous mass of living darkness. The knife was lost, buried in the flesh of the creature that had attacked him. The single-shot pistol seemed so very small in his hand.

He swept the lantern around the chamber again, and for a second caught a glimpse of those terrible eyes—dozens of pairs of them, in every shadowed corner. The crawling, scurrying movement of slender, pale bodies was visible only for a moment, and was then gone so quickly it appeared to be a trick of the light. The creatures, whatever they were, scrambled away from the light, hissing each time it fell upon their gleaming eyes.

John felt the shadows converge upon him, the creatures taking heart in their superior numbers. He was surrounded, but he was not through yet.

John unfastened the lantern and threw it hard against the floor near the pile of crates. Glass shattered, oil flowed, and the chamber filled almost instantly with firelight. The creatures checked their advance, shielding their unnatural eyes and screaming with rage as they tried to turn from the heat and light. There were twenty or more of them, naked and muscular, with skin so pale it was almost translucent. Some had grotesque, bulging deformities, whilst others had the unsettling look of half-rotted cadavers. They grunted and hissed in some guttural language, if indeed it could be called a language at all. Soon they inched closer, growing more used to the light by the second; whatever their aversion to the flames, it was passing rapidly.

John's eyes alighted upon the crates, which were filled with work-tools. He snatched up a heavy steel wrench before the fire could spread to them, swinging it about in a wild arc to fend off the creatures that even now snarled at his back. He squeezed a round into the chest of the nearest creature, which fell to the ground. The shot rang around the chamber deafeningly, silencing the creatures for a moment. And then the felled thing staggered back to its feet, a gaping, bloodless wound in its cadaverous chest. It glared at John with a look of such unimaginable, bestial hatred—with such an intelligent malevolence—that he was momentarily unmanned.

John did not hesitate again. He turned and raced to the top of the stairs, but one of his pursuers scurried up the wall beside him with jerking, spasmodic movements, like a hideous crawling insect.

John barged into the door at the top of the stairs, but it was locked. He kicked at it, feeling it give, trying to ignore the pain that flared up his leg. The monster dropped from above him, its marble-white face twisted with fury. John smashed the wrench into the head of the creature. It fell with a crunch. With one last effort, he kicked open the door, and flung himself through it. Too late, he saw another creature had almost caught up with him, and it sprung at him with terrible force, sending the two of them crashing through the doorway in a deathly embrace.

They ploughed into the midst of a workshop of some kind, and half a dozen night-shift workers were standing gobsmacked at the sudden intrusion into their world as John skidded across the room, flat on his back with a ravenous beast atop him.

John raised the wrench, using it to push the creature off him by its throat. He scrambled upright. He fumbled for a weapon atop the nearest workbench, finding a large glass bottle, smashing it and jamming the broken glass into the creature's throat. With a bird-like screech, the creature released its hold and scurried away towards its fellows that were already cautiously entering the workshop. John waved his empty gun around threateningly.

'Now look here, you'd all better—' he began. But he did not finish. Another creature tore into the room, crashing into a workbench, before leaping upon the first workman that crossed its path and tearing into his throat with its large, uneven teeth. Another monster entered close behind, and then another, to cries of terror from the workers. John raced for the exit with the rest of the men, who were taken one by one by the creatures. The workshop was hot as hell, with smelters and peculiar apparatus set up all around; vials of bubbling pinkish fluid boiled away on workbenches, discarded ammunition moulds scattered alongside them. John realised at once that he had stumbled upon yet another of the Majestic's dark secrets, but there was no time to explore it further, or to gather evidence. Instead he flung open the workshop door and staggered into the courtyard beyond, wrenching free of a labourer who clung to him pleadingly with calloused hands.

'I'm sorry,' John grimaced. He kicked the man hard in the midriff, sending him crashing backwards into the press of his colleagues. John pulled the door closed on the scene of terror. The last thing he saw was the creatures feasting upon human flesh. This time, the flesh of the living.

'It was you or me, old chap,' John whispered.

But he soon saw that he had more pressing concerns. Dozens of factory workers were gathered in the yard, and were staring at him. Some looked merely curious at the sounds coming from the workshop, although they were fast subsiding.

A group of burly fellows began making their way over to John; he half hoped they would rush to his aid, seeing the state he was in, but he knew at once that was not to be. The closest man brandished a sledgehammer with menace.

John stepped backwards to the door of the workshop, an insane plan forming in his mind. As more workers plucked up the courage to advance, and their shouts began to ring out in the night air, John surveyed the courtyard. A main thoroughfare; two factory buildings, one large, one small; a row of five workshops similar to the one behind him; sundry sheds and shacks. Most importantly of all, a stable.

As the men drew almost within arms' reach, John flung open the door. The factory workers suddenly checked their advance on the shed, from which the smell of meat and death wafted into the yard. Then the growling came. A pair of violet eyes appeared; then another. John regretted his decision the moment he had reached it, but it was done. He leapt aside, scrambling for cover before the workers knew what was happening.

In another instant, the creatures had barrelled into the yard. Men fled, or tried in vain to wrestle with the monsters, which were now so smeared in gore that they resembled red-skinned demons. If the factory workers did not know otherwise, then they probably thought the creatures were the very hellspawn from the Rift.

John did not stay to witness the terror he had wrought. He ran as fast as he could—little more than a limping jog—towards the stables. A man stepped in his path, and John struck him with the wrench, knocking the labourer to the ground. A creature gained on them, and upon hearing its snapping jaws and guttural grunts behind him, John spun around with the tool, cracking it into its sloping, malformed head. The monster let out a low, keening howl, and pulled itself along the ground towards John, its oversized jaws gnashing, and its noxious breath steaming in the winter air. John smashed the wrench into the head of the blasphemous thing, again and again, until he was as gore-smeared as the thing itself.

He looked up. More men were racing past him towards the courtyard. John hazarded a look back over his shoulder. Across the courtyard, from the shadow of the factory, strode a tall, thin, figure in black. With imperious sweeps of his arms, the grotesque creatures retreated from their half-devoured victims, like chastised hounds shrinking from a stern hunt-master. What mysterious power this Majestic held over the foul beasts, John knew not. And he did not intend to stay and find out.

By the time John had found a dray horse, led it from the stable and hauled himself onto its back, a gang of workers had almost reached him, with a hue and cry and demands for vengeance. That their master had brought such misery upon their fellows was evidently lost on them. John spurred on the horse, barging through the mass of bodies. He stole a look over his shoulder, and saw the Majestic striding towards him, porcelain face twisted into a bestial snarl that was too much like the pale-skinned beasts for John's liking.

With another kick at the horse, John was away through the great gates of the factory, and onto the road that twisted through the black forests.

Cold air filled his lungs. John knew he had to return to London as soon as he could. The Majestic—whoever or whatever he was—posed a threat greater than John could have imagined. He thought of the beasts in the subterranean lair, and of the strange liquid in the workshop—most definitely etherium, the most dangerous substance on earth. He had to tell Sir Toby all that he had seen.

EXTRACT FROM THE KEYNOTE SPEECH OF
DR. WILLIAM CROOKES, ROYAL SOCIETY, 1873

There were many who doubted my own assertions that Catherine and Margaret Fox were possessed of genuine psychical ability, and that doubt extended beyond the point of all reason, when science had clearly illustrated the truth of the matter. We can now look back on the events of September last, however, with utmost certainty. Those events have become called, in the popular press, 'the Awakening', and this is as apt a name as we of the Royal Society could hope to coin.

We now know that approximately ten per cent of the population of England, and some smaller proportion of people around the world, were in some way affected when the woman known colloquially now as Kate Fox performed her infamous séance by royal appointment. The proportion of those affected was higher still among those in attendance, although thankfully Her Majesty the Queen appeared unharmed by the procedure. In revealing what she called her 'spirit familiar' to an unsuspecting public, Kate Fox inadvertently widened the Rift, with a twofold effect.

First of all, the number of adverse psychical phenomena involving the Riftborn more than trebled worldwide. So-called demonic possession of vulnerable personages became almost commonplace—an alarming trend that escalates daily. Secondly, in a somewhat violent mass spiritualist event, reported simultaneously across the world from Edinburgh to Timbuktu, many thousands of people began to unlock hitherto hidden potential, becoming preternaturally excellent in myriad fields of academic, artistic, technical and esoteric expertise. For many, this 'Awakening' manifested itself as a brilliant but limited skill—an improved or suddenly prodigious aptitude for music or painting, for example, an uncanny aptitude for any number of academic disciplines, from botany to linguistics, or deep insight into ancient philosophy. But more crucially, the fields of engineering, physics, chemistry, and medicine have been bolstered by an influx of minds now brimming with untapped knowledge, who claim to receive their brilliant insight from, and I quote, 'beyond the veil'. This uncanny reception of knowledge has led to their collective designation as 'Intuitionists'.

The doors of every great society in Britain have been flung open to these brilliant men—and even women— and as a result the very landscape of our great nation is changing. The railways expand at an exponential rate; bridges of unprecedented length span rivers and lakes; the fledgling London Underground is fledgling no more. Even the most impecunious households are now illuminated at night by electric light. The first horseless carriages have taken to our streets. Passenger airships are but a handful of years away from completion, they say. Steamships larger and faster than anything we have ever seen are even now being constructed at Portsmouth. In our hospitals, diseases are being cured that were once thought fatal. Doctors have new apparatus at their disposal so frequently that they barely have time to learn its use before it is outmoded. Truly, even the greatest minds of our time must look at these Intuitionists in awe, for by their hands is humanity set upon a course of unprecedented change.

Yet for every ounce of potential offered us by the Intuitionists, great danger is presented by their counterparts. Who among us does not know of at least one man or woman cursed by the Awakening? Poor wretches touched by visions of the Rift so powerful that they have been driven irrevocably mad? Some few of these poor souls have maintained a semblance of control over their esoteric abilities, but they represent a dark reflection of Kate Fox's vision. Spiritualists of unprecedented and unrefined power, telekinetics, *chiromancers, psychometrists, and a host of other classifications of psychic that we are still struggling to define. They treat with spirits and read minds, they ply their trade within a twilight realm that they call the 'Eternal Night'.*

Kate Fox, indeed, calls these people the greatest gift to the world as we know it. She calls them 'Majestics'.

I, gentlemen, have seen the danger that they pose to the very fabric of reality.

I call them the greatest threat to the safety of our world since the bubonic plague.

SIX

The Awakening was a phenomenon aptly named, as it had certainly awoken something in Sir Arthur, not to mention countless others around the world.

As a boy, Arthur Furnival had but one 'talent' of note, though he himself had thought it a curse. Sometimes, when he held an object close, he would become enraptured by such a violent glimpse into its past as to send him into a fit, and give him night terrors for weeks afterwards. The doctors did not know what to do with him; how could he have explained to their satisfaction that he received visitations from shades of the long dead? He'd become an object of ridicule at Harrow. He'd learned to fight—both physically and politically—at public school. Those talents at least had consistently served him well since.

The family physician had thought that some time in the seminary would ease Arthur's troubled mind. He might as well have sent him to Zululand to see a witch doctor. As the youngest of the three Furnival sons, it was his duty to enter the clergy upon leaving university. Yet fate took an altogether different turn, taking Arthur's brothers early, and thrusting a troubled youth into an inheritance for which he was ill prepared. His extensive reading of theology was all for naught, and the awkward, pensive youth entered a whirlwind life of society balls and philanthropy. Not that he embraced such at all. Despite the baronetcy and the prestige it brought, Sir Arthur Furnival mourned his eldest brother, Horace—the second to depart this earth—for the longest time. It was that very process that drew him to Spiritualism. And it was his new-found status that had opened doors to audiences with the American prophet of that church, Kate Fox.

Arthur had been inducted into mysteries profound, learning that the powers that had for so long been a weighty source of misery had a name: psychometry, the power to sense the history of an object through touch. The visions, he was informed, were 'echoes' of powerful emotions, vibrations left by an owner, and channelled through the afterlife itself to the waiting medium. It was not a pure gift, like the clairvoyance that Fox herself possessed, but it was strong in the baronet nonetheless.

All that had changed with the Awakening. Like so many others who laid claim to the most modest psychic talents, Arthur's powers had increased a hundredfold on the day that Kate Fox lost control of her 'spirit guide'. Tragedy and miracle both; lives were for ever changed, and the world had not been ready. Then, and since, Sir Arthur had performed his duty for Queen and country. He had travelled the globe many times in the name of that duty. In truth, he preferred far-flung assignments, for leaving London these days was more a blessing than a curse; an opportunity to see clear skies, and perhaps to feel a modicum of peace rather than be plagued by the repercussions of his uncanny powers.

Arthur only wished he could be less troubled. In the years since the awakening he had seen things that would have driven lesser men mad. He had seen, he believed, the very denizens of hell spill forth into the world, and had done his part to turn back the tide of evil that could surely only signal the reckoning. Judgement Day.

Something terrible was coming: he could feel it in his marrow. What had happened in the Dials, and what had happened to

John Hardwick in the north... He shuddered, nodding his thanks to Jenkins, who solemnly withdrew the syringe from his master's arm. So-called 'mundane' etherium, the only thing that could bring him peace after he had used his powers. The only thing that could quiet the voices in his head. Sir Arthur dismissed his servant, and leaned back in his chair, closing his eyes until respite washed over him, enjoying the moment's silence, while it lasted.

He and Lillian had seen horrors indeed. And yet the creatures had been flesh and blood. They were not the ravening things that couched behind the veil, scratching for egress into the world of men. They were something else. Sir Arthur Furnival, with his long experience in Apollo Lycea, had an idea of exactly what they were.

Saturday, 18th October

THE APOLLONIAN CLUB, LONDON

'You mean to say that there is a... creature... on the loose in the Underground?' Sir Toby Fitzwilliam, that staunch and unswerving Lord Justice, frowned at his agents from beneath his bushy, greying eyebrows.

Lillian was about to reply, when Arthur beat her to it.

'It is uncertain,' Arthur said. 'What we stumbled upon was a construction tunnel for an aborted line. Although it was closed off, I'm afraid the Board of Works believe it to be connected to further tunnels, and to the old sewers, via maintenance shafts. In short, the creature could be anywhere.'

'It is wounded,' Lillian offered, with optimism. 'It has the use of but one arm.'

'And a lot of good that does us.' Gazing out of a large sash window across St. James's Square, was the Minister for Defence, Lord Hardwick, formerly Brigadier Sir Marcus Hardwick. To the populace he was the most important man in England, the man who would revive a cursed empire and lead it back into the light. To Lillian, he was simply her father. He had not spoken until now. Even so, he did not turn away from the window.

Agents Furnival, Hardwick and Hardwick stood to attention, side by side in Sir Toby Fitzwilliam's office. From this unassuming cloister did the judge exert control over Apollo Lycea—the Order of Apollo—the most powerful covert agency in the Empire. Lillian glanced askance at her brother; she had barely spoken to John before the meeting, and he had seemed most strange in his manner. He had been overjoyed to see her but remarkably stand-offish when asked about his mission. He was usually tight-lipped about official business, even with other agents—the pillar of integrity, some said—but this was different. He was troubled.

'I shot it,' Lillian said at last, when any wisp of clever retort eluded her. 'It may be dead.'

'The reports do not tally on that matter,' said Sir Toby. 'As far as we know, the creature is alive, and is even now posing a threat to the citizens of London. However,' his tone softened, 'we are a step closer to discovering who is behind the killings. You have other avenues to investigate, do you not?'

'We—' Lillian began.

'Yes, Sir Toby,' Sir Arthur interrupted. 'The cabman, Dresden, is currently under watch. We think he was lying about his involvement with the killer.'

'We should bring him in. What do you say, Cherleten?'

A third official leaned forward from a plume of cigar smoke. 'I concur,' he said, his voice rasping. 'Let's hand him to my Nightwatch. I'll have them poke about in his head for a bit. Whatever secrets he's keeping will soon come tumbling out, eh, Sir Arthur?'

If it was a jest, it was a mirthless one. But Lord Cherleten was famed for his black humour. He sat smoking fat cigars in the corner of the room, always away from the light of Sir Toby's desk-lamp, somewhat theatrically, Lillian thought. He was the Order's foremost keeper—and discoverer—of secrets. Lord of the armoury, and founder of the Nightwatch. Spymaster supreme, and second in command of the Order of Apollo.

'I'm sure you know best,' said Sir Arthur, with an air of distaste. Lillian fancied she saw Cherleten smirk before vanishing into the shadows again, his tufts of pale red hair the only thing to distinguish him. She knew Arthur was the only field agent who could get away with speaking his mind to Lord Cherleten, due primarily to his title, but also to his prodigious psychical gifts. Even her brother would think twice before crossing Cherleten, though heaven knew he'd considered it often enough. Lillian wondered why Cherleten was at the debriefing at all.

Sir Toby looked up at them from beneath bushy eyebrows the colour of gunmetal. 'Agents, you have been brought together because your reports contain several disturbing correlations. It would seem that the suspects in your seemingly disparate cases are connected, if not, indeed, the same person.'

Lillian looked at John—he seemed as perplexed as her.

'Lieutenant Hardwick returned this morning from Hyde, where he was investigating certain irregularities in the army's munitions supplies.' Sir Toby passed a pair of grainy photographs to Arthur, who handed them in turn to Lillian. 'These pictures were taken less than a week ago by Corporal Henry Moreton, of Debdale. The army sent him to take a look at one of their munitions factories near Hyde. You see, it ceased production a month ago, citing an outbreak of fever amongst its workers, and thus it failed to fulfil the month's orders. Dockets were sent to the War Office and the Admiralty defaulting on the agreement to supply shells for at least another month. And yet, as you can see from Mr. Moreton's photographs, the factory is very much operational. The photographs were sent with a note, explaining that the factory is not only functioning as expected, but is also working through the night, every night, with goods coming in and out regularly. And yet, we do not know where those goods are going. A telegram was sent to Moreton the day before yesterday, to which he did not respond.'

'Has he been found?' Arthur asked.

'What was left of him, at any rate,' John replied.

'I see,' Arthur said.

From the look on Arthur's face, Lillian guessed he was remembering the scene in the Dials; it was certainly not far from her own thoughts.

'Lieutenant Hardwick managed to trace one of the most recent deliveries to the factory,' Sir Toby went on. 'A consignment of guncotton; a very large consignment. It began its journey at a freight-house in Faversham, and ended up being packed into weapons of war in Hyde, for purposes unknown.'

Faversham was Lillian and John's old family home, before their father's promotion had brought them to London. At its mention, Lillian glanced over at Marcus Hardwick. He stood in silence, his back to the three agents, thrown into silhouette by the roiling red sky through the window.

When had the sky first started to burn? It seemed like for ever ago.

She ought to remember—the Great Catastrophe had marked the end of her childhood, and the loss of her father as she knew him. She blinked the thought away—it was pointless to wish her father back. They were worlds apart now, it seemed.

'Although Lieutenant Hardwick was unable to retrieve any physical evidence, he also stumbled across an etherium distillery. An unlicensed etherium distillery.'

Lillian noted Arthur's unease at mention of the Majestic drug.

'I'm sorry, Sir Toby,' Arthur said, 'but is this not a military matter? Why this is the business of the Order?'

'Because I decided it was,' growled Lord Hardwick. He turned away from the window, and the hellfire beyond illuminated his weathered face in a most ghastly fashion. 'Have you any idea of what is happening in the north?'

'A little, sir,' Arthur said, coolly. Lillian was surprised by her father's tone. Arthur usually commanded more respect, even from his superiors in the Order. She hoped the unpleasantness was not on her account. Arthur went on, 'The tearing of the veil has affected northerners most terribly, and disease and dispossession run rife. I have heard talk of insurrection, in some quarters...'

'Insurrection... indeed; and what if I told you that in every great hub of industry in this realm, rebellion has begun to take hold? What if I told you that the people of Manchester, Sheffield, York and Newcastle—among others—no longer respect the Crown, or the government? That no metropolitan force or yeomanry dare to even try to enforce law and order?'

'How... how could we not have heard of this?' Arthur asked.

'Because,' Sir Toby picked up the thread, 'we cannot allow anyone to hear of it. We face the most terrible crisis mankind has ever faced. Demons prey upon the weak, the dead do not rest easy in their graves, and more and more people succumb to the madness that stalks our streets with each passing day. To allow news to spread that political factions are on the verge of fracturing the country would be the final straw. There has to be law, here in London at least. You ask why Lord Hardwick has entrusted the Order with this matter? Because it is a delicate operation indeed. We believe the munitions factories are being targeted by a group of well-organised political dissidents, who wish to use their possessions to hold the Crown to ransom. Can you imagine if these rebels managed to manufacture weapons of mass destruction to use against our own armies in our own country? Or sell them to our enemies? What began as mutinous grumbling from petty councillors and labour unions has become something dire indeed. This game is a political one, and the factories are the tipping point in the balance of power.'

'John's—Lieutenant Hardwick's—assignment in Cheshire has undoubtedly uncovered part of this terrible plot,' said Lillian. 'But I do not understand how it links with the murders in the East End. What has poor Molly Goodheart to do with this?'

'Nothing,' said Marcus Hardwick, 'but her killer may have everything to do with it. Your brother uncovered the identity of a man we believe to be a prime agitator in the north, and has long evaded the law—operated above the law, in fact. His name is Lord Lucien de Montfort, though his claims to the peerage are tenuous at best. He belongs to a group calling themselves the "Knights Iscariot"—a cabal of occultists and aristocrats who claim to be older even than our Order. When he is not lobbying for devolution of political power to himself and his allies, he has been known to indulge in… somewhat salacious and even barbaric activities here in London. If your cabman can admit dealings with de Montfort, then our suspicions will be confirmed.'

'Until now,' Sir Toby said, 'our enemy has hidden in the shadows. It is your job to unmask him, and drag him kicking and screaming into the light.'

'De Montfort is a man of prodigious power,' John said. 'I stabbed him and he did not bleed. He was physically strong and fast, and yet also possessed powers of foresight. What manner of man is he?'

'Barely a man at all,' said Cherleten. 'A Majestic, yes; but something more, also.'

'There are forces at work here that threaten the very fabric of our society,' Sir Toby said. 'You three agents are the first of our Order to make contact with these creatures in over a century. They are growing in number and audacity, but what exactly they are planning is unclear. De Montfort is the key to their plans, we believe, but his true motives are known only to him.'

'Please, Sir Toby,' Lillian said. 'If you will forgive my bluntness, you are speaking in riddles. What are we dealing with and what must we do?'

Sir Toby almost smiled, Lillian thought. *Almost.*

'Do not be so keen to get back into the field, Agent Hardwick,' he said. 'That these monsters are not from the Rift is troubling indeed, for if they did not tear their way through to us like the other creatures of the night, then they must have been among us all along. I trust you understand the implications.'

In spite of everything that had befallen the Empire—indeed, humanity—in the last few years, Lillian had never heard Sir Toby talk in such a manner.

'How do we know that they are not from the Rift? What are they?' Lillian grew impatient. More than that, her shoulder was throbbing, and she was starting to feel nauseated. She realised that the sensation had been growing gradually since she had first set foot in the room, and as soon as she had thought this, it became harder to push her discomfort from her mind.

'It is not easy to explain,' said Sir Toby. 'So I will begin with our more recent evidence, and you can draw your own conclusions. It began with wild reports of bodies being desecrated in funeral parlours and churchyards. Increased reports of bodysnatching followed and then, just two months ago, human remains were discovered by the Yorkshire constabulary in a small village on the edge of the moors.'

'I remember reading about that in the newspapers,' Lillian remarked. 'They attributed the killings to an old legend about a beast on the moors, did they not?'

'They did. And no one took it seriously, except perhaps to wonder if it was the work of the Riftborn; if perhaps the bones belonged to some Majestic who had overdosed on etherium.' At those words, Lillian felt sure Arthur shifted uncomfortably. 'And yet,' Sir Toby went on, 'when the same phenomenon occurred five more times, around York, Whitby and even Manchester, it came to the attention of Apollo Lycea.'

'I had not heard of any other cases,' said Lillian. Sir Arthur remained silent.

'Then that is testament to the integrity of your fellow agents,' replied Sir Toby. 'I asked them to conceal all evidence of the crimes, lest it cause a panic, and to keep speculation about monsters and cannibals out of the newspapers. Isn't that right, Sir Arthur?'

'Indeed, Sir Toby,' came the reply.

Lillian turned to look at Arthur. The only rule in the field was discretion. If Arthur had investigated a case without her and been sworn to secrecy—as was so often the custom—she could hardly hold it against him. And yet she did anyhow, for how could he withhold such information from her if he thought it might have any bearing on their own case?

'What our agents discovered,' continued Sir Toby, 'was a string of disappearances—of both the living and the dead—in a pattern across the north. Mostly unfortunates and beggars, but all in most mysterious circumstances, and with no real regard for secrecy when disposing of the remains. Bones chewed, flesh eaten and, in some cases... well, Sir Arthur can explain better than I.'

Arthur cleared his throat, probably feeling the hole that Lillian's eyes bore into him more keenly than most. 'Of course, Sir Toby. As I stated in my last report, the final victim we discovered was in a less defiled state. A young woman, an unfortunate taken from the slums we think. The body was found in a crypt beneath York Minster, seemingly drained of all of its blood, and partly... eaten.'

Lillian observed that Sir Arthur looked uneasy at the memory. She guessed that he must have used his powers to discern something of the victim's history, and perhaps had gleaned more than he'd bargained for. Whatever gruesome discovery he had made in York perhaps explained his hesitation yesterday.

She snapped her attention away from her partner when she realised that Lord Cherleten was standing right next to her. He had a way about him that was sly, and a tread that was silent as a cat. He reached across her, holding out a box of cigars to Sir Arthur, who took one gratefully and lit it. Lillian fancied it was to steady his nerves. She wished she could partake too, as the close proximity of Cherleten made her skin crawl, but that was not the done thing. No, for all of the systems of rank and military swagger of Apollo Lycea, it was still based in a gentlemen's club, and Sir Arthur Furnival was a gentleman of high standing, not a mere soldier to be ordered about.

So what does that make me?

'We encountered a great deal of superstition from the locals about the murders,' Sir Arthur went on once his cigar was lit. 'I confess, at first glance it was tempting to write it off as the work of the Riftborn; yet my own intuition and Smythe's examination—'

'Beauchamp Smythe?' Lillian interrupted, instantly regretting her outburst as all eyes turned to her. In her experience, the surgeon Beauchamp Smythe was a popinjay, so absorbed in promoting his fledgling theories of 'forensics' that he often lost sight of the goals of Apollo Lycea. She felt the strangest sense of betrayal that Sir Arthur had been on a secret assignment with an agent she disliked.

'Yes, the same,' Arthur replied, the look on his face one of puzzlement and amusement both. 'As I was saying, Smythe's examination of the cadavers led us to believe that the killers were certainly flesh and blood. And I suppose now we've seen the evidence with our own eyes.'

'Or perhaps you do not see it all,' said Cherleten. He always had an air of eccentricity about him—eyes wide, red hair dishevelled. Every sentence uttered seemed to hang in the air, as if he were waiting for imaginary friends to finish it for him. Perhaps he was trying to be enigmatic. Lillian snuck a glance at Sir Toby, whose eyes belied an annoyance at his peer, if only for a moment.

'Agent Smythe has been of singular use again,' Sir Toby interjected, dismissing Cherleten's jibe. 'He has already examined the remains that you found in the Dials. Beneath Miss Goodheart's fingernails was a small amount of necrotised flesh, like as not clawed from the attacker in her final moments.'

Both Lillian and Sir Arthur had heard many times over how Smythe believed that one day criminals would be apprehended by the scientific method of examining skin, blood and hair left at the scene of their crimes. And yet, they had also listened to Smythe bemoaning how such advances in forensic science were beyond the reach of the medical fraternity at this time.

'This cannot help us identify the killer, surely?' asked Lillian, lending voice to her thoughts.

'So we would have said previously, were it not for Lieutenant

Hardwick's struggle with de Montfort. You see, as the lieutenant has told us, de Montfort did not bleed. The flesh beneath the girl's fingernails was also curiously bloodless. Smythe has examined the girl, and the severed hand that Agent Hardwick and Sir Arthur discovered. He believes the flesh beneath the fingernails was not from the creature Agent Hardwick shot, although most like from its… kin.'

'Kin? You cannot mean de Montfort.' John sounded incredulous.

'The flesh had been treated with some type of bleach. And it had been, in Smythe's professional opinion, dead for longer than the unfortunate herself. That is to say, it looked as though it were taken from a corpse.'

'But you said it was likely from her killer,' Lillian said.

'Indeed I did.'

Arthur was quickest to comprehend. 'It has to be some new devilry of the Riftborn,' he said.

'I am afraid not, Sir Arthur,' Sir Toby replied. 'We entertained several theories at first, but eventually had to accept the truth of it. Events that we had long hoped would never come to pass have been set in motion. The Order's learned opinion is that the creatures you three encountered are not of the Rift, but are indeed of our world—though they are not entirely flesh and blood. Lord Cherleten is here today because he has something of an insight into the case, having collated intelligence from several… sources… over the years. I do not mean to beat around the bush, but it is difficult for me to believe what I am about to tell you, even though I have already seen the evidence for myself…' He trailed off, as if trying to gather his thoughts. *The old man is rattled,* thought Lillian. From the corner of her eye, she saw Cherleten smirking. *God, but he loves to hold all the cards.*

'What do you know of vampires?' said Cherleten, blurting out the question gleefully.

Sir Arthur almost choked on his cigar. John only half-managed to suppress a scoff. Sir Toby did not so much as blink. Lillian took the bait, if only to bring a swift conclusion to Cherleten's game.

'They are a fiction, dreamt up by gypsies and peasants from Bohemia and beyond, and served up in the penny dreadfuls by the more sensationalist writers. Unless you are suggesting that the things we all encountered yesterday were... vampires?' She scorned the notion. Lord Cherleten remained unruffled.

'A fiction, indeed? I suppose I would say the same, were I prone to denying the evidence of my own eyes.'

'I'm sure Agent Hardwick means no offence,' Sir Toby intervened. 'Likewise, I am sure that we can both understand her incredulity.'

Cherleten smiled and returned to his seat, leaving a coil of thick cigar smoke in his wake that made Lillian's eyes flutter. The oppressive atmosphere of the room was affecting her. *Damn this corset, I can hardly breathe.*

'I dislike the word "vampire" as much as you,' Sir Toby said, 'but Lord Cherleten has persuaded me of the truth of it. In your reports you both used the word "degenerates" to describe the creatures. You were not wrong; only, they were not degenerate humans that you faced, but degenerates of another race. They are ghouls—flesh-eating monsters—descended from their blood-drinking kin as surely as the common mongrel is descended from the wolf. It may not be entirely accurate to call these creatures "vampires", but if the glove fits, as they say.'

Lillian was finding it increasingly hard to concentrate. The cigar smoke was irritating; the pain in her arm was intense. She wanted nothing more than to go home for a hot bath and a hearty meal. But instead she had to listen to news of yet more horrors let loose upon a world already saturated with evil.

Lillian was thankful when John answered for them. 'You mean to say that the Majestic I saw at the factory could have been a vampire himself? One of the *living dead*?'

'It seems a strong possibility, particularly as you say that he commanded the creatures so easily. But understand this: we have had very few confirmed sightings of vampires. In fact, this

Majestic represents only the second of his kind that we have ever heard of, the first being so long ago it is barely given a credible place in the Order's records. And believe me, from what we know, these creatures are not the romantic, blood-sucking revenants of the penny dreadfuls. Beneath the veneer of humanity they are lifeless, soulless, and without compassion or mirth. Isn't that right, Lord Cherleten?'

'Oh, for the most part,' the peer replied. 'Though I wager they take their pleasures in their own particular way. I imagine they made a bit of sport of these two. How fortunate for us that they underestimated the intrepid lieutenant.'

How long must we suffer his prattling? Lillian swayed slightly.

'These creatures are not merely the blood-sucking undead that the more fanciful stories tell of. And their origins may be somewhat more natural than you would care to believe,' Cherleten was only getting warmed up, it seemed. 'Tales of vampires have been told around the world since before the birth of Christ, and indeed the Knights Iscariot claim to be descended from the very disciple for whom they are named—the blood of Judas is said to run in the veins of the creatures who control the ancient order, which makes their treachery against the Crown today hardly surprising. Tales of vampires, however, long pre-date these so-called knights. The Anglo-Saxons of our own isles spoke of nocturnal, blood-drinking half-men. Across Europe they are the *upir,* the *wampyr, the dearg-due* and the *strigoi;* in Africa the *ramanga;* in India the *vetala.* Even in South America, the most ancient cultures that we know of told of vampires called the *cihuateteo,* dead creatures that would impregnate the living with their spawn. I like that one in particular... so deliciously depraved, don't you agree? Although I suppose the best of all are the *lamia* of Greece; for how poetic that our warriors of Apollo should be battling ancient Hellenic monsters?'

'A goodly number of legends, my lord,' said John, 'but no evidence to link these creatures of the night with our man in Hyde; beyond, that is, some pickled flesh.'

'And if vampires are indeed real,' Lillian interrupted, 'we need only know two things: where they are, and how to kill them.' From the corner of her eye she saw John smile.

Cherleten pursed his lips and said simply, 'Your father's daughter, I see.' Lillian winced at that. Lord Hardwick did not react. 'For now, Agent Hardwick, you will have to show uncustomary patience in this matter, for there is more work in store for the three of you beyond common brawling. But heed my words; it is no coincidence that so many ancient cultures across the globe speak of vampires. These creatures are as real as you or me, and have perhaps been among us since the first man walked the Earth. Some say Adam's first wife, Lilith, was one of them, and her offspring brought the darkness into the world. Vampires are older, it seems, than womankind.' He chuckled at his observation. 'They are real, but you'll be pleased to know that we are developing weapons in the armoury to combat this new threat. When next you meet our flesh-eating friends, you will perhaps be better equipped. I shall see to it.'

'Please, Sir Toby, may I ask when I am to return to Hyde?' John cut out Cherleten, who looked unperturbed.

'You are not,' said Sir Toby. 'At least not yet. We already have an agent en route to the north.'

'Might I ask who?' John said.

'If you must know, Lieutenant, Agent Smythe left an hour ago. We need to find out quickly just how far the corruption has spread amongst the industrial towns in the area, and a… lighter touch is required for the task. Besides, Smythe is keen to observe a live specimen of these—*ahem*—"ghouls", for study.'

'Oh, for pity's sake…' Lillian muttered. This time her father did turn, with a frown that bore more a warning than outright disapproval.

Sir Toby ignored her, and addressed John directly. 'You and your sister will be assigned to a lighter duty, though of no lesser importance, while you recover from your injuries.'

John's indignation at that spilled over at the same time as

Lillian's. Despite feeling light-headed, she found herself saying, 'There are questions that must be answered, and justice that must be delivered!' She tried to sound confident, but Sir Toby looked concerned, ignoring John's protests and Sir Arthur's resigned sighs, looking instead straight at Lillian.

'Agent Hardwick, are you well?' he asked.

'Perfectly, Sir Toby. I am simply eager to receive instruction as to our next objective.'

Sir Arthur stepped forward and stubbed out his cigar in an ashtray.

'Gentlemen,' he said, 'I fear we have allowed Agent Hardwick's status as our equal here to blind us to good manners. She is still a lady, after all.'

'Oh, no, there's no need—' she began to protest, but it was too late. Sir Toby had already mumbled an agreement and stubbed out his cigar too, whilst the elder Hardwick propped open a window. 'Agent Hardwick; Lieutenant,' Sir Toby said. 'You have both been injured in the field. There will be no immediate return for either of you, although you will be needed again for this case, I assure you. Take tomorrow to recover; report to the club physician, and be ready to leave on Monday at first light.'

John looked as surprised as Lillian felt. She knew he'd be angry at being replaced on an assignment he'd made his own.

'Leave? For where, sir?' John asked.

Sir Toby reached into his desk drawer and handed an envelope each to John and Lillian.

'Your new orders. While you recover from your last ordeal, you will be assigned together on a diplomatic mission. It is a mission of great import, but should at least be free from unnecessary... exertions. Lieutenant, I would ask that you escort your sister home. We shall resume this discussion upon your return.'

'But... the vampires. The arms deals?' Lillian said, almost disbelievingly. Another wave of weakness rushed over her.

'We have your reports, and, rest assured, action will be taken. But for now, I suggest you take time to rest before your next mission.'

It was meant kindly, but it caused a flash of petulance to cross Lillian's features. By the time she had composed herself, Sir Toby had already turned to Arthur.

'Sir Arthur, if you would stay a while longer, there is a separate matter that requires your attention.'

'Of course, Sir Toby,' Arthur replied. He glanced at Lillian guiltily.

'Agent Hardwick, Lieutenant—you are dismissed.'

Sir Toby waved them both away. Sir Arthur opened the door for Lillian and John, sympathy writ on his face as she passed him.

'Lillian, there was more to be had from that exchange. Much more!' John's frustration bubbled over. 'How could Cherleten have been working on new weapons without test subjects? What is the relationship between the Knights Iscariot and those creatures? Who is de Montfort and what do we know about—' He stopped short, glancing furtively around, presumably to ensure no other clubmen were about to overhear his outburst. The pause seemed to bring about a change in his demeanour. 'Dear sister, forgive me; are you feeling all right? I think sometimes I forget what—'

'What a weak woman I am?' she finished, sounding far stronger than she felt. A flash of anger had lent her temporary strength, but she felt as though she might be sick.

John threw up his hands. 'That is not what I was going to say, and you know it.'

'I know, it's just... blast it! This corset is going to kill me, I swear.'

'Well, best not deal with that here, or some of these old fellows will keel over with apoplexy.'

Lillian steadied herself on the handrail of the grand stair, trying not to laugh despite her discomfort. John looked like he would hug her, but thought better of it.

She faltered. The prickling sensation behind her eyes, the

light-headedness, and the hot pain in her shoulder conspired to almost make Lillian faint. She stumbled forwards, catching sight of the floor of the marble hall over the balcony, which seemed too far away, and caused her to become more disorientated. John steadied her, and looked concerned.

'Lillian, you know there's no one I'd rather have by my side in a tight spot; but by God, you can be stubborn. You need to rest—we both do—and then we'll "get back on the horse", so to speak. I don't know what's in these envelopes, but I hope it'll be light duties somewhere sunny, and you should damned well hope for the same.'

Lillian tried desperately to compose herself. The pain and nausea passed, and she straightened up, knowing her brother was right. Lillian looked down at the grey-haired clubmen loitering in every nook of the great hall below them. 'Look at them, John,' she murmured. 'They talk of literature, of law and philosophy, and dine on the finest fare. They pretend, as ever, that the club is still just a place for social gatherings, free of Apollo Lycea, that they can continue as they always have, in a world that has changed beyond recognition.'

'I envy them their fantasies, sis. You should too. You're in the real world, where they don't have the heart to live.'

'Perhaps... I can't change everything at once,' she said, with a half-hearted smile.

He offered her his arm. 'Dear lady, let me escort you to a carriage. The hour is late, and the weather is dreadfully inclement.'

With the best smile she could muster, she accepted, and together they descended the sweeping marble stair of the Apollonian. She leaned on her brother more heavily than she'd have liked, but was safe in the knowledge that he would never tell anyone about her moment of weakness. He was her true ally in the club—the only man who saw her side of things, and who could honestly understand what it was to bear the Hardwick name.

SEVEN

Lillian had not returned home as instructed. Instead, she had gone with John to his home in Hackney. John knew only too well the worry her condition would cause their dear mother, and so became complicit in the deception, sending a message to Dora Hardwick informing her that Lillian was in rude health, but was to be retained for several nights on investigative duties. John fussed around Lillian like a mother hen. He made her comfortable, and prepared a light supper of soused herring and bread.

Lillian perused John's bookshelves, which groaned under the weight of hundreds of volumes, from poetry and great literature to the latest sensational stories. John had fancied himself a writer in his youth, even having a few poems published in *The Graphic*, before he had given up such aspirations to follow in their father's footsteps and join the Order. She turned from the books and surveyed the unkempt flat, dozens more books tossed around the living room beside piles of dirty linen and unwashed dishes. John lived the life of a carefree bachelor, but his abode was more like that of a scatter-brained academic in his senior years.

'The state of this flat is… unseemly,' Lillian said, picking up a crumpled shirt from the chaise before taking a seat.

'You know you're always welcome here, dear sis, but I am a bachelor, and must be afforded certain allowances. Besides, the maid doesn't call again until Monday.'

'And you wonder if your antics will shock me?' Lillian needled her brother. 'I do not think you are quite the scandalous spy you aspire to be... not yet, anyway.'

John laughed. 'It seems I'm doing a better job than you of staying out of mischief. What is this now? Four assignments, and wounded in three of them? I think perhaps you should try the subtle approach from time to time, like I do.'

Lillian looked at him gravely for a moment, and then forced a smile. 'You are as subtle as a coster's call,' she replied. 'Too much of a popinjay for subterfuge.'

'I resent that, madam!' he said, feigning injury. 'With one look at my honest face and impeccable wardrobe, the enemy simply spills his secrets into my ear. Which is a damned sight better than trying to tear it off.'

Lillian scowled at that. He referred to her last ill-fated assignment to pursue a foreign ambassador with a criminal bent. It had resulted in an altercation with a burly punisher, during which the man had twisted Lillian's ear so hard it had needed stitching back into place. The man had received a sharpened hairpin to his manhood for his trouble, but the ambassador had escaped the scene. She blamed Beauchamp Smythe for that; the surgeon had been blindsided, and in a bid to save him from his own carelessness she'd paid a painful cost.

'It still pains me in the cold weather,' she replied, ruefully; more ruefully still upon taking another mouthful of herring that tasted of little other than vinegar.

'Hark at you, like an old, wounded soldier. Father would be proud.'

Lillian tried to ignore that.

'Anyway, have this.' John tossed a small parcel across the room, which she caught deftly. 'Got you a present. Didn't have time to give it to you before they packed me off to Hyde.'

Lillian unwrapped the coloured paper to reveal a jewellery box. 'John, you shouldn't have.' She opened it up, to reveal an ornate silver locket, quite large. Clicking it open, she was a little dismayed to find a small portrait of her father staring back at her. Her mother graced the other side, but it was Marcus Hardwick's stony features that made Lillian's heart sink. 'You really shouldn't have.'

John snorted back a laugh. 'That, my dear sister, used to be grandfather's best pocket-watch. He gave it to Father on his twenty-first birthday, who gave it to me on mine. I've rather broken with tradition by not having sons of my own first... anyhow, that's not important. I had a chap on Bond Street remake it into something a bit more to your taste.'

It was not really to Lillian's taste at all, but she forced a smile. 'You had a family heirloom... remade?'

'Yes, especially for you. But that's not the best part. See it still has the watch-winder? Give it a twirl.'

Lillian looked again at the locket, bemused by John's idea of an appropriate gift for her. All the same, she twisted the winder, which clicked and came loose. Pulling it, a thin wire unfurled from within the locket, extending to almost eighteen inches as she pulled it taut.

'A garrotte!' John beamed. 'That's an extra special modification courtesy of a pal in the armoury.'

'Oh, John,' Lillian said, smiling genuinely now. 'You do know me after all.'

'Just want to see you equipped for any eventuality. It seems fitting, given what happened yesterday.'

'There is something seriously amiss, John. You feel it too?'

'Yes and no. I mean, it's an awful business, but just because these cases are connected doesn't mean we're on the brink of Judgement Day. I mean, the world doesn't revolve around us, much as I'd like it to.'

'It's more than that, though. I mean, Father's recent trip, the secrecy around it... aren't you worried? Or in the least bit curious?'

'Well, I... um...'

'You know something!' Lillian gasped.

'Not really. It's more something I… overheard.'

'Which is?'

John sighed. 'Father spent some time in Alaska, at a research facility in the middle of nowhere. He also travelled to the Confederacy, to strike some deal with President McClellan, and meet with some top scientists over there. I don't know much beyond that, except that it's to do with the Rift.'

'Has he found a way to close it? I can't believe it! And why treat with the Americans first? Why would he not—'

John held up a hand. 'I don't know, sis. Probably not, or I'm sure he'd be making more of a song and dance about it. No, you're right that there's something going on, but beyond what I just told you I have no idea—the fellows at the card table had no further gossip, and Father said nothing more.'

'Really, John, the one time I need you to… oh, never mind. I don't suppose you know if this new mission is related to Father's secret dealings, do you?'

John shrugged. 'Maybe. I try not to ask too many questions. Protocol and integrity and all that—you really ought to try it.'

'But why are we to go to Portsmouth?' she said, looking again at the orders she had received. 'I have to believe there's more to it than just nannying a foreign dignitary. Is this what it has come to?'

'Ah, careful, sis,' John said. 'The orders do not expressly say "dignitary". It could be a political prisoner, an undercover agent, or Sir Toby's favourite hunting hound for all we know. The most telling part of orders, I always find, is the part that is omitted.'

Lillian scowled at the papers, an expression that was becoming a fixture of the evening. John was right, of course. He only had a couple of years' more experience as an agent, but his successes spoke for themselves. His misadventure at Hyde was probably the only time he'd put a foot wrong in the field, so far as Lillian knew.

'Who is this "Tesla", anyway? And why on earth are we delivering him to Cherleten and not to Sir Toby?' That the orders were signed by Lord Cherleten was a source of much indignation, and she was aware that her protests against this had been perhaps too ardent on the ride home.

John shrugged. 'Engineer? Scientist? Surgeon? Must be one of those if Cherleten needs him. Undoubtedly an Intuitionist. And if they're sending two agents of our great notoriety, I'd say he's important.'

'Now you're making assumptions. It might be a woman.' Lillian poked at her meal, before observing, 'Father's name is on here too.'

'Well, like it or not, it is Father's doing that Cherleten swaggers about so much. He's made himself invaluable to the War Office, and so Father's influence protects the spiteful old fop. I imagine Sir Toby is looking forward to the day when Cherleten slips up, so he can bring him down a peg or two.'

'It seems we've both gone down in the world. I daresay Lord Cherleten will want to tell us all the things we field agents are doing wrong, and how his precious armoury personnel can do it all better and faster, and at less expense.'

'What was it Father always said? "The Order of Apollo is a first-rate warship, but Anthony Cherleten is a privateer, sailing the fine line between nobility and piracy." Whatever he has in store for us, just remember where your loyalties lie, or he'll end up stealing us from old Toby.'

'I will not be one of Cherleten's toadies,' Lillian said.

'Just try not to insult him to his face,' John replied. 'If you're going to poke the anointed pig, do so from behind the fence.'

'I simply cannot stand being in his presence; I swear it was his leering that made me feel faint, rather than the pain.' She looked at John, and realised that he'd been rubbing at his ribs for a while, making her feel terribly guilty that all the talk had been of her feelings and injuries. 'How are you healing?'

'I'm still sore. But I'm trussed up in one of Smythe's fancy girdles, tighter than a Tyburn tippet. A goodly number of cracks and bruises, but no breaks, thank heavens. You complained of your corsetry back at the club—I rather think I know what you mean.'

'Are you quite sure you'll be fit for duty on Monday?'

'Of course. And even better, this girdle makes me look leaner, don't you think? Mind you, I hope I don't have to get my suit adjusted.'

Lillian could not help but laugh at her brother's vanity. 'You always find a way to see the best in things,' she said. 'You'll be wearing the girdle long after you've recovered if it improves the look of your wardrobe.'

'Hmm?' John turned sideways, admiring himself in the mantel mirror.

While he was distracted, Lillian held out a forkful of herring to John's cat, Chuzzlewit. The runtish ginger tom had entered noiselessly through the kitchen window; the cat turned his nose up at the merest sniff of the fish, and retreated whence he had come.

Lillian whipped the fork back to her plate as John turned back to her, perhaps realising belatedly that he had been insulted. 'And what of your injuries, sis?' he said, evidently deciding to ignore whatever it was she'd said.

'I am fine,' Lillian replied curtly. 'Granting me an extra day's rest is nothing but chauvinism on Sir Toby's part. I could have gone to Hyde immediately.'

'Smythe would have liked that,' John said. Lillian scowled at him. 'Mind you, he was deuced sheepish when I told him... oh, never mind.'

'Told him what?' Lillian's eyes flared.

'Oh... damn. It's nothing. I was gaming with him in the club last night and... it's nothing!' He spread his palms and smiled, but his protestations were too vigorous.

'What are you hiding?' Lillian asked.

John sighed. 'You know I shouldn't say anything. You're putting me in a jolly unfair position.'

'You shouldn't *know* anything; and if you hadn't been so loose-lipped over cards and cigars, you still would not. Honestly, John Hardwick, I would expect better of you than carousing with the Bullingdon boys.' It was one of the things that Lillian could not rise above at the Apollonian, no matter how hard she tried. Despite graduating from the academy with distinction, while in the club she could partake of neither alcohol nor tobacco in the company of men, and she certainly could not play cards. If she desired a glass of wine after a hard day, she was banished to the ladies' drawing room, to gossip with the wives and daughters of distinguished clubmen, while her peers sat in offices and traded information that she should be privy to.

'It was a bagatelle, if you must know. And I am lucky that the "Bullingdon boys" let me anywhere near their gaming tables,' John grumbled. He sighed and looked resigned. 'Look, Smythe *might* have told me about his next assignment and... and that he hopes very much that you will not look upon him unfavourably in the future as a result.'

Despite being subjected to Lillian's best withering glare, John's eyes twinkled. It seemed that no matter how old they got, he would always enjoy teasing her.

'He knew he was taking over from Arthur and me? How?'

'He... ahem... requested the assignment, for purely academic reasons, you understand. Although he was deuced disappointed when he learned you weren't fit enough to go with him.'

'Oh, for heaven's sake. Did he request the assignment for the advancement of his scientific endeavours? Or did he... well...'

'Just want to be close to you? Perhaps we'll never know. But you realise that a lady of action such as yourself could do a lot worse—'

John did his best to dart out of the way, but Lillian's aim was true and a hunk of bread hit him square between the eyes. He laughed. She glowered at him, and rubbed her injured shoulder. That stopped John, and he went over to his sister, though cautiously.

'Let's have a look at that, sis. Oh... it looks angry. I think it'll heal all right, but it's little wonder you aren't yourself. I think you should go to bed.'

'I'm perfectly—'

'No you are not. Just for once will you do what's good for

you? What would Beauchamp Smythe say, I wonder? In his professional capacity, of course.'

'I'm sure I couldn't care less.'

'Then abed with you. I suggest that a good night's sleep followed by a hearty breakfast will do you the power of good.'

'Don't tell me you're going to make breakfast?'

'Why... no. Cook will be here first thing.'

'Then it is a wonderful suggestion. I feel better already.'

Lillian jumped awake, her heart racing and her nightdress clinging to her, damp with cold sweat. Her mind was filled with images of slavering jaws and sparkling, violet eyes, cold, pale, naked forms scuttling along the walls and across the ceiling, shimmering in the darkness as they hunted for her, the rank smell of fresh human flesh still on their breath.

Worse, a voice had called to her. It pulled at her as inexorably as the moon pulls the tides. She had felt it resonate deep within her; in her blood.

It had called her name.

At first, the shadows of the strange room brought panic to her, but gradually as the wisps of nightmare relinquished their hold, she remembered that she was at her brother's lodgings, and calmed herself. Her shoulder throbbed more than ever, and a few spots of blood stained her nightdress where they had seeped through the dressing, but her nausea had gone.

She lit her candle and padded over to the sideboard to wash her face. She poured a glass of water and drank thirstily. The nightmare had been vivid indeed. The monster in the tunnels had shaken her more than any encounter in recent memory, for it could so easily have killed her. And what would have become of her then? Would she be another corpse for Smythe and Lord Cherleten to unearth, to feed their fanciful tales of vampires and ghouls and goodness-knows-what?

Feed. A poor choice of word, she thought.

Lillian took another long drink, and looked around the room. The dim crimson glow of the skyline shone through the thin curtains. She went to the window and opened the sash a little. John had closed it so that she didn't catch a chill on top of everything else, but she needed air. Not that she'd get much fresh air from the city this night. Ghostly wisps of fog flowed into the room, as if grasping for Lillian with ethereal fingers. She sighed, and closed the window again. The next day would doubtless play host to a London particular, and she would be housebound whilst the world outside was suffocated by the stifling smog. She felt like a ship set adrift, waiting for a change in the wind to push her from the doldrums so she could beat to quarters once more.

Monday had not come quickly enough, though after another restless night Lillian began to regret her eagerness to take up her next assignment. When she had awoken that morning with bags under her eyes, and a nightmarish voice whispering to her in the darkness, she had set about masking her unrest so that John would not look upon her with undue concern. Lillian had long learned to conceal fatigue and injuries from her mother, who was at least twice as observant as John, and so that morning she had washed in elderflower water, before applying a concoction of rosewater and sulphate of zinc to the dark rings about her eyes.

John was in high spirits, though Lord knew why. They had left his flat at an ungodly hour to receive a briefing from Cherleten, and since then they had been confined to a carriage, which bumped and jolted their way out of the city. The details of their mission were skeletal at best, and what instructions they had received had been enough to frustrate Lillian—an outcome that doubtless filled Lord Cherleten with no small amount of pride. And yet, John was all smiles, despite being as much in the dark about their ultimate goal as Lillian.

'Oh, come now, sis, surely you can manage a bit of cheer? I think of this as an adventure, don't you?' John sat across from

Lillian, beaming at her like a child on Christmas morning.

'We are to be confined to this coach for an interminable duration, and we haven't even been entrusted with the details of the mission. You may call that an adventure, but I call it going off half-cocked.'

'Oh dear, it seems you do not thrive on mystery. Perhaps an occupation outside of espionage might be more your forte?'

'In our business, a lack of intelligence is dangerous.'

'I'm sure we'll receive further instruction in good time.' John sighed. 'Mind you, given the state of us both, I'm surprised you aren't glad of a little light duty for a day or two.'

Lillian scowled again. 'I did not join the Order of Apollo for light duties. I would rather be facing an enemy than be escort to some stranger.'

'If it's righteous vengeance against Cherleten's monsters you're after, I'm sure you'll get your chance. We all have to set aside personal vendettas in the name of Queen and country. I'm sure these missions are vital, too, in the greater scheme of things.'

Lillian held her tongue; she had forgotten how much she disliked working with her brother. They got along famously at home and in the dojo, but when he was on duty he adopted a superior air that infuriated her.

The coach jolted violently for the umpteenth time, causing the windows to rattle in their panes, and an icy draught to be sucked into the compartment. Lillian turned away and looked out of the grimy window. They were approaching Streatham, their first stop, where the driver would change his team ready for the cross-country leg of the journey.

'I never thought I'd crave a train journey,' Lillian said at last, more to herself than to John.

'Aside from the romance of this antiquated mode of transport, it is the safest way to travel. We command our own schedule, and can change our route at the drop of a hat. Trains run to timetables, and our journey could be predicted by the enemy.'

'What enemy?' Lillian asked.

John shrugged. 'Whichever. Just because we are used to facing creatures of a more... metaphysical nature, it doesn't mean that the Empire has no real enemies left. In fact, I'd wager that's the reason for Cherleten's clandestine manner.'

Lillian found that almost reassuring. She would rather believe that shadowy foreign agents plagued their every movement than trust Anthony Cherleten not to be toying with them for his own amusement.

Minutes later, the carriage pulled into the courtyard of a coaching inn. The driver jumped down from his seat and tapped on the window. Lillian pushed it down to address the portly man, whose face was red from the cold wind.

'Stopping 'ere for a moment, miss, to change the 'orses. If you'd like to take some time in the inn, that'd be agreeable. Otherwise, I'll have this team swapped around in barely a minute.' He said this proudly, confident in his skill with the horse and tack.

Lillian saw that John was about to get out to stretch his legs, and immediately replied: 'No, Selby, that won't be necessary. I think we should be on our way as quickly as possible.'

'As you wish, miss. I'll be done in two shakes.'

Lillian closed the window, happy at her brother's minor discomfort. John reached for his newspaper and pretended he didn't want to leave the coach after all.

'We're damned lucky to get Selby,' John remarked, pretending to look over the obituaries. 'Fastest whip in England, by all accounts. Five hours is a devil of a time to reach Portsmouth by road.'

Lillian wished he hadn't reminded her. Five hours seemed interminable. She knew that she would have to disembark at their next stop, no matter how satisfying it felt to score points against John.

The carriage was an odd way to travel; Lillian half wondered if it would attract undue attention in and of itself. Even here, in a traditional coaching house, automated perambulators were parked outside unused stables, and the stertorous murmurings of new-fangled electrical generators could be heard from within. Jim Selby, a coachman of some note, was anachronistic in his passion for the carriage and horse.

She had barely reflected on this when the coachman rapped on the window again.

'All done, sir, miss.'

'Very good, Mr. Selby,' Lillian replied. 'Let's make hay while the sun shines.'

Selby grinned and hopped back into the driver's seat with an agility that belied his stout frame, and the coach jerked into motion once more, rattling from the cobbled courtyard and picking up speed at an alarming rate as soon as the gates were cleared.

'A minute and a half to change the team,' John said. 'He's taking his time today. But this is where you'll see Selby in action.' John had a boyish look about him. 'According to *The Times*, he achieved twenty miles per hour on this next stretch during the record-breaking run. We should be lucky if he does that today!'

Lillian looked through the window as the uniform terraces of Streatham rattled past, the greenery of the old village poking between them at intervals. Though she would not admit it to John, there was something romantic about taking a stagecoach; a hearkening back to a simpler time when the fastest a body could travel was on the back of a horse. A time before Majestics and Intuitionists, etherium and Riftborn. The great march of progress and the downfall of the natural order had gone hand-in-hand, it seemed. Indeed, the rise of the Intuitionists had seen much of the world industrialised faster than had been thought imaginable just a decade prior.

Before long the London outskirts gave way entirely, first to rough wasteland and then to fields and dark forests, the crimson caste of the sky mellowing to a golden hue, almost dawn-like. The great airships that monitored the meteorological conditions of the burning sky were specks on the horizon behind them; the last perambulator passed by the coach, its range insufficient to take it further beyond the city limits. The driver of the 'automobile' waved to the stagecoach, as if Lillian, John and Selby were adventurers, taking the path less trodden into unknown territory.

'Next stop, Godalming,' John said. 'Almost seems like a bit of a jaunt, eh? Wonder how Smythe's getting on up north? And Sir Arthur, for that matter.'

'Perfectly well, I'm sure,' Lillian replied. Though in truth, she was not at all sure. Arthur had been retained by Sir Toby after their last meeting, and although she had sent him a note on Sunday morning inviting him to tea, he had not responded. The secrecy of the club made forming bonds of friendship inadvisable; any one of the thirty-two active field agents of Apollo Lycea could find themselves in deadly pursuits at the drop of a hat. John was right—their current assignment did seem like a jaunt, and she only hoped that, while she and her brother rattled through sleepy countryside, Sir Arthur Furnival was not in danger.

Monday, 20th October
FROGMORE HOUSE, LONDON

Sir Arthur held back a respectable distance, though endeavouring to keep in stride, and earshot, of his estimable host. The Queen walked slowly through the gardens of Frogmore, towards the great ornamental lake, with Lord Hardwick at her side. The old soldier was tall, straight of back and broad of shoulder, striding slowly with Her Majesty, hands folded behind his back. He stooped respectfully to bend his ear to the diminutive monarch, and spoke only when spoken to.

To Arthur's left, her presence felt even when it was not seen, walked Kate Fox, the royal adviser. The catalyst, or half of it, at least. The American was slender and fey; her dark eyes bore into the back of Arthur's head when he was not looking at her—even, he fancied, when she was not looking at him either. And when he did turn to her, to show diligence or exchange some pleasantry, he was forced each time to look away hastily, lest the myriad crawling things that slid into his peripheral vision and surrounded the woman drive him to distraction. She was a conduit for spiritual energy, the mother of all Majestics, and she alone remained untouched by the persistent attentions of the Riftborn. Or, if not untouched, at least unharmed.

'And you are sure, Lord Hardwick, that the Earl of Beaconsfield is agreeable to your plan?' the Queen asked. 'He was most agitated when last we spoke, and I could not sanction any course of action that the Earl did not support. As he would say, the people would not have it.'

'Of course, Your Majesty,' Marcus Hardwick replied, his demeanour more respectful than Arthur had ever seen. 'I have apprised the Earl of Beaconsfield of the situation, and will meet with him later today.'

'And you are sure it will work?'

'I am afraid there are no certainties in this world any longer, ma'am. All I know is that what I saw in Alaska gives me hope. Hope that there is a way out of these times of darkness, and a brighter future ahead. My experiment will, one way or another, settle the matter.'

'And this Intuitionist is the key to your experiments?'

'Nikola Tesla is, they say, the greatest Intuitionist in the world. His grasp of electrical engineering and his theories about the use of Rift energy are unparalleled, especially in one so young. He has some... eccentricities... but I believe he represents our best chance of success.'

Arthur strained his ears to listen to the conversation, giving only the most cursory replies to Miss Fox, who was making monotonous chit-chat. In fact, Miss Fox did not seem to be truly engaged in their conversation either, though Arthur was sure she was not eavesdropping on the Queen and Lord Hardwick like he was; no, it seemed to Sir Arthur that the dark-eyed woman's mind was altogether elsewhere, and he did not like the thought of that at all.

'I hope you are right, Lord Hardwick,' the Queen went on. 'It took a great personal favour from Emperor Alexander to secure Mr. Tesla's release—and were it not for the Earl of Beaconsfield, the Russians may not be so well-disposed to us at all. They believe the young man in question to be a danger to all around him.'

'Youthful exuberance, ma'am, I am reliably informed, nothing more,' Hardwick replied. 'Tesla has been granted incredible knowledge, undoubtedly by the grace of God, and such gifts in one so young have led to unfortunate accidents. In our facility he will be trained and kept in check, until his wisdom grows in accordance with his talents.'

Queen Victoria nodded thoughtfully, and appeared satisfied with Hardwick's answer. Arthur, however, was more troubled than before. He had not previously heard of Tesla being a dangerous man, and as far as he knew no mention of this fact had been made to anyone in the Order. Arthur wondered if Lillian was aware what she was getting herself into.

'Who is Lillian?' Kate Fox asked, her voice flat, its rhythm slow.

Arthur cursed himself; between Miss Fox's dreamy prattling and his own eavesdropping, he had lowered his guard, and his thoughts had been transmitted to the most gifted psychic in the world as surely as if he'd written her a note. And had he imagined it, but did Lord Hardwick's ears prick up at the mention of his daughter's name? By God, the man had the senses of a wolf. Had he not spent several years training within the secret service, Arthur might have blushed. As it was, he merely cleared his throat and said, 'I'm sorry? Oh, a fellow agent—Lord Hardwick's daughter, in fact. She and her brother are away presently.'

'I cannot see her,' Miss Fox replied, as though it were the most natural thing in the world to say.

Arthur looked at her, and shuddered as he saw a strange, shadowy black tendril whip up from behind the woman's back and coil around her pale throat. And yet, when he tried to focus on the thing, it was not there. It remained in his mind's eye nonetheless, as did the fingers that probed about her dress, and reached across to tug at Arthur's sleeve. He dismissed them at once, and set about building his mental defences more firmly this time. Soon he could not see the creatures at all, but he fancied he could hear a voice in the back of his mind.

We shall take your woman and claw-gouge her eyes...

'Tell me, Lord Hardwick,' the Queen was saying, 'what news from the north? I have received most disconcerting reports from my government.'

'I cannot lie, ma'am, the situation appears less than satisfactory, though we do not yet have all the intelligence we require.'

'I would normally hold you accountable for any lack of intelligence when it comes to England's security, Lord Hardwick, but it appears on this occasion that even Miss Fox's vision is clouded by the matter. Isn't that so, Miss Fox?' The Queen stopped and turned towards her adviser.

'Forces are arrayed against us,' Miss Fox replied in her dreamy, detached tone. 'Whether they have shrouded themselves from me, or whether it is the Other's doing, I cannot say. I see only shadow.'

The Queen nodded, and began to walk again, everyone else following suit at once. 'There is another, is there not, who has previously helped us when Miss Fox was sadly unable? One who intervened when my dear Albert was almost killed. Can you perhaps not consult with him again?'

'Alas, ma'am, I am afraid that is quite impossible. That man has not been heard from for some time.'

They're talking of the Artist, Arthur thought, though he shielded those thoughts from Miss Fox, whose shadowy familiars squirmed in his peripheral vision in ever-growing numbers. How the celestial would be able to assist the Order in this matter when Kate Fox could not baffled Sir Arthur.

'A pity,' the Queen said. 'So what are we to do, Lord Hardwick? I hear that our ships are being turned away from our own ports, and that our army is facing worldwide shortages as a result of closed munitions factories. Why, the Prime Minister has even advised us not to travel to our beloved Balmoral for the foreseeable future. Am I, the Queen, not safe in my own country? This will not do.'

'Of course not, Your Majesty,' said Lord Hardwick. 'You will pleased to hear, I hope, that agents of Apollo Lycea are in the north as we speak, and I expect their first reports any time now. Once we have intelligence, we will act swiftly and decisively, you have my word.'

'Lord Hardwick, your word has ever been sufficient. I will speak to the Earl of Beaconsfield and advise him most strongly to lend you support in this matter. But we must have results, and quickly.'

Lord Hardwick bowed courteously. The Queen was impossible to read; Arthur wondered if he would be able to divine her true intent even if he were to use his powers. Of course, such a question was moot, especially given the presence of the formidable Miss Fox.

The circular walk continued, with the Queen commenting further on the state of the north, and Lord Hardwick holding his cards firmly to his chest in the most cordial manner possible. When finally they reached the courtyard of the country residence, they were met by several servants of the royal household, and a small gig was brought about to take Sir Arthur and Lord Hardwick back along the drive. Their perambulator awaited them a mile down the lane, for Queen Victoria would not allow the machines within earshot of her beloved horses.

'We were glad to meet you, Sir Arthur,' said the Queen. 'The Nightwatch has ever been a valuable jewel in the Empire's crown.'

'I... that is, I am not with the Nightwatch, Your Majesty,' Arthur replied, with a glance towards Lord Hardwick's impassive features.

'Indeed? Then perhaps Lord Hardwick and Sir Toby have finally seen sense and afforded their Majestics a more central role in the Order.'

'Sir Arthur's talents have proved indispensable, ma'am,' Lord Hardwick interjected.

'He is a great seer,' said Miss Fox. Her interruption would have been indecorous, but appeared to be greeted eagerly by the Queen. 'The Other takes great interest in Sir Arthur Furnival, but I foresee that his end shall not come at the hands of the Riftborn. Sir Arthur is too canny an opponent for such a fate.'

Lord Hardwick straightened. Arthur shuddered a little. He was not altogether certain he wanted to discuss the manner of his passing at all.

'My lady is too kind,' Sir Arthur said, and against his better judgement he took her—mercifully gloved—hand, and bowed. Though he was well guarded against involuntary visions or intrusions into his thoughts, there was an exchange of energy between them, like an electrical charge, and he heard Kate Fox's voice clearly in his mind, though she did not speak aloud.

Take care of your lady. A time will come when all that she is will depend upon you. And if you fail, the Other shall be waiting...

Sir Arthur pulled his hand away, perhaps a little too sharply. No one else seemed to notice any form of exchange, but as Arthur looked up at Miss Fox's dark eyes—rather sad eyes, he thought—he could have sworn he saw a whip-thin tendril of shadow unfurl itself from her throat, and retreat once again behind—or, rather, into—her back.

'May I speak freely, Lord Hardwick?' Arthur asked when they were safely away in the growling automobile.

'I suppose you will do so anyway.'

It seems to me that I was brought along today for no better reason than to sweeten Her Majesty's disposition.'

'Oh?' Lord Hardwick raised a bushy eyebrow.

'Indeed. The Queen's preoccupation with Majestics is well known. However, I resent being paraded before her, and not just her, but Kate Fox. That woman's powers are quite beyond my own—to associate too closely with her is to court... unintended consequences.'

Lord Hardwick considered this.

'I had presumed you were skilled enough to handle the matter,' he said. 'That is, after all, why Sir Toby spared you the rigours of the Nightwatch, is it not? You are right—in part at least. The matters I put to the Queen this afternoon were delicate ones, to say the least. And I confess I hoped that you'd provide some distraction to the Fox woman. You certainly succeeded on that score.'

Sir Arthur frowned at that. What he had seen—what he had felt—had been most discomfiting.

'I said you were partly right,' Lord Hardwick continued. 'There was one other reason I asked you along today.'

'Which is?'

Lord Hardwick leaned forward in his seat. Arthur heard the man's leather glove squeaking as his fist clenched around his walking cane. His face was as stone, his stare intense—this was not the elder statesman, this was Britain's war leader, until recently a decorated, serving soldier, forged in battle. He spoke to Sir Arthur plainly, in almost a growl, so there would be no mistaking his meaning.

'I do not know if what I have heard in the upper clubrooms is true or not, but the fact that I have heard such things at all displeases me. It displeases me a great deal. I shall say this to you once, and only once, and I shall say it as one man to another, so that our rank and titles may not muddy the waters: stay the hell away from my daughter.'

EXTRACT FROM *THE DAILY NEWS*

7th September 1860—In a statement issued by the Palace, Queen Victoria has today publicly endorsed the growing Spiritualist movement, which has until recently been mostly confined to practices in the Americas. Her Majesty the Queen revealed that a recent telegram received from a leading Spiritualist figure, one Catherine Fox, accurately diagnosed a hitherto undetected medical condition of the Queen's Consort, Prince Albert. Through further consultation with acolytes of Miss Fox, the Prince is said to be on the road to recovery from what could have been an otherwise fatal illness.

The Queen has extended an invitation to Catherine Fox and her sister, Margaret, to visit England and hold the first Royal Spiritualist Society meeting at Buckingham Palace. Whether the invitation will be accepted remains to be seen, but there is already talk in Parliament of extending the freedom of the City of London to the two American sisters.

EIGHT

illian jumped awake as the coach jolted.

'Back in the land of the living?' John said. 'You missed Godalming altogether.'

'What? You should have woken me. Where are we?' Lillian craned her neck to see out of the window.

'Coming up on Havant. Last stop. I didn't have the heart to wake you. You seemed to be having a nightmare again. Oh, don't pretend—I've heard you calling out in your sleep the last couple of nights. Something troubles you.'

'It's nothing,' she lied. 'But we really must stop soon so I can make myself presentable.'

John nodded. 'Ten minutes at most. Selby hasn't set a new record, but he's come deuced close, I can tell you.'

Lillian was cross with herself for nodding off, but troubled at yet another nightmare. She hoped she hadn't been too fitful. Even now, she was possessed of a sense of dread, and when she closed her eyes she could see the creature that haunted her dreams; the creature with the pallid skin, sharp claws, and those shining, violet eyes that glittered like amethysts in twilight. She could hear the voice, too, whispering to her from some place far away. A place she knew and yet had never been.

She shook her head, as if to shake away her own foolishness.

At that, she realised John was looking at her curiously. She ignored him. If the nightmares became worse, she knew she should confide in her brother, though it crossed her mind that she might need a Majestic rather than a confidant.

Presently, the coach left a wide, gritted track and began to rattle once more over cobbled roads, which proved enough to shake the last of the sleep from Lillian's head. A minute later, they drew into the courtyard of a half-timbered inn called the Bear, and Lillian alighted without waiting for Selby to bring the step. It was late afternoon, and the inn looked fairly quiet.

The sky was not clear, but it was also not as fierce as back in London, and Lillian took a breath of fresh air before heading into the inn to refresh herself.

Less than half an hour later she was sitting in a cosy snug drinking strong coffee, earning a disapproving glance from the landlord's wife, but caring little. A fire crackled low in the hearth. John sat opposite her in a comfortable armchair, stretching himself after being cooped up for so long.

'The lad has just returned, sir, ma'am,' the landlord said, poking his head around the timber frame of the snug. 'Your carriage will be here in ten minutes, I reckon.'

'Thank you, Denton,' John replied. 'I trust the settlement for your services is satisfactory.'

'Aye sir, more than satisfactory. Your agency can always depend on us.'

Apollo Lycea, under various guises, had safe-houses across the country, with staunch men and women from all walks of life ready at a moment's notice to act as servants to the Order, knowing only that, in some small way at least, they served the Crown. For Denton, like so many others, that was enough. That, and the fact that the Order paid them well. Lillian wondered if the safe-houses in the north were still loyal to the Crown—whether such folk as Denton hid their allegiance from those who would oppose England's authorities, or if they had been compromised by whatever forces were sweeping the land. She wanted nothing more than to head northwards to find out for herself.

'I see our boys are in a spot of bother in Caboul,' John said, rustling his newspaper.

'Afghanistan… Father will be vexed, though I imagine it shall get worse until we can mend this situation with the munitions supplies.'

'Yes, I rather suppose you're right,' John said, his brow furrowed. 'Better finish our coffee. When the carriage gets here we'll have to be off to the docks.'

'I wonder if this Tesla fellow even speaks English,' Lillian mused. 'Could be an awkward journey back to London otherwise. My Russian is not up to scratch.'

'*A nam ponravilos*, dear sis,' John said with a wink.

'My, you are full of surprises,' Lillian replied, somewhat annoyed at her brother's apparently fathomless skills.

'If you knew where and why I'd picked it up, you wouldn't be half so impressed. Now come along and finish your coffee. We have another carriage ride to look forward to, and then we'll finally meet our mysterious charge.'

The great Russian ironclad that awaited them at Portsmouth's naval docks was an imposing if outdated vessel; an oversized reminder of Imperial Russia's fading glory, rusting, creaking, belching smoke and steam, and yet bristling with cannon and swarming with regimented sailors who laboured like clockwork men.

The two sailors who flanked the Russian naval captain on the gangway were straight out of an adventure novel—striped shirts, cocked berets and near-identical square jaws and barrel-chests—standing to attention as though they alone represented the pride of the Imperial Navy. The captain himself, a stern-looking fellow named Novikov, returned John's salute when the latter was introduced as a lieutenant. Novikov's eyes did not so much as glance towards Lillian.

A small party of Royal Marines stood with the two agents, eying up their Russian counterparts as a curiosity, for few soldiers and sailors from these two great nations had encountered one another during the uneasy peace that had followed the Awakening.

Lillian wondered at first where Tesla was; there appeared to be no civilians present as John exchanged pleasantries. That was, until she observed a mass of unruly black hair poking out from behind one of the Russian marines, followed by a pale, gaunt face. It was a young man, barely twenty years of age if his wispy moustache was any indication, and now he leaned most comically around the burly sailor, looking about twitchily like a newborn fawn. He eventually saw that Lillian alone was looking at him directly, and flinched back behind the sailor, who pretended not to notice he was playing mother doe. Slowly, the young man gathered himself and stepped out into the light, dusting his palms down the front of his ill-fitting suit jacket, and trying to act nonchalant. It was only then that Lillian saw his manacles.

'If you will sign here, Lieutenant,' Captain Novikov was saying, 'and the consignment will be yours.'

John took a hefty docket offered to him by the nearest Russian sailor. There were scores of pages of neat, printed text, which John looked at confusedly.

'What is all this?' he asked.

'A formality. Do not worry about the details; they have been already agreed between our superiors.'

Lillian spoke up at last. 'Why is this man chained?'

The Russian captain looked at her with an air of distaste. 'Madam?'

'Agent,' she corrected. 'Why is this man chained? I did not understand him to be a prisoner.'

'Then perhaps you do not understand much about these… "Intuitionists", you call them? He is chained for his own safety, and for the safety of my vessel.'

He spoke to Lillian like a child or, worse, an inferior. She glared at him boldly, and without taking her eyes from his, said quietly to her brother, 'Sign the papers, John, and let us take our leave. I should like to be back in the bosom of enlightenment before midnight.'

John did not turn around, but Lillian saw from the tensing of his shoulders that she had put him in a predicament. Much as she regularly cursed the limitations of her sex in London society, she was thankful she wasn't serving with the likes of Captain Novikov, who seemed only to acknowledge her under sufferance.

Tesla was pushed forward—looking more bewildered than frightened—and one of the English marines took him by the shoulder. The Russian sailor presented his counterpart with the key to Tesla's manacles.

Lillian checked to make sure that John had signed the dockets and, satisfied that he had done so, gave her orders to the marines, loudly and clearly, for the captain's benefit.

'Release this man, and show him to our carriage. He is to be treated as a guest.'

'Yes ma'am.' The marine obeyed, but did not salute—unlike many other agents of Apollo Lycea, she had no rank, not even an honorary one. Another disadvantage of her sex, but one that she rarely allowed to hinder her; as the daughter of Lord Hardwick, her social status and reputation often proved sufficient.

Lillian turned to the captain, who was trying to ignore her. 'Good day, Captain,' she said, with a thin smile and all the courtesy she could muster. 'I trust your voyage home will be an uneventful one.'

He clicked his heels together and bowed his head sharply. 'A pleasure, my lady,' he lied.

As Lillian walked along the gangway to terra firma, she was dimly aware of John exchanging words with the captain and his men in Russian, followed by low laughter from all of them. It was his way to ease tensions with jests; she fancied, rather scornfully, that the jest was about her.

A Royal Navy doctor had been allowed five minutes to examine Tesla, passing him as fit to travel irrespective of whether he was or not, and then the Intuitionist had been bundled onto the Victoria. He had requested a cup of tea, but had been denied—time for that, Lillian had informed him—when they reached Havant. It was dusk, and it had already been a long day.

Soon they were underway back to the Bear, where Selby and his team of horses would be waiting.

'The sky here is so strange,' Tesla said, popping his head out of the carriage.

Lillian remembered that he had been aboard a ship for goodness knows how long. Had he even been allowed on deck?

'It is worse in London,' she said. 'But surely the sky burns the world over.'

'Oh, in Moscow most certainly,' the young man replied. 'But I have not seen a city for some time. I am in Siberia for...' He moved his head rhythmically, counting to himself. 'Three hundred-and-seventy-one days. We still see the stars in Siberia, when they let us outside.'

'Your countrymen leave a lot to be desired,' Lillian said.

'They are not my countrymen. I am Serbian,' he replied, puffing out his chest with affected pride.

'What? Then how did you end up their prisoner?'

'I work in Austria when the—what do you say?—Awakening happen. My parents try to hide my talents, try to stop me building things. They want me to go to America, to work for the great Thomas Edison, though I think he is not so great these days, no? But the Russians hear of the things I can do, and they pay the government much money. My steamer to America is intercepted by Russian warship, and I am put to work in a secret project in Moscow.'

'And... what is it that you build, that makes you so valuable to the Russians?' John asked, hesitantly.

'Generators,' Tesla replied.

'We have generators. Lots of them. What is so special about yours?'

'My generators do not need fuel, or even cables. With my

first prototype, I create power for my village before even your great London had electric lighting. It lasted for ten days before it explode, but I think I know what go wrong. My new creations will produce a hundred times more power than the largest electrical generators anywhere in the world. Perhaps more, given the correct conditions.'

John stole a glance at Lillian before continuing. 'If there are no cables, how do they conduct power?'

Tesla let out a small sigh. 'Through the air, of course. I send it, and I trap it, between metal coils—I call them Tesla coils.'

'Of course you do,' muttered Lillian.

'You do not like the name, dear lady?' Tesla said earnestly. 'For you, I change it!'

'And the Russians,' John went on, 'they had you building these Tesla coils?'

'Big ones, yes, but they say it take too long. So they send me to a factory where I work eighteen hours a day, and I build other things for them.'

'What other things?'

'Weapons, mostly.'

John shot another look at his sister. Lillian guessed he was wondering what their father had in mind for the scientist: generators, or weapons.

'So you never finished your generators?' Lillian interjected.

Tesla shook his head ruefully.

'How do you know they'll work this time?'

He looked up at her with a sudden twinkle in his eye. 'I just know. We receive this knowledge, no? And men may call us "genius" for it, for they assume the knowledge lies within us all, and only we Intuitionists can unravel it. But what if I tell you that the knowledge comes from out there?' At this, Tesla gesticulated theatrically, fluttering his fingers outwards towards the horizon.

'Out… where?' Lillian asked.

Tesla shrugged heavily. 'Beyond the veil between universes. Between worlds. Beyond time itself, or our understanding of it.'

Lillian studied Tesla's thin face. Her father had surely hired a madman.

'Between universes?' John interjected. 'And… ah… how does it come to you, then?'

'Through the air,' Tesla replied with gusto. 'In invisible waves of energy. Transmitted, much like current can be transmitted between two points—between my electrical coils. It can come to anyone, at any time. You would call it "inspiration". But I simply call it knowledge. You may not know that you have received this energy, for the clarity required to understand it is dependent on the quality of the receiver, yes? Like a telegraph, or a signal station. What use is a telegraph station without a telegrapher? What, then, is the use of inspiration without the right brain to think of a practical application?'

Lillian spoke again, slowly, as though talking to an imbecile. 'So… you receive messages from the future, or from other worlds, and they tell you what to invent?'

'If you would have it so, dear lady, then absolutely,' said Tesla, with equal parts enthusiasm and condescension.

'It is not a new theory,' John said. 'There are several philosophers who argue that Intuitionists receive a form of divine inspiration; just as the Riftborn have come from elsewhere, so too does the extraordinary knowledge of our Intuitionists.'

'This is not philosophy,' Tesla said. 'This is fact.'

'Oh? You can prove this theory empirically?' Lillian asked.

'Prove? No.'

'Then how do you know it for a fact?'

'Because I can see it,' Tesla said.

'See what, old chap?' asked John, with a sly wink to his sister to indicate he was humouring the man.

'The transmissions, of course,' Tesla said. 'All around us. They come to me, and to you, and to Miss Hardwick, too. Never deny the evidence of your own eyes. My father said that to me. Now, is it almost time for tea? I must have some of this Indian tea that I have heard so much about.'

* * *

'How is the tea, old chap?' John asked.

The three of them sat in a private room at the Bear, taking refuge from the inclement evening before embarking again with Selby.

'It is not at all like Russian tea,' Tesla said, wrinkling his nose. 'I think perhaps it would be better without milk. And maybe with lemon and honey instead of sugar. Yes, that would be better.'

John looked at Lillian and shook his head with a wry smile.

'So, Mr. Tesla,' Lillian said, 'it must be good to be free at last.'

'Oh, yes, it is—but I would have found a way out sooner or later. It was fortunate that Lord Hardwick heard of my work, though of course he was not the only one.'

'Only one what?' Lillian asked.

'The only one who ask me to work for him. There are not so many Intuitionists who know the things I know.' There was no trace of egotism in his words; he was assured of his genius as a matter of fact, not hubris.

'So you had your choice of "rescuer"?' Lillian asked. 'Why choose our father?'

'Lillian...' John warned. She ignored him.

'Lord Hardwick has many associates in the Americas,' Tesla said. 'One in particular, he promised to introduce to me. A Mr. John Keely. He is an inspiration to me. When offered an opportunity to work with a man such as this, I could not refuse. Your father is a very influential man, no?'

'No... I mean, yes, he is. Who is John Keely?' Lillian began to form a picture of what her father had been doing abroad these past months.

'You have not heard of him?' asked Tesla. He swallowed a mouthful of sandwich, and swilled it down with tea, making a face as he remembered that he didn't care for it. 'John Keely is a genius—a man who has created devices capable of generating perpetual energy from little more than etheric vibration.'

Lillian looked at John, who stared at her blankly. Tesla sighed. 'He make... how can you say? Electricity from the thin air.'

'I see,' said Lillian. Though she did not.

'Without John Keely's theories,' Tesla went on, 'I would never have started upon this path in my own work. And to think, he is not even an Intuitionist. A normal man with vision can achieve much, no? John Keely think he has reached the limitations of his study, but I show him that he require only a simple adjustment to the polyphase—'

'And you are to use your theories of... perpetual energy... for my father?' Lillian cut short Tesla's scientific babble.

John's look changed from amusement to a warning glare. Any information about Tesla's purpose within the Order was classified; even the offspring of Marcus Hardwick were not beyond protocol. Lillian pretended not to notice.

'Among other things, I expect so. I have many ideas that will help your Great Britain. Eventually I build generator for Lord Hardwick. The biggest in the world, although maybe one half the size would be sufficient, no? But he knows what he wants—I am but a servant humbly in his debt.' Tesla shrugged, sipped at his tea, and made a face again.

'You said "eventually",' Lillian prompted. 'Is the generator not your only task here in England?'

'No. I am to meet another honoured lord first. A... Charlton?'

'Cherleten,' Lillian said, attempting to mask her distaste.

'Yes, Cherleten,' the Serbian beamed. 'He wants what all men want from me—a weapon. But in this case, I agree to help, for the cause is just.'

'What kind of weapon?'

'Lillian,' John said sharply. Lillian ignored him again.

'A weapon to use against the dark things,' Tesla said. 'What you call the "Riftborn". And worse.' For a second, his expression changed from one of enthusiasm to one of sadness.

'Worse than the Riftborn?' Lillian asked.

'Oh, the Riftborn are not so bad. They are demons, yes, but

they are beasts too. They do what is in their nature; they cannot help it any more than the fish can help swimming. And they are only here because we bring them here, no? In my homeland, they say that the wolves do not come unless the farmer leaves out food for them. It is the same.'

Lillian shivered at the thought, despite the inn's fire. She couldn't help but think of Arthur as food for wolves. For the Other.

'Back home,' Tesla went on, 'the elders tell us old Ottoman legends. They speak of monsters that lie in wait in the darkness. Eaters of flesh. Drinkers of blood.' Lillian looked at John, who had stopped his fidgeting and now drew in close, shoulders hunched and arms folded, as he too guarded against an imaginary chill. 'When I leave my homeland, I find that these stories are true. In Russia, the monsters are known. In Siberia, they are not only known, but seen. They prey on the weak, dragging children and old people away into the night. But these creatures are not like your Riftborn; they are controlled by men—not entirely human, I think—but men, nonetheless. They have evil purpose by design, not because it is in their blood.'

'You've seen them?' John involved himself at last in the discussion.

Tesla nodded solemnly, suddenly looking twice his tender age. 'Briefly. In the camp in Siberia we suffered many losses. The guards could not protect us, and so we had to protect ourselves. The monsters attacked, more than once—horrible, white-skinned creatures, like corpses, naked even in the coldest weather. We find that they cannot easily be harmed. But they can be burned well enough. When we discover this weakness, we light great fires at night, and whenever we hear the monsters howling in the storms, we stay near the flames, ready to fight.

'One time, when the monsters came in great numbers, there was another amongst them: a man with strange eyes, riding a horse. He shout curses at us, and tell us we are cattle, to be slaughtered at his will. His words strike fear into us all, and we flee inside and barricade the doors. To our shame, the oldest amongst us did not make it, and were taken.

'After that, I begin to develop a way to protect us. I think that if fire can harm the creatures, then so can electricity. The guards, afraid of the enemy, fetched everything I needed. Soon, our work camp was ringed by fences, all charged with electrical energy, through which nothing could pass without being horribly burned. We were safe behind those fences at night. The villagers thereabout were not so lucky.'

'Do you know who the man on the horse was?'

'No. But I hear talk that he was a knight of the old country. An immortal, they said, from an ancient order who have stalked the earth since the time of Christ.'

'The time of Judas,' Lillian muttered.

'Then you have heard it too,' Tesla said. 'The Knights Iscariot. If I can help to destroy them, I will do so. I have vowed it.'

There was silence in the little room, punctuated only by the crackling of the fire.

'You said that your weapons could be used against the Riftborn,' John said. 'Do they use electricity also?'

'Yes,' said Tesla. 'The weapon is one and the same, by fortunate happenstance. With some adjustments, I believe I can equip agents such as yourselves with these creations. Here, I show you.'

Lillian and John exchanged glances as Tesla rummaged around in the kit bag that contained all his worldly possessions. He eventually pulled out a construct of metal and tangled wires, which protruded crudely from a pistol grip. It looked like a revolver that had been taken apart and reassembled by a lunatic with a penchant for copper wire.

'It is an early design. I have not tested it yet, but I am sure it works,' Tesla said proudly, swinging the strange weapon outwards as he did so, so that the barbed 'barrel' pointed first at John, then at Lillian. Both agents in turn ducked out of the way instinctively.

'Oh, fear not!' Tesla chuckled. 'I have not primed the device. Look.'

Nikola Tesla showed John and Lillian the small crank-handle on the side of the weapon. 'This must be turned until the charge is primed,' he explained. 'The two coils rise up until they are aligned. When there is a steady spark between the coils, the gun is ready to fire. That is when you point, and shoot.' He indicated two rods, each topped with a steel ball and wrapped in tight coils of thick copper wire.

'It is, ah, that is to say… a little cumbersome?' John ventured.

'And slow to fire,' Lillian added.

Tesla looked somewhat indignant. 'It is not perfected,' he said. 'I make this on board a ship, with nothing but scraps from the engine room, and tools I had to make myself. With your Lord Cherleten's help, I will make it smaller, lighter and more efficient.'

'And… how does this work against Riftborn?' Lillian asked. 'As far as we know, nothing of this earth can harm them—only Majestics, and that is a risk in and of itself.'

'Ah, but ask yourself *why* the Majestics can harm them,' said Tesla, his confidence growing. 'I tell you. It is because their powers are increased by imbibing etherium. The essence of etherium flows through the Majestic, augmenting his power. In its raw form, etherium feeds the demons; but when enervated through the Majestic's innate abilities, it can repel them, even wound them, because it is the very stuff of which they are made.'

'The stuff of nightmares,' Lillian said.

'Precisely that!' Tesla said, not interpreting Lillian's rueful tone. 'Now, imagine that instead of enervating the etherium by using a poor Majestic as a vessel, we instead use electricity. This is the genius of Mr. Keely, whom I mentioned before. He had the idea long ago of a vaporic gun, creating energy from water and air—I have perfected his idea, and made the theory a reality, only I use etherium instead of water. Look here.' He turned his strange device about, and flicked out a small compartment that sat behind the barrel, between the two strange coils. 'I have had to guess at the measurements based on my reading,' he said, 'but this chamber should house a cartridge of etherium. You are familiar with these, yes?'

Lillian nodded. She carried etherium rounds for her pistol at all times. They could not kill, banish or severely harm the Riftborn, but they did slow them down enough that an agent could escape a demonic attack. She had seen this once with her own eyes, when Arthur had fired at one of the horrors during their last assignment in Paris—and she had caught the briefest glimpse of the indescribable Riftborn as it squirmed beyond her sight, beyond her understanding. She hoped never to see it again.

'The current passes through the chamber,' Tesla went on, 'and the charge is carried outwards in an arc of enervated etherium. It will burn the Riftborn as surely as it will burn flesh.' He handed the gun to John to inspect, before sitting back in his chair, arms folded, a look of triumph on his thin face.

John passed the gun to Lillian, who turned it about gingerly in her hands before passing it back to Tesla.

John checked his pocket watch. 'Mr. Tesla,' he said, 'we must get underway soon. I am sorry we can offer you little hospitality after your voyage, but once we are back in London I am sure you will be more comfortable.'

'My friends, this has been fine indeed!' Tesla exclaimed. 'The comforts of a warm fire under a solid roof are more than I have seen in a long time. I am content.'

At the coach, Tesla harangued Selby with questions, pointing out the inefficiency of the horse as a means of transport, and yet appearing impressed both by Selby's passion for the art of coaching, and his record-beating abilities.

Lillian turned to John and whispered, 'How did Cherleten—or Father, for that matter—know of Tesla's encounter with the vampires?'

'I don't know,' John replied, his expression grim. Much as he had disapproved of Lillian's questioning of their guest, he was also intrigued. 'More pertinently, how long has Father been planning this operation? How long has he known about the Knights Iscariot?'

Lillian nodded. 'If I were allowed to gamble, I'd wager Father is doing what he does best.'

'Oh?'

'Preparing for war.'

NINE

Night fell. The coach hurtled along remote lanes; tendrils of low mist, sparkling like gold in the faint amber glow of the weak emblazoned firmament, fled from the path of the snorting horses, whose hoofbeats provided staccato accompaniment to the carriage's monotonous rattle.

Lillian Hardwick looked around the swaying compartment. Her brother entertained the gaunt Serbian with tales of merriment and adventure in far-off lands, the sound of his own voice amusing him perhaps a little too much. The Intuitionist appeared captivated by John's wit; though a young man, the male heir to the Hardwick name already had ample experience in the field, both in battle and in the varying strata of social dalliance—equally deadly, in their own way.

Lillian pulled back the curtain a little, gazing out into the gloom. Dark trees and hedgerows blurred past them. Then a solitary gaslight passed by, followed by the dark shape of church steeple and, finally, a sign. South Harting. She brought her focus back into the compartment, and studied the Serbian. By the dim glow of the coach's small lantern, the pale man's face looked sickly, blue-white veins standing proud at his temples and throat. It would be so easy to reach out, to snap the man's neck, to feed…

Lucien de Montfort opened his eyes, breathing in deeply and casting off the vestiges of the Hardwick girl's mind, until his own thoughts were uncontaminated once again. He had seen everything he needed to see through her eyes; felt everything he needed to feel. It was good to feel, sometimes.

Yes, she would be perfect. His masters would get more than they bargained for with this one. And de Montfort relished the opportunity to take revenge on the girl's troublesome brother.

He looked about the dark chamber, at dozens of pairs of glittering eyes in the darkness, and smiled. The time was nigh.

'I say, sis, are you all right?' John asked, pausing in his story when he noticed Lillian jump.

'Oh… I must have been dozing. Do forgive me.' She rubbed at her shoulder.

'Wound giving you gyp?' John turned to Tesla. 'We've both had close shaves with the Knights Iscariot,' he explained. 'I've seen what their leaders can do first hand, and—'

There came at once a knock on the roof of the coach. John pulled down the window, ignoring the icy blast of wind that caused his eyes to water.

'What is it, Selby?' he shouted up to the coachman.

'Another carriage, sir,' Selby called back. 'Half a mile behind us, and keeping pace.'

John leaned further out, and looked back along the dark road. The last village was long gone, and they had entered a long stretch of bumpy track. Sure enough, two pinpricks of dancing green light could be seen a good way back: carriage lights.

'Keep going!' John shouted. 'Stop for no one.' He pulled his head back inside and closed the window. Lillian was already checking her pistol.

'It's probably just a local cabbie on his way back from the

last village,' John said. 'No need to shoot anyone.' He cracked a smile, though he wasn't entirely convinced himself. Lillian looked at him with annoyance; she was not convinced either.

Lillian looked out of her own window. When she next turned to John, her cheeks were ruddy and her hair out of place. 'I believe they are gaining on us.'

'They must have extra horses,' John said. 'There's no way they can pass us... we should slow, and let them catch up. Then we'll know for sure.'

'I'd like nothing better than to face them head-on,' said Lillian, 'but we have Mr. Tesla to consider.'

John thought about that for a moment. 'You're right, but we have nowhere to go. To leave the main road would be folly. We could make it to the next safe-house, but if these fellows mean us ill, we would still have to fight.'

'But at least it would be from a position of strength,' Lillian argued.

'Very well.' John reached into his jacket pocket and took out a small book, in which was printed page after page of coded lists. He found what he was looking for quickly.

'What is it?' Lillian asked.

'The next safe-house is in Liphook.'

'That's almost twenty miles.' Lillian looked to John, to Tesla, and back again. 'We won't make it,' she said. 'It looks as though we shall have to fight, assuming they're enemies.'

'We must assume that,' said John. He leant out of the coach window again and shouted up to Selby. 'Mr. Selby—we must try to reach the safe-house in Liphook. Do not let this other coach pass us!'

'Aye, sir!' came the reply, lost almost instantly on the wind.

Nikola Tesla was watching the two agents closely, his expression open, expectant.

'Do not worry, Mr. Tesla,' John said. 'We will not allow anything bad to befall you.'

Tesla looked solemnly at Lillian. 'I fear it is too late for that,

Lieutenant,' he said. John did not have to look at Lillian to guess her reaction.

Selby gave his horses the whip, and the coach sped up, dangerously so for the condition of the road. The three passengers held on as the coach jostled and rocked harder than ever, almost throwing them about the compartment.

'Apologies for the inclement conditions,' John said, pulling down the window once again. 'Good Christ...' He sat back in his seat again, and immediately drew his own gun.

'What?' Lillian asked.

John tried to remain calm, so as not to alarm Tesla. 'They are gaining on us more quickly that I'd anticipated,' he said. 'They'll be with us in minutes.'

'You're sure we'll not reach Liphook before they catch us?'

John shook his head solemnly.

'Then we fight,' Lillian said.

John had not argued with her, and Lillian had taken his silence as tacit approval. She removed her skirts and bustle—at which Tesla's eyes had almost bulged out of his head until he had seen the breeches she wore beneath—and braced herself on the opposite bench, drawing down her window and taking up as stable a firing position as she could.

Outside, through the mist and darkness, the other coach thundered towards them. Six great black horses pulled it onwards at a furious pace, a coachman fully shrouded in heavy black clothing urging them on. There was no longer a possibility in Lillian's mind that the other coach contained a mere traveller in a hurry.

She took aim at the enemy coachman through the carriage window, ignoring the bitter cold. The coach edged ever closer, gaining stride by stride. Lillian's finger tensed on the trigger, but then she stopped. Inexplicably, she could not take the shot. Her hand began to tremble; her eyes watered, her vision blurred.

Let me in.

It was a voice in her head—or, rather, not a voice, but a queer feeling that quickly became an idea, fully formed. An external influence that was, in an instant, coalesced into Lillian's own will. An instruction. Something was coming; she had to let it in.

'Lillian?' John's voice was faint, as though it came from a mile away, carried on the wind.

Lillian blinked, and stared into the darkness, at the coach driver who was now so close she could make out his silhouette clearly. He was like a bundle of dark rags, his face obscured by a black muffler and wide-brimmed hat. Lillian fancied that he had no face at all, but she stared anyhow at the shadows where his eyes should be. Was his the voice she had heard in her mind? Was his the will that opposed her own?

Let me in.

It came again. Stronger this time, and accompanied by a vision, a flash of something like a snatch of memory from long ago. Lillian was a child, staring up at a cloaked man. A man with oiled black hair and a face like alabaster. Was this a memory? Or a premonition?

'It begins. Your sister is in thrall to the monsters!'

Tesla? Lillian heard the Intuitionist's voice like an echo in fog.

Pain shot through Lillian's shoulder, the wound burning. She cried out and fell back into the compartment.

'Lillian!' John's cry came again, louder this time, and he jumped across to tend to her, his face swimming in and out of her vision.

Through the strange fug, Lillian heard a thud, and gawped dumbly as a large depression appeared in the cabin roof.

John dropped low onto the floor of the compartment and fired two rounds into the roof. The shots were followed by an ear-piercing scream. Lillian felt it as much as heard it, the noise drawing her from her waking dream.

At once, she recognised what was happening. Had she not been through this at the academy countless times? A Majestic was asserting control over her. It was stronger than anything she had ever been tested with, but the pattern was the same: the call; the false memory; the breaking down of her defences. But Lillian Hardwick was stronger than that. She shook her head briskly and focused hard, envisioning nothing but a brick wall through which the probing powers of a Majestic would have to break. She pushed herself up, and again leaned from the window, pistol in hand and determination renewed. She saw the coach almost within touching distance; heard the crack of Selby's whip behind her. She aimed the pistol, but at once realised that her efforts came too late.

Crawling things moved swiftly from the clattering coach behind them, leaping from the cabin and forwards to the horses like ghastly white spiders, making their way nimbly towards her. She fired, taking one of the beasts in the chest, but it did not relinquish its grip, instead screaming in pain and rage, and hanging on to the carriage's yoke before recovering all too quickly. She heard a cry, and turned to see John struggling at his window on the other side of the compartment, before firing three shots into the night. When she looked back at her target, it was gone.

From nowhere, a hideous, hairless face confronted her, inches from her own. The creature was scarred and bestial, an arrowhead hole where its nose should have been, its ears large and pointed, eyes glittering in the darkness under their own luminescence. Its huge maw gaped, screaming at Lillian, its breath assailing her like the stench of a thousand corpses. One wickedly clawed hand dug into the side of the carriage, the other grabbed at Lillian's wrist and tried to yank her through the small window. Lillian pulled back, squeezing the trigger of her gun. As she did, the beast roared louder and with a violent tug wrenched Lillian against the carriage door. The catch gave with the impact and the door flew open. For a stomach-churning moment Lillian thought she would be dashed beneath the wheels of the carriage, but she managed to cling to the door even as the monster held her other wrist. Her heels skittered against the road; briars whipped at her face and pulled her hair, and the pistol fell, a flash of silver vanishing into the night.

For a moment, Lillian's hand flailed at thin air. The pain in her shoulder flared again as the pale creature yanked her upwards, climbing effortlessly onto the roof of the moving carriage. Her left arm was wrenched away from the door, her feet kicking at it as it flapped about below her. She heard John shouting something, Selby too, but their words were lost on the wind. She was hoisted upwards, face to face with the grotesque gargoyle, a man-beast that resembled a skeleton wrapped in wrinkled parchment. She knew beyond all else that it was controlled by the very voice that had called to her, and that it aimed to take her to him, whomever and wherever he might be.

Monday, 20th October, 8:30 p.m.

KENSINGTON, LONDON

Arthur knocked at the door again, more urgently. A light went on in an upper window next door, and a face glared out; the wealthy inhabitants of the crescent were unused to having their peace disturbed. Arthur turned back to the door when he heard the sound of bolts being withdrawn, and presently he was faced by a stern-looking housekeeper.

'I must see Sir Toby at once,' he said.

The housekeeper made some protest, but Arthur did not let her speak before barging into the grand hall of the Georgian townhouse. A butler approached from the next room, and Arthur met his look of disdain simply by handing him his card and declaring, 'Sir Arthur Furnival to see Sir Toby. It is of the utmost importance.'

The butler was not cowed; clearly he was used to people excusing their rudeness thusly, and was perhaps about to argue the matter when Sir Toby himself appeared at the landing.

'That will be all, Carter,' he said. 'Give us some privacy, will you? I shall ring if I need you.'

The butler bowed curtly and ushered the housekeeper away.

'Now, Sir Arthur, what is the meaning of this intrusion? You know as well as I do that my home is off-limits to club business.'

'And I would respect that for any other matter, Sir Toby, truly I would. But I have... I have received a premonition.'

Sir Toby raised an eyebrow. 'Oh?'

'It regards Lil— the Hardwick siblings.'

'And this is not a matter that should be presented to Lord Hardwick?'

'I... that is to say... I thought it best I should report directly to you, sir. You are our commander, after all.'

'You mean you feel unable to call on Lord Hardwick. That is quite understandable; he is my friend, true enough, but he is hardly the most approachable of men. Come, step into my study; you had best tell me what is so urgent that it could not wait until morning.'

They entered the small ground-floor study, and Sir Toby lit an oil lamp, eschewing modern electrical lighting, just as he did at his club office. The room was cold, the fire having died out hours ago.

'Whiskey?' Sir Toby asked.

'No, thank you.'

'Mind if I do?' The Lord Justice took out the glass and decanter.

'Not at all.'

'So, you'd best spit it out—what has you so agitated, Sir Arthur?'

'I have received a premonition. A fearful one. I believe that something is amiss with the Hardwicks. Particularly, Lillian is in danger. I can sense it most keenly.'

'She is in particular danger? Or she is the only one you can sense?'

Had he spoken with Lord Hardwick? Or was he simply every bit as astute as his reputation suggested? 'I... I do not know for sure. The former, I believe.'

Sir Toby Fitzwilliam looked thoughtful, his craggy face crumpling as he pondered something, though his thoughts were unfathomable, even to one such as Sir Arthur Furnival. In the end he exhaled deeply, and seemed to come to some decision. He pointed to the corner of the room.

'Within the parcel over there is a painting. It arrived this afternoon.'

At first, Sir Arthur did not take the judge's meaning, but then it became clear. 'A painting... from *him?*'

'I've been expecting as much. That cabman you sent to the Nightwatch... Dresden? It transpires that he did take our suspect to one more destination the night Molly Goodheart was killed.'

'The House of Zhengming?'

Sir Toby nodded. He set down his whiskey and strode to the parcel. He removed the paper from the two-foot-high canvas, and held the revealed painting to the light. Sir Arthur did not move—he would not touch an object created by the Artist. The celestial had a damnable power, and given Arthur's unique skills in psychometry, nothing good could come of it. His eyes widened as he took in the painting; its complexity and detail astonishing, its mood resonating through the room as though it were painted in pure emotion rather than merely oils.

'I am afraid your powers are slipping, Sir Arthur,' the commander of Apollo Lycea said. 'I already know of the dangers ahead. The appropriate authorities have been notified, and the Nightwatch stands ready. But there is little else to be done.'

'Send me. If I leave now I could find them, and—'

'You will do no such thing. Lieutenant and Agent Hardwick will survive this night; of that I am certain. I will not risk the life of another agent to confirm what our psychic intelligence has already divined.'

'How can you be so sure? Even the Nightwatch cannot—'

Sir Toby held up a hand. 'This is not the only painting dispatched by the Artist today. Lord Hardwick has one, as does the Home Secretary. And we intercepted two others. They form pieces of a puzzle—one that the Artist, for reasons of his own choosing, wishes us to solve.'

'What would you have me do, Sir Toby?' Sir Arthur asked.

'Nothing. Go home and try to get a good night's sleep. I will see you at the club bright and early tomorrow, because if what we have learned is correct, something portentous is about to happen. I am sure you would not have the events depicted here come to pass?'

As Sir Arthur made his way home, his thoughts were crowded by the ominous painting. A castle on a high cliff, burning, the flames spiralled high into the dark sky, forming great tendrils, around which winged Riftborn swooped. The landscape stretching out before the castle was made entirely of corpses. And over it all, standing at the forefront of the chaos, with a face so impassive it might as well have been sculpted of marble, was Lillian Hardwick.

Monday 20th October, 8:30 p.m.
NEAR ROGATE, HAMPSHIRE

John grappled with the thing at the window desperately, fending off its claws and gnashing teeth. He saw Tesla from the corner of his eye, flailing about as the coach went over yet another hillock and veered around an awkward bend. John heard Lillian cry out in alarm, but he could do nothing but fight for dear life, and try not to be scratched for fear that whatever had befallen his sister would also befall him.

With all the strength he could muster, John finally wrenched his left arm away from the beast, and smashed his elbow into its face. It thrust an arm into the carriage to save itself from falling, but for the scant seconds John was free he had reached to his ankle and snatched out his knife. With a vicious backhand swipe, he drew the blade across the monster's throat and it fell from the window, but the immediate avian croak it gave was a sure indication that the creature was not dead, even if it was out of the running.

John slammed the window shut and clambered at once to the other side of the carriage, dismayed to find no sign of Lillian. Tesla, on the other hand, was rummaging through his kit bag.

'Mr. Tesla,' John said, 'if there is anything in that bag of tricks that can help us, now would be the time to find it.'

'A minute,' Tesla said.

That was more time than they had. More time than Lillian had. John took up his pistol and looked out of the flapping door, out into the gloomy countryside that sped past them at a rate of knots. With a deep breath he hauled himself into the cold air.

The hunchbacked creature—Lillian still could not bring herself to think of it as a 'vampire'—hoisted her off her feet. Lillian looked over its sloping shoulders and saw the rumbling carriage with its faceless driver hurtling after them through the mists. She tried to prise the creature's clawed hands from her collar, but it was possessed of a strength that belied its scrawny frame. She kicked at it, but drew little more than a flinch and the hideous, throaty growl that she had come to associate with her nightmares. She did not understand how the beast remained upright on the moving coach, and feared they would both be thrown from the roof at any moment.

Do not be afraid. Let me in and we can be together.

In her panic, she had allowed her defences to slacken again. But the voice no longer filled her with dread, nor did she feel any compulsion to obey it. If anything, it made her realise that the goal of the monster before her was not to hurt her, but to abduct her.

Lillian gambled on her intuition, and let go of the creature's arms, staring fearlessly into its sparkling, violet eyes. It did not drop her, but instead hissed, tilting its head to scrutinise her. The fetid stench of the thing's rotting flesh was nauseating. Lillian reached up for her hairpins slowly, focusing all the time on her mental defences, to mask her intention from the Majestic who whispered to her. Her fingers closed around the delicate weapons.

'Lillian! By God!'

John had clambered up to the coach roof. The creature started, and turned its attention away from Lillian to face this new threat, and in that instant Lillian struck. The two pins slid into the beast's papery hide, either side of the throat, thrusting upward into its skull. With an ear-piercing scream that caused Lillian physical pain, the creature fell limp, and rolled from the roof of the carriage as Lillian fell onto the roof face-first. She looked up to catch the briefest glimpse of a naked, lily-white corpse vanishing beneath the wheels of the pursuing vehicle, before she began to slip from the roof. Terror gripped her as she struggled for purchase. She was half-over the stowage compartment, staring down at the muddy road, when she felt a hand grip her arm, and finally she steadied herself. To her great relief, it was John who now held her, and not another creature.

'Get back!' she yelled. 'I'm all right, and I know what to do.'

He tried to argue, but she silenced him with a hard glare. John ducked as a low-hanging branch whipped over his head, nodded to his sister, and swung himself back into the coach.

Don't be a fool. Let me in, or you all shall die.

Looking at the black coach that pursued them, Lillian felt the call strongly. The voice in her head presaged the throbbing of the wound at her shoulder, and she knew the two were linked. Was de Montfort aboard that coach, she wondered? Was he the creature that even now exerted influence over her? Or was it some other who tugged at her, impelling her to join them? She wanted it to be so. She felt her heart lurch at the realisation that she was no longer in command of her emotions. Deep down she ached to be united with whatever dark lord summoned her. And that thought sickened her, made her grit her teeth in determination, and drove her to fight. She would not allow some inhuman creature to sway her from her course.

The shrouded coachman cracked his whip once more. Another wiry, pale figure emerged from the carriage, crawling spider-like along its side, and onto the horses that panicked, wild-eyed at the thing's touch. Something inside Lillian told her to give herself to the creature, to let it carry her off into the night and end the chase. She glowered, and instead reached down and took out the derringer from her boot, holding the small gun tight. She stared down the violet-eyed beast that jerked and scuttled over the team of horses towards her. It reached the lead horse, and crouched low, ready to leap at Lillian. She took aim at the horse.

Before she could pull the trigger, her defiance turned to surprise as a loud fizzing noise filled the air, accompanied by a flash of blue light that—for a second—turned the night to day. A coruscating arc of electrical energy flashed from below her, from the coach window, and struck the pale creature in the chest. Its gleaming white skin charred and peeled instantly. Its body was wreathed in bands of lightning, which leapt from the horses to the ghoulish beast in flickering bands. As the creature fell between the animals and into the road, the horses shied off to the right, crashing through a dark hedgerow and falling in a tangled, whinnying heap. The carriage itself broke away, bouncing over a ditch and flipping end over end, the black-swathed driver flying through the air.

Lillian barely had time to register what had happened when she was almost thrown from her position by another jolt from their coach as Selby fought to keep his own team from panicking.

She grabbed the ropes of the stowage tight, and shouted back over her shoulder as loud as she could. 'Selby, pull up! Pull up, I say!'

It took some time to come to a halt, and when they did the enemy was out of sight. Lillian climbed from the roof of the coach, fighting the urge not to be sick.

Tesla disembarked nervously, still holding the strange weapon, which smoked ominously. John followed, Webley revolver in hand.

'Selby, everything all right?' John called.

Jim Selby climbed down from his seat, legs visibly shaking.

He took off his hat, clutching it tight as he nodded to John.

'We need to search the wreckage,' said Lillian, pointing back along the road.

'I'm not sure, sis. Maybe we should make our getaway while we can. That was a damned close-run thing.'

'No, John,' said Lillian, gritting her teeth. 'We need to go back there, and make sure there are no survivors.'

She could not—would not—say that she wanted to put a stop to the voices in her head, to the nightmares. Perhaps John knew; he nodded assent. Lillian led the way, treading down long, damp grass, wading knee-deep through it as the cold wind picked up, causing the black field to ripple like a vast lake, and the upended coach to creak, its one good wheel spinning awkwardly on its axle in the breeze. Her hands were held outwards from her sides, each holding a small knife, as she trod cautiously, deliberately, towards the wreck.

Lillian remembered a time, long ago when, as a little girl, she had stolen from her bed in the middle of a winter's night, and had walked through the long, wet grass of the fields behind her old family home. She had not thought of that episode in the longest time, except in her dreams. She had been caught up in a terrible storm that night, and had awoken lost and frightened, cold and soaked through, almost a mile from home. Her enduring memory was of being swept up in her father's arms, having almost drowned in the river. Marcus Hardwick had seemed impossibly huge, enfolding her in the bundles of his overcoat and running back home with her. She had almost died of pneumonia shortly afterwards. She vaguely remembered her mother and father and older brother sitting in a dimly lit room, their faces lined with worry. When she had pulled through, something within her had changed. Her parents did not notice it at first, but eventually they came to know that their daughter was no longer the carefree girl they had known. The brush with death had taught her, even at that tender age, to pursue her goals relentlessly, and hang the consequences. This had often brought her into conflict with her father. Indeed, the last time she remembered feeling any true bond of love between them was when she had been carried back to the house in his arms.

The creature before her now was like a parody of that memory. A pile of heavy black cloth given form and life, a ragged creature dragging itself away from the wreckage of the coach. It redoubled its efforts when it sensed the approach of its enemies, and began to crawl more frantically when John put a bullet in the head of a pale-skinned monster that hung limply from the window of the coach wreck. Lillian saw that the driver's legs were shattered—he was dragging them piteously.

She marched over to the stricken man, kicking him over onto his back. He lashed out at her with a large hand, which she at once knocked aside and trod upon. He grunted, but said nothing.

At Lillian's signal, John stepped forward and tore the muffler and hat from the man's head. No monster was revealed beneath, and Lillian knew without her brother's confirmation that this could not be de Montfort.

He was a man, large and sallow-skinned, face podgy and devoid of expression. He babbled something incoherent, and then said only, 'Mercy.' Lillian knew at once that he was a simpleton, some poor imbecile employed to the cause of the Knights Iscariot because he could know no better.

As if to confirm her thoughts, Tesla spoke. 'It has always been the way,' he said. 'The Knights Iscariot can rarely pass for normal men—those of sharp wits fear and despise them. So they look to these poor unfortunates to do their bidding—brain-damaged wretches whose only experience is servitude.'

'What shall we do with him?' Lillian wondered aloud, half to herself. She had come to the wreckage with murder in mind, but she had not the stomach for that now.

'Innocent or no,' John said, 'he is not our concern. The Knights Iscariot know where we are—we must at least get to the safe-house before any more come for us, and return to London at first light. If all these stories are to be believed, further travel by night would be folly.'

'I'm not sure how safe this "safe-house" shall be, judging by their strength and tenacity.'

'Then we'll have to pray that there are no more to come. The Knights Iscariot are a power in the north, but not here. If they had more creatures to spare, perhaps they would have sent them already, but do you really want to take that chance?'

Lillian looked into the pleading eyes of the coach driver. 'You are right,' she said to John, the words sticking in her throat. 'We leave him. Let's go'.

TEN

THE APOLLONIAN CLUB, LONDON

When Lillian Hardwick entered the marble hall of the Apollonian, it was all Arthur could do not to rush to her, take her hand, and declare his relief that she was well. Yet above him, looking down from the upper balcony, was her father. And so even as Lillian made to greet him with utmost familiarity, and with a twinkle in her eye, Sir Arthur Furnival stepped towards her, cutting short her approach and bowing to her brother and their companion before greeting Lillian.

'Lieutenant; Agent Hardwick. I am most pleased to see you returned safely.'

'Really, Arthur, there's no need to be—' She stopped short. She peered over Arthur's shoulder, up towards the balcony. The briefest scowl crossed her features, and she said only, 'Your concern is appreciated, Sir Arthur. We suffered some minor inconvenience on the road, but nothing to worry about. May I introduce Mr. Tesla, of Serbia.'

Arthur was unsure how to respond—as was so often the case, he could not tell if Lillian was cross with him, with her father, both of them, or neither. If only his powers gave him more of an insight into the workings of the female mind. He extended a hand to the stranger and said, 'Pleased to make your acquaintance, Mr. Tesla. I hope your journey was a pleasant one.'

'It was not,' replied Tesla, ignoring Arthur's hand. The man's mind was clearly elsewhere. He craned back his head and spun slowly on the spot, gazing in childlike wonder at the great domed skylight that cast the white marble hall in a pinkish hue. Tesla's eyes flittered around the great hall briefly, before finally alighting upon the man before him. 'But it could have been worse. You are a Majestic, no?'

'I... yes...' replied Arthur, puzzled.

'I can always tell.' Tesla smiled proudly. 'You have the look of men from ghost stories,' he explained. 'Except you carry the ghosts with you always.'

'Please, won't you come this way,' Arthur said, changing the subject hastily. He held out his hand in the direction of the stairs.

'We are to meet Lord Cherleten,' Lillian said. 'I expect he will be in the armoury.'

'I am afraid not, Agent Hardwick,' Arthur replied, hiding his dismay at the coolness that had come between them masterfully, thanks to a lifetime in high society. 'Lord Cherleten is waiting upstairs with Sir Toby... and Lord Hardwick.'

Lillian said nothing, but simply strode past Arthur, not even looking him in the eye, and Tesla followed. As John passed Arthur, he winked.

'Don't worry, old boy. I'm sure she won't be cross with you for ever.'

With the little entourage shepherded towards the waiting Lord Hardwick, and the loud clicking of Lillian's heels echoing through the hall, Arthur followed suit, not entirely sure why Lillian should be cross with him at all; a feeling he was somewhat accustomed to.

* * *

John was tired, and utterly famished. He sat as straight-backed as he could, and tried to look attentive whilst his father, Sir Toby and Cherleten took it in turns to question Tesla, but in truth he was exhausted. Lillian appeared fully engaged with the proceedings, despite their father's rebarbative disposition towards them both, and he had no idea how she managed it.

They had spent a restless night in the safe-house at Liphook, which had become a veritable fortress when the landlord heard that agents of the Crown were in danger. Lillian's sleep had been fitful, and John had elected not to wake her for a turn on watch duty, instead maintaining a vigil over her, terrified that the mysterious Knights Iscariot had managed to take some control over his sister. He had not seen her in such a feverish state since her bout of pneumonia many years prior, and it pained him to see her so again. Upon their return to London, John had insisted on looking after Tesla while Lillian went home to dress as propriety dictated for the debriefing. He had half expected her to slap his face at this suggestion, but instead she had acquiesced. The truth of it was she was not herself, and John only hoped that her thoughts could not really betray them to the enemy. More than that, he had already told her all he knew about their father's secret work—it was not much, but it was more than anyone should know. He felt sick that, through his beloved sister, he might have inadvertently betrayed their father. But he had to believe Lillian; if she said she was over the worst of it, then he would trust her.

There had been no further attacks—if the monsters had come for them, they had decided against assailing the safe-house, with no easy ingress and armed men within. Or perhaps they had some other reason for allowing the agents to escape. It was now well past three in the afternoon; they had lost an entire night boarded up in a roadside inn far from their destination, sleeping in a single room like fugitives.

'Lieutenant? Are you paying attention?'

John snapped to his senses when he realised that Sir Toby's

eyes were upon him. 'Yes, Sir Toby. Sorry, sir.'

'You have first-hand experience of Mr. Tesla's weaponry—do you believe it to be effective against the... vampires?'

'*Wampyr*,' Tesla corrected, though no one paid him any heed.

'Is it more effective, or can we afford to delay its development a while longer?'

'I'm sure I'm not qualified to offer an opinion, Sir Toby,' John said. Though he hadn't been listening, he was sure that Sir Toby was playing peacemaker between his father and Lord Cherleten, as usual, and John would really rather not take sides in that particular spat.

'Yes, the weapon is effective,' Lillian said. She had not been asked directly, but since when had that ever stopped her speaking up?

'Go on,' Sir Toby prompted. The old man often encouraged Lillian; John was glad of it, most of the time. At other times he'd rather Lillian kept her head below the parapet rather than risk their father's ire, which only ever added to their poor mother's burden.

'The creatures, be they vam—*wampyr*—or no, are strong and fast, though susceptible to mortal wounds to the head. Little else seems to hinder them—even the loss of a limb only slows them for a time. Mr. Tesla's weapon not only killed one of the creatures outright, but caused sufficient collateral damage to bring their pursuit to a halt. In short, a single shot from such a weapon did more than a sustained assault by Lieutenant Hardwick and myself.'

Sir Toby looked thoughtful.

'And this "collateral damage",' Lord Hardwick said, his voice lowering to a growl as he became more displeased. 'Is it worth the risk of discharging the weapon in less favourable battlefield conditions? When innocent lives may be at stake?'

'A simple modification is all that will be required,' Tesla said, unaware of the glare he drew for his interruption. 'I could not create a focusing array with the materials I had aboard ship. With your assistance I am sure the Mark II Tesla pistol shall be much more precise.'

'There you have it, Hardwick,' Lord Cherleten said, a self-satisfied smile accompanying his overly familiar address. 'Your secret project will have to wait. The Riftborn increase in power daily, it is true, but the Knights Iscariot are the more immediate threat—and a global threat, too, if Mr. Tesla's story is accurate. They are organised, powerful, and according to Smythe's initial assessment, they have transformed the north of England into a lawless waste right under our noses. Do not fear, you can have Mr. Tesla back for your "great work" soon enough. A few weeks in the armoury should be sufficient for a man of his talents.' He spoke as if the argument were already won. John could scarcely believe that his sister's testimony had swung the argument in Cherleten's favour. If it truly had, John made a mental note to steer well clear of his father for a while, as the old dragon would be like a bear with a sore head for the foreseeable future.

'Of course, we are lucky indeed that Mr. Tesla brought his talents to London at all,' Lord Hardwick said, throwing an accusatory look in the direction of his offspring. 'It appears he saved himself, in the end, by virtue of his genius.'

'Come now, Lord Hardwick,' Sir Toby said, 'they acquitted themselves as well as could be expected, given the circumstances.'

'We almost lost Mr. Tesla, and it was not superior intelligence that alerted the enemy to their position.' Lord Hardwick turned and fixed his daughter with an icy stare. 'Within these walls, with the Nightwatch on hand, I would wager we are safe from the predations of the Knights Iscariot. But otherwise it would appear that you draw them like moths to a flame, and for how long this breach of security will be manifest is unknown.'

'I... it is passed. I am certain. It is all to do with this blasted wound. But it heals by the day, and I have felt no further adverse effects.' Lillian faltered, and reddened.

'We have nothing but your intuition for that,' he replied. 'An advantage that you have over your male counterparts, perhaps, but not enough to stake the safety of our prized assets upon.'

'If I may speak,' Tesla interrupted again, helping himself to a biscuit from a nearby plate. 'In my experience, the influence of a Majestic wanes over time. It is a battle of wills, which the lady seems well equipped to win.' For a second, Tesla averted his eyes bashfully, and shoved the biscuit whole into his mouth.

What is it about my little sister that makes such asses of men? John mused.

Sir Toby and the two lords looked first at Tesla, then at Lillian. Cherleten spoke first.

'Agent Hardwick is likely correct in believing that her wound is the cause of her lapse in mental defences. From my studies, I would say it was possible, although I have never seen it in practice. But then, this de Montfort is a most unusual foe. That cabman—Dresden, was it? When my people delved into his thoughts, they found residual psychic controls in place that prevented the man from revealing de Montfort's true designs. I have never seen anything quite like it. A truly remarkable—'

'What do you suggest, Lord Cherleten?' Lord Hardwick interrupted.

'Get that wound healed. Have Agent Hardwick observed by the Nightwatch.'

Lord Hardwick nodded and spoke curtly. 'This is what I think too. You are dismissed, Agent Hardwick. We may have made a grave mistake in admitting you to this meeting at all, and we shall not discuss concrete plans until we are certain you are free from the enemy's influence. When you leave here you will submit yourself for examination by the Nightwatch before undertaking any further duties.'

'Now, let's not be hasty!' Sir Arthur spoke up.

'I hardly think—' Lillian started.

'Do I make myself clear?' Lord Hardwick snapped, silencing them both.

Lillian ignored Arthur, and instead looked to John for support, but he could offer little; instead he nodded at her, urging her to comply.

'Perfectly clear... Father,' she said.

John wondered if their father had a point, although he had never known any Majestic to exert such power over another across great distance. And through a simple wound? The suggestion was ludicrous—that one creature could transmit some psychic force to another being through a scratch, as if it were some contagion?

Lillian stood. 'Gentlemen,' she said. With that, she turned and made for the door without another word.

Their father was unreadable, as ever. Sir Arthur cast his eyes downwards, jaw tensing and fists clenched by his sides. John watched his sister, wondering whether there was time to say something. He did not have to. Lillian barely made it through the great polished doors when she stepped back sharply. A man blocked her path, flustered and breathless. He stopped only to apologise, before darting into the room. It was Carrington, the club secretary. John had barely recognised the man, such was his unusually troubled demeanour.

'Carrington?' Sir Toby said, worry creeping into his tone.

'Sir Toby, my lords, gentlemen... madam; please forgive this most improper intrusion,' Carrington said, wringing his hands, 'but this is a most improper occurrence. I must ask you all to come with me at once, for this is a matter for your most urgent attention.'

John looked past the forlorn figure of Carrington at his sister, who stood in the doorway, a look of grave anticipation etched on her face. They all rose, and followed Carrington out, past Lillian, who fell in behind like a soldier. Her banishment was, for the moment, forgotten; John had a grim feeling that every agent would be needed for whatever lay ahead.

Arthur did not need to see the scene with his own eyes. He sensed death; it was redolent in the air, in the motes of spirit-light that spiralled from the great glass dome above them and down between the elegant columns that lined the marble hall. He assembled with the others on the balcony all the same, and peered down.

In the centre of the hall was a box, a square parcel. Around it, in a wide circle, grey-haired clubmen gathered nervously, unsure what to make of this intrusion into their sanctuary. From the box, a dark pool of liquid seeped like oil, washing the polished marble floor a deep red-black as it ebbed outwards.

No one spoke—not the old clubmen below, nor the Apollonian luminaries assembled beside Arthur. Carrington mopped his brow with his handkerchief, before handing a letter to Sir Toby.

'It was delivered with the... package,' he explained.

Sir Toby took it, a look of distaste on his face as he noted the spots of blood upon the envelope.

'Who delivered it?' he said, opening the envelope.

'I did not see them, sir,' Carrington said. 'The porter said it was a rough-looking man, a labourer or some such, who barged his way in, deposited the box, and said nothing. His manner was threatening. When the porter saw...' His words caught in his throat. 'He summoned me, and I thought it best to inform you directly.'

Sir Toby scanned the letter, and looked up at Carrington. 'You did the right thing, Carrington, though I would have preferred it if you had exercised more discretion. Please escort the ordinary members to the public rooms and ensure they receive the best hospitality. The hall is out of bounds until further notice.'

Carrington patted his oiled hair into place and, looking something more like his usual self, flitted down the stairs to relay Sir Toby's wishes to his staff. Soon the ordinary members of the Apollonian, who amongst their number counted some of the great thinkers, writers, theologians and reformers of London society, were shepherded away to have their frayed nerves salved with brandy and tobacco, leaving only the clique upon the mezzanine balcony and a few junior agents of Apollo Lycea in the hall, along with a few trusted servants. The agents looked up expectantly.

Only when he was certain they had some privacy did Sir Toby pass the letter to Arthur.

'Read it aloud,' he instructed. 'And... see what you make of it.'

Arthur removed his gloves, somewhat hesitantly, and took the letter. He at once frowned and squeezed his eyes shut. The vision was fleeting—suspiciously so for a Majestic of his power—but it was telling all the same.

'This letter was written by a man in fear for his life,' Arthur said. 'He knew he would be executed after writing it, but he wrote it anyway, for his tormentor had some hold over him. The identity of that tormentor is hidden from me—that in itself suggests he was a Majestic, and a good one.'

'I doubt there is anything good in this affair,' muttered Sir Toby. And then, louder, 'Read it.'

Arthur cleared his throat and began to read.

'Honoured gentleman, lords and ladies of the vaunted Apollo Lycea, I offer greetings from an order more ancient even than your own—the order of the Knights Iscariot. It would seem that our paths have begun to cross, and we already appear to be adversaries, yet this need not be so. Our goals may appear at first to oppose your own, but in truth we seek only a greater peace for the British Empire, and believe that we may yet reach a resolution that is agreeable to both of us. However, for that to happen, we would treat with you in person, tonight.

'At midnight, an emissary of the Knights Iscariot will arrive at the Apollonian Club. We request that all those in a position to hear his words, and to carry them to the highest authority, are present. We expect nothing less than the presence of representatives from the Cabinet of Whitehall, the royal family and household, the British Army, and, of course, Apollo Lycea. In return for your cooperation in this matter, we promise a full and frank exchange, so that our terms are not misunderstood. Our chosen emissary is but a humble diplomat, yet he speaks for the whole of our order.

*We presume that he will be afforded full diplomatic rights
and protection.*

'*Though it pains us to resort to petty threats, we
understand fully that we are, rightly or wrongly, considered
your enemy. That being so, we send to you a symbol of our
utmost sincerity. In the box you will find what remains of
one of your operatives—a spy—uncovered in our midst. If
our terms are not taken seriously, or our emissary waylaid
in any way, I can only promise you that a hundred more
such boxes shall be delivered to the Apollonian, Horse
Guards, and Buckingham Palace before the next day is
through. And that will be but the start, for our influence is
vast, and our supporters myriad.*

'*But let us not dwell on such unpleasantness, for tonight,
we shall parley, and put all of this behind us, for the good
of all.*

'*Yours, &c., Lord Lucien de Montfort, Master of the
Knights Iscariot.*'

Arthur rubbed his temple and handed the letter back to Sir
Toby. 'What… who… is in that box?' he asked, weakly.

Almost as soon as he had voiced the question, Lillian
Hardwick started down the stairs. She was halted at once by Sir
Toby, who placed a hand on her arm.

'Smythe?' she asked. She had a look in her eye that was,
Arthur thought, equal parts rage and sadness. That look usually
preceded an act of folly or violence.

Sir Toby turned instead to her brother. 'Lieutenant, if you
would,' he said.

With a nod, his complexion ashen, John Hardwick took the
stairs to the marble hall. The junior agents and trusted staff
gawped at him—for a young man, he had already made for himself
a reputation for steadfastness and resourcefulness. But none of
them had ever witnessed anything like this—the possibility that
one of their own had been executed by an unseen foe.

John stepped gingerly around the tendrils of blood, until he was able to grab the box and drag it towards himself, smearing crimson trails behind it. As John opened the package, Arthur observed Lillian leaning forward expectantly and, to his shame, realised he was doing the same.

The view of matted hair and pallid flesh was unmistakeable. The box contained a severed head. Sir Arthur Furnival, never one for ghoulishness, stepped back.

He heard John's heels on the marble floor once more and then, finally, his voice.

'It is not an agent,' John called up. 'His name was Massey—an innkeeper. He managed the safe-house in Hyde. Without him I would not have escaped so easily.'

Sir Toby hung his head ruefully. 'A humble servant. This will do more to sway the common man against us,' he said. 'It was calculated to show our supporters in the field that they are in mortal danger.'

'But what of Agent Smythe?' Arthur asked. 'Do we know he is safe?'

'We received vital intelligence from Agent Smythe only this morning,' said Sir Toby. 'It is no guarantee of his safety, but he is expected to return to London tonight, or tomorrow at the latest. Only then will we know for sure.'

'Is he alone?' Lillian asked.

'No. We sent an apprentice with him—Hanlocke.'

'The cracksman?' Lillian said. 'Forgive me, Sir Toby, but right now the north is no place for a novice.'

'Indeed,' said Sir Toby, his patience clearly wearing thin. 'Which is precisely why you are here, and not there.'

Lillian turned away from Sir Toby sharply. It had not been an easy day for her. Arthur wanted to take her aside and offer some words of comfort, but now was not the time.

'Come up, Lieutenant,' Sir Toby called down to John. 'Carrington—recall all of our agents from the field, no matter where in the Empire they may be. I want every one accounted for by morning. Find out if the late Mr. Massey had any family. They will need to be informed and well compensated. And arrange for this—for Massey's remains, I mean, to be—I mean, with all due ceremony…'

'Right away, sir.' At a clap of the secretary's hands, there came a flurry of activity as the club servants mobilised for duty.

'What do you think, my lords?' Sir Toby turned to Lord Hardwick and Cherleten.

'I rather think I'd like to take this "emissary" by force of arms, and use Mr. Tesla's inventions upon him until he tells us all we need to know,' growled Marcus Hardwick.

'Folly,' said Cherleten, still utterly calm despite everything. 'The insinuation was that the Knights Iscariot have a hundred more targets in mind for decapitation, and there is no telling who they are. Would you want to be responsible for the Queen waking up to find her maid's head in a box?'

Lord Hardwick sighed. 'Would that it were just a bloody maid.' He looked about, his expression changing as perhaps he realised how callous he sounded. 'Very well, we parley with these so-called "knights", but we do so under strictest security. I'll line the damned streets with soldiers: let them see what we can command at a moment's notice.'

Sir Toby nodded. 'I will talk to the Prime Minister and see who he can spare to represent the Cabinet at this meeting. Lord Hardwick, you can no doubt speak for the army. But what of the royal family?'

'There are three princes in attendance at St. James's,' said Lord Hardwick, 'I may be able to arrange a favour. I will certainly not risk Her Majesty's life in this venture—for all we know we are inviting a suicidal assassin into our midst.'

'Do not tell the Queen of the danger,' said Sir Toby. 'She would not put even one of her sons in harm's way if she knew your doubts.'

'Agreed. But there is no time for discussion, and we must set to work. I shall not receive these creatures in this sanctuary of

Empire without thorough preparations. Cherleten, can I entrust upon you to see to our... esoteric defences?'

'Oh, indeed, Hardwick,' Lord Cherleten smiled. 'And more besides. I think these events somewhat prove my earlier point, do they not? The Knights Iscariot are indeed the immediate threat; Mr. Tesla belongs with me.'

For a moment, Hardwick and Cherleten locked eyes like stags in rut, sizing each other up. Arthur was surprised when Lord Hardwick nodded, and turned away, looking back down to the scene below them.

'Sir Arthur, might I request your assistance?' Lord Cherleten said. Arthur grimaced inwardly; he knew what was coming.

'Of course, my lord,' Arthur replied. In truth, he wanted no part in assisting with the Nightwatch, which was almost certainly what would be required of him; but when called upon, he was a Majestic first and foremost, and his extended freedom came only through voluntary service.

There was not a chance that the Knights Iscariot, nor anyone without full and considered membership of the Apollonian, would be allowed to the upper floors. The building had five stories, and a sixth that was hidden from view beyond the balustered rooftop. But the gleaming façade of the club was a mere illusion as to its true size—several secret rooms and one entire wing protruded from the upper floors, interlocking seamlessly with the imposing Regency buildings either side and behind. Lord Cherleten's armoury was another case in point; no mere field agent knew for sure how many levels of tunnels, laboratories, storerooms and workshops stretched beneath the clubhouse, but there were always more personnel down there than anyone ever saw admitted by the main entrance, and some said that, should one sit in the tranquillity of St. James's Square after midnight and listen carefully, the distant, muffled sounds of industry could be heard rumbling and buzzing ceaselessly until the dawn.

Tonight, all of the civilian functions that were once the heart of the Apollonian were closed. The dining rooms and public bar, the ladies' room and picture gallery, the billiards, music and drawing rooms, the famous library, the gymnasium and swimming pool, the snugs and bedrooms. Things felt very different; different from any time Lillian had ever known during her short association with the Apollonian.

The walk along Pall Mall had been eerie. No one, not one member of the various clubs from the Reform to the Athenaeum, was on the streets at half past ten when Lillian returned to the Apollonian. Outside every door was a soldier on sentry duty. Soldiers and policemen were stationed at intervals along both the parallel roads of Pall Mall and Piccadilly, all the way from Regent Street in the east to St. James's Palace in the west. Inside the club, the armoury had equipped every available agent with weapons, and they made themselves very visible now; some pretended to be servants of the club, or casual members; others were very much playing their role as combatants, ready at a moment's notice to take up arms against hostile intruders. Lillian was relieved to note that the blood of the Cheshire man, Massey, had been removed without a trace. Somewhere behind the scenes, connected to life-assisting machinery invented by Intuitionists like Nikola Tesla, were the Nightwatch. They, undoubtedly, would feel the resonance of the unfortunate Massey's death for some time to come. Given the current state of emergency, Lillian had not submitted herself to their scrutiny, nor did she intend to.

Lillian marched unhindered through the marble hall, between the great classical pillars, past the sweeping staircase, and through to the banqueting hall, which was now transformed into an emergency meeting room. John and Sir Arthur gravitated to her at once, doubtless to shepherd her out of sight of the illustrious gathering at the far end of the room. No one seemed to notice her arrival, not even her father.

'Are you quite sure you should be here, Lillian?' asked Arthur, his voice low. She responded with her best withering look, which she had practised often on men who questioned her abilities or her right to do as she pleased. It had lost some of its efficacy on Arthur over the last couple of years, true enough, but it had the desired effect now.

'Look here, sis,' John said, 'I for one think you're as much a part of this as anyone—we both do, isn't that right, Sir Arthur? I heard Old Toby say as much earlier, and that's good enough. I've had a word with the Nightwatch's handlers, to make sure there are no… ah… interferences with your faculties, you understand.'

Lillian turned her look to her brother, and intensified her withering glare somewhat. John fumbled. Lillian was pleased.

'Oh come now, I was doing you a favour. If there is a risk, it'd be a deuced bad time for it to manifest, don't you think, with the bloody prince here and all.' The thought had not really occurred to her, but now Lillian peered over John's shoulder and saw indeed that, at the end of the room, Prince Leopold stood with her father, Sir Toby, and several advisers and other men whom she did not recognise. She sighed and nodded acceptance. John looked relieved, and went on, 'The Nightwatch can keep a lid on all of that, leaving us to focus on what's important. When this diplomat fellow arrives, we are to meet him at the door and escort him in. We take positions near the prince and our people and make sure there's no funny business. Just stick by us, and no one shall question your presence.'

For a moment, Lillian dropped her guard, for she realised that these two men were her only friends in this place; possibly her only friends anywhere. 'Thank you,' she said at last. 'Both of you.'

John kissed her on the cheek. Arthur managed the first smile she had seen from him all day. Perhaps, she mused, she should show a little gratitude to them more often if the effect was so telling.

By ten minutes to midnight, the guards within the club were visibly on edge. Other than John, none of them had ever seen a member of the Knights Iscariot up close, and the guards did not know what to expect. Lillian only hoped that the emissary would not be accompanied by any of their foul, cadaverous monsters. It seemed unlikely that they would sully proceedings by bringing along those hideous ghouls, but who could know for sure? John had said that de Montfort had exercised some control over the creatures back in Hyde, so perhaps they could be tamed. The thought of Hyde made her uncomfortable, for she still did not know if Beauchamp Smythe was safe. She told herself that she did not care overmuch, but she had said some unkind things about the surgeon the other night, and when she had believed his head to be in the mysterious package she had regretted them. Most of them, at least—the man was still unbearable.

John had gone to the door to check for any signs of the visitors. Before he even turned back, Arthur, standing beside Lillian near the rear of the hall, said, 'They are coming.'

Lillian was thankful that she sensed nothing. She had not voiced this concern to anyone, but secretly she feared that if de Montfort was near, she would feel his insidious influence in the back of her mind. She was certain it was de Montfort, even though they had never met. A fragmented picture of the mysterious Majestic had started to coalesce in her mind, piece by piece. Though she was afraid of what might happen should they ever meet, part of her relished the chance to purge him from her thoughts once and for all; to kill him. If the diplomatic talks went badly, she might yet get her chance.

John entered through the front doors and strode down the hall towards her.

'There's movement outside—a right royal entourage by the looks of it, arriving in three growlers. Bloody heraldic seals on the sides; of all the arrogance.'

'Well, their leader is apparently a lord,' said Arthur. 'It stands to reason they have some station.'

'If what Cherleten says is true, they aren't even human,' said John. 'Besides, so far as I can tell, Lord de Montfort is using a defunct title. I doubt there's any nobility in him.'

Arthur shrugged. Lillian was glad to see her brother so agitated—he clearly had a score to settle.

Two minutes past midnight. The doors of the Apollonian Club swung open. Lillian realised she was holding her breath, and felt at once foolish. Releasing it, however, gave rise to a fluttering in the pit of her stomach.

Four men entered the marble hall, very much human as far as Lillian could tell. They took up positions briskly, standing at either side of the door. They were dressed as footmen, in full livery, but all four were large men with a slack look about their features that set Lillian in mind of the poor coachman they had encountered the previous night. The men all had rough-shaven heads, with visible scars beneath their stubbled scalps. What had been done to them?

Lillian had little time to muse on that, as four other men entered, this time fanning out into the hall in regimented fashion. These four were certainly not human, and the club servants and even several agents shuffled away from them instinctively. All four were clad head to toe in black, smart suits and ruffs of a somewhat antiquated style visible beneath long coachman's cloaks. Their movements were unnatural, jerky, their limbs sharp and angular; sparkling violet eyes set within deep, hollow sockets scanned every face, peering into every corner. Their strange, snub noses sniffed the air as if the creatures were wolves hunting prey. They were completely bald, and their skin pale as alabaster. Their jaws were overlarge and curiously scarred, but they were not as deformed as the monsters Lillian had previously encountered; indeed, something in their eyes betrayed a keen intelligence, though they appeared almost ape-like in aspect. These were surely the masters of those degenerate beasts— kindred, perhaps, but a breed apart.

Lillian felt her grip tighten around the handle of the derringer, which was tucked into the holster at the small of her back. One of the creatures turned to her at once, as if sensing her aggression. Its nose wrinkled in something like a snarl, head cocking to one side as it examined her. She released the pistol at once, and the creature's face smoothed instantly into something almost human, and it nodded to her in acknowledgement.

A loud tapping sound came from the covered portico beyond the doors. And into the hallowed halls of the Apollonian came the emissary of the Knights Iscariot, tapping his steel-tipped cane on the marble.

'It's not de Montfort,' John muttered into Lillian's ear. But she already knew that.

The creature before them looked as though it had walked straight from another time. It was a man, ostensibly, whip-thin and tall, with a grin etched on his pallid face that was almost too wide, too grotesque, and somehow too perfect all at once. He was dressed in a fashion a hundred years out of date, as though he was en route to a Venetian masquerade. His velvet raiment was the colour of claret, with accents of ruffled black lace. He swept a long cloak from his shoulders and handed it to a trembling club servant, followed by his stovepipe hat, revealing a powdered wig atop a powdered face, which looked as ridiculous as it did anachronistic. The hideous grin did not fade as he looked about the hall, eyes hidden behind small, dark spectacles, but unmistakeably fixing upon each assembled face with deep scrutiny.

Behind this man was a woman; demure, small, timid. She too was bedecked in Georgian fashion, but there was no flamboyance about her. Her violet eyes had no sparkle. Her expression was tired, her bearing laggard. Where the male was proud, grotesque and garish, this creature was lolling, awkward, her features lumpen, as though beneath the powder and wig lay some great deformity. Like nothing else Lillian had ever witnessed, from Riftborn to the bestial servants, these two creatures frightened her.

'The Right Honourable Sir Valayar Shah, Prince-in-exile of Ahmednagar, Knight of the Ancient Order Iscariot!' The declaration was abrupt, and loud; it came from one of the human serfs who had entered first, and the baritone announcement—

too eloquently delivered for the look of the man—reverberated around the hall.

Lillian looked again at the grinning 'prince', and frowned. He was announced as 'Right Honourable', but he was certainly no privy councillor, no peer deserving of the honorific. Now his title and rather exotic name had been revealed, however, she realised there was something of the colonies about his features, even though his skin was white as a moonlit sail. Whatever race of men that he claimed his brethren, however, was irrelevant. He was not human.

'A prince, no less,' John whispered. 'I believe that is our cue.' He stepped towards the centre of the hall, Sir Arthur beside him. Lillian, as they had planned, stayed close. The eyes of the four bald creatures fell upon them as they approached their master. This close to the emissary, Lillian was greeted by a sickly smell, the pungent odour of dried flowers left to hang for far too long, of embalming fluid and strong cologne. She stopped a pace short of him as her senses were assailed.

'Sir... um... Valayar,' John said, meeting the creature's gaze. Lillian knew her brother was far too professional to be fumbling about his words, and his memory far too keen. He was being subtly disrespectful, and Lillian loved him for it. 'Welcome to the Apollonian Club. I am your liaison officer, Lieutenant Hardwick of Apollo Lycea, at your service.'

'We know who you are,' said Valayar Shah, his voice as thick as a desert wind. He was a full head taller than John, though much thinner, and looked down upon the agent with that rigor-mortis grin almost unmoving. Lillian could barely keep her eyes from it; those teeth that looked too large and white to be real, and dozens of tiny cuts and scars across Shah's face, covered by make-up, as though his visage was nothing but a carnival mask. In fact, she had the disturbing impression that his smile was carved into his flesh, and could not be relaxed even if he wished it. 'We know this one, too,' the emissary continued, looking directly at Lillian. 'My dear lady, Lord de Montfort sends his regards, and wishes me to convey his great disappointment that he is unable to make your acquaintance at this time.'

'The regret is mine,' Lillian said, her words dripping venom. She managed a small curtsey all the same. Shah's eyes lingered upon her for a second longer than was polite, before turning to Arthur.

'Ah… the free Majestic, the great novelty of Apollo Lycea. Sir Arthur Furnival, is it not?'

Arthur nodded. Lillian saw that Arthur had taken as much of a dislike to this creature as she had. The look in his eyes suggested that he was studying Shah for signs of weakness; perhaps, she thought, he had taken offence on her part. For once she was glad of it.

'Sir Valayar, our delegation is gathered just through here, as per your request,' John said, indicating the double doors at the back of the hall. 'Let us not keep them waiting.'

Shah bowed low, but his eyes were, at all times, upon Lillian. Lascivious. Impertinent. Threatening. When he straightened, he stepped past John, following the line of his extended arm towards the doors, which were also flanked by club guards. Shah curled a beckoning finger nonchalantly behind him, signalling for the strange woman to follow, which she did at once, tottering unsteadily, her vacant stare suggesting she was in some fug, either of intoxicants or mere mental deficiency. The other members of Shah's entourage remained where they were, the bald creatures as one staring coldly at Lillian and her two companions. She had half hoped they would try to enter with their master, for she already relished the thought of pitting herself against them, but it was not to be. The creatures would be confined in the great hall, and would remain there, if they knew what was good for them.

Lillian took up a position at the side of the room, next to Arthur, ignoring the look her father gave her when he finally noticed that she had prised her way into the meeting. She expected to face his ire later, but for now she would say nothing, as would he. Agents of the Crown and royal guards lined the room. No chances would be taken this evening, and it dawned on Lillian that, as far as her father was concerned, she represented as great a security risk as Shah, given Mr. Tesla's assertions.

John announced Valayar Shah, who bowed to his hosts and took a seat at one end of the long table, his attendant—or whatever she was—standing beside his chair. The men at the other end of the table were introduced in turn: Lord Hardwick, Lord Cherleten and Sir Toby; Lieutenant-Colonel Sir Edmund Henderson of the Metropolitan Police; General Askwith of the British Army; the Right Honourable Richard Cross, Home Secretary; and last of all, seated at the head of the table upon an ornate chair reserved for state visits, Prince Leopold. The prince was a young man in his middle twenties, with a thin, pale face and small, neat moustaches. He had dressed for the occasion in ceremonial garb and, despite his tender years and diminutive stature, looked every inch the noble. It was not the prince, however, who opened proceedings, nor even Lillian's father, but Sir Toby Fitzwilliam. He was commander of Apollo Lycea, and this was his territory; just as a ship's captain would brook no challenge aboard his own vessel, Sir Toby would not relinquish control.

Not even to a privateer, Lillian thought, glancing at Lord Cherleten.

'We bid welcome to Sir Valayar of the Knights Iscariot,' Sir Toby said, standing. 'Every courtesy under the conditions of parley will be extended on this night, but the noble emissary must be under no illusion—the actions of his order thus far have not endeared them to us. Indeed, today's "gift", sent by a certain Lord de Montfort, constitutes the latest in a long line of criminal acts committed or endorsed by the Knights Iscariot. We may have agreed to Lord de Montfort's conditions, but tonight's talks will involve a discussion of reparations for his actions. That is *our* condition.'

Shah stood, gathering his full height and tilting his hideous, grinning skull-like head to Sir Toby. 'The honourable gentlemen is right to be angry, of course; but be aware that I am not a representative of any individual, but of a species with its own royal line, its own government and, we hope, its own sovereign state.'

'I beg your pardon?' Sir Toby dropped the cordial tone and furrowed his imposing brow.

'Surely you understand the nature of the Knights Iscariot by now?' Shah said. 'By the laws of men, indeed you may believe our people have transgressed against you. But we are not men, sir. We are something else entirely. For too long now—centuries, in fact— we have hidden in the shadows, our purpose at times intersecting with nations of men, either fortuitously or by design. But for the most part we have stood alone, looking inwards to protect ourselves from a world that could never understand us, and never accept us. But with the rise of the Riftborn and the thinning of the veil, we have spied an opportunity to end our long, self-imposed separation. It is men who have brought about this calamity, and men who fail to control it. And so it falls to us to act. The time for hiding is at an end. We seek a truce, and a place in this great empire of yours. We seek nothing more than a home, and in return we shall place at your disposal all our great esoteric knowledge, which will assist you in combating the growing terrors of the Rift. When presented thus, does not the desire for retribution against my Lord de Montfort seem… petty?'

His voice was lilting, soothing. Only when he had finished speaking did Lillian realise that Shah had left his position, and had moved half a dozen places along the table, so that he was now close to her. No guards had moved to stop him. At the same moment she realised this, the other agents also tensed, as if nodding awake from a dream. Shah spread out his palms in a gesture of apology, his smile doing nothing to assuage their fears; the smile lingered again on Lillian, Shah's dazzling eyes fixing on her over the brim of his spectacles even as he turned away. As Shah retreated back to his seat, his movements fluid and elegant, Lillian looked about the room to see that only one man had reacted during the emissary's entreaty. Lord Cherleten was not in his seat, but was standing near the head of the table to Prince Leopold's left, where he would have been able to intercept Shah had the emissary attempted any misdeed.

Lillian breathed easy. More than that, she saw Cherleten in a different light all at once. He'd had presence of mind enough— or perhaps even some trickery from the armoury—to shake off the almost soporific influence of Shah's sing-song tones and uncanny will, and Cherleten had used that composure to put himself in harm's way to defend the prince. Lillian found that admirable, if not reassuring; he was, after all, a greying man of middle years, with not half the formidable military training of her father or Sir Toby.

And it was Sir Toby who spoke next, choosing, Lillian thought, to ignore whatever odd experience they had all just shared.

'Sir Valayar, you seek to move the discussion from what you call "petty" matters to one of global import. Under normal circumstances, with a normal guest, I would applaud your audacity and perhaps approve of the sentiment. But in this matter I—and, I imagine, all of those fine gentlemen assembled here— find it hard to overlook the criminal acts to which you allude. Accusations of murder fall at your door—at the door of Lord de Montfort, whose title, I might add, the honourable House of Lords does not recognise. The death of at least one servant of the Crown preceded your arrival, the admission of guilt signed by de Montfort himself. And lastly, but most certainly of greatest consequence, there is the matter of the nature of the Knights Iscariot. Yes, we do indeed understand your "nature", if it can be called natural at all. And as we understand it, your kind is sustained only by the blood of the living—specifically, the blood of human beings.'

Lillian felt a chill run through her veins at the very words, and saw from the reactions of those around her that she was not alone.

'Sir Toby, your directness and astuteness befit your estimable reputation,' the emissary replied, 'but I would indeed ask you to overlook the things that you may personally find distasteful, and think instead of the greater good. Think what we might accomplish together, as one united force.'

'I cannot see for a moment what we might accomplish,' Richard Cross interrupted.

'Please, Home Secretary, have your say,' said Sir Toby.

'This… "Sir" Valayar,' Cross said, clearly angry, 'brings to us promises of peace while not denying that his people prey on ours, and will doubtless continue to do so if Lord Cherleten's intelligence is correct.' At this, Shah's eyes—and his unsettling smile—fell upon Cherleten, who still had not moved from his position by Prince Leopold. 'I agree wholeheartedly with Sir Toby's sentiment: this is not a matter for diplomatic talks. Indeed, I cannot understand why we are here at all. The emissary merely seeks to bargain for amnesty for his master—a master who is too cowardly to submit himself to the Queen's justice.'

'Ah, but my learned friend makes a mistake,' said Shah.

'Mistake?' spat Cross, indignation writ large across his craggy features.

'A mistake, indeed. Firstly, there is the false assumption that one of the Knights Iscariot, such as my master, is subject to the justice of your Crown. As I said, we pay tribute to a royal line far older than your queen's, and thus consider ourselves subjects of another sovereign.'

'While you are within this great kingdom, sir, you are subject to the laws of its ruler. Whether you choose to recognise them or not is irrelevant.' This time the speaker was Prince Leopold, who remained seated, eyes narrowed and fingers pressed together. His tone was regal and, Lillian was surprised to note, laden with no small amount of menace.

'Forgive me, sir, for I meant no disrespect,' Shah said, at once bowing low. 'I merely attempt to explain our position, as it was explained to me.' A plea for leniency, it seemed; Lillian fancied that Shah played the humble messenger only when it suited him.

'Enough of this,' said Sir Toby, 'It is high time you explained to us exactly what your master brings to the table. Perhaps he promises an end to the killing of innocent men and women, which apparently is a long tradition of the Knights Iscariot.'

'That, Sir Toby, we cannot promise,' said Shah, his softly accented voice purring from behind large white teeth. 'The taking of blood is not a tradition, as you so delicately put it, but the means of our survival. Since before the time of Christ, we have lived thus, and through certain... peculiarities of our race, we could not change even if we desired it.'

'Blasphemy!' growled Cross.

'And do you?' Prince Leopold asked, leaning forwards in his chair. 'Do you wish to change?'

Shah cocked his head and held the prince's gaze, looking more and more like a grotesque ventriloquist's dummy, his white skin waxen-looking. 'Does a tiger desire the fruits of the earth when the deer are plentiful?'

'You believe us... prey?' The prince glowered.

Lillian blinked hard. Was Shah several paces from his seat once again? When had he moved? It seemed that the emissary's words, if not his rictus grin, were hypnotic.

'Do not be insulted, my prince,' said Shah, extending a long, bony arm in a supplicating gesture. 'You have undoubtedly heard many folk tales designed to scare children to their beds of a night. But the truth is that we have always been, and always shall be. Most of us rarely need to feed in the manner that causes you such concern, for we are old and our dependence on human blood wanes with each passing winter. The younger members of our order, however, have certain... needs. Yet even these are mostly sated by common men who give of themselves willingly, eager to be a part of a tradition spanning two thousand years.'

'Most, but not all,' Sir Toby said.

'Transgressions are unfortunate,' said Shah, 'but far less common than murder and violence amongst your own kind. Our order polices itself.'

'I suggest you step back, Sir Valayar. I suggest it most strongly indeed.'

At the sound of Lord Cherleten's voice, which was uncharacteristically set and forceful, Lillian blinked again. The emissary had reached the other end of the table, almost within striking distance of the prince, and the agents and even the gathered dignitaries seemed not to have noticed—most were looking abstractedly at the table. Cherleten alone stood before Shah, his expression fierce. Someone had to act, and Lillian was first to respond.

Darting past Sir Arthur and two other agents, her movements seeming to wake them from their reveries, Lillian was beside Cherleten in a heartbeat, derringer drawn and aimed at Shah's head. The emissary of the Knights Iscariot looked down at her, his expression fixed. Perhaps he could not change it if he wanted to.

'Return to your place, Sir Valayar,' she said. 'If you please.'

'Ah, misplaced loyalty,' said Shah to Lillian, his eyes darting to Cherleten and back. 'Ever is it the bane of your kind.'

The strange woman who accompanied Shah at once sprang to life, her feline movements affording her an inhuman quality as she stalked to her master's side. Sir Arthur and the other nearby agents intercepted the woman at once, at which she let out a long hiss, which tailed away into a low, staccato sound that put Lillian in mind of the bestial ghouls with the parchment skin.

As it dawned on everyone in the room what was happening, a general clamour was raised. The dignitaries, Cross and Sir Edmund Henderson foremost amongst them, leapt from their seats and harangued the visitor, while their trusted attendants rushed to their sides. Only Leopold remained seated, and as Shah and his vile creature were escorted back to their places at the other end of the room, he held up his hands and demanded silence.

'Please, gentlemen—and ladies—none of us wants any violence here today. Is that not correct, Sir Valayar?'

'It is indeed, sir,' Valayar said, bowing. 'I was merely stretching my legs, as is my peculiar manner. I forgot myself.'

'My learned colleagues asked you a question earlier, Sir Valayar,' the prince went on, 'which you have still not answered to their satisfaction. What is it that de Montfort offers, which is not already our right as rulers of these isles?'

'Knowledge, power, peace, prosperity. We offer you two thousand years of ancient lore—enough to make the long-dead librarians of Alexandria weep with joy. We offer the very secrets of the Knights Iscariot, secrets that will cure myriad human frailties, and help you to fight the Riftborn that even now gather at the threshold between worlds, waiting to grow fat on your mortal souls.'

'Not your souls also?' Leopold asked, an eyebrow raised.

'Indeed not, my prince, for the Knights Iscariot have long possessed the means to battle esoteric forces. It is why Sir Toby's pet Majestic, Sir Arthur Furnival, even now seeks ingress to my thoughts, but is able to find none.' Sir Valayar shot a glare at Sir Arthur, who had been touching his fingers to his temple in concentration, and now was forced to stop awkwardly as all eyes fell upon him. 'Are not these secrets worth a hearing of our terms?' Shah asked.

'Let us hear these terms, and then we shall decide,' Sir Toby said.

Shah bowed once more. 'You are quite right, Sir Toby,' he said. 'It is time for the pleasantries to be concluded. As I can see it suits the honourable gentlemen, let me speak plainly, so that I shall not be misunderstood, and so you all might return to your beds the sooner. In exchange for our cooperation in all matters, the Knights Iscariot require a place to call our own. A home. As we have made our business in the industrial north, that is what we want: the north. Henceforth, we request that Yorkshire, Lancashire, Cheshire, Westmoreland, Durham, Northumberland and Cumberland are seceded to our rule, and recognised as a single independent principality, under the rulership of my masters, for whom Lord de Montfort is the recognised representative. In return, the shipyards and mining works of Northumberland will be subject to a trade agreement, granting the British Crown exclusive contractual rights to services provided by our operations. The stipulations are written in great detail in the treaty that my lord has already drawn up, to be studied at your leisure. These, gentlemen, are our terms, and they are non-negotiable.'

There was uproar in the room. The prince's advisers clamoured around him, vying for his attention; the others shouted their outrage, slinging insults at the emissary, who swayed his head slowly, snake-like, grinning throughout. Sir Toby quelled the assembly. As he stood, he looked more commanding than the royal prince, or any of the elected officials present.

'What you ask is madness. More than that, it is tantamount to a declaration of war. You know that?'

'No, no, Sir Toby. What I ask is necessary to *avoid* violence,' replied the emissary.

'A ransom, then. And what of the people of the north? The *human* subjects of Great Britain; what of them?'

'Lord de Montfort assures me that all of your officials—your magistrates, councillors, clerics, clerks, soldiers and any other notable personages of your choosing, will be allowed to leave our lands, or stay on in exile. The remainder of the common citizenry not so named will be... ours. Our subjects. Our servants.'

Lillian saw Sir Toby's fists clench, and yet his rage barely manifested as he replied, 'And if we choose to reject your proposals... forcibly?'

'You will lose,' came the reply, matter-of-factly. 'We have already treated with the Scots. So far seventeen local magistrates have agreed a policy of non-intervention in return for our support after the secession. There is barely a farm, factory or fishery left in Scotland that has not signed some agreement or other with our agents. In short, gentlemen, you can expect no help from north of the border, not even from those regiments you believe loyal to your queen. Likewise, other emissaries have already petitioned Austria-Hungary and Russia to recognise our right to secede. When our negotiations have concluded, we have no doubt that the Prussians, French and Dutch will support our claims, too. In exchange for our business and, more importantly, our assistance in ending the unholy terror of the Riftborn, they are willing to end trade agreements with the British Crown, and provide military aid to protect their... new investments... from English aggression. We will be a fledgling sovereign state, and we have already taken steps to secure our autonomy.'

'Our allies would not dare turn on us for the likes of you!' Richard Cross spluttered.

'Not alone, this is true. But united, and knowing that the Knights Iscariot already have a foothold on English soil... you will find there is little they would not do in exchange for our knowledge, and our industrial wealth. I put it to you, Home Secretary, that you would be wise to do the same.'

'Do not propose to lecture me—'

'Please, gentlemen,' said Prince Leopold, taking to his feet, 'let us not give in to anger. It would seem to me that Sir Valayar's proposals, even with the support of our supposed allies, are insufficient for his needs. Not only that, but the treaty he has mentioned has not yet appeared. Therefore, I presume he has more to say, unless, of course, he wishes to find himself taken into custody by Sir Edmund's constables.'

'His Royal Highness is as astute as he is genteel,' said Shah. 'We have, of course, made certain assurances far in advance. This is the first time we have thrown ourselves upon the mercy of an uncaring world; it would be folly to do so without preparation, for our people have ever been feared and even persecuted over the centuries.'

Cross muttered something disparaging, though everyone else pretended he'd said nothing.

'I come to you today on your territory, as a gesture of good faith,' Shah went on. 'But the treaty shall be signed in the north. My masters suggest gathering at Scarrowfall, a great estate that has become the home of our kind this past decade. Every hospitality shall be extended, and your delegation shall have all the time they need to review the treaty before signing. We shall welcome Her Majesty the Queen to our home.'

'The Queen?' This was the first time Lord Hardwick had addressed the diplomat directly, his voice full of displeasure.

'Of course, Lord Hardwick. I said before, did I not, that my masters are of a royal line, more ancient than any on this earth. They will brook no substitute for their agreement than the Crown, whose rulership extends over the Empire by the grace of God.'

'Are you honestly suggesting that we send the Queen of England into a vipers' nest full of your degenerate monsters?' Hardwick asked.

'You wound me, sir, with your insults. But I shall forgive you, for they are born not of true enmity, but of superstition and ignorance.'

Hardwick's eyes flared at the slight. 'It is impossible. It will not be done.'

'The treaty shall be signed by one of the royal line, Lord Hardwick,' said Shah, confidently.

'Or else?' glowered Lord Hardwick.

'Or those assurances I spoke of shall come into force, immediately. Do you have any idea how many of our loyal servants live and work in London? Do you have any notion of how tirelessly they have worked these last years? What if I were to tell you that almost a third of the etherium harvested outside the capital has passed through our hands? That a tenth of London's supply is directly controlled by subsidiary companies owned by the Knights Iscariot? Do you have any idea what we might do with that etherium... what we have already done? I am sure Lord Cherleten can guess. I am likewise sure that your new pet, Tesla, could think of all manner of destructive uses for the wrong type of etherium thrust into the vein of the wrong arm.' Shah threw a quick glance at Arthur.

'You would not dare...' Lord Hardwick did not sound so sure of himself any more.

'Have I not already explained, Lord Hardwick, that we do not fear the Riftborn? I offer a great opportunity for you to share power with the Knights Iscariot, and heal this world together. The alternative, of course, is for us to rule alone.'

'Alone with no food source,' Cherleten said.

Shah shrugged his narrow shoulders. 'None near the epicentre of the catastrophe that would ensue,' he said. 'Believe me when I tell you that we have no desire to rule a world of ash and brimstone, where we are forced to be masters to a slave-race that used to call itself humanity. That is a vision I know has been visited upon many Majestics since the Awakening. It is the undeniable truth of what will happen should the Rifts expand and the Other walk abroad freely. It is an outcome that can be prevented by accepting our offer. I doubt very much any of you noble lords would knowingly allow such a terrible thing to befall your beloved country.'

'We would barely have a country left,' said Sir Toby. 'You would hold us to ransom.'

'No. I would persuade you to see reason. And now that my cards are on the table, as you Englishmen say, I must have your answer. I am sure you understand that I cannot wait for ever—dawn approaches, and the journey ahead is a long one.'

There was a moment's silence. Then Prince Leopold spoke, his firmness somehow reassuring.

'My mother will not sign your treaty, nor will she set foot in Scarrowfall.'

Someone at the back of the room gasped. Sir Toby and Lord Hardwick looked askance at the prince as though they had already decided that compliance was the best way forward. That surprised Lillian, and she liked the prince more by the second.

'Dear prince,' said Shah, 'I pray that you reconsider—'

'There is nothing to reconsider. My mother the Queen shall not treat with your masters. But I will. I will speak in her stead, and have no doubt that my words will be her words, and as binding as any that she would speak.'

'Your Royal Highness, I urge you—' Cross protested, but the prince raised a hand, and the Home Secretary was at once silenced. Shah studied the prince's resolute face. Lillian held her breath. She had thought the prince at first stubborn and rash, and had admired him for it. Now, it seemed he was instead brave, and noble—though Lillian had thought that a fight was inevitable, perhaps the Knights Iscariot's threat was too grave. Leopold would shoulder the burden of ignominy rather than put his mother in harm's way. Would she do the same for her father? She was ashamed when she realised, truthfully, that she likely would not.

'It seems the prince has made up his mind,' Shah said.

'Wait!' The command was imperious, gruff and rumbling. Lillian's father got to his feet. 'His Royal Highness speaks for the Queen, but it was Her Majesty who requested that I be made Minister for Defence of this nation, and protector of her interests—and of her family. I would offer a counter proposal.'

'Do go on, my lord,' said Shah.

'His Royal Highness the prince shall meet your people on neutral ground. Aboard the royal train—while it is in motion. You shall come aboard when the train reaches Yorkshire and say your piece, and have until it reaches the Scottish border to come to an accord. If your talks are not concluded within that time, then we will all see what happens next, will we not?'

There was moment's silence. Shah cocked his head like a nanny bemused by a precocious charge. Leopold raised a thin eyebrow, and Lillian fancied she saw him stifle a smile.

'Do you find this satisfactory?' Prince Leopold asked, breaking the awkward silence.

Shah seemed to consider for a moment, before finally bowing lower than ever. 'More than satisfactory,' he said. He straightened. 'We have an accord, gentleman—the bargain is struck. I shall take my leave of you immediately, with your permission, and with God's speed, I shall inform my master Lord de Montfort of your decision before morning.'

'But there are still details to discuss, a great many details,' the Home Secretary spluttered.

'I will send a messenger to you tomorrow to discuss the formalities,' said Shah. 'I have only two stipulations, mere trifles, which Lord de Montfort has bade me communicate to you all. The first is that a certain agent of Apollo Lycea, one Lillian Hardwick, is to accompany the royal delegation. Lord de Montfort is eager to make her acquaintance. The second is that the good lady's brother, one Lieutenant Hardwick, for transgressions made personally against my lord, is not to set foot in the north, on pain of death.'

Lord Hardwick began to turn the colour of an angry bruise, and his large hands clenched into fists. Lillian was uncertain whether he was angry about her, or John, or both. More likely it was neither, and that he was apoplectic only because his family name had been drawn into this affair. Sir Toby, on the other hand, nodded grimly.

'When do you expect you will be ready to greet His Royal Highness's delegation?' he asked.

'Soon—three days hence.'

'Three days... That gives us no time!'

'Time? What time do you require, when the outcome is already assured? Gentleman—and lady,' he said, glancing once more at Lillian, 'I bid you good night. When next we meet, I trust it shall be as friends.'

Lillian only scowled, an expression as etched upon her face as the vampire's grin. With that, and with objections still being vocalised within the room, Shah took the hand of his strange companion, and turned away from the stunned dignitaries. Only when the doors had closed behind him did the true discussions begin. The formulation of a plan to topple the Knights Iscariot.

ELEVEN

Friday, 24th October

THE ROYAL TRAIN, NEAR LEICESTER

The royal train was seldom used, and when it was its movements were a closely guarded state secret. It was nine carriages long, each one gleaming black and adorned with discreet painted livery, appointed with fitting finery for the British monarchy. It was armed and armoured, from the indomitable war-engine to the triple-layered glass windows of the sleeping cars. The rearmost carriage held a garrison of ten soldiers drawn from the prince's household guard, who made the total crew complement of the train—sans royalty—thirty-nine.

From her private booth in the guest car, Lillian gazed through the reinforced window at the sky beyond, which was already paling to a hazy orange as they neared the Midlands. They were far from the largest conurbations, which attracted the baleful energies of the Rift. She mused on the fact that her father had kept her assignments largely domestic, especially since her ill-fated mission in Paris. She had spent more hours travelling these last few days than she had for the whole of the previous six months, confined as she had been to the Home Counties. Still, there were worse ways to travel—this was a world apart from the bumpy ride of Selby's coach. The royal train was both mobile fortress and luxury hotel on rolling stock, forging through the blasted expanse of the countryside on rails cleared in advance of humble passenger and freight cars. It did not stop except by royal decree, and so they would rumble on for nearly two more hours until Hull, where the enemy delegation would come aboard. From there, the train would take the less-used lines along the east coast and across the North York Moors, travelling on to Edinburgh uninterrupted. This would give the Knights Iscariot more than four hours to make their case, by which time, Prince Leopold had ordered, the negotiations would be concluded for good or ill.

The thought of it made Lillian's skin crawl; these creatures, these murderers, were to treat with the prince. She scowled, and checked her weapons. A pistol was concealed within her dress, along with a belt of ammunition, both standard and etheric. A derringer was hidden up her right sleeve, a slender knife within her left boot. Only one gun was on show—a snub-nosed Webley at her breast holster, which she was not usually permitted to carry openly. 'Unladylike, and liable to provoke trouble,' her father had said. She checked herself in the mirror of her compartment once more, and tied up her hair into a chignon of sorts, slipping an eight-inch, razor-sharp hairpin into position to complete her arsenal. She had been commanded—more than once—to avoid confrontation with the northern delegates. But Lillian never went unprepared for any eventuality. Moreover, she never went unprepared for a fight.

She looked at herself carefully in the mirror. Though she was weary, and troubled, she had managed to conceal it well—the rings beneath her eyes and the tired complexion were hidden at least as well as the weaponry she carried. But there was something more, something that all the powders and lotions in the world could not disguise. There was a shadow about her—she could almost see it coalescing around her reflection. Every mile the train travelled was accompanied by swelling fear in her breast and, more than that, a tingling sense of anticipation. She would meet de Montfort today. She felt she knew him intimately; that she would recognise him instantly. What she could not say, what she had not said, was that she was not wholly anxious about the meeting, but curious, and even a little thrilled. Lillian buried these feelings deep, for she thought they were not born of her own psyche, but of some residual suggestion placed within her mind by the Majestic.

There came a soft knock at her door.

'Enter.' Lillian turned away from the mirror, confident that her array of deadly weapons was masterfully concealed. She almost looked the lady her mother wanted her to be.

Arthur entered the carriage, took one look at her and said, 'Really Lillian, we're on a diplomatic mission. Must you really carry the weight of London's ordnance on your person?'

Lillian tried to stifle a laugh, and put her hand over her mouth.

'You shouldn't use your powers on your friends, Arthur,' she said. 'That is not very gentlemanly.'

'Nonsense,' Arthur said. 'I require no second sight to know your ways, Agent Hardwick—merely simple deduction. The only time you ever wear a bustle is to conceal a gun belt.'

Lillian smiled, and stood to face him. 'Then it's for the good that our guests do not know me half so well as you.' She reached out and straightened his cravat. 'You really must learn to dress yourself without the aid of Jenkins.'

In the confines of the compartment, they stood close. Lillian fancied Sir Arthur reddened a little around the collar.

'I, um... I came to say that they're serving tea in five minutes. I believe the prince will be joining us—be rude not to show.'

Lillian held Arthur's gaze for a second longer than was proper, before turning away. 'I will be there shortly, thank you,' she said.

Sir Arthur nodded, hesitated, and then left.

Lillian sighed. She chided herself for playing games—whatever was between her and Sir Arthur was in the past. A missed opportunity; a forgotten moment. If it were not for her father's unwarranted rebuke, and her brother's patronising warnings, then the past was where these feelings would remain. But as in all things, Lillian could not help but rebel. She often disliked herself for it. But she did it regardless.

'Not long now, chaps, and we'll be in the north,' the prince said, as the train clattered between the ironworks of the Erewash. '"The north",' he added. 'Honestly, people talk about the bit of the kingdom north of the Humber as though it's another country. It's not like anyone's thrown up a bally great wall or anything, eh?'

Lillian sat taking tea with a group of gentlemen, who all seemed as comfortable in the train carriage as they would have been at Clarence House. The train was furnished with plush carpets, settees, mahogany tables and crystal chandeliers. It was warm, having none of the customary draughts that characterised normal passenger coaches. It smelled now of brewing tea, Turkish tobacco and warm buttered teacakes. Comforts of home that were singularly out of place given the nature of the mission.

'The Knights Iscariot are little more than degenerates, Your Royal Highness, and impudent ones at that,' said Sir Robert Collins. The man was not much older than Sir Arthur, with prematurely greying hair, but he had already secured a position as comptroller of the prince's household. He always seemed to know the right thing to say, except to Lillian, for whom he appeared to reserve only a casual sneer and disapproving glance. She had taken an instant dislike to the man, for it seemed that his quips and apparent wisdom were a thin veneer for the jingoism and conservatism within. There was nothing they could say about the Knights Iscariot that Collins would not dismiss with some jibe about the 'whiff of the foreigner' or the 'half-witted scheme of the diseased imbecile'. Lillian hoped that, when the time arose, he would not so brazenly underestimate the enemy.

'Quite,' said the prince, reclining on a plush settee. 'And yet, there's already a strange feeling in the air, don't you agree? It is like we have all been blind to the goings-on in the north, as though whatever strange spell the Valayar creature worked on us at the Apollonian has somehow been performed *en masse*, disguising the workings of the Knights Iscariot while they strengthened their position. What do you think, Sir Arthur? Could this be the work of a Majestic?'

Arthur had not been expecting the question, and set down his teacup quickly, dabbing his small moustache with a napkin to afford himself a little thinking time. Even a baronet could not speak entirely freely in the presence of a prince.

'It cannot be ruled out, Your Royal Highness,' he said. 'Although I would grant that one Majestic would be incapable of such a feat. Even the whole of the Nightwatch combined could not befuddle half the nation.'

'Or so you believe,' said Collins. 'I mean, how would any of us know?' He let out a thin laugh at his own joke, which everyone was impelled to copy when the prince laughed out loud. 'If it is not Majestics at work,' Collins asked, addressing the whole carriage even though his question was clearly intended for Arthur, 'then what? Some devilish power born of the Rift? The hypnotic gaze of the legendary "vampires".' He chuckled again. Arthur was about to answer, but Lillian stepped in first.

'We have no evidence that they possess any such powers,' she said. 'In fact, I would say it is more likely that they have friends in high places, who have helped obfuscate their plot.'

Collins stared at Lillian as though a servant had just addressed him unbidden. 'Friends in high places? You mean, in government?'

Lillian ignored Arthur's imploring expression, and took the bait. 'Who else could exert sufficient influence?' she asked. 'We have evidence that this Lord de Montfort has visited London on—'

'My dear lady,' said Collins, raising his voice to cut her short, 'you venture dangerously into the realm of politics, a subject that no woman other than Her Majesty the Queen has ever sufficiently grasped. To have such self-destructive corruption within the hallowed chambers of Whitehall would be unthinkable, leaving it the least likely of the options we have discussed. Now, humour me... I understand that your father has given you a position within Apollo Lycea, but why would you feel qualified to make such assumptions about these Knights Iscariot?'

All eyes were on her now—the prince, Arthur, Collins, the two diplomats, the three guards at the door, even the servants.

'Because,' she said, allowing her indignation to grant her courage, 'I have killed more of them than any man on this train.'

There was silence. A brief glower crossed Collins' features, but he had no time for further witticisms at Lillian's expense before the prince clapped his hands together slowly.

'Bravo, madam, bravo!' he said. 'Killed more of 'em than any man here, you see, Collins? The lady is as fearless as she is pretty. If we indeed have a modern woman in our midst, then we must be modern men also, eh?'

Collins cleared his throat and nodded. 'Quite so, sir,' he said. 'I would say that Agent Hardwick is a rose amongst thorns, but it appears she is thornier than any of us.'

Leopold laughed at that, too. Lillian forced a smile. The conversation had made her the centre of attention, for all the wrong reasons.

'I am sure we will find out more than we need to about the Knights Iscariot shortly,' said Arthur, gallantly intervening. 'And should things turn sour, we should all be glad of Agent Hardwick's particular expertise.'

'Hear, hear,' said the prince. 'Although I should hope the guards will prove capable. Isn't that right, Colonel Ewart?'

The large Scotsman, who had remained thus far silent, now set down his own tea, the bone china cup looking comically tiny in his broad hands. 'My men are prepared for any eventually, sir, although if our job is done correctly there'll be nae need of hostilities.'

'Spoken like a true soldier,' remarked Collins, shooting another glance at Lillian.

'Allow me to be candid, Agent Hardwick,' the prince said, the mirth draining from him instantly. Lillian nodded, for she was unaccustomed to dealing with royalty, and the company made her even more uncomfortable than the formal attire. 'You said you have fought these creatures before, and you have my sympathies. It is with deep regret that any brute should lay hands—or claws, or teeth, or whatever they possess—upon a lady, and one so young.' Lillian felt herself blushing. It was ridiculous—Prince Leopold was not far her senior. 'Know this,' he continued, 'it would give me no greater pleasure than to see the Knights Iscariot hung for treason, to exact revenge on them for the wrongs they have done you, and have done to others under the Queen's rule. Colonel Ewart has been fully briefed on effective combat measures against the Knights Iscariot and their pets, and I would dearly love to set him loose on them. However, I must advise caution. In less than an hour we will be joined by their representatives, and I am honour-bound to treat with them peacefully, and reach an accord if at all possible. Our personal feelings must be set aside for the good of the nation, don't you agree?'

Lillian had the unpleasant feeling that word of her reputation, such as it was, had reached the prince's ears. Or perhaps he was merely referencing her part in the unpleasantness with Shah. Was this a warning for her to keep a level head? If anyone else had said it, she would have fought her corner tooth and nail, but from Prince Leopold? It was a battle she would not take on. And so she nodded, and said merely, 'Your Royal Highness is correct, of course. Sir Arthur and I are here as representatives of the Order, not as soldiers.' She picked up her cup as casually as she could, and took a delicate sip of tea before presenting her comeliest smile to the prince, just as her old nanny had taught her many years previous, before being driven to her wits' end by Lillian's tomboyish ways. The prince returned her smile and nodded approvingly.

'What I can't stand,' said Collins, changing the subject, 'is all this skulking about in the dark. By the time we reach Hull, evening will be upon us. Is it true then, what they say about the bastards being vulnerable to sunlight?'

'Please, Sir Robert,' said the prince, 'remember that there is a lady present.'

'Of course, sir, I was… forgetting. Sir Arthur, you will know more of this I'm sure—can sunlight kill the creatures?'

'I am afraid we don't know for certain,' Arthur said. 'Lord Cherleten is the foremost expert on the Knights Iscariot, and his knowledge is limited to hearsay and snatches of old texts. The arrival of Tesla has increased our knowledge dramatically, but there are still unknowns. To answer directly, we believe that sunlight merely hurts their eyes—perhaps even blinds them—just as it would a nocturnal creature. Beyond that we do not know.'

'It seems Apollo Lycea knows very little about the greatest threat that ever has been to our national security,' Collins said.

'Forgive me, Sir Robert, but we do have some knowledge of the vampires' vulnerabilities,' Lillian intervened, 'as Colonel Ewart can attest.'

'Ah, yes—fire and electricity, isn't that so, Colonel?'

'It is, sir, yes,' replied the colonel, looking awkward in such estimable company. Lillian had spent much of the previous day in the company of Ewart, his men, Cherleten and Tesla, going over the known methods of killing the pale creatures that accompanied the Knights Iscariot—creatures that the Highlanders had dubbed 'gaunts' upon seeing one of the corpses laid out on a dead-room slab. 'The surest way of killing them, though, is tae strike them in the heed, firm and sharp. Or stab them through the brain wi' a long blade, as the lady has done herself.' He nodded acknowledgement to Lillian. 'There's nae mistake then.'

Lillian had gained the impression yesterday that Ewart was embarrassed by his countrymen's stance on the Knights Iscariot. Half of his regiment was still north of the border, where it seemed they would remain even if civil war broke out across England. Ewart and his battalion, however, were stationed in London, where they were assigned to ceremonial duties as guards of the Tower and royal residences. Ewart was not an officer born—he had risen through the ranks, and Lillian was touched by his humble attitude and his great shame that his regiment would not heed the Queen's call to arms if required. Lillian had wondered what had become of the royalty who resided in Scotland; were they attempting to sway public opinion against the Knights Iscariot, or were they sheltering within their palace walls for fear of reprisal?

'We may ever depend upon the colonel for a colourful description,' said Collins.

'Let us hope such action is not called for today,' said the prince. 'Although,' he added with a wry smile, 'I am certain there is no man more suited for the task of "striking heads" than Colonel Ewart.'

'It all depends, one supposes, on whether all of the Knights Iscariot possess the hypnotic abilities that we witnessed at the Apollonian,' said Collins. 'I mean, are our defences sufficient to prevent them from toying with our minds?'

'Cherleten assures me so,' said the prince, 'and I trust his expertise, as should you.'

'Sir.' Collins nodded.

'Our man Tesla has worked wonders on the royal train,' offered Arthur. 'The etheric defences have had their efficacy increased tenfold. I have tested these defences myself—my own humble abilities have been dulled almost to mundanity. Within the confines of the train, we are protected from any psychic intrusion.'

'As long as we remain in motion,' the prince added.

'Indeed, sir. Tesla's modifications are powered by gyroscopic devices within the wheelset. When we stop to allow the Knights Iscariot to embark, we should all be on our guard, for that is when we will be most vulnerable to a Majestic attack.'

'Then how fortunate we are to have you aboard, Sir Arthur,' said the prince.

Lillian saw Arthur's hand brush his left-hand jacket pocket, where she knew he often carried his etherium, and that made her tense. The use of the sinister drug could increase a Majestic's powers tenfold, but the dangers—physical and otherwise—were myriad. Arthur had struggled with his dependence on etherium in the past, leaving him somewhat frail. Etherium provoked encounters with the Riftborn, and that could take a terrible toll on a Majestic's sanity. She knew that Arthur would be cursing his failure to overcome Valayar Shah's influence, and that might be enough to tempt him into injecting the fluid once again. She resolved to tackle him on the subject later, though those conversations had never previously gone well.

Lillian withdrew into herself, wanting no more part of the social sparring with Collins, allowing instead he and the prince to talk of matters between themselves. It appeared to her that the prince was not being entirely forthcoming, which was perhaps fitting, given Arthur's idea that the Knights Iscariot had friends in high places. Leopold was difficult to warm to, but her respect for the prince only grew as she listened to him. He seemed to trust Collins' advice, but had no truck with the man's acerbic and often impolitic jibes. Though he had as much as admitted that he might sign away part of the kingdom—if indeed he truly had the authority to do such a thing—Lillian read in his eyes resoluteness and pride. She felt certain that, if the Knights Iscariot overstepped the mark, Prince Leopold would be willing to go to war rather than appease them. She realised that the look she saw in his eyes was not dissimilar to the 'Hardwick look'. If that was not enough cause for concern, she mused, then nothing was.

The delegation had been given some time to prepare as the train rattled through Nottinghamshire. Arthur sank back into his seat, letting the needle fall from his arm, exhaling slowly as time seemed to slow around him. Every sound became muffled—the gentle, rhythmic clunk of the wheels faded away into a distorted bubbling, as though Arthur had submerged his head in deep water. Or, more accurately, as though he had climbed back into the womb, warm and safe, with nothing but the distant echoes of the world beyond his limited scope. The sensation lasted longer than usual. At least, he thought it did. Tesla's psychic defences held at bay the onrush of Riftborn visions that always fleetingly, horrifically, flooded his senses after each administration of raw etherium.

Snip-crack; snip-crack; snip-crack your bones...

He almost missed it. The pain, the voices, the moments of utter madness. It was penance—the price he had to pay for absorbing the hateful fluid that so many of his kind suffered to produce. The process should not be without discomfort, but this time it was. He wondered if this was what the dragon-chasers experienced when they injected opium. The warm embrace of oblivion.

Still, it passed all too quickly. There was no euphoria, no nausea, nothing; Arthur Furnival felt only a thrumming inner strength, somewhere deep in his mind. He was prepared for the worst the world could throw at him now. Perhaps, when the train stopped and Tesla's defences powered down, he would experience the terrors belatedly. Deep down, he hoped so.

Once he had recovered, he picked up his tiny syringe—another innovation of the Intuitionists—cleaned it, refilled it, and put it away carefully beside a row of tiny phials in its small leather case. He rolled down his sleeve, put on his jacket, and placed the case in his jacket pocket.

Arthur blinked hard, suddenly feeling cold and vulnerable as the gentle buzz of the etherium tuned out all around him, his senses returning as the numbing sensation of the drug left him. What remained was an acute awareness of his surroundings. He felt the air moving, as though his skin was conductive material in some Intuitionist laboratory, and energy flowed in and out of him as surely as his breath. He was aware of everything and everyone on the train, and all the space in between, and all the spaces between the spaces, in which invisible things lurked and slithered. He was safe, for now, but he could feel it all the same. He blinked again, dispelling the last of the iridescent shapes that floated and flashed before his eyes. The muffled sounds of the half-world he'd inhabited just moments earlier vanished with them, and the rhythmic sound of the rails returned sharply.

Snip-crack; snip-crack.

Though the light outside the carriage window still had its pinkish hue, the sun was almost certainly setting. His respite must have taken longer than the half-hour he'd allowed. Arthur checked his pocket-watch; it was nearly four o'clock. Outside, the landscape had changed once more—mills and refineries blotted the horizon. Quarries and warehouses slid past the carriage window, and numerous grey-stoned hovels huddled together in tiny villages, clinging to rugged hills against the inclement weather. He could see the cold sea beyond those hills, with dark rain rolling in off it ominously. They were almost at Hull, he was sure. Why hadn't Lillian come knocking at his door? Embarrassed, he wondered if she had, and if so whether she had guessed what he was doing. Still, it mattered not—ultimately he had to be prepared for anything, even though Tesla's inventions had reduced the risks.

When Arthur eventually found Lillian, she was in conversation with Colonel Ewart, along with three members of the household guard. They were laughing when he entered; she was guffawing as though she were one of the soldiers. The laughter dried up almost instantly.

'Sir Arthur,' Ewart greeted him.

'Colonel; Lillian.' Arthur only nodded at the other men. One of them, whose name escaped him, stood apart from the others. Arthur recalled that the man had come off rather badly against Lillian during the previous day's training—a turn of events that his comrades had likely not allowed him to live down.

'Sir Arthur,' Lillian said, with formality, 'I was just telling Colonel Ewart about the rigours of psychic defence. We arrive at Hull in a quarter of an hour—I trust you are prepared?'

Arthur doubted very much that psychic defence was what they'd been discussing, and the veiled chiding about his tardiness was not lost on him. Arthur half-wished his skill at telepathy was as pronounced as his psychometry, so he could ascertain what Lillian was really thinking.

'My preparations are complete,' he replied stiffly. 'All being well, Colonel Ewart and his men shall be free to concentrate on our guests without fear of any fell influences.'

'Aye. All being well,' Ewart repeated. 'If the situation turns ugly, mind, it'll be this wee lassie I'd rather have wi' us. No offence, Sir Arthur.'

'None taken. But might I remind you that Agent Hardwick is the daughter of Lord Hardwick, and as such is surely unaccustomed to being called a "wee lassie".' Arthur had no idea why he was making an issue of the colonel's manner—he certainly didn't think Lillian needed rescuing. If anything, she appeared to be getting along famously with the Highlanders. Rather, he'd had the strangest buzz of intuition, and as a result had taken a dislike to Ewart most abruptly, when earlier he had thought the Scot earthy and dependable.

Ewart held Arthur's gaze for a moment, the smile playing on his lips suggesting he was somewhat amused at being challenged by such a slight fellow. Finally he turned and bowed to Lillian, and then to Arthur. 'You are right, of course, sir. My lady, my humblest apologies for any offence. I am but a simple soldier, after all.'

'No offence taken, Colonel,' Lillian said.

'Well, if ye don't mind, we'll take our leave. We must arm ourselves before we reach Hull.' Ewart stepped towards Arthur, his men following him. He paused. 'Be ready, Sir Arthur. I hear these beasties are full o' surprises, even for one such as you.' With that, and looking oddly pleased with himself, Ewart strode from the carriage, his men following.

'Really, Arthur, you are such a stickler for etiquette. Was it really worth the quarrel?' Lillian asked.

'No... I mean, yes. There's something not right, but I can't place it. Damn Tesla's wizardry: it has left me blind to my own intuition.' Arthur was behaving irrationally, and he knew it. The etherium was coursing through his veins, heightening his sixth sense, and fighting almost painfully with the 'Tesla field' around the train. He had to get a grip—there were only minutes left before he would be the last line of psychic defence on board. He had dallied too long already.

'Colonel Ewart is not your enemy, Arthur,' she said gently. 'There are malign influences at work, certainly, but they are without, not within.'

'Are they?' He said it without thinking. She looked unsure of her convictions, and Arthur gleaned a sudden sense that Lillian was not wholly free of the vampires' grip; that thought chilled him to the bone. Lillian's featured hardened.

'The train is slowing,' she said. 'They're here.'

The doors were opened onto a grey platform, preceding a blast of icy wind that caused Lillian to realise just how artificial the environment was aboard the train. The draught carried with it the smell of saltwater and smoke.

The prince stood before the door, in dress uniform, with Sir Robert and Colonel Ewart beside him. Behind them stood the prince's private secretary, and behind him Leopold's valet and two of the household guard. Two other soldiers flanked the carriage door.

Lillian, standing further along the corridor with Sir Arthur, leaned over to get a better look at the platform through the thick glass windows. The steam was clearing, and from its swaddling embrace loomed a huddle of black-clad figures. She knew Shah at once, even as an indistinct shape amidst the silver-white plumes, his towering yet skeletal form unmistakeable. She caught movement from the corner of her eye, and looked left along the platform to see three of the bald vampire bodyguards in their long black coats, sniffing the air alongside the train, squinting into the windows with sparkling eyes. When one drew level with her window, it stopped and stared directly at her, cocking its head to one side in contemplation. They resembled the squat ghouls in many respects, though these creatures were straight-backed, and a keen, malign intelligence lurked behind their eyes. Lillian stared back, willing the creature to understand her intent: she would kill it given half a chance.

She heard voices, the exchange of formalities. The entourage of the Knights Iscariot were announced, though Lillian could not make out the names. A rolled document was passed to Colonel Ewart, who presented it in turn to the prince. And then a man stepped into the carriage, bowed his head, and shook the prince's hand. He turned to look along the carriage aisle, to where Lillian and Sir Arthur stood, and she knew him at once.

Lucien de Montfort.

He was tall, though not strong of stature. His face was smooth and angular, white as driven snow, with a thin black beard. He wore a topper, a fine brocade suit of dark green and a black coachman's cape. His eyes met hers for only a second, peering over tiny spectacles. For the briefest moment, trepidation washed over her, as though he had issued a threat aloud. She looked to her right and saw that Arthur had taken a step backwards; his head was lowered, but his eyes were fixed upon the foppish de Montfort. The blue veins at Arthur's temples stood out; he was concentrating hard, to the exclusion of all else.

De Montfort was shown into the next carriage, away from the agents of Apollo Lycea. Next came Shah and his lolling companion, then a burly human servant, with eyes even more vacant than the vampire woman. Finally, a single bald man stalked aboard, head jerking all about, a faint growl emitting from his throat. Apparently satisfied, the thing followed its master into the next carriage, and the soldiers closed the doors. No more of de Montfort's party were admitted. As the prince and his own delegation followed their inhuman guests, a whistle sounded outside, and the train's wheels squealed as it jolted forward.

Lillian looked at Arthur, who breathed a sigh of relief, the colour returning to his cheeks.

'Are you all right, Arthur?' she asked.

He nodded, somewhat gingerly. 'Come,' he said, 'let us take our stations. The journey ahead is long, in more ways than one.'

'Father, tell me what to do,' John demanded. He tried to stop himself from pacing back and forth across the drawing room, but was otherwise unable to mask his agitation. His mother sat in her usual chair, eyes red, pretending to concentrate on the cross-stitch that she had been fiddling with unconvincingly for the last half an hour.

'There is nothing you can do, my boy,' Marcus Hardwick replied. He stood with his back to the room, staring at the mantelpiece absently as the dying fire warmed his legs. 'I have important work to see to that will leave me indisposed for some time. I cannot have you along. You are an agent of Apollo Lycea, and you have your orders.'

'That's just it, Father—my orders are to do nothing,' John retorted. 'Lillian is away in the north, in the lion's den, and I am here, with no mission, and no way of knowing if—' He stopped short, knowing that his mother was listening; knowing that her distress at her daughter's absence consumed her. He was surprised that his father had not conducted this discussion in his office rather than here, where Dora could hear.

Lord Hardwick took up the poker, and prodded life back into the coals.

'When I spoke to Sir Toby, just an hour ago, we agreed that you should take some leave, John.'

'Take some leave...' John was exasperated. 'And do what?'

'Whatever you see fit,' said his father. Lord Hardwick turned now, to face his son, locking eyes with him. 'Sir Toby informs me that Agent Smythe has returned from Cheshire. Smythe shares your concern for your sister. Perhaps the two of you should... take that leave together. Neither of you are required for a few days. It would be well if you should make yourselves scarce for a while. If you take my meaning.'

John could hardly hide his surprise—this was most out of character for his father. He wondered now if his mother had talked some sense into the old man. It would certainly explain her presence.

'I understand completely,' he said, studying his father's face for any further hidden instructions, but finding none. 'You may not hear from either of us for a short time.'

'It will do you good to get away,' Lord Hardwick said. 'Find your own path.'

'I will leave immediately,' John replied. He was aware of his mother standing, and walking to him. She took his hands in hers, and he bent to receive her kiss.

'God speed,' she whispered.

John stepped away, nodded a farewell to his parents. Shah had told him to stay away from the north, on pain of death. In that case, he reasoned, he had better call at the armoury first.

'You see now the extent of our grip on lands that were traditionally subject to the Crown,' de Montfort said. 'The Knights Iscariot are no longer a tiny sect, but rather a large, diverse line of politicians, businessmen, nobles and, dare I say it, warriors. We have made our home here, and our numbers are set to grow beyond imagining. And yet there has been none of the chaos and bloodshed that your advisers may have warned against. Through commerce and good governance we have brought peace and prosperity to the north.'

'Peace at what cost?' asked Leopold, wearily. They were going around in circles. 'What of the liberty of the people? What of their choice in the matter of their governance?'

'Of course, Your Royal Highness, if you feel so strongly about the future of your subjects, they will be given the choice to leave the north,' de Montfort said.

They had already spoken at length. The prince had stated his case most passionately, becoming more animated than Lillian believed possible of a member of the royal family. De Montfort remained, throughout, measured and immovable. At every turn he brought the discussion back to the minutiae of his precious contract, refusing point-blank to be drawn on matters of morality and philosophy, willing to negotiate only over specific terms. The greatest source of disagreement was, naturally, the loyal subjects of the Crown who resided in the northern counties.

'You make the north sound like little more than a townstead, whose people, only mildly inconvenienced, can relocate to the capital at the drop of a hat. The reality, Lord de Montfort, as I am sure you are aware, is that hundreds of thousands of poor people will be dispossessed. They will be forced from their homes—homes which are the only ones many of them have known for generations—and they shall become migrants in their own land, refugees.'

'My dear prince, you speak of refugees as though we were at war, but there is no war. There is no threat. These people will be allowed to live as they have always done, albeit with some... adjustments.'

'By adjustments,' growled Sir Robert Collins, 'you do of course mean that they shall be hunted across the moors like game before the hounds.'

'Sir Robert, you insult our way of life—our very existence— with such a crass assertion,' de Montfort said. 'There will be nothing so vulgar as a hunt. As Sir Valayar stated when last you met, we will take our nourishment from willing volunteers, and servants of our order. The people who wish to remain in their homes shall do so unmolested, and under far greater protection than they would enjoy in London, whose rate of crime eclipses all the cities under our control combined.'

'Under your control?' Collins spluttered. 'They are not under your control yet.'

'Are they not? Who do you believe polices the north? Who controls trade? Who keeps the lands free of the taint of Riftborn?'

'And who kills innocents in the north by unleashing an army

of monsters upon the land?' Collins retorted.

De Montfort glowered at Sir Robert, before turning once more to the prince. 'Sir, we have been over these details several times now; our time grows ever shorter. Are you any closer to reaching your decision?'

De Montfort was right—time was now of the essence. York was some way behind them, and they had branched onto the line to Darlington, cutting across the North York Moors, which even now stretched out as a great purple expanse beyond the train's windows. Once past the great industrial works of the north-east, the royal train would reach its top speed, and would run unimpeded to Edinburgh, by which time de Montfort's negotiations would be over.

'I grow nearer with each passing second, Lord de Montfort,' said Prince Leopold, 'though I fear you will not be pleased with my response to some, if not all, of your conditions.'

'Your Royal Highness,' said de Montfort, coolly, 'I would urge you not to make any rash decisions. You know full well the repercussions of denying us.'

'Do not dare to lecture the prince!' snapped Collins.

'Save your bluster,' de Montfort said. 'I answer to a higher authority, and we are just as unwilling to be browbeaten.'

'And who is this authority you so often mention?' asked Collins. 'What is this ancient line of royalty whose members have seen fit to place you at the head of their affairs?'

'The King makes himself known to no one. He is the Nameless King, who has ruled the *wampyr* nobly for as long as any can remember. He will treat with you himself, when the time comes. For now, know that I speak for him, as the prince speaks for your queen.'

'Yes, yes,' said Collins, with growing impatience, 'but who—'

The squeal of brakes and the scream of the train whistle cut Collins short. Lillian struggled to keep her feet in her heeled boots as the train lurched sharply; it did not stop, but slowed considerably.

'What the devil...' said Collins.

The household guard rushed to the prince's side at once, although none of the Knights Iscariot moved a muscle. A smile rippled across de Montfort's lips. Seconds later, everyone noticed that the prince was staring out of the window, and all eyes followed his.

Outside, against the pale glow that bathed the moors in a pinkish twilight, ghastly silhouettes began to appear. A forest of tall, sharpened stakes, some straight and proud, others at awkward angles. As the train ploughed on, the number of them increased, as did their proximity to the tracks, until their grim purpose was revealed. Lillian's anger grew along with her revulsion, as she saw the stakes topped with heads, torsos, even entire cadavers. Men, women and children. Some were masked by clouds of buzzing flies, the corpses rotten. Others had slid down the stakes, leaving trails of fresh blood behind them on the rough wooden shafts. Others still were all too recent, the butchered bodies still twitching, mouths releasing agonised groans that could not be heard by the passengers aboard the opulent royal train, but which were sickeningly apparent.

'I imagine this must shock you.' De Montfort did not have to raise his voice to be heard in the deathly quiet carriage. 'Whether you agree to the cessation of the north or not, know that we have already assumed control. What you see before you are the consequences of treason.'

The prince tore his eyes from the scene. 'If that is so,' he said, in a thin voice, 'you shall not leave this train alive.'

At those words, the household guard reached for their weapons; the bald-headed servants of the Knights Iscariot did likewise, crouching, ready to strike. Lillian had her Webley in her hand, and was already marching along the carriage aisle, sights fixed firmly on Lord de Montfort, when the train lurched once more and she almost lost her footing.

The door at the forward end of the carriage opened, and a frantic-looking man in rough clothes barged in, red-faced and breathless.

'There's a train on the line ahead!' he shouted. 'We must stop. There's a... oh...'

He stopped as he saw the scene unfolding before him. The prince behind guards with weapons ready, inhuman creatures hissing with bestial rage. He turned and ran the way he had come.

Lillian reacted first, single-minded. She recovered her footing quickly and squeezed the trigger, aiming at de Montfort's forehead. The bullet hit a black shape, as one of the bald creatures dashed in front of its master, lightning fast.

The train lurched again, and the squeal of brakes pierced the air. The lights went out. The carriage was plunged into darkness, only the dim glow from the fiery horizon casting any illumination. The gentle, rhythmic thrum of Tesla's etheric field began to slow and stutter like the heartbeat of a dying man.

Something big barrelled into Lillian, knocking her to the ground and landing atop her, heavy and smothering. She heard shouts all around, the reports of revolvers, and saw muzzle-flashes from the corner of her eye. But the thing upon her was hissing and chittering, and she smelled grave-rot. A cold, bony hand was upon each of her wrists; she struggled, twisting, trying to get free. More shouts—someone called to the prince. She heard Ewart roaring. Good. The big Scot was a formidable soldier by reputation.

She pushed her knee into the chest of her assailant. She felt its teeth snapping towards her face like a hungry wolf. She could see little more than the outline of a bald head in the wan light from outside, but the gnashing teeth sounded far too powerful, too large, for the human-like creature she had seen board the train. Again it snapped, this time its teeth brushing her nose as they closed, and again Lillian pushed hard with her legs to keep the beast at bay.

Another muzzle flash lit the creature; a white ghost-like head smashed like an eggshell. Lillian's ears popped at the proximity of the gunshot, a piercing whistle replacing all other sound. Her world became dark once more, and she was dimly aware of the weight leaving her, of a dead weight rolling off her onto the floor, and of someone yanking her to her feet.

'Lillian. Lillian!'

She snapped to attentiveness, her hearing returning in a rush like bathing water leaving her ears, and she knew that Arthur had her, was pulling her away from the sounds of violent struggle. The train had slowed to a crawl. She heard the wet sound of a blade hacking at flesh from somewhere in the gloom.

'No!' she protested. 'The prince!'

'Lillian, you don't understand. We are betrayed…'

Arthur's warning had barely registered when, with a faint murmur, the generators started once more and the lights flickered back to life.

The bald creature that had attacked Lillian was lying in the aisle, a white ooze pooling from a gaping wound in its head. Its jaw was massive, distended—dislocated perhaps—and sparsely filled with large, half-rotten, jagged teeth. A few feet from it, lying dead or dying, were four soldiers. The other bald creature was busily tearing into one of them with a wicked, oriental-looking blade. The creature was soaked in blood from head to toe. Lillian would have engaged it, were there not more pressing concerns.

De Montfort stood as overseer to the carnage, unsullied by what had transpired. Shah, his rictus grin turned to the two agents of Apollo Lycea, stood by his side. The female courtier, usually so stupefied, bent low over the prince's valet. She had clamped a rubber tube, some three feet in length, onto his jugular with a set of shiny metal pincers and fastened it to her mouth by similar intrusive means. Lillian could barely comprehend the grotesqueness of it, this artificial process that visibly transformed the valet from man to husk.

Worse still was the position of the prince. He appeared unharmed, but was held in the restraining grip of Colonel Ewart, whose burly arms at once held Leopold fast, and prodded a sharp knife to the fleshy pouch beneath his left eye.

'Lillian,' Arthur whispered in her ear, 'we must flee.'

Lillian was dumbfounded. She stared first at de Montfort, whose sly smile was somehow more sinister than the one that was surgically etched onto Shah's face, and then at Ewart.

'Don't look at me like that, lassie,' he said. 'I'm done takin' orders from the likes o' you, and this pompous ass. These fine gentlemen offer Scotland a chance o' freedom, and I'm takin' it.'

'Your countrymen don't look so proud right now,' Lillian said, forcing as much bravado into her tone as possible.

Ewart winced. 'Traitors to the cause, lass. True to the queen till the bitter end.'

'Where are the others?'

'Locked up in the barracks car, safe and sound. Unlike these poor wee saps, the other lads'll get a choice.'

'Join or die?' Arthur offered.

'Aye. Did ye read my mind, Sir Arthur?'

'Enough of this,' said de Montfort. 'Drop your weapons and come quietly. There is no need for further killing. Cooperate, and you shall not be harmed. Resist, and the prince loses an eye, and you lose your lives.'

Don't make me do this, Lillian. The voice in her head said. Had it ever really gone away since the night she'd escaped with Tesla? In any case, it was louder now, and at the forefront of her thoughts. *All you need do is let me in.*

The train was still moving, but slowly, and Lillian knew the Tesla field was much diminished in power. She became aware that Arthur was breathing heavily, in great concentration. Was he battling de Montfort on her behalf? Or was it something else?

'I said drop your weapons,' de Montfort repeated.

'Do it, Lillian,' Arthur whispered from behind her. She knew by his tone that he was up to something.

Lillian un-cocked the Webley and dropped it.

De Montfort was holding out a hand now. 'Come to me, Agent Hardwick,' he said. 'It is over.'

Lillian hesitated. She could see no way out. She could perhaps escape the carriage, though the vampires were fast. She could fight—she still had weapons concealed about her person—but she could not risk the prince's life. Even if her actions led to him being maimed, regardless of whether or not he survived, the consequences for her would be dire. And de Montfort was persuasive. Far too persuasive...

'Lillian, run!' Arthur made the decision for them both. Upon his shout, everything seemed to happen at once. Ewart pushed the prince to the ground and went for a pistol. De Montfort leapt towards the rear of the carriage, leaving Shah and the female vampire to look aghast at the two agents—if, indeed, they were capable of the expression. For a split second Lillian didn't understand what they had all seen, then it became apparent. From the corner of her eye she saw Arthur raise the pistol—a strange contraption of brass and steel, with two coils atop it buzzing with electrical power. A Tesla pistol.

Even as Ewart jerked his revolver from his belt, Arthur's finger squeezed the trigger. The lights in the carriage flickered and died once more. There was a click, a fizz, and a coruscating arc of blue-white energy leapt from the Tesla pistol, striking the space where de Montfort had stood a heartbeat earlier, and illuminating the ghastly grin of Valayar Shah, which did not fade even as lightning danced about his scarecrow body, and even as he fell, screaming, into a charred heap.

Shouts, curses, hisses and roars followed. The wail of Shah's companion was audible over all of them, high-pitched and keening. A pistol fired. Lillian felt a tug at her arm, and needed no further encouragement. She turned and followed Arthur, fumbling along the aisle. Another shot rang out; she felt the whip of air as the bullet kissed her face, sparking as it ricocheted off the far wall. She heard shouting—de Montfort—but could not make out words. She knew there was someone, or something, close behind her, and from the shrill screaming sound she knew at once that the female creature was giving chase.

She heard the clunk of a heavy compartment door-handle ahead, saw a shaft of pale light and felt the rush of cold air as it opened. She bundled through the door even as another shot rang out, deafening, and squeezed past Arthur as he slammed the door shut and turned the handle. The vampire thudded against the door, muffled screams and scrabbling talons falling upon the steel in impotent rage.

'Keep going!' Arthur said. His voice was laboured. Lillian knew the psychic exertion could take it out of him, and prayed for once that the etherium would be enough to keep him going.

They moved on into the next carriage, laid out like a palace drawing room, with card tables, bookcases and even an upright piano. The lights flickered on again, and the sound of metal clanging against metal rang out behind them as their enemies wrestled with the door. The carriage was devoid of inhabitants, and so they sped onwards as the train swayed like a steamship. They had to move to the rear of the train, towards the barracks car, where Lillian hoped they would find some assistance from those Highlanders still loyal to the Crown. The human Crown.

Arthur flung open the door to the dining car, with tables arranged along the sides, and a narrow aisle between them. Arthur pulled up and moved to the side, and Lillian saw that, up ahead, in the flickering electric light, a bald vampire had entered the carriage. It was hunkered low, sniffing the air, a quiet, guttural growl issuing from its throat. It saw the agents at once; its violet eyes flashed, and it bounded towards them, wolf-like and low to the ground.

How did it get ahead of us?

Arthur cranked the charging handle of the Tesla pistol furiously, but the creature was far too fast, bearing down upon them with astonishing alacrity. Lillian leapt forward, blades in her hands, and used the creature's own momentum to lend force to her strike, slashing the vampire across the chest before twisting out of its path. It bundled to the ground and let out such a hate-filled scream that Lillian's blood froze.

It leapt at her again, with such strength in its limbs that Lillian was barged aside, only by some miracle keeping to her feet. It slashed with a taloned hand, yanking out a handful of her hair as she ducked the blow and stabbed forwards with her blade, taking the creature in its side. It was about to slash down at her with its other hand, which she had no time to dodge, when Arthur jumped at it, dragging it back by the trailing arm.

The creature hissed, turned, and raked Arthur's chest with its claws. He grunted with pain, and stumbled back, trying desperately to fend it off as it snapped for his throat with vicious teeth.

Lillian recovered quickly, taking up both blades and punching them into the monster's back, ducking again beneath its flailing arms as it swung back at her, and finally delivering the *coup de grâce*—an uppercut with an eight-inch spike. The tip of the blade entered beneath the monster's chin, and pierced its skull. It staggered and flailed, before falling to the floor.

This time, Lillian helped Arthur up.

'We have to move,' she said. 'If we can make it to the barracks—'

Arthur's eyes widened. 'By God... they're all over us.'

She followed his gaze, and saw dark shapes scurrying outside the windows, scrabbling along the train's armoured exterior like great spiders. She sucked in a breath—there were too many. But where had they come from?

Stop running. Come to me.

The voice pierced her mind, and Arthur looked at her as though he had heard it too. A loud metallic clunk sounded behind them, and the door opened. Ewart was first through the door, struggling to hold back the harridan whose sole purpose now seemed to be vengeance for Valayar Shah.

Lillian pushed Arthur onwards, and, leaving one blade for lost in the head of the vampire, she took up her concealed revolver from her bustle as she hurried after him. She had a sense that there were more pursuers now, but she could not stop to take stock. Instead she pointed the gun behind her and fired indiscriminately, willing Arthur to move faster.

As he slammed the next door behind them and locked it, he pushed his back to it, panting for breath and clutching a hand to his chest. Blood oozed between his fingers.

'Arthur…'

'No time,' he said. 'We must keep moving.'

'If you're scratched, they'll find us no matter what.'

He shook his head. 'It's not the scratch I'm worried about.' He took his hand away from the wound. Blood flowed from a small hole four inches beneath his right arm.

'You're shot.'

He nodded. 'Ewart,' he said.

On cue, a pounding came at the door behind them.

'Give it up; there's naewhere for you tae go!' Ewart bawled, barely audible through the thick door. As he shouted, the train lurched, metal panels creaking, and it began to pick up speed, slowly but surely.

'He's right,' said Sir Arthur. 'They're crawling all over the train, and even if we reach the barracks car there's no saying the soldiers won't join Ewart.'

'Arthur, will your injuries permit you further struggle?'

'Why? What is your plan?'

'I plan to get off this train, immediately.'

They ran from the door, along what they realised now was the kitchen car, where servants huddled behind cooking apparatus in fear and confusion, crying out in alarm when they realised two armed agents were amongst them. They cried out louder when they saw black-clad creatures scrambling over the outside of the moving train, peering inside with inhuman eyes, claws scraping thick windows. Lillian knew they would find no aid here; these poor servants were soon to be victims. She wished she could save them, but knew they would only slow her down.

So will Arthur.

Was that her own thought, or de Montfort's? It was getting harder to tell.

As she reached the end of the kitchen car, Lillian paused. Through the glass panels set in the iron doors, she could see that the way was clear. Outside, the train was indeed moving faster, though still not up to full speed. If they were to jump clear, it would have to be now.

She pulled down the window of the external door, and poked her head out, half expecting to face a nightmarish creature riding on the outside of the carriage. There was none. Instead, she saw the train moving around a shallow bend. There was another engine in front of theirs; a red-painted, unliveried locomotive, which had been the cause of their sudden slowing. Now it led the way, picking up speed; an escort to an unknown destination. There was nothing but moors stretching out beside them. A few hundred yards ahead, on the inner curve of the track, the hard ballast began to give way to scrub, until it dropped into a heather-covered decline, leading to a stretch of boggy ground. It would be their best chance.

She pulled her head back inside. Arthur had just finished charging the Tesla pistol for another shot.

'There's a soft landing up ahead,' she said. 'We have to go now. But that gun could be dangerous—electricity and water don't mix.'

There came a heavy thud above them, as of a clumsy footfall on the train's roof.

'Then I had better use this shot before we jump,' Arthur replied. 'You go first; I shall cover your escape.'

Lillian nodded and, her own pistol at the ready, swung open the outer door. She peered over the treadplate, at the dark ground that sped past faster than it had previously appeared to, and wondered if this were really such a good idea. As if to lend her urgency, she heard a loud bang behind her, which almost startled her into falling over the edge.

'Lillian,' Arthur shouted, 'they're almost through. Go now!'

With a deep breath, and hardly daring to keep her eyes open, Lillian stepped into thin air. But she did not fall.

A strong hand held her by the back of her jacket, and hoisted her upwards as her legs kicked at nothingness. She landed hard on the roof of the train, her arms and knees scraping metal, and then slipping, sickeningly, across the smooth, gently sloping roof. She did not know what scared her more: the three pairs of black-clad legs standing around her, or the fact that there was nothing to grab, nothing to grant her purchase as she started to drift sideways off the roof.

A hand grabbed her by the hair and yanked her head back. It was enough. Lillian leapt upwards against her assailant, trusting that he was trying to take her alive and thus had a firm grip upon her. She still had the revolver, which she had managed to hold on to, and at once unloaded five chambers into the other two creatures. One moved with alarming speed, only taking a flesh wound to the arm. The other flew backwards as it took a bullet to the chest, and another to the side of its face, shattering its ugly, jutting cheekbone. The vampire that gripped her now pulled her up to her feet, attempting to wrestle the gun from her grasp. With one last effort, Lillian twisted and turned, jabbing the heel of her boot into the creature's foot, throwing both off them off the train in a deathly embrace.

Arthur's stomach lurched as he saw Lillian fall through the air, wrapped in the arms of a black-coated attacker. They twirled in the air like wounded crows shot from the sky by a farmer's gun.

The pain in his side was overwhelming; he'd lost a lot of blood. The handle of the door behind him squealed as de Montfort's minions forced it open. The barrage of psychic attack that Arthur had fought against had lulled as the train began to move faster, but the physical threat was all too real.

Arthur looked down. Lillian and the monster were almost out of sight, a tumbling mass of black cloth rolling into the thick heather. If he didn't jump now, he wouldn't make it at all. But he wanted a parting shot.

The door behind Arthur burst open, and the she-creature barged through, almost falling over in her haste to spring at him. It was all the encouragement he needed. Before de Montfort or the others could reach him, Arthur pushed himself backwards from the train step as hard as he could, pulling the trigger of the Tesla pistol as he went.

There was the smell of burning air and copper, and a blinding light that arced in his descent into thin air. He was sure he had hit his mark—the freezing wind was filled with high-pitched screams. Time seemed to slow. Motes of ghost-light drifted about him like dust, clinging to him as his proximity to the realm of the dead drew nearer.

Arthur smiled. How strange a thing, he thought, to be flying. To be buffeted on the cold winter air, not knowing whether life or death awaited him upon landing. *Morte d'Arthur*, he thought.

My wound hath taken cold; and I shall die.

TWELVE

'Lillian! Lily!'

She remembered her father shouting her name over the roar of the storm, over the biting wind and hammering rain. She remembered clear as day the taste of river-water filling her lungs, and the knowledge, even at that tender young age, that she would probably die. She had wondered what death would feel like. She was already so cold that she was numb, and so scared that she could not be any more afraid. She thought she was thrashing in the water, trying to swim to shore, but she could not feel her arms and legs, so she could not be certain.

She did not really know why she had wandered off. She had always believed that, beyond the garden gate, there was a secret land of fairies and gingerbread cottages. Her brother had teased her, and said that if there was anything out in the woods, it was evil goblins and prowling wolves. When the storm came, John had remarked that the fairy castles would be swallowed up and the wolves would devour all within. And so Lillian had stolen away in the night, with her father's iron key, unlocking the garden gate and running across the field to the forest. She had perhaps hoped to prove her brother wrong; or to save the fairy-folk. Or perhaps she just wanted to show that she was not scared of goblins or wolves or storms or anything else.

When her father had scooped her up in his arms and held her close to his chest, she had thought he was a giant. He had never seemed so big or enfolding. Her father cried, 'Lily! Oh, my girl!' He had thought her dead, and she was too weak to tell him otherwise.

She remembered being bundled into her father's overcoat, and carried through the woods and across the field, staring up at the clouds as she went, the rain falling on her face. They returned to the cottage that they called home, on the edge of a large tract of farmland near Faversham in Kent, where the smell of smoke rising from oast-houses always hung in the air.

On this night, there was no warm welcome, only the cries of Lillian's mother, and a house that felt as though it were mourning a little girl on the edge of death.

Lillian remembered dreaming of a great dragon that set the house alight and carried her off far away, and dropped her into a fathomless ocean. Between fits and nightmares, she woke to see faces, some familiar, some strange, peering at her. Her mother, with eyes reddened and sore; John, asleep at her side; Dr. Harthouse, who always smelled of cigars; the nanny; some strangers. She heard talk of 'pneumonia', and how something was very 'grave', and remembered Dr. Harthouse telling her mother that she ought to 'prepare for the worst'. She did not remember where her father was during that time.

When Lillian finally woke, and asked for a drink of water, her mother had cried and kissed and hugged her until she thought it might never end. The doctor had been called. Nanny went away to fetch water and food. Lillian's mother went to find her father. Only John had been left behind in the little bedroom. Her brother had looked much older than his twelve years; wise almost. Something had changed in him. He had squeezed her hand and leaned close. 'You should have asked me to come with you, Lily. I would have come. You could have died.'

'I wasn't afraid,' she had said, defiant even then.

'I know,' John had replied, gravely. 'But the day will come

when you cannot stand alone. And on that day, I shall stand with you.'

Lillian dragged herself from the boggy water, detaching her skirts as she went so that she could better climb free of the embankment in her breeches. Her heart pounded so hard she thought it might burst from her chest; she coughed and spluttered stagnant, freezing water from her lungs. She was hurt; her legs and stomach gouged and slashed, ribs aching as though she'd been kicked by a horse. The taste of her own blood rose in her mouth, salty and warm. She spat out a tooth.

Another lecture from Mama. I shall no doubt deserve it this time.

She reached the crest of the bank. The trains had not stopped, and now they were a distant collection of dancing carriage-lights, their twin plumes of steam barely visible against the glowing night sky. Lillian glanced back to the pool of water from which she'd barely emerged with her life. She could just make out the creature's bald head, luminescent in the darkness, bobbing upon the black water, the corpse floating face down. She had saved one bullet in the chamber, and was glad of it, but it had still been a desperate fight. She made a mental note that the Knights Iscariot did not need to breathe underwater, if at all. Unfortunately, she did, otherwise she would have gone looking for the pistol that she had dropped in the deep, murky pool.

Another thought, more pressing, hit her at once. Lillian had no idea if Arthur had made the jump. She had been dimly aware of a flash of light as she had rolled into the water in what she had thought was a deathly embrace. It had to have been Arthur, but what had befallen him afterwards was anyone's guess. The thought that he could have been captured, or killed, was the final straw. The pain from her wounds, the cold, the tiredness in her bones, the abject failure to protect the prince, and the possible—no, probable—loss of Sir Arthur Furnival, was too much. Lillian fell to her knees in the damp heather, and sobbed. How dare de Montfort take everything from her?

She breathed and tried to calm herself. She could not allow herself to be defeated. Granted, she was far from home, on the edge of an inhospitable moor, with no money or food, and only the clothes on her back, one concealed blade, and a tiny derringer. She squinted against the darkness, looking about and seeing nothing but scrub and field for miles. She could not recall how long ago she had noticed the last station they passed—it had been nothing more than a hut-like station building and a distant church spire. What was it? Commonford? Commondale? It was miles away, regardless.

Lillian knew she stood upon the fringe of the moors. She could follow the rail tracks west, which would give her surety of direction, but would in essence lead her towards her enemy. What if they came back for her?

With bitterness, she reflected that John would know what to do. He always had a plan. She'd often told him that requiring more than one plan was the same as expecting to fail. How she regretted that now.

She would, she decided, do as she always did, and take one step at a time. She was shivering now, and knew she had to find shelter rather than wander the moors in soaking wet clothes. But even before that, she had to search the area for any sign of Arthur.

'Get back, Smythe, for pity's sake,' John hissed.

John yanked Beauchamp Smythe into the shadows as a black-clad creature stalked past them. The surgeon squeezed himself flat against the rough brick wall of the station waiting room, and looked rather sheepish.

As soon as the coast was clear, John slipped from their hiding place, beckoning Smythe to follow, treading along the platform silent as a cat to the little ticket office. He froze momentarily, Smythe almost bumping into him, as the creature up ahead stopped to sniff the air, turning its head from one side to the other as if dimly aware of some hostile presence. When the bald-headed guard continued on its way, John quietly clicked open the door to the ticket office and crept inside.

The office was small, cramped, full of papers and copybooks, and unoccupied. The entire station was deserted, except for the Knights Iscariot, whose agents were seemingly everywhere. John pointed to another door near to the side of the office.

'Keep a watch,' he whispered. He ducked low behind the little ticketing window, and shuffled the papers on the desk, looking for the most recent documentation. There was nothing to suggest the passing of the royal train; John had not really expected as much. Even if the station had been running as usual, the arrival of Leopold's delegation would have been a state secret. John sucked at his teeth as he considered what to do next.

There came a soft thud from behind the side door.

'There's someone in there,' Smythe whispered.

John crept to the door, and signalled to Smythe that he would open it, and that Smythe should be ready to shoot whomever came out of it. Smythe readied a pistol dutifully.

John opened the door quickly, pressing himself against the wall, expecting Smythe to shoot. The surgeon did not, but almost instantly lowered the gun. John stepped from behind the door and looked inside a dark store cupboard, in which was sitting an old man with white whiskers, wearing a railway uniform that had seen better days. He was tied to his chair, and gagged with a kerchief.

'Well,' said John. 'This explains why things are so quiet around here.

The old man looked up at the two agents of the Crown pleadingly.

'All right, old boy,' said Smythe. 'Just keep quiet, and we'll get you out of here in a jiffy.'

* * *

'I don't care if they find me, sir, I'll not be going back there. Upon my oath!' The old stationmaster, Cottam, was stubborn as a mule, and rightfully angry at his predicament.

'There now, old fellow,' said John, 'no one is going to make you go back. But those men on the platform are going to be more than a little confused when they find you're no longer their prisoner.'

'I couldn't care less, sir, beggin' your pardon. And they ain't what I'd call "men", neither.'

'Quite,' said John. He slurped his tea.

They sat in Cottam's meagre flat, overlooking the murky waters of the River Hull. A sea-mark chimed softly in the distance. The stationmaster had explained to the two agents that he had been forced to turn a blind eye to the dealings of the Knights Iscariot for long enough. When he had refused to put the entirety of the station at their disposal, they had subdued him until their work was done.

'There's a fog dropping,' John said, gazing through the small window.

'Sea fret,' said Cottam. 'Rolls in along the 'Umber, fast as you like. Some days you can't see your hand in front o' your face when the fret's up.'

'Fortunate,' said John. 'We might need to move about the city discreetly.'

'You get bumblin' about out there in the fret,' said Cottam, 'and ye'll as like run in t' one of *them*. They'll kill you sure as God made little green apples.'

'You're lucky they didn't kill you,' said Smythe. 'I've seen them butcher men for less.' Smythe was keeping his tone steady, but John could tell he didn't trust the old timer.

'Pah!' spat Cottam. 'What's the use o' killin' an old man like me? Besides, they can't just go around killin' folk, can they, well, not folk who keep the trains runnin' and the ships sailin', and the docks loadin'. They threaten us, they control us. But when they go too far, they find that a man'll fight back, 'specially if they've took everything from him.'

211

John frowned for a second, and then followed the old man's gaze to the cluttered mantelpiece, where a faded watercolour of a woman took pride of place. It was the kind of daub that a street artist would do for a penny, but the man's reverence for the portrait was unmistakeable.

'Mrs. Cottam?' he asked.

The old man nodded. 'My Maud. Took 'er a year ago. Said at first they was 'oldin her at Scarrowfall, but as time went on I knew she were dead. No one 's goes to Scarrowfall ever comes back. Everybody knows that.'

'I'm very sorry for your loss, Mr. Cottam,' John said. He was struck by a sudden sadness as he thought of this old man, alone in the world thanks to the Knights Iscariot's cruelty, now clinging to a penny-portrait as if it were a masterpiece; the only thing he had to remember her by. It made him angry.

'Mr. Cottam, we need to follow the royal train, to ensure it reached its final destination. You are certain it left via the western route?'

'The Moorlands Line,' he said. 'Aye, I'm sure. And it were bang on time an' all. I heard it leave at a minute past the hour, an' there've been no other trains today.'

'Do you know when the next Moorlands Line train will leave?' John asked.

The old man shook his whiskered head. 'There's a train first thing in t' morning, but the station'll be crawlin' with them devils. Always is when the trains come in, even in the daytime. You'll not get by them.'

John wasn't so sure about that, but he certainly did not wish to create a commotion needlessly. For now, secrecy was their greatest ally.

'Then we need another way out of Hull,' John said.

'Do you know of any coachman who might be trusted?' Smythe added. 'Or perhaps an ostler who might have horses we can buy?'

'No one who'll risk his neck fer the likes o' you,' said

Cottam. 'Not without Pickering's say so.'

'Pickering?' John asked.

'Aye. He's the only man who's not been cowed by the Knights 'scariot. Anyone round 'ere who's true to England answers to Christopher Pickering.'

'Wait, I know of him,' said Smythe. 'He's the shipping magnate, is he not?'

'Aye. His fleet controls most o' the trade in Hull. He survives because the Knights can't afford to lose him. Mind you, if they only knew what he got up to behind their backs, I imagine they'd cut their losses.'

'And what does he get up to?' asked John.

Cottam allowed a satisfied grin to cross his wizened features. 'He *resists*, Lieutenant. 'Im and 'is fleet, and as many men 's he can summon. He resists.' He nodded knowingly.

'A fleet is hardly the thing we need right now,' Smythe said, almost to himself. 'But the man must have considerable resources, I suppose. Perhaps he could help us.'

'I'll be going to him as soon as I can, sirs,' said Cottam. 'Figure there's no one else will help me now, 'cept Mr. Pickering. I'd advise you to come with me—I doubt you'll be safe elsewhere.'

'I daresay you are correct,' said Smythe. 'And besides, it would be remiss of us to enter enemy-occupied territory and not show our support for the resistance, eh, Lieutenant Hardwick?'

'Indeed, Agent Smythe. Most remiss indeed.'

Arthur woke. He was not dead; at least, he did not think so. He certainly could not see anything, except perhaps crawling shadows on the edge of darkness. A sweet smell drifted to him, comforting almost, the night-scent of flowers, mingled with damp earth. He was cold.

When the voice of the Other came, it was almost a relief. If it pursued him still, then he was alive. But that it had found him meant that his relief would be fleeting.

You are ours now, little blood-sack.

Arthur blinked against the night, trying desperately to come to his senses. Shadows moved around him, the icy cold numbed him. His fingers closed around something wet and slimy; he at first recoiled, but then identified clumps of vegetation. He felt now the damp seeping through his clothes, felt needle-sharp pains all over his body, and the sticky warmth of the bullet wound, from which his strength seemed to flow into the cold ground.

Relinquish the spark of life and come to us, blood-sack. The Other cajoled him, the voice in Arthur's head sounding soothing, alluring.

He tried to shake it from his thoughts, but it was there still, scratching at the inside of his head. Arthur realised that his limbs would barely move, that he must be injured badly. He knew that if he lay there too long, so suffuse with etherium, the Other would claw its way after him greedily. He willed his body to move, willed his hands to grip the coarse bushes beside him and his arms to pull him upwards. His wound burned like fire, his own blood feeling impossibly hot in the freezing air. He crawled at first, wriggling and undignified, every inch of ground covered causing him more pain than he'd thought possible.

Where are you running to, little blood-sack? We hunger.

Arthur's vision swam. Slowly but surely he began to make out shapes and colours; a dark sky, a pale pink horizon, foliage washed with purple hues, picked out by the weak light from a cloud-covered half-moon. He pushed with his legs, his crawl becoming a clamber. His feet sank in deep puddles of mud, making every step laborious.

We will find you, and we will snip-crack your bones...

He could see the Other in his mind's eye now—a half-glimpsed mass of writhing terror, upon which his thoughts could not linger lest he be dragged to madness. Arthur steeled himself, his freezing fingers poking into his pockets, fumbling for his syringe case and the phials of etherium. It was still there, but he would not use it unless it was absolutely necessary.

Snip-crack; snip-crack; snip-crack...

Louder and louder, closer and closer, the Other stalked him. Arthur knew he had taken too much etherium. In the cradle of the Tesla field he had felt safe, knowing that his powers would need to be increased tenfold if he were to combat de Montfort. But now, out here, he felt more vulnerable than ever. He was a candle in the darkness, a feast of rotting flesh for the lord of flies.

That thought spurred him onwards—if he were to die, it would be on his own terms. He knew he could outrun them, at least for a while—the Other would try to break through the veil, to create a Rift within the fabric of the universe, but that would take time and energy that the Riftborn often failed to muster. By staying on the move, a Majestic could lead the Riftborn a merry dance until finally, he hoped, the demons lost the energy to break through. If he were to tire before them, however...

Where are you? Blood-sack, blood-sack... where are you?

There were other options. He fingered the syringe case, but knew that it was a desperate gambit, a last resort. Mundane etherium. Not etherium at all, but something perhaps more sinister, dressed up with a fanciful name to make its use more palatable to the general populace. No, the source of mundane etherium must remain a closely guarded secret, known only by the Nightwatch and their masters. Arthur pushed such thoughts from his mind—all thoughts, indeed, for only a clear head could hold the Other at bay. But he was in no state to bar the doors to his psyche. He could feel long, probing fingers picking away at the psychic defences he had so hastily formed. He had to keep moving.

Where are you?

The voice was louder now. A sharp pain jabbed at Arthur's skull, and he felt the trickle of blood from his nose. The after-effects of etherium were often violent. The attentions of the Other more so.

The ground became less even. Arthur scrambled up a steep bank, grabbing clumps of tough heather to pull himself upwards.

His vision began to return to normal, the dark moors coalescing into focus. The cold night air pricked at him relentlessly.

Where are you?

Arthur reached the top of the bank, and a stronger breeze pushed at him. Before him was a wide bed of heavy gravel, and a pair of rail tracks. His memory flooded back to him, piecemeal at first, then faster. He remembered the creatures aboard the royal train; the Tesla pistol—where was it now? He remembered falling from the train. He knew he was lucky to be alive.

Arthur straightened up as best he could, and the agony of his wound almost forced him to his knees. He could not bear to touch it, for he knew he might pass out, and there was no telling what would happen then. He locked his mind, visualising ironbound doors and barricades, fortified against the raging demons beyond. They hammered at his mental defences, and howled with hatred.

'Where are you?'

The voice was loud, and close. Head spinning, Arthur steeled himself for a confrontation with his old enemy. The cat-and-mouse game they had played since the Awakening was almost over.

'Arthur! Where are you?'

He saw the figure stumbling towards him, slender and black against the dark moors.

He saw Lillian Hardwick. Even as she reached him, he fell into her arms, weak and limp, and laughed until he wept.

'Arthur, we have to find somewhere to stop,' Lillian pleaded. 'You must rest.'

'No,' Arthur said, though speaking at all seemed too much of an effort for him. 'The Other... we have to keep moving.'

In truth, Lillian was starting to think about her own injuries. She was tired and weak, but Arthur was leaning on her more and more heavily. She could not complain—he was half-delirious, raving about the Other. Several times now, when he had grown more distressed, blood had flowed from his nose, and he had suffered terrible convulsions. They had been forced to stop each time, Lillian cradling him as though he were a babe in arms, soothing him with soft words until his agitation passed and he was able to resume their flight.

She had no cause to disbelieve Arthur about the pursuit of the Riftborn, but she also knew that he had lost a lot of blood, was weak and near insensible, and had taken a large dose of etherium already. Not only that, but she had far more pressing concerns. Arthur was in no physical state to travel, but he was also in no mental condition to offer any advice on their options. Of their partnership, Lillian had always relied heavily on Arthur for carefully considered strategy. Her plan had been a rushed one, for the Knights Iscariot had clearly not intended to leave the two agents to their fate on the moors. They were in pursuit.

A howl echoed through the night, rolling to a high-pitched crescendo that tailed into a staccato, avian shriek. It was getting closer.

Spurred on by the knowledge that they were being hunted, Lillian had opted to follow the rail tracks back east, towards the last village she remembered. She hoped there was more to it than merely the station and church she had seen—much of the nearby environs had been masked by woodland, she recalled. If they could only find a cottage, or an inn—somewhere to take shelter from the creatures at their heels.

The shriek came again, and this time it was answered by another, more distant. They were closing fast. Lillian wondered if these were the same creatures that had been crawling over the train, perhaps stowed away waiting for their master's command, or whether the Knights Iscariot had their ghoulish, bestial creatures prowling the moors for runaways. She guessed that de Montfort—or his mysterious 'Nameless King'—would be able to exert a measure of control over the beasts even at a distance.

Lillian dropped Arthur as gently as she could into a pile of heather beside a rocky outcrop, sheltered from the wind—and, she hoped, from the view of their pursuers. She took stock of her weaponry again, more out of habit than hope. The situation was dire. She had a single-shot derringer, with five rounds including the one in the chamber. Only one of her hairpin-blades had survived the battle, which presently did a poor job of controlling her dirty, tousled hair, and she had a small knife stashed in her left boot, weighted for throwing. Arthur had his standard-issue pocket knife, heftier than her own but short-bladed, and four etherium bullets for a pistol he had lost. He sat on the damp ground, muttering incoherently to himself. Or rather, Lillian realised with a shudder, chanting some strange litany against unseen terrors.

She had lost track of how long they had stumbled through the scrub. Behind her were many miles of moorland, punctuated by tall, craggy rock-piles. Ahead, the horizon terminated at an indistinct, black forest, some half a mile away at least.

Lillian heard a growl so close she could almost pinpoint it, and she scanned the darkness behind her. At first, the moors seemed just as they had seconds before. But she quickly looked back again as she realised the vertical stones that erupted from the landscape had increased in number. Thin black shapes, stock-still and full of menace, stood amongst the rocks. So unmoving were they that Lillian was almost ready to discount their appearance as a trick of the softly undulating flames that glowed as ever on the horizon to the south. But then she saw two tiny pinpricks of purple light flash briefly from one of the figures; violet eyes gleaming keenly and, surely, seeing her.

'Arthur, it's time to go,' she hissed.

Arthur murmured something akin to a protest, but allowed himself to be pulled to his feet and guided onward in a pitiful limp. He leaned less heavily on her now, which was a small mercy as she tried to overcome the intense chill in her bones that made her limbs feel like lead. She glanced over her shoulder. The figures had multiplied—where there had been two, there were now four, and they were closer. They remained still as statues, their flickering eyes the only signs that the creatures were alive at all.

What are they waiting for? Lillian did not wish to find out. Instead she picked up the pace as best she could, half-dragging Arthur with her. The pain in her side flared up; she was certain she'd broken a rib or two, but she could not stop. Her mission had surely changed—her sole objective now was to get Arthur to safety, and find a way home. Arthur was starting to gibber incoherently, the volume of his mutterings increasing. Even though the enemy was upon them, and surely aware of their location, Arthur's ravings made Lillian feel exposed, and she tried her best to hush him, to no avail.

They covered another fifty yards, torturously, and Lillian heard a snarling sound all too near. She turned again. There were five of them now, and they had moved once more, fanning out into a horseshoe formation, herding their prey ever eastwards. Whenever Lillian looked at them, even if she tried to spin quickly and catch the monsters unawares, they were stationary once more; yet each time they had taken up a new position. These were the bald-headed creatures with some semblance of intelligence, the snuffling, prowling hunters of the Knights Iscariot. Their long overcoats transformed their silhouettes into ominous black monoliths on the windswept moors.

Lillian could not tolerate the idea of being pushed into a trap. She considered what would happen if she were to make a stand. As if in answer, the black statues were joined by something else, something that made Lillian's heart sink. A low howl rang across the wastes, and the pale, hunched forms of a dozen hideous ghouls now approached, what Ewart had called 'gaunts', crouched at their masters' feet. They were so close now that their grunts and hideous cries were plain to hear. Lillian knew that if she tried to fight they would overwhelm her. Would they spare Arthur? After seeing de Montfort in person, she rather doubted it; it seemed she was part of some sadistic game.

She forged onwards, staggering up a sudden incline, tripping on the uneven ground. As she did so, something snapped at her heels; she turned at once, ready to fire her weapon, only to see a pallid form scurry backwards, eyes fixed upon her until they vanished into the shadows. As she crested the rise, her heart skipped a beat. Protruding above the dark forest ahead was the unmistakeable spear-tip of a church spire and, nestled beneath the jagged black canopy of the skeletal woods were small, yellow lights. Lamps glowing at windows. An inn, perhaps; sanctuary, or a trap.

There was no other choice. Lillian pulled at Arthur's arm and started towards the village, but this time he gave out a pained cry and fell to the ground, clutching his side. At this, the snarls in the night grew louder, and one of the pallid creatures, unable to contain its bloodlust, leapt forward. Its jaws were upon Arthur's wound before Lillian could react, a wet, snapping sound as of a beast rooting within an animal carcass, lapping at fresh blood, grunting and snuffling greedily.

Lillian fired the derringer, which was shockingly loud upon the still moor. The beast uttered a hoarse, hate-filled scream as the small bullet struck its neck; it tumbled away from its prey, scrabbling in the heather, bounding and snorting like an injured bull. Sir Arthur cried out too, in agony and fear, and Lillian knew at once that there was more at stake than a mauling at the jaws of the vampire beasts. An orb of amber light, small at first, but growing by the second, began to form in the air above Arthur's stricken form. Within the hazy orb was a brighter, jagged flash of white, which began to open like a wound, revealing something hideous beyond, something red and blood-slick, infinite and terrible, with a million flurrying claws and pin-sharp teeth.

The Other.

The vampires shrank back from the light, hissing at the approach of a new enemy. Lillian grabbed Arthur by the collar and hauled him from beneath the amber glow, which was already the height of a man, hanging in the air some six feet off the ground. Black tendrils probed from the Rift, smoke-like, but gaining solidity by the second. Thousands of pairs of eyes peered into the world, shining like stars—perhaps they *were* stars. Lillian saw but the briefest glimpse into the Other's realm, that fabled veridical plane, and what she saw frightened her in the way that darkness frightens small children, instilling within her breast an absolute certainty of the horror lurking in the unknown.

The black-clad hunters moved at last, circling warily, seemingly uncertain whether to press their pursuit of Lillian and Arthur, or to face the new threat. When they turned as one to the Rift, Lillian had the sudden epiphany that they did not want her dead; that the vampires would protect her, save her.

But for what worse fate?

A sound like snapping bones and squelching flesh assailed Lillian's ears, accompanied by a horrendous cacophony of screeches. She felt her teeth and bones vibrating, and for a second she felt as though she were falling into deep water, and was overcome by the absolute conviction that she was to be swallowed up by the Rift—that she could somehow be *shaken* into another world entirely.

The amber light grew. The vampires' avian clicks became snarls. The tearing of the veil between worlds was audible, and with it came the smell of brimstone, and of fresh blood, of ash and decay. Arthur screamed again, and clutched his head. Lillian could not look—she felt the light upon her, like it was the warmth of a new day's sun. From the corner of her eye she saw the pallid shapes of the Knights' minions scuttle past her like enormous spiders, scurrying towards the new foe. Somehow she willed her body to move, tightened her grip on Arthur's collar, and pulled him away.

Behind them, claws slashed, teeth snapped, and inhuman screams echoed across the moors.

The church had been locked. Lillian gave it up as futile, and moved on quickly along the narrow lane, searching for the lights that she had seen burning from the moors.

Crossing a footbridge over a shallow brook, she saw it at last—an inn, half-timbered and dilapidated, the first in a short row of village shops on what appeared to be a long-forgotten road. Lillian chanced a look behind her—of the Riftborn and the Knights Iscariot, there was no sign.

Arthur had calmed, although he was by no means himself. He breathed raggedly. Lillian wondered just what he had seen, in his mind's eye. To her shame, she realised she did not really wish to know.

With soothing words, Lillian encouraged him to follow her to the inn. The metal sign creaked softly on the cold breeze, emblazoned with a heraldic raven pecking the eyeball from a dead soldier. The name of the inn, the Ravengill Arms, was painted above the grisly scene in a faded, uneven hand.

She stood on tiptoes and peered through a grimy, leaded window. Within, a large oil lamp that looked as though it had been taken from a ship hung from the soot-stained ceiling, giving off a smoky, yellow light. The bar that it illuminated appeared deserted. There was no fire in the hearth, so why leave an oil lamp burning? Such a waste was surely beyond the means of a humble innkeeper in so remote an establishment.

Lillian went to the door and hammered firmly upon it. There was no reply. She tried again, and went to the window once more to see if she had stirred movement within. Not a soul was to be seen.

She stooped and took up a handful of grit, and cast it against an upstairs window. After a second, the curtains twitched, and she was sure she spied a face within.

'Please,' she shouted up. 'Let us in. We are in urgent need.'

The face retreated; the curtains fell back into place.

Lillian scowled. This time she picked up a larger stone, and threw it at the window, smashing a hole through the bottom corner of the pane with a satisfying crack.

'Let us in, in the name of the Queen!' she shouted.

Quick as a flash, two internal shutters were slammed fast,

making further attempts upon the window pointless.

Lillian at once returned to the door, and pounded on it even harder. Before long, a muffled male voice floated from the other side.

'Go 'ome! There's nowt for you 'ere.'

'Will you not help two strangers in need?' Lillian shouted. 'We are injured. My friend is close to death. Please, where is your Christian charity?'

'This is not a Christian land, miss; not any more. Move on now… I've a gun, and I'll use it.'

Lillian heard the unmistakeable sound of a shotgun barrel snapping shut from somewhere behind the door, punctuating the voice's threat. Lillian took three steps away from the door instinctively, and looked along the street. Her eyes alighted on a peeling sign beneath the street's only gas lamp. It read:

D. K. GALTRESS, POSTMASTER. POST OFFICE,
TELEGRAPH, CHEMIST.

'Arthur, just a little further,' Lillian said. 'We have a new plan.'

THIRTEEN

Lillian pulled the stitch tight, wincing as Arthur struggled not to scream. Blood flowed down her arms, making her hands slick and the work she did even more difficult. The tiny back room of the post office smelled of rubbing alcohol, which was all she had been able to find to disinfect the wound.

Arthur bit down hard on the wooden handle of a postmaster's stamp. His pain was writ large across his face. He grunted and wheezed. When at last she tied off the final strand of waxen thread, Arthur's head thudded back to the tabletop with relief.

'Is it… done?' he asked, his voice very thin. The pain of Lillian's somewhat amateurish surgical skills had at least brought him from his delirium and restored some lucidity, though now he was weaker still.

'It is,' she said. 'Hush now. Thankfully the bullet passed straight through, and the wound is closed, but you need to stay as still as possible. You need a real surgeon.'

'That should not be a problem,' he said, forcing a smile upon his ghastly pale features. 'I feel as though I have been kicked by a mule. No… an elephant.'

Lillian smiled back, trying to ignore her own throbbing ribs. 'Rest easy, Arthur. I must attend to other matters.'

'Lillian… I cannot let you carry all the burden. What can I do?'

'There is nothing you can do, unless you feel able to build a barricade. I must send a telegram to the Order, and inform them of what has transpired.'

'Let me do that, at least. I have always been better at writing code.' He winked. She appreciated it took him a great effort to appear light-hearted. The Other had invaded his mind, if only for a moment, and had clawed its way into the real world because of him. That would scar him, perhaps for life, if what she knew of Majestics was correct.

'If you insist. It will have to be done from memory... Are you sure you are in the right frame of mind?'

'Lillian, I am fine, I assure you. The... episode... has passed. I can no longer feel the presence of the Riftborn, and must assume that the Knights Iscariot have banished them.'

'At least they weren't lying when they said they had that power. But it means they shall be after us sooner rather than later,' Lillian said. 'Here, take these, and hurry.' She handed him a copybook and pencil, and helped him to sit up against the wall, before beginning the important work of barricading them in the little post office for the night.

No one had answered their pounding on the door, and they had broken in to find the building deserted. There were four rooms downstairs—the shop itself, an office, a large kitchen that appeared to double as a storeroom for medicines, and a tiny, unkempt lounge by the back door. Stairs led off that room to an attic bedroom and wardrobe. Lillian assumed that the accommodation was not often used; perhaps the postmaster lived elsewhere, and did not often stay overnight.

She did not feel in a fit state for physical exertion, but set about her duties with as much enthusiasm and efficiency as she could muster. First she washed down the makeshift operating table around Arthur, and scrubbed her hands and arms scrupulously free of blood. She closed and locked the shutters at the bedroom window. She upended the bed and pushed it down the stairs, blocking the back door. The mattress followed suit. Once she had fought past her handiwork to return to the kitchen, she toppled all of the furniture behind her, to make the porch completely inaccessible, either from the back yard or from upstairs, without a struggle. There was a key in the rear kitchen door, which she turned as soon as she had finished in the back.

'How is the message coming, Arthur?' she asked.

'Almost there—it is not easy without the cypher, as well you know.'

Lillian had struggled in her code-writing lessons at the academy. Though she knew enough to get by, Arthur had far more experience, and she was thankful that he was up to the work. Apollo Lycea used various systems of code when sending telegrams or letters, depending upon where the operation took place. On British soil, the Burmese system was preferred, for hardly anyone in Great Britain was familiar with the language of Myanmar. Messages were first translated into Burmese, and then carefully transcribed into a standardised, phonetic form. This in itself could be transcribed once more into numerals, using a substitution code, which was far harder to crack than one written in a familiar language. Anyone who got that far without a cypher would not only need to understand Myanmar, but also recognise it from the Romanised form.

Arthur only needed to write a line or two to convey their dire predicament to headquarters, but it was painstaking work. She shifted uncomfortably as he scrawled, listening carefully for any noise from outside.

At last, Arthur handed back the copybook. Lillian tore out the finished message—a series of numbers—and placed the rest of the book in the kitchen stove and lit it. Once she had sent the message, she would do the same with the page she had, in case the Knights Iscariot had the means to understand the code.

She went to the shop floor and, with one eye on the window, installed herself at the telegraph. It did not take long to send the message, after which she returned to the kitchen and, with no small effort, moved the dresser to the door, toppling it so that it was firmly wedged between the door and the dining table. Finally, she stoked the kitchen stove in the hope of bringing some warmth to the room. With that, she could do no more, but slumped into a chair, so exhausted that she shook.

'Lillian, I am sorry,' Arthur croaked.

'For what?'

'I could have done more. I should have predicted what Ewart would do. I should not have got myself shot. Most of all, I am sorry that you are the one protecting me, rather than the reverse.'

'Stop it, Arthur. You understand our roles as well as I. Much as it may challenge your notion of the gentler sex, I am the "muscle" in this partnership.'

Arthur's laughter rattled in his chest until it turned into a hacking cough. Lillian forced herself to her tired feet and at once brought him water, which he gulped thirstily.

'That's not what I meant,' Arthur said once he had recovered. 'Do you remember what happened in Paris?'

'Please, Arthur…'

'No, let me finish. This has gone unsaid for too long. I promised you then that you could always depend on me, and I meant it. I have been distant, aloof, in the time since then, but my feelings have not changed. I have not denied them because of your father; I want you to understand that. I have merely buried them deep, out of duty, and because I want to protect you.'

'Protect me from what?' Lillian asked, cradling Arthur's head, drawing near to him.

'From me,' he whispered. 'From the danger that surrounds me. You saw it in Paris—it is why your father disapproves of me so.'

'If I remember rightly, we escaped the Riftborn, and saved a hundred people that day.'

'At great cost! At too great a cost, some would say. I took a risk in Paris, and I took that risk because I saw you were in danger, and all I could think about was saving you, while I should have considered the consequences. Lillian, you have seen tonight why I can never lower my guard; I can never find love like an ordinary man. At any moment my life can turn on a sixpence—I could descend into madness, or be torn from this world by things beyond our ken. I could be cursed to walk the Eternal Night for ever. And anyone... close to me... would be taken with me.'

'Perhaps... that would not be so bad,' Lillian said, softly. 'Perhaps it is not something you should face alone.'

'There is no other way to face it, my dear Lillian,' he said. 'We who were awakened must walk this path alone, in this life and the next.'

Lillian took his hand in hers. 'Arthur, I want you to know that I care about you very much. Let us just see this night through, before we speak of the afterlife.'

'You hesitate to say that you love me,' he said. He sounded rueful.

'Is it fair to say anything of the sort, given the circumstances? And is it fair to expect such a thing of me, given what you have told me?'

'No. It is not fair; it is selfish. You are younger than me, and you are free of this curse that lesser men call a gift. I cannot offer you the life you deserve; I cannot offer you a bright future. And yet I wish I could, and I wish to God I could hear you say that you desired it also.'

Lillian's eyes turned downwards. How often had she wondered if this moment would ever come? How many times had she questioned her own heart on the very complicated matter of Sir Arthur Furnival? She did not know her own mind, and that made her feel very foolish. And so she squeezed Arthur's hand, and he tried to return the gesture, but weakly.

'I can forgive your selfishness, Arthur. And I am sorry I cannot give you what your heart desires, not yet. Perhaps, if you will be patient, there may yet be a future for us. But for now, we must simply survive this night, and pray that the new dawn brings us sanctuary.'

Arthur nodded. He was a sickly shade from the blood he had

lost, and his eyelids drooped as he fought to stay awake.

'Sweet Lillian, you are ever the stronger one of us, and you are right, I ask too much, and the moment is inopportune. Forgive me.'

'There is nothing to forgive. Will you sleep, Arthur, please? Take some rest, and we shall talk more when the danger is passed.'

He nodded. 'Yes... I think I shall. Please wake me when it is my turn to take watch.' His words were already slurring as he grew drowsy.

'I will,' Lillian promised, knowing full well that she would not.

'Lillian...'

'Yes?'

'I never got you a... birthday present...'

'You can buy me an extra big one when we return to London. Now sleep.'

Arthur finally gave in and closed his eyes. Lillian sat back in the kitchen chair, checked her small, inadequate pistol, and leaned her head against the wall. She would stay awake; she had to. She only hoped that, should it come to it, she would have the strength to fight.

'As I said, Lieutenant Hardwick, I am thankful beyond measure that we finally have government men taking an interest in our plight. But the simple fact is that we are but few here, and we cannot get you out of Hull by rail or road.'

John sighed. He had hoped for a more determined—and certainly more numerous—resistance effort. What he instead found was a crumbling warehouse occupied by a band of fishermen, some thirty strong, all in the employ of Christopher Pickering. The businessman was not so very experienced, perhaps not even in his fortieth year, although his face was well lined through worry and toil.

'Mr. Pickering, you have heard Mr. Cottam's statement that

the royal train passed through Hull earlier today,' John said.

'Aye, we know all about it,' Pickering replied. 'Figured one of their royal highnesses was talking with our self-proclaimed masters. To what end, I'd rather not consider, given the short shrift the north has received this past year.'

'Matters have come to a head, Mr. Pickering, and Prince Leopold himself has been sent to treat with the Knights Iscariot. I believe the prince wishes to wrest control of the north from their hands.'

'Chance'd be a fine thing,' Pickering said, furrowing his brow. He was not a boorish man, nor a rebarbative one, John had found, but he had a confidence that came from spending his days in charge of others, and dealing with the same. Added to his forthright manner, common amongst the men of the region, it made Pickering to appear somewhat gruff in his demeanour.

'Nevertheless, Mr. Pickering, it is imperative that we catch up with that train. If anything were to happen to the prince, the repercussions would be grave indeed.'

Pickering stroked his beard. 'We are hardly enjoying a time in the sun here, Lieutenant. I have worked all my life for the benefit of this city, and yet now I must endure the yoke of oppression, and watch my fellows live in fear for their lives. And while this shadow has fallen over us, not once have we received aid from London.'

'We did not know the extent of your troubles until now, Mr. Pickering. My agency, among others, is only now taking matters in hand—'

'Pish!' Pickering snapped. 'Do you think I have rested idly, boy? Do you think I have not sailed out of here myself to raise the alarm? We are not cut off from the world—we have telegrams and letters and ships and trains. For all my influence, there are a dozen powerful businessmen here who would deny all knowledge of the Knights Iscariot, and label me mad. Then there are the scores, if not hundreds, of councillors, magistrates, army officers, and eminent peers who would swear nothing is amiss, and that they are still loyal to the Crown. The resistance is too few to contradict the Knights Iscariot. From what I understand, there are traitors even in Whitehall, who would keep secrets from the government. Or perhaps Whitehall knows full well what is happening here, but have chosen to do nothing.'

John considered this, and his stomach knotted as he realised it must be true. He had suspected it all along, though he had not wanted to admit as much. Maybe, with the Riftborn providing a more immediate threat, it had been easy for the government to ignore the repression of a few villages, or the business dealings of a shadowy group who some accused of being vampires. But now that the great industries of the north had fallen almost into full control of the Knights Iscariot, action had been taken. He wondered how much the Order had known. Had they sent him to Cheshire to gauge how far the rot had spread? Had his father known about any of this, or suspected? He felt sick at the thought.

'I say, that's a rather nasty accusation—' Smythe started, but John touched his arm and gestured for him to be silent.

'We understand your position, truly we do,' said John. 'Whatever circumstance has rallied the Crown to your cause is no concern of ours—we are agents, soldiers, here to do our duty. But know that we are on the same side. I have no love for the Knights Iscariot, nor even for Prince Leopold, if truth be told, but I am here for a reason far beyond mere orders.'

'Oh?' Pickering said.

'My sister is on board that train, Mr. Pickering. My little sister. And I believe—nay, I know—that she is in danger. I would find the royal train, and I hope beyond hope that you will help me do it, for there appears to be nowhere else to turn.'

'Now, there's some honesty,' said Pickering, his face softening. 'Diplomacy be hanged; we all are here for personal reasons, Lieutenant, for there is no greater motivation to face mortal peril than the defence of a loved one. What do you say, Cottam?'

'I trust 'em, sir. They might have left me at the station so as not to give them away. But they rescued me all the same. If'n you can 'elp 'em, and in doing so 'elp me to repay a debt, I'd be grateful fer it.'

Pickering turned back to the two agents. 'Well, gentlemen, it seems you have an advocate. Cottam is one of ours, and a useful man to have about. If he says you're all right, then all right you are. I will help you if I can, but I state to you again: there is no way out of this city by road or rail—the Knights Iscariot control all the routes except for the sea. Beyond the Humber, I maintain my freedom.'

'Why don't you just leave, then?' Smythe asked.

Pickering fixed Beauchamp Smythe with a measured gaze. 'Why do you follow this man, when it is his sister on that train and not yours? We all have our reasons for doing apparently foolish things, Agent Smythe; and sometimes those reasons are better left unsaid.'

Smythe looked admonished. John stepped in while the relations were still friendly.

'If there is no passage from Hull, what aid can you offer us, Mr. Pickering?'

'I can put a telegraph at your disposal, if that would suit.'

'It would.'

'And I can smuggle you aboard one of my stamps and sail you along the coast. North or south; I shall leave that decision to you.'

'If we were to go north, is there a place we could be free of the Knights Iscariot? And from where we could take a train unmolested across the moorland route?'

'Bridlington would have been the best place to pick up the train,' Pickering said. 'But now that the Knights have made their home at Scarrowfall nearby, it fair crawls with traitors.'

'I would suggest Scarborough, sir,' said Cottam. 'I know the stationmaster there, and he is true to his kind still, if I am any judge.'

'And the train?' John asked, with growing frustration.

'Aye, sir, ye'll get your train from Scarborough, and more

direct, too, but not until morning light.'

'Then I would suggest we make arrangements quickly,' said John. 'Mr. Pickering, I would send a telegram to London, and then would ask that you take us to Scarborough. Is that possible?'

'It is,' said Pickering. 'I will not sail in the dead of night, for that is when our enemies are most active. The sea fret is up, too, and it will only hinder us. If we leave at sun-up, you'll make your train, have no fear.'

John considered this. Pickering proposed that they wait almost eight hours before getting underway, and he already had a bad feeling about the fate of the royal train. But he knew he had no choice—to make haste out of Hull was to attract the enemy to their presence, and if there were no more trains out of Scarborough until the next day, then there would be no advantage gained in courting unnecessary danger.

'Very well,' he said. 'I thank you, Mr. Pickering, for all your help. Now, about that telegram...'

Pickering nodded and led the way through the warehouse, past a covered boat shed, and across the other side to a small harbour building. Inside was a surprisingly well-appointed office, with desks enough for several clerks and assistants. At the end of a row of benches sat an electrical telegraph machine, a sight that raised John's spirits.

'Do you require an operator to assist you, Lieutenant?' Pickering asked.

'No, sir, thank you. We have been fully instructed in the use of the machine.'

'Then I shall leave it at your disposal.'

Pickering left John and Smythe to their own devices. Smythe at once took a small copybook from his breast pocket, and began to create a coded message at John's dictation.

To: Lord Hardwick, M.
  HAVE MISSED THE TRAIN STOP SETTING
SAIL NORTH STOP JOURNEY SHALL CONTINUE

Lillian's eyes opened and she jumped awake. She blinked several times, rapidly gathering her wits. The windowless kitchen was dark—the paraffin lamp had gone out, and the warmth from the stove was barely enough to keep the shivers from her bones. Everything was washed with grey.

As her eyes slowly adjusted, she peered towards the table on which Arthur lay. A bundled black shape told her that he still slept. His shallow breathing was the only sound she could hear; she thought that a good sign.

Lillian stood, placing her hand upon the nearby sideboard to steady herself. She felt around for the book of matches she'd left there. She'd forgotten to check the oil in the lamp, but she knew there was a candle nearby that would suffice for now. As she felt for a match in the darkness, she stepped towards the shelf that housed the lamp, but her toe bumped something hard and uneven on the floor, almost tripping her. She cursed under her breath, steadied herself, and then froze. There had been nothing on the floor in front of her earlier, she was sure. The outline of something square and dark lay before her now. Finally finding the matches, she struck one.

In the bright fizz of the match-light, the shadows of the room retreated in a sinister dance. On the floor before her was a planked trapdoor, open, the kitchen rug folded back with it. In her groggy, weakened state there was almost too much to take in all at once: the black space beyond the trapdoor; the suggestion of stairs leading down into a cellar; the hood over Arthur's head and the binding at his wrists and ankles. And then the creak of floorboards behind her.

Her training gave instinctual life to her leaden limbs. She turned to face whatever threat came at her in the gloom, but she was weakened by her ordeal. She saw a scrawny face—a human face, a man—loom momentarily towards her, and etched upon that face was a look of fear or, more closely, desperation. A hand was raised high, and crashed down towards Lillian's head. Pricks of light like sparkling cascades of Chinese fireworks filled her vision. Her eyes rolled back into her head and she felt herself go weightless, falling, seemingly for ever, as the lights, along with her senses, blinked out one by one like London streetlamps snuffed before the dawn.

Part 2

The mirror crack'd from side to side;
'The curse is come upon me,' cried
The Lady of Shalott.

ALFRED, LORD TENNYSON

COVERING NOTE FROM 'A FIELD STUDY OF CROOKES' NECTAR AND ITS EFFECTS ON MAJESTIC AGENTS', BY DR. F.W. MCGRATH ADDRESSED TO LORD CHERLETEN, 16TH JUNE 1876

Sir, on the subject of etherium—that powerful stimulant of Majestics known among the common folk as 'Crookes' Nectar'—I can offer no comfort such as I know you were hoping for. My studies of the Nightwatch, and of lesser Majestics in the field, both licensed and otherwise, have shown quite clearly the dangers of this drug.

Of the thirteen subjects that used etherium on a regular basis, seven have shown signs of pronounced mania, with a clear danger of developing further into forms that will certainly cause harm to themselves or others. The remainder have all exhibited various physical ailments, from brain fever to wasting disease. All have become insomniac, only finding respite after receiving a higher than usual dose of narcotics. They fear sleep, claiming that it is a gateway to the 'Eternal Night', a supposed netherrealm from which one day they may not return. Those Majestics within the Nightwatch are no longer capable of independent function, and their promised rehabilitation into society now seems impossible.

I enclose within my report additional statistical analysis conducted by Dr. William James, of Rift anomalies and their correlation with Majestic phenomena. These data illustrate clearly the increased probability of Riftborn incursions into our world while the loci are under the influence of etherium.

The harvesting and distillation of fluid from the pineal gland is a distasteful process in itself; the properties inherent in the Majestic form of this fluid is unstable, its effects upon the Majestic psyche unpredictable, and its attraction to the Riftborn irrepressible. The mooted development of 'mundane etherium' will only serve to compound the underlying dangers of etherium dependency. After discussing these matters extensively with Dr. James, I have reached a decision. It will be my firmest recommendation that the use of etherium—in any form— by agents of Apollo Lycea be prohibited immediately.

FOURTEEN

L illian drifted upon a warm ocean current, her eyes closed; she was suspended, weightless. Water lapped her naked body. It felt like the womb, like a memory from before her birth.

All at once she knew that it *was* the womb. She was an infant, dreaming of a life yet to be lived. She breathed not air, but her mother's life-giving fluid. She almost panicked, but knew instinctively that it was the natural way of things; that she could not drown. She opened her eyes but saw nothing. Darkness, and the warm liquid, within and without...

Lillian awoke, and the feeling of calm that had so permeated her being moments before drained from her in an instant. She saw nothing, but she was drowning.

Warm fluid filled her lungs. There was something in her throat, some foreign object pumping liquid into her. There was a bag or sack over her head. Her hands were tied behind her, her feet tied fast also, and she tried to struggle, scream—do something, *anything*—but found she was helpless.

The liquid filled her gullet, her belly, her lungs, warm and salty. Seawater? She gagged and heaved, the taste of her own bile mingling with the brackish fluid. Her nose was pinched closed so that nothing could escape her. Each time she heaved, the fluid rose up into her mouth, only to be forced down again. She could not breathe, only swallow whatever was being pumped into her; whatever was killing her.

Lillian's throat burned with pain. Every muscle strained against her bonds. She knew she was crying, and it felt like the only thing she could do; the only thing she had left to prove to herself, and to her killers, that she was fighting. And then, in the moment that she felt she was truly mad, that she could take no more without dying of sheer horror, she was dragged violently from the darkness, into the light.

Momentarily, she was blind. White light filled her vision. And then she was falling, feeling for a second as weightless as she had in her dream, until a hard, cold floor rose up to meet her.

The light shrank away into orbs somewhere above her. She now faced a grey expanse, a heavily stained lime-ash floor, onto which she spilled the contents of her stomach and her lungs.

Only then did it occur to her that she was not alone. Her bonds had been cut. She tried to shake the lethargy from her limbs, to bring circulation into hands and bare feet to save her from slipping around on the wet floor. Wet with blood. Bare feet... She was naked. The sudden shame of that sensation, the feel of rapidly cooling liquid on her skin, of air rushing over her, was numbing.

Lillian tried hard not to focus on the pool of wine-red liquid that had poured from her. She whimpered as something was pulled from her, from deep in her throat and out of her mouth, and she saw a slick red tube whip away across the floor, snake-like, leaving undulating trails in the pooling blood that she had regurgitated. Through watery eyes, she struggled to focus upon the scene before her, her mind lagging some distance behind the proof of what she saw, comprehension wilfully evading her. She followed the whipping movement of the tube, and saw where it led. In that moment she forgot all else; the shame of her nakedness, the desperation of her situation, the utter perversity of what had been done to her. How could any of it make sense when confronted by depravity and cruelty of such proportions?

Sitting upright in a chair to which he was bound, was Sir Arthur Furnival. He was unconscious—at least, she clung to the hope that he was not dead. His head drooped lifelessly to his chest. His skin was pale and greying in the cold light. The rubber tube was attached to him, penetrating the bulging, blue vein of his left arm, where he so often injected himself with etherium.

She tried to say his name, but no words would come. Her throat was claggy from what she still could not admit was Arthur's blood.

Lillian's own arm was adorned with a similar apparatus, and as her thoughts cleared, and her eyes traced the path of the second hateful tube, a weak, lilting laugh reached her ears. She looked towards the sound, the lights burning her eyes, until she saw a dark figure, seated, which slowly came into focus.

Lord de Montfort was laughing at her. His posture was an idle one, like an opium addict spent too long acting the epicurean, and now barely able to summon the energy to face his daily reality.

Black shapes moved around de Montfort, amorphous at first, then coalescing into the forms of his cohorts. Two black-clad figures—women, as diminutive and subservient as the one that had followed Valayar Shah—helped de Montfort to his feet, and gently removed the tube from his mouth, where, unlike Lillian's, it had been clamped in place with painful-looking metal clips. One of the women dabbed at de Montfort's mouth dotingly with a handkerchief.

'Your face is a picture,' he said. His voice was tired, breathless, though he tried to disguise his discomfort with a sardonic tone. 'I could barely guess how you would react to the process; you are the first, after all. But the agony, your sheer terror... exquisite! If you only knew what was to come, you would embrace this moment, savour it, for it is the last time you shall truly *feel* anything.'

'Wh... what have you done to him?' Lillian surprised herself with her own voice. It was raw, phlegmy, but stronger than she had expected.

'To him?' De Montfort cocked his head to one side, and then tossed it back as he laughed again, musically, beautifully almost. 'Oh, my dear girl, you really are priceless. You stand upon the precipice between life and death, salvation and damnation, and yet your first thought is for the Majestic?'

Lillian tried to raise herself from the floor, but her body behaved as though it were not her own. She could barely feel her own limbs, nor anything else save the cold of the room. Electric lights hung high overhead from long cables. The walls were wooden, and old.

She gave up trying to stand, or even to crawl, and instead curled herself up into a ball, rubbing at her blood-slicked arms to aid the circulation.

'Is he dead?' she asked, her voice finding strength. Fear and revulsion began to part before her growing anger like the sea before Moses.

De Montfort shrugged, infuriatingly nonchalant. His consorts helped him on with his jacket. 'Maybe. If not, he soon shall be. We are both beyond caring about this little blood-sack.'

'Where am I?' Lillian needed to keep de Montfort talking while her senses returned. She could not fight like this. She did not even know if she had the heart to ever fight again. She was soiled irrevocably. She felt barely human.

'Irrelevant,' he said, a look of amusement upon his alabaster features. Lillian began to take in more of the room; the searing lights became a manageable glow, and the shape of a large barn manifested about her, appearing to solidify all at once. Dark forms stood silently around the edge of the cavernous space— the hunters, perhaps the same ones who had pursued her and Arthur across the moors. At that, she felt horribly exposed. She was fumbling upon the dirty floor like a newborn calf.

'What have you done to me?'

'Ah, now at last you ask the only question that matters. Now perhaps you are ready to see.'

'See what?' Lillian's eyes flicked to Sir Arthur's prone form.

She thought she saw his chest rise and fall, but weakly. She hoped it was not wishful thinking on her part.

'Life, in all its savage glory, as it was meant to be seen. As it was meant to be experienced.' De Montfort nodded to one of the women, who padded across the pool of blood—Arthur's blood—towards her, bare soles sucking at the wet floor. Lillian saw that the creature was clothed only in a robe, pinned loosely at the breast, but was otherwise naked. Her skin was ghost-white, and her body hairless from bald head to clawed toe. As the vampire drew nearer, Lillian discerned uncountable scars upon the creature's body, criss-crossing her skin, some horribly deep and puckered, others shallow slits. The creature's head was malformed, with bony protrusions jutting from the back of her skull, half her nose missing, and another great scar that ran vertically down the centre of her face, so deep that Lillian fancied she could see the skull beneath. Even over the stench of blood, Lillian could smell the woman, a heady, musky scent, with the underlying odour of a hospital; iodine and antiseptic, masking a sweet, gangrenous decay.

The creature stopped a single pace from Lillian, pausing as if expecting an attack. Receiving none, she stooped and draped a cloak around Lillian's shoulders. Lillian's eyes were level with the creature's navel, which was pierced with a long, metal barb. With disgust, Lillian observed similar adornments across the creature's body, from its forearms to its scarred legs. Blades, hooks, the sharp teeth of predators, carved ivory fetishes, hoops of gold, all pushed through the necrotised flesh, deep and sore-looking.

Lillian allowed the creature to fasten the cloak about her with a pin, and only watched as it withdrew slowly, padding backwards, with blood from Lillian's matted hair staining its pale waist. The creature ran long nails through the blood lasciviously, sucking it from bony fingers, her large, glittering eyes locked with Lillian. Lillian wanted to stand, to find her strength, to kill the thing with her bare hands. But she surprised herself once again, and began to sob. Her shoulders heaved, and she fell forwards, using all her strength to hold herself up from the bloody floor, which served now as a repugnant reminder of both her greatest failure, and her greatest shame.

'Do you know how the Knights Iscariot came to be?' de Montfort asked.

Lillian looked at him, her body trembling, full of hate. He mistook her silence for curiosity, and began to pace around her in a circle, carefully avoiding the spreading blood-pool.

'The oldest of us still living remembers the Roman Empire; fought for the Romans, some say. The gift of immortality was given to him by creatures older still, who some say lived long before the Christ-child ever trod the earth. They say that Judas Iscariot himself was one of us, but he cast aside his true nature in order to follow Christ. In return, the Messiah stripped him of his weaknesses—his aversion to sunlight, his morbid degeneration— and promoted him to the ranks of the blessed disciples. Judas, having been denied the pleasures of the flesh for all of his long life, sinned and fornicated, creating progeny who were, to his dismay, ugly beyond measure and filled with the bloodlust of which he himself had been freed. He asked Jesus Christ why his offspring were cursed so. Christ told him that he had been spared his ill fate not to further his foul race, but to serve God, and in doing so to seek redemption for the impurities of his kind.

'From that day forth, Judas Iscariot plotted against Christ, trying—and failing—to find his own cure for the cursed bloodline he had spawned. At last, frustrated, he betrayed Jesus, and saw him crucified. When he visited his former lord on the cross, Judas was overcome with remorse, and yet Christ forgave him. In that moment, Judas knew that Jesus Christ was the perfect being, and that within his veins lay true divinity. And so he gave in to his base urges, and drank of the rivulets of blood that flowed down the True Cross. He was for ever changed.

'Judas left the Holy Land, and travelled west. For several hundred years he tried to bring salvation to the race of vampires which, he found, subsisted across the world. Legend has it that, possibly due to the blood of Christ within him, he was able to create others of his kind, made almost in his own image. These creatures were the first born—the Blood Royal, and a handful of them still survive to this day.

'Judas founded a cabal of vampires from all walks of humanity—warriors, sages, holy men, slaves, farmers... it mattered not. But he elevated all of them to be his equals, and shared with them his knowledge—most of it, at least. He never shared the secret of creating others of the Blood Royal, and every attempt by one of Iscariot's progeny to sire an heir ended in disaster. These offspring always bore terrible deformities that Judas believed were the work of the devil, and punishment for disobeying the express wish of Christ not to continue his line. Eventually, Judas left—perhaps he grew tired of enduring the centuries in a world that would only ever shun him, surrounded by ugliness and increasing depravity. He left behind scant fragments of knowledge, upon which our kind built a sacred code of laws. The Blood Royal—the first of them—scattered similarly. The most devout, the chosen few who followed the teachings of Judas Iscariot most resolutely, distinguished themselves during the Crusades, where they lent their formidable powers to a human cause. Perhaps they sought absolution for the sin of being born? In any case, the Knights Iscariot were founded, blessed by the Vatican, no less, and thus believing themselves finally to be free of the curse.'

De Montfort paused in his slow, circuitous path when he reached the slouched form of Sir Arthur, stopping by the chair and running a finger down the baronet's sallow cheek. Lillian felt her blood boil in rage, but said nothing.

'It was not so,' de Montfort continued, looking absently at Arthur. 'The craving for blood—the necessity for it—did not pass. The vast majority of their offspring still bore deformities, and were little more than beasts; walking dead, trapped between life and the grave. The Knights Iscariot, for the longest time, kept to their cloisters, refusing to sully the earth with their kind. But they saw the ongoing struggle between their kind and humanity, and they knew that, should the truth of their nature come to light, they would be hunted to extinction by the very Christians who had elevated them to knighthood. And so they began to take control of all vampire-kind, to establish themselves as rulers of a degenerate race that lived a pitiful existence in the shadows. They came to love these creatures as their children—in essence, many of them were exactly that: children, grandchildren, cousins… spreading across Europe and the east, living in crypts, caves, sewers and crumbling ruins. Those of us who herald from the Old Country call these poor creatures *vârkolak*. You might call them ghouls—the eaters of the dead.'

Lillian was starting to recover some semblance of her wits, though de Montfort's prattling was serving as its own kind of torture. She tried to block out his lilting, sardonic tones, and focus on Arthur, on thoughts of vengeance. She needed that thing she had always struggled to improvise: a plan.

'So what are you?' she blurted. She needed to buy time, even if it meant listening to more of his diatribe. De Montfort paused, a flicker of annoyance crossing his features. He raised an eyebrow. 'Are you one of the "Blood Royal"?' she asked. 'Have you walked the earth since the Roman Empire?'

'Not nearly so long,' de Montfort snapped. He folded his hands behind his back, and pursed his lips. She had forced him to lose his place in his narrative. 'No, I have lived for over a hundred years, and the Blood Royal does in part flow within me, but I cannot claim to be one of the chosen. I am… a poor cousin.'

'But you lead the Knights Iscariot?'

'No. I speak for the King. There is a great difference.'

Lillian was wracked abruptly by a hacking cough, and more blood was expelled from her body violently, adding to the ever-growing lake beneath her.

'Wh… what—'

'Do not fear, child, it shall pass.'

'What is happening to me?'

'I was coming to that,' de Montfort smirked. 'When a human concubine gives birth to one of our own—the *wampyr*—it is to a mewling, vicious infant, which more often than not kills its mother on its entry into this world. If the child is a boy, then within the first hour of its life, the decision must be made to grant it the gift of un-death, by allowing it to suckle the Blood Royal, or to cast it aside as a ravening, mindless beast—a mad cousin—whose only hope is to be trained as a hunting hound, the taste for human flesh nurtured within them so as to better aid their masters in sport. We pity them, for are they not our kin? Females, on the other hand, are raised to maturity, in the hope that they can birth a pureblood, raising the offspring of their own father in an attempt to preserve the sanctity of the lineage. Yet the true curse of our kind is that our women are almost always barren, and so we must stoop to mating with humans if our line is to continue. Can you understand the ignominy? It is an act akin to bestiality, or playing with one's food. Can you imagine if humans could reproduce so? Copulating with apes for the sake of their species' survival? Perhaps Mr. Darwin would be first in line for a hairy bride to vindicate his own theories, though somehow I doubt it.'

'I don't understand...' Lillian was hardly listening any more. But she managed to bring her legs up beneath her, and for the first time since her release from bondage she felt enough strength in her legs to support her own weight. She concentrated on that; she might yet have to fight her way out of here.

'Of the male children, perhaps one in a thousand can pass as human, though we certainly are nothing of the sort. It is a freak accident, a circumstance of our birth. If we are deemed worthy to complete our transformation, we grow to join the hallowed ranks of the Knights Iscariot. But none of us can create a pureblood vampire. Few of us would want to, for the Knights Iscariot have become so single-minded in their doctrine that they view what was once a gift as a heresy against their purity.

The secret of transforming a weakling human into one of the *wampyr* was lost with Judas. Until now.'

'You have... you have made me like you?' Lillian could not breathe. Everything closed in on her dizzyingly.

'Vampires who can pass for human, in a certain light, are of great usefulness to the Knights Iscariot, but only as agents, go-betweens, middlemen. I, on the other hand, was elevated to the upper echelons of my house for one very specific reason. When the Awakening swept the land, I was gifted great insight. I am what you would call an Intuitionist, and, for my sins, a Majestic. A rare coupling, no? And unique in my kind; a quirk of fate no doubt inherited from my human mother. My field of expertise was medicine—I studied at Geneva with some of the greatest minds of my age, and yet all of that learning paled in comparison to the whispers that reached my ears from the Rift. I set about creating a series of experiments, all of which bore early promise, and have now come to fruition. For the first time in millennia, perhaps the first time in history, humans—your pitiful, weak race, can become so much more. I have blessed you, child. Before you woke, you took the distilled essence of the Blood Royal from my veins. It should have killed you, but you triumphed over death. You repaid my faith in you. You, Lillian Hardwick, are the first recipient of the Iscariot Sanction. You are the first of many more to come. *You are wampyr!*'

Lillian could not believe what she was hearing. De Montfort raised his arms aloft as though proclaiming her eternal salvation, yet she knew that, if what he said was true, the opposite was the case. She wanted to weep; more than that, she wanted to die.

'It is a shock to you, I can see it writ large on your face. And yet we have whispered this secret to your government. The Queen knows it. The Prime Minister knows it. Your father knows it. This is the true reason that they would not outright deny us. The real threat of the Knights Iscariot is that we would turn all of you into vampires, and usurp the human race. What few of your kind remained would be little more than cattle. This is the first experiment in a long line, and who better to serve as an example than the daughter of Lord Hardwick? Who better to bring our message to the great and the good of London society? The time of humanity is in decline, Lillian Hardwick, and has been since the Rifts began to open. The time of the Knights Iscariot is dawning. And what a glorious dawn it shall be!'

She tested her limbs. Strength was returning, but not sensation. Other than a sense that she was very cold, her flesh was numb, and that lack of feeling gave way to a rising fear. Even so, she flexed the muscles of her legs, and forced herself to stand.

'I am impressed,' de Montfort said. 'I did not expect you to take so readily to your new condition. You are, after all, a child given the form of a god. You are—'

Lillian did not allow another word to cross his thin, hateful lips. She rushed towards him, surprised at her own speed and strength. De Montfort looked, for a moment, surprised. He backed away, and tried to step aside gracefully from her desperate lunge, but she managed to pre-empt him, twist towards him, and grasp his throat with her left hand. She squeezed. It was hard as iron.

'Oh, this is wonderful!' he cried. 'This really is—'

Lillian pulled him towards her as her right arm delivered a straight punch to the bridge of his nose with all the force she could muster. It was a manoeuvre direct from the dojo, her target point not the man himself, but the space behind him, so that her full impetus was directed *through* him. His nose crumpled. He reeled backwards, tearing himself from her grip.

She crouched low, preparing to pounce. In an instant, the two lithe she-creatures were upon her, dragging her back into the slippery pool of Arthur's blood. She flailed and fought, but they were stronger than she. She turned and bit one of them on the face, tearing a chunk of bloodless flesh from its cheek, and drawing no more than the smallest grunt of pain, if indeed it could be called such.

'Witch! Abbess! Adventuress!' de Montfort cried, holding his nose.

'What do you want?' Lillian screamed, vision blurring through tears as she wrestled impotently against the two women. 'Do you want my thanks?'

De Montfort glowered at her. 'Perhaps I expected too much of you,' he growled. 'But you should indeed thank me.'

'I'll kill you,' she said.

'I am already dead, girl, as are you. Unlike you, however, I died within an hour of my birth, and never knew the comforts of human feeling, the taste of good food, the full heat of the summer sun upon my skin… You have lived a life, and now I hope you will find something even more wondrous in the walking death I have granted you.'

'Murderer!' Lillian screamed, her voice ringing in her own ears. And the tone with which it was delivered was more one of sorrow than of hate.

De Montfort laughed. 'Oh, Lillian, I did not think such humour possible, but you have instilled in me great joy. For that, it is I who should thank you. You love this man? This Majestic? I never knew, even though I have shared your heart and mind these past days. Oh, how delicious the pain you must be feeling. How I wish I could feel it too.'

Lillian broke down in tears, the strength draining from her in her grief. Her feet slipped in the blood, and the she-creatures dropped her to the floor.

'I will kill you,' she whispered.

'Listen to me!' de Montfort snapped. 'I have done you the greatest service imaginable. Oh, do not look at me so; I speak not of the gifts you have received, for I am sure you will find them as much a curse as a blessing. No, I speak of the fate that would have been yours were it not for my intervention. You recall the time that I was in your head? The time that I tracked you and spoke to you, though many miles lay between us?'

'How?'

'A quirk of my Majestic gifts. The poor creature that scratched you was a distant relative—on my mother's side, of course. From then until the wound began to heal, I called to your blood, and it answered. However, my power is not quite unique. There is one other of my kind whose telepathic skills surpass even my own. When you and I shared our... special bond... there was another eavesdropping on our thoughts. The Nameless King, the true leader of the Knights Iscariot. He was so taken by your courage and guile, that he selected you as his own, his bride—one of many. He would have taken you as a human concubine, destined to be torn apart by his spawn once he had finished with you. But now, your destiny is greater. Now, you are of the Blood Royal!'

'Like you? A go-between? A servant?' she asked, the words as ash in her mouth.

'Ah, not quite. There is more to my little experiment, but that is for another time. I am sure you have reached the limit of your understanding... for now.'

Lillian had indeed reached her limits; she had done so some considerable way through de Montfort's speech. She looked up to see de Montfort treading gingerly through the blood towards her. His nose was broken, though he did not bleed. He stooped in front of her, taking her chin in his hand and raising her eyes to meet his.

'The time has come to set you free. Remember your experiences in Commondale; the postmaster of that backwater was warned of your coming. He hid in the cellar until such time as he could strike in our name. Our servants are everywhere—our eyes, everywhere. You will see us no more, but we shall know your movements. Now, listen to me carefully: what I do now, I do for your own good, though I am sure you will not understand. When next we meet, I hope it will be under better circumstances, for I really am very fond of you, believe that. Sadly, I fear your... rebirth... will make trouble for us both. When you leave here, you shall be all alone in the world, for the time being. You shall experience such agony, and such madness, that you may wish for death, but death has no dominion over you, and never shall. When finally you are able, you will fly home, little bird, and show your old masters what you have become. And then, when they reject you, you shall return to me, and embrace your new family. You may not believe a word of this, you may think you hate me and will never join me; but you are wrong. It is in your nature now.

He leaned in closer, and kissed her on the cheek. As he did so, he whispered in her ear so quietly that she almost did not hear it.

'I am being watched at all times. When next we meet, I shall explain all, and you will find me a valuable ally. Trust me.'

He withdrew, the congealed blood from Lillian's face on his lips. The darting of his sparkling eyes suggested that the dark figures around the room were not just his servants, but his warders. Lillian knew not what she was now involved in, and hardly cared; she had far more pressing matters to concern her.

De Montfort stood. As he did so, there came a soft groan from behind him. He turned; Lillian's eyes widened. Sir Arthur Furnival stirred.

'Arthur...' Lillian managed. That Arthur was alive, beyond all hope, gave her more will to resist.

'Impossible...' de Montfort murmured. He snapped his attention back to Lillian. 'I am sorry you will not have the chance to say goodbye,' he said. He nodded to someone behind her. 'I am truly sorry.'

Lillian did not follow what was happening, but for the second time that night a sudden pain exploded in the back of her skull, knocking her once more into the black depths of unconsciousness.

John gazed across the bay towards the Scarborough docks as freezing salt-spray hit his face, which was already chapped and pinched. He felt nothing.

He had sat upon the foredeck of the *China*, Pickering's swift little steamer, for much of the journey from Hull. He had willed the going to be quicker, and yet every toss and bob on every wave had felt like a laborious mountain to climb. Their progress had appeared to John so ponderous that they might as well have set sail into an ocean of treacle.

He still clutched the telegram from his father in his hand, the paper crinkled from exposure to the rough coastal elements. He glanced down at it, crumpled within his clenched fist. He did not need to read it again.

PRINCE IS LOST STOP TWO AGENTS MISSING
STOP LAST MESSAGE RECEIVED MIDNIGHT STOP
COMMMONDALE ON YORK MOORS STOP CAUTION
ADVISED NAZELING

John shook his head ruefully. Caution advised. 'Nazeling'— 'do only what is necessary'. And yet his father had just told him that Lillian and Arthur were missing in action. Marcus Hardwick remained resolute even in the knowledge that his own daughter was lost behind enemy lines.

John had been sent into an impotent rage by the missive, for Pickering would not be swayed from the agreed plan. And so, a full eight hours after Lillian's last message had been received, John had set off on what seemed like an interminably long voyage to Scarborough, in the hopes that passage aboard a westbound train could be secured.

Unsteady footsteps fell on the deck behind him, and John felt a firm hand squeeze his shoulder. Smythe stood beside him, resting his hand on John's shoulder as much to steady himself on the choppy waters as to provide comfort. He said nothing; there was nothing to say.

The picturesque bay arced before them, its tall, gaily painted houses and small fishermen's cottages clustered beneath the cliffs, the pink sky making them appear to glow beyond the veil of grey drizzle, like imprecise daubs of oil on canvas. The promontory above them was but a ghost of an outline. A few gulls braved the elements, riding the bluster above the boat, heralding the coming of the enemy in shrill cries.

The boat turned towards the harbour, heading for the small commercial dock. The equable, chugging rhythm of the steam engine slowed, taking on a deeper resonance and causing the grey water about to foam and chop as the *China* dropped its speed. John pulled up the collar of the battered overcoat that he had been given to conceal his identity. It smelled like herring.

'Keep your chin up, Lieutenant,' Pickering called out from the wheelhouse. 'You'll be away soon enough.'

John remained sullen; it would not be soon enough. Not by a long chalk. Now he did unfold the telegram and scan it again, and felt Smythe reading it over his shoulder. What did his father mean when he said 'missing'? Had Lillian and Sir Arthur been separated from the others, or was the entire delegation missing? Had Lillian sent a telegram home, or had someone else sent the message? In the latter case, was Lillian even alive? That thought chilled John more than the cold sea air ever could. Surely his father would have forewarned him if that were so? Or perhaps grief had clouded the old man's reason. John became gripped by the thought that Lillian was dead, perhaps Arthur too, and he read the lines over and over, expecting each time to hit upon some hidden meaning that would explain all.

'We'll find her, Hardwick,' Smythe said at last. 'Probably still at Commondale, wherever that is. Middle of nowhere, I expect, well away from trouble. Don't you worry, we'll find her.'

John knew Smythe's feelings about Lillian all too well. He knew his fellow agent was trying to reassure himself more than anything, and by his tone he was doing an inadequate job of it. By the time the boat landed at a small wooden dock, John had started to fear the worst.

John and Smythe loitered in the shadows, dressed in scruffy fisherman's garb and carrying all their belongings in old kit bags. John imagined from the odd glance they received that they resembled tramps, or homeless stowaways from a merchant ship. Over by the train sheds, Pickering and one of his men bargained with a crook-backed railwayman, who glanced in John's direction periodically with a look of deep suspicion.

'I've seen neither hide nor hair of the enemy,' Smythe muttered. 'And there's nobody about in this inclement weather. I'd rather we simply chanced our luck at the ticket office and procured first-class tickets to this backwater village.'

'I'd normally agree with you,' said John, 'but we must trust Pickering. If he says there are traitors about, we have to be careful. He should know, after all.' Smythe sighed, and John found it hard to fault his companion's feelings on the matter. In the scant years that he had served the Crown, John had rarely had to 'rough it', always preferring to play whatever role would secure him the best rooms and the finest cuisine. This affair was different: this was Lillian, and John would do whatever it took to find her safe and well. Travelling third class would be a small price to pay.

'It is done, Lieutenant,' Pickering said as he approached. 'Mr. Dawkins over yon has pledged to make an unscheduled stop at Commondale. It cost a pretty penny to arrange, I can tell you.'

'I can assure you, Mr. Pickering, money is no object, and you will be reimbursed in full,' John said.

Pickering held up a hand. 'It does not matter a jot to me. All I care about is that the plight of the north is at last recognised by this so-called government. Assuming you return to London in one piece, may I have your word that you will relay our situation accurately, and tell those in Whitehall that a resistance, though small, waits for the word to rise up?'

'You have my word, a thousand times over,' said John. He extended a hand, and Pickering shook it firmly.

'Once is enough, Lieutenant, for I see in your eyes that you are a man of honour. I am sorry I could not secure you more comfortable travelling conditions, but the journey is a short one.'

Pickering nodded towards the man, Dawkins, who loitered nervously next to a pair of wood-planked freight cars, one of which was emblazoned with Pickering's name.

'A freight train?' Smythe groaned, echoing John's feelings on the matter. Third class suddenly seemed like a dream long wished for.

'It transpires we were wrong about the enemy's hold in Scarborough,' Pickering said, ignoring Smythe. 'Their eyes and ears are everywhere, particularly at the station, and even the coaching inns hereabout. The hotels have closed early, for no holidaymaker would travel here and risk being waylaid on the road. Yet the Knights Iscariot leave the freight alone, for now. Perhaps I am too cautious, but I guessed you would rather that than the alternative.'

John nodded. 'You were wise to be so, and I thank you. I shall take no risks where my sister's life is concerned.'

'The train will arrive at noon,' said Pickering, checking his pocket watch. 'You must be aboard and well hidden before it gets here. Dawkins will couple these cars and speak with the driver. When it stops, it shall be for but moments, and you must alight quickly. Is that understood?'

'Noon?' John's heart sank. 'There is no other way?'

'There is not,' said Pickering. 'I am sorry, Lieutenant—I know this matter is urgent, but there is no point in getting captured, is there? You must look after yourself if you are to find your sister.' John and Smythe both agreed, though reluctantly. 'Now, I am sorry I cannot be of more assistance, but I must be away—my absence will be noted if I'm not back in Hull by sundown. I shall leave you in Mr. Dawkins' hands.'

John and Smythe grabbed their kit bags. 'Thank you again, Mr. Pickering,' John said, 'for everything.'

'Fare well, Lieutenant; Agent Smythe. God speed.'

With that, the two agents took their leave of their benefactor, and made for the draughty freight car, both of them hoping that their mission would soon be over.

* * *

Lillian awoke numb and cold. Her head throbbed. Weak shafts of light filtered through gaps in weathered boards, stinging her eyes. The smell of livestock, of muck and blood, assailed her. She lay on a hard floor, draped only in a cloak, and the sight of it brought back recollections of the horror she had experienced. There was no blood on the floor, but the pinkish stains beneath her were unmistakeable—no amount of scrubbing could clean away such signs of butchery. Thick, dried blood congealed beneath her fingernails, and dried on her pale skin like mud. She did not want to look about her, for she knew what she would see, and wanted nothing more than to deny her ordeal as anything more than a nightmare.

Lillian Hardwick had never shied away from life's harsh realities, and it was not within her to start now. She turned her eyes upwards, blinking hard as they adjusted.

The chair in which Arthur had been bound was overturned. The ropes lay loose on the floor, frayed where they had been severed. Scuff marks and a claret smear led away to the far wall, near the outline of a door in the gloomy barn. Any hope Lillian had that Arthur had escaped died when she saw the body.

It was slumped against the door. It was unmistakeable.

Arthur was dead.

Lillian was almost beyond feeling; she had thought him dead twice already, and her heart had broken anew each time. Her detachment from her present situation hung over her, a void as terrifying as the Rift. She ought to feel more; she ought to feel something.

She tried to stand, but her legs felt as though they belonged to someone else, and shook so tremulously that she went to her knees. There was no one around to witness her weakness, and little option but to suffer further indignity in private, and so she crawled towards the door, towards the body.

A small knife gleamed on the floor beside Arthur's corpse. He had clung to life longer than anyone had a right to. She guessed that he had stirred after Montfort had gone, and had managed to free himself. But why had he dragged himself to the door rather than tend to her? Had he even seen her in his weakened state? Lillian could not bear the thought that Arthur had been all too aware of what had happened; that he had been repulsed by the very sight of her in his final moments, this creature that had once been his heart, and was now glutted upon his very life-blood.

She crawled to him, cradling his cold head to her breast, trying hard not to see his ghastly, almost desiccated appearance, the sallow skin and shrunken gums now making him resemble an Egyptian mummy rather than the proud man she had known. The man she had loved, yet had never told as much. It had taken de Montfort to make her realise it—no, he had known it, even before she had known it herself. The thought that de Montfort had shared so intimate a bond with her, when the man she loved never had, filled her with resentment. For de Montfort. And for herself.

'It's like a ghost town.'

John had to agree with Smythe's assessment. Commondale was a wraith of a village. Its dwellings were in poor repair, its business premises locked or boarded up.

The two agents walked with caution down the cobbled main street, which sloped and curved meanderingly towards a copse of dark trees, from where the babbling of running water was the only sound to be heard. They walked past a handful of half-timbered premises, whose render had long since cracked and chipped, and whose roofs were riddled with holes.

John and Smythe rapped upon several doors to no avail. Soon, they passed a shopfront proclaiming itself 'Post Office, Telegraph, Chemist', and paused to peer through a grimy window.

'Hi-ho,' said Smythe. 'I'd say we have a clue here.'

John squinted. Within the dingy shop was a scene of destruction. Tables and chairs overturned, displays ransacked. Furniture and stock seemed to have been piled high against the front door, and hastily cleared again, just enough to make an exit.

'If I were on the run behind enemy lines, this is just the kind of place I'd make for,' John said.

'And if the enemy were on my tail,' Smythe followed, 'then maybe barricading the doors and praying for a new day's light would be the sensible option.'

John's brow furrowed. 'In the best circumstances, Lillian would not hide from anyone. Or anything.'

'I know,' Smythe replied. 'So if it was Lillian who made this mess, I'd say her situation was desperate. Perhaps the barricades are cleared because she left as soon as she could.'

'Let's not think about the alternatives, or speculate too rashly. We should take a look inside. You go around the back and I'll—'

John stopped as a new sound floated up the lane from beyond the trees. A low, mournful singing. It took a moment for either of the agents to recognise it.

'Church,' Smythe said. 'So that's where everyone is.'

'On a Wednesday afternoon?' John asked.

Smythe shrugged. 'Funeral?' The sound was certainly too solemn for a wedding.

'I have a bad feeling about this place,' John said, speaking quietly even though the entire village appeared deserted. 'But I never look a gift-horse in the mouth. If everyone is preoccupied at church, let's take a look in here, and be quick about it.'

The post office was in a poorer state inside than it had appeared from the window. Not only was every stick of furniture rammed against the doors front and back, but the entire premises was filthy, every surface coated in a carpet of dust such that it looked as though the village truly had been abandoned.

In the kitchen, they found a few plates and mugs that had evidently been used recently. John's face turned pale when he noticed the state of the kitchen table, for although a cloth had been thrown over it and sundry pots and pans placed upon it, pinkish splotches had started to seep through the linen from the underside. Smythe saw it too, and quickly cleared away as much of the large table as he could, before peeling back the cloth.

'Blood,' he whispered.

'Human?' John asked.

'There's no way of telling, not without my laboratory,' Smythe replied. 'However, the positioning is consistent with an abdominal wound, assuming the marks at this end of the table are boot-scrapes. The droplet pattern is still visible, even though it has been cleaned. There's a faint odour of alcohol and stains in the wood where such a chemical might have indelibly marked the wax—I would adduce that some surgery has taken place here.'

Smythe's observational skills were mocked and respected at the club in equal measure, and John would have been more impressed had there not been the suggestion that Lillian was the recipient of this slipshod surgical procedure.

'Can we be sure it was... them?' John asked.

'Not from this alone, although it is an educated guess that someone from the royal train would end up here. Let us search some more—if they were here, we need to find out where they went.'

Smythe was taking the lead, and John allowed it, gratefully. As Smythe busied himself searching through decrepit cupboards and shelves, casting his magnifier across every surface, John walked around the kitchen, running his fingers absent-mindedly over cupboards, boxes, and the large stove. He paused, and more out of a need to busy himself than any intuition, he opened the stove and checked the grate.

'There's been a fire here recently, I'd wager,' he said. 'Oh...'

Smythe came over to see what had given John pause. The fire had been made with kindling and coal, but there was paper on it too, some of which was mere remnants. John had fished out a tiny, burnt fragment, some half an inch across, and now held it up to Smythe. The surgeon squinted, and then his eyes widened as he saw what John had seen: one tiny Burmese character.

'They were here,' John said. With that simple statement, his fear grew. Either Sir Arthur Furnival or Lillian had been wounded, and stitched up in this very room. Now they were gone, and there was no way to tell if it had been by choice, or under duress.

'We need to tear this place apart,' said Smythe, his jaw set with uncharacteristic determination.

'Agreed. You carry on down here, and I'll...' John stopped, inclining his head to hear better.

'What?' asked Smythe.

'Didn't you hear that? Listen.'

The two of them stood in silence for a moment, until the sound came again. A distant, muffled voice. Less of a discernible language, and more of a high cackle, as of some pantomime crone. The sound appeared to come from beneath the two agents, and as Smythe stooped to determine its source, it came again, and this time was accompanied by another, more guttural voice. It was again unclear, but more recognisably the shout of a man.

Smythe went to the pantry door at once, looking inside for any sign of a cellar door. John began to look about the kitchen floor, throwing back the large rug that covered much of the floor space. The rug was nailed to the boards at one end, and as John tugged at it, it lifted up, and a trapdoor with it. As an entrance to a set of cellar stairs was revealed, John hissed at Smythe to come at once.

'There's someone down there,' Smythe whispered.

'Or some*thing*,' John said. 'Neither sounded much like Lillian.'

'Well, there's only one way to find out, old boy.'

John took up a paraffin lamp he had seen earlier, and lit it. Smythe pulled out a pistol as John reached down for the trapdoor. Without a word between them, John threw back the trapdoor fully and hung the lamp as low as he dared into the black space beneath, while Smythe pointed his pistol at the narrow stairs that stretched below them.

There was no movement, and the muffled sound stopped at once.

John took out his own pistol, nodded to Smythe, and

proceeded down the stairs, squeezing as close to the brick wall to their left as he could, allowing Smythe a clear shot if anyone were to attack.

When Smythe joined John at the foot of the stairs, they saw a cellar laid out like a pauper's living room—two small armchairs with grubby antimacassars draped over their headrests, a threadbare settee, a table, a crocheted throw, huddled groups of church-candles almost burned down to nothing, and a rickety sideboard upon which were laid hunks of cheese, stale bread and a pitcher of water.

As John cast the light about, he noticed a door at the far end of the cellar, and almost as soon as the agents had seen it, a strange voice came from the other side—a croaking, childlike voice, rasping with age and lilted with madness.

'Old Father Long-Legs can't say 'is prayers; take 'im by the left leg, and throw 'im down the stairs.'

'Silence, woman!' A second voice, unmistakeably male.

Some domestic disagreement seemed to be taking place beyond the door; at the very least John was relieved that it was not vampires he was dealing with.

'Open the door!' John shouted, the full weight of his frustration and anger behind his command.

He was met with silence.

'Open the door or I shall—'

The door flew open with such force that Smythe's aim was thrown off. His shot was deafening in the small space, though it hit nothing but brickwork. A tall, thin man, eyes wild, hair thin, screamed like a demon, brandishing a rolling pin as if it were a battle-axe.

Something made John refrain from the pulling the trigger. He wanted the man alive. He tried to step out of the way and tackle the man instead, but with his hands full all he could do was shove the gangly lunatic aside. The improvised cudgel missed John's head by an inch, catching his shoulder lightly before its bearer pirouetted clumsily towards the stairs.

John dared not drop the gun, knowing the madman was not alone, and so he set down the lamp and grabbed at his assailant. The man looked at John over his shoulder with wide, sly eyes, his aquiline nose and bulbous head accentuated in ghastly fashion by the flickering yellow lamplight. He was not just mad, but terrified.

'Stop! You don't have to be afraid,' John said, but his words fell on deaf ears. The man kicked out, forcing John back. He twisted, hurling the rolling pin at the agents, before scrambling up the stairs as fast as he could, looking more spider than man.

Before John could react, another shot rang out from behind him. He saw a puff of blood and torn fabric ripple from the back of the gangly man's thigh, but it did not slow him enough. His feet vanished through the trapdoor, and they heard his footsteps over their heads, a stumbling, limping gait. John was relieved that the fugitive had not thought to close the trapdoor and lock them in the cellar.

When his ears stopped ringing from the gunshot, he heard the woman's voice, growing louder and more incessant: a nursery rhyme, punctuated by cackling, hysterical laughter.

'Old Father Long-Legs can't say 'is prayers; take 'im by the left leg, and throw 'im down the stairs. And when 'ee's at the bottom, before 'ee long has lain, take 'im by the right leg, and throw 'im up again.'

The room beyond the far door was small and dingy, lit only by tallow candles. The air was thick, and smelled of sweat and unemptied chamber-pots. A bed was pushed into one corner, in which sat a woman of middle age, light hair greying, several teeth missing. She sat upright on filthy pillows, rocking gently back and forth as she recited her nursery rhyme.

'Ah... hello?' Smythe ventured.

The woman laughed as though he had made a joke.

'What was the name on the sign outside?' John whispered to Smythe.

'Began with a "G"... Galtress? Yes, that was it.'

John stepped forward. 'Mrs. Galtress?'

The woman stopped, and squinted pale eyes at the agents.

'Oo wants ter know? Can't be 'aving no gentleman callers at this hour. I'm a married woman! Respc'able.'

'Agent Smythe,' John said, 'would you be so good as to check on things upstairs whilst I speak with this fine lady?'

Smythe looked uncertain, but acquiesced; with the gangly man on the loose, time was not on their side.

'Fine lady!' the old woman repeated.

Once the surgeon had left the room, John dragged a stool over to the woman and sat beside the bed. She was thin, malnourished, and looked old before her time. Her eyes were almost lifeless, and never alighted on anything for more than a second before fading to stare into the middle distance.

'Mrs. Galtress, I apologise for the, ah, lateness of the hour,' John said. 'This is a matter of utmost importance. I have been sent by... the Queen.' He chose the words carefully, scanning her features for any glimmer of recognition, or of betrayal. What he saw was an expression of happiness, though fleeting.

'God save the Queen!' the woman said, with enthusiasm.

'Yes. The Queen is very pleased with your work here, and says she's going to come and save you all. From... *them*.' He nodded at her knowingly. It was a gamble, but John imagined that the woman's hardship was due to the draconian rule of the Knights Iscariot, and that the gangly man—presumably her husband—was to blame for their misfortune.

She looked at John pitifully. 'Them as comes in the night,' she said. 'Will the Queen save us all?'

'She will, but only if you tell us what we need to know.'

'God bless 'er!'

'Mrs. Galtress, there was a woman here last night. Perhaps accompanied by a gentleman. They were in trouble. Do you know who I mean?' John was in no mood to beat about the bush. It was not a great distance from the post office to the church, even if the messenger was wounded.

'I cannot say, sir, I cannot. Don't make me!'

'I can only help you if you help me,' John said, trying his best to maintain a gentle tone. 'This woman—a girl, with brown hair—she is the Queen's servant, and I have been sent to find her. The Queen will be most cross if anything untoward has happened to her.'

At this, the woman quailed. 'Not cross wi' me, sir, oh no! I never did nothing! It were all his doing!'

'Who?'

'Old Father bloody Long-legs! Oh, I curse the day I married 'im.'

'Does your hus—um, Father Long-legs—work for them? For...' he leaned forward to whisper, 'the *Knights Iscariot*?'

There was a sharp intake of breath. 'We do not speak that name! They'll 'ear us, and then we'll be for it!'

'No one can hear us, Mrs. Galtress, I promise. The Queen's men are about. Now, what did your husband do?'

'I never knew, not till after, I swears. Never, never. 'Ee went creepin' up the stair, quiet as a church mouse, an' 'ee bashed 'er over the 'ead.'

John tried to hide his dismay. 'Did he... did he kill her?'

'Oh no, no, no! Old Long-legs is a coward, sir, and a tyrant, too, but 'ee ain't no murderer. I 'eard 'em come in, and they talked. They gave my foolish 'usband a purse o' coin, and took them poor folk away.'

'Where? Where did they take them?' John had not heard anything from upstairs, and grew increasingly agitated.

'Cattermole,' she said, matter-of-factly.

'Cattermole?'

'Aye, Cattermole.'

'Mrs. Galtress, I don't understand.'

'Top Farm,' she snapped, transforming in an instant from fragile imbecile to stern battle-axe. 'Cattermole!'

'John!' Smythe called from upstairs, and John looked in the direction of the shout. When he turned back to Mrs. Galtress, she was staring blankly through him, and holding aloft an object in her gnarled old hand. John reached out and gently took it from her.

It was a silver locket, engraved with the Hardwick crest, with an unusual watch-winder upon its side. A lump came to John's throat.

Smythe called again, the tone more urgent.

Mrs. Galtress resumed her rocking and laughing. John sighed—he hoped he had enough to go on. As he dashed from the room, he heard a soft singing resume behind him, and the tale of Old Father Long-legs went on.

The street outside was still deathly quiet, but was no longer abandoned. A short way down the hill, twenty or so men, armed with tools and farm implements, stood gathered, silent, watching. At their head was the postmaster, Galtress, crooked and unsteady due to the gunshot wound in his right leg. Further up the hill, a smaller group of men, similarly armed and quietly assembled, glowered at the two agents with malice.

Between the two groups, John and Smythe stood back to back.

'Any bright ideas?' Smythe whispered. 'Your sister would probably just shoot her way out.'

'Let's not resort to guns just now,' John replied. 'We don't know how many of these fellows might be carrying firearms. We'll try the official approach first, shall we?'

'Be my guest, old boy.'

John straightened his collar, rolled his shoulders, and stepped towards the largest group, fixing Galtress foremost with his most imperious stare. 'Now look here,' he shouted, 'we are on official business, and shall not be hindered. Return to your homes at once. If we have need of you for our enquiries, we may call on you in good time. Off you go!'

There was no movement from either group, no glances exchanged, no shouts or even whispers as far as John could tell.

Smythe leaned towards John and whispered, 'Off you go?'

'Well, it works on Father's dogs.'

'I rather think these dogs are loyal to another master,' Smythe muttered.

'Looks like you're far from home,' called Galtress. 'You should have stayed on that train, because this is the end of the line for you.' His weak pun was met by a ripple of thuggish laughter.

'Up the hill?' Smythe suggested, already backing up towards the smaller of the two groups.

'Quite,' John replied. He turned and marched briskly away from Galtress's thugs. He reached into his pocket and his hand closed around the grip of his pistol. In the field, John liked to carry a snub-nosed Webley loose in his pocket, and a Beaumont-Adams in his breast holster. 'Don't shoot unless you must,' he said. 'We'll run out of bullets before they run out of men—we must be clever about it.'

The men remained motionless, until at last John and Smythe moved to within a few yards of them, and they began to crowd together, closing ranks.

'Stand aside!' John called.

They did not stand aside. Instead, they took a step forward, with almost military coordination. A great roar went up from the crowd further down the hill, accompanied almost at once by the thudding of heavy boots. John was of two minds about how to proceed, and hands were upon him before he had decided on his course. He had built a reputation for never getting caught in sticky situations like this, and yet not for the first time this week he found himself in mortal peril. Flustered, he fired his pistol through his jacket pocket. The crowd shrank away; a man screamed in pain. From the corner of his eye, John saw Smythe fumble for a gun. Over the shoulder of the nearest thug, he saw the gleam of a shotgun barrel raised into the air.

John shoulder-barged the wounded man out of his path, and took out his pistol, trying to force his way through to the gunman—their last hope, he felt, was to be the only men on the street with firearms.

The closest thugs stepped away as their fellow fell to the

ground, clasping a bloody wound at his hip. No one wanted to be next in line to be shot, but as pounding footsteps approaching from downhill grew louder and more rapid, the entire crowd took heart, surging forwards.

John's Webley discharged again, but this time harmlessly into the air as his arm was pushed upwards. He was aware of Smythe disappearing under a wave of bodies, fists flailing and legs kicking. Someone hit John hard in the stomach, taking the wind from him. He was pulled about so that he was face to face with Galtress, whose head bobbed about upon a long neck as he shouted a spittle-flecked invective into John's face. His sharp eyes and pointed nose gave him the look of a heron, jabbing its beak at a thrashing fish.

'You shot me!' he screeched, then, to the group: 'We'll be paid well for this. They'll regret coming here—they'll regret crossing us!'

All of the villagers shouted in agreement. Strong hands twisted the gun from John's grasp, and a moment later he was being carried along in an irresistible tide. Smythe was alongside him, face swollen and bloody. They were being dragged down the hill, and before long John saw their likely destination.

Outside the inn on the corner of the street, another two men were waiting, the cellar doors of the pub held open, ready for their prisoners. John tried to steady his breathing, and thus his thoughts; to formulate a plan. His eyes darted about, looking for a way out.

Across the road from the pub was a small farrier's yard, and tethered next to the gate was a horse. It had no saddle, but was tied to a post by its halter. As they were wrestled closer and closer to the beer cellar, the options available decreased dramatically. John knew the horse was their best chance of getting away from the mob; he also knew that neither of them had been searched thoroughly. He just needed a free hand to go for his second gun.

He feigned a stumble and, on cue, the thug who had hold of his arms yanked him upright. As soon as John's hands were level with the man's chest, he flicked his wrist, and one of Cherleten's favourite gadgets came into play. A derringer on a spring-loaded device was propelled from his jacket sleeve, and appeared in his right hand. The thug barely had the time to register the tiny gun's presence, and John gave him no chance. The pistol flared, so close that the man's shirt was powder-burnt before the blood began to flow.

The shot was not a powerful one, but the weapon's report was enough to send the surprised group scattering, swelling away from the two agents like the ripples of a lake around a cast stone, and converging again almost as quickly. John wrenched his pistol from his holster, cracking his elbow into the nose of the first man who tried to take it away from him. Smythe, more badly beaten, staggered towards John, groping about for a weapon of his own.

The crowd parted as a bearded old farmer levelled his shotgun. John shot him dead where he stood, with a ruthless precision born of hundreds of hours on the practise range. He did not relish the killing, he never did, and he was acutely aware that these were poor folk in thrall to monsters. Yet even if John's mission was not of national import, it was personal. They had turned Lillian over to the vampires, and would do the same to John and Smythe. He would kill as many as it took to rout them, and count the moral cost later.

The death of the farmer scattered the crowd, though none of the men ran far.

'The horse,' John hissed, and ran at once across the street. Smythe followed close, but awkwardly, finally finding a small-calibre pistol that had been secreted at his ankle. The surgeon waved the gun in the general direction of the crowd, causing half the men to duck as the barrel swept across their lines.

John helped Smythe onto the back of the unsaddled horse. Already the crowd had begun to reassemble, making a desperate bid to block their escape route. The horse shifted beneath John and whinnied with panic as the men began to circle her. That panic turned to self-preservation when Smythe fired once again, and the sound of the gun spurred the horse on, through the crowd and up the hill, with the two agents holding on for dear life.

The crack of a shotgun sounded behind them; masonry billowed from the front of the post office as the agents rode past. Soon, the sound of the crowd's shouts and jeers were lost, and all John could hear was the crisp echo of hooves on cobblestones. Smythe patted him on the back to let him know he was all right, and with grim determination John took the horse into a canter, his only aim now to find the Cattermole farm, where Lillian had been taken.

Lillian sat for what seemed the longest time, trying not to doze, for when she did she was beset by terrible dreams, of bestial things howling in darkness, of running with packs of malformed monsters with sloping backs and twisted limbs. She struggled to stay awake, and watched lines of shadow slide across the barn floor as the weak sun marched its progress across the sky.

Strength began to return to her. With it came hunger. It was unlike anything she had ever known: a deep, voracious hollow forming within her belly, as though she had been starved for days. The stench of death drifted to her nostrils, although it must have been there all along, and with a nauseated revulsion Lillian pushed Arthur's body aside. It rolled away from her into the dirt, and for a second she fancied the eyes had life in them yet. The face contorted and twisted, as though Arthur were trying to form words, to speak to her one last time. She set aside her horror and leaned towards Arthur's shrunken face, unsure of her own senses. The pangs of hunger began to overwhelm her, reaching up from the pit of her stomach like a hand forcing its way through her gullet, grasping for any morsel to sate it. And the word she fancied came from Arthur's dead lips terrified her.

Feed.

She shrank away from the body, scrabbling backwards on

her hands and knees, eyes wide, her entire body shaking. When the convulsions came, they were violent and painful. She was thrown to the ground as if by unseen hands; she thrashed about, slamming her knuckles into the barn wall so hard that wood splintered, her head cracking upon the floor. Her vision swam, and became a vista of liquid purple flame, blocking out reality. Gibbering Riftborn and phantoms plagued her; spirits of the long-dead spoke to her in voices cold and measureless; every surface writhed and moved, the life of mould and woodworm and hitherto invisible creatures now revealed to her, as though everything upon which she gazed was through a magnifier of unprecedented power and clarity. She could smell hay rotting in the loft overhead, the damp grass from outside, the bovine stench of nearby farm-sheds. She smelled most of all the rot of Arthur's body, and with it came the hunger again, the insatiable desire to claw at him, to gnaw upon his bones. Had de Montfort not warned her of the 'ghouls'? The eaters of the dead? Had his experiment, this 'Iscariot Sanction', gone horribly wrong, and she had become such a creature? She saw a vision of herself, staggering through a mausoleum, heaving stone slabs from sarcophagi as she went, tearing parchment-dry flesh from skeletal remains, cramming it hungrily into her mouth.

She was going mad.

When the hunger returned, she bent double and vomited, before staggering away out of the barn, head spinning in delirium. She fell, and was immersed in freezing water that brought her to her senses so quickly she felt her brain jolt in her skull. She dragged herself from an algae-ridden pond, fingers clawing at sodden earth as she heaved herself onto a mossy bank, and closed her eyes until the visions and voices subsided. When next she dared open them, the barn in which she had been held was a black shape upon a hill some five hundred yards away. Behind her was a dark copse of skeletal trees, and the vista in between was of rolling fields in mist, dotted with livestock, and of the endless moors that stretched beyond the fields up to the swirling rose-blushed horizon.

She saw farmhouses in the far distance with a clarity that seemed impossible. But those havens were too far away; Lillian's need was too immediate, overwhelming. She did not think, only acted. She fixed her huntress eyes upon the indistinct shapes of a small herd of cattle nearby. As she moved towards it, staggering at first, her weaving path became straighter, her poise more confident; her bare, wind-chapped legs at last felt strong as iron, carrying her towards the only thing in the world that mattered.

Blood.

FIFTEEN

inding Top Farm had not been easy. Several hours spent riding the lanes on an unsaddled horse, hiding from other travellers, had proven laborious. Logic dictated that the name was a colloquial one, and probably referred to the farm's physical position, and so John and Smythe had wended their way along the high lanes, looking for hillside farms bordering the moorland around Commondale. The first farm they had tried as a likely candidate had proven deserted, save for two vicious dogs shut up inside that threw themselves at the doors and windows ferociously. The occupants of the house had been dead for some time, their bodies drained of blood and left to rot on the kitchen floor, where the dogs had gnawed at their bones. One of the dogs was so sick that John killed it as a kindness. The other, he set free—better it take its chances on the moors.

As sunset approached and the two agents were succumbing to tiredness and hunger, Smythe's keen eyes had spotted a small wooden sign in a hedgerow, pointing up a tree-covered bank. HILLTOP FARM.

They had not been far from the village—their path had been a winding one, taking them to the limits of the district and then back, dangerously close to Commondale. They had decided that, even if Hilltop Farm was not the one they sought, they would have little choice but to rest there for the night. When the door was answered—somewhat cautiously—by an old woman named Cattermole, John almost laughed giddily out of sheer relief.

'Might as well 'ave some stew as you're 'ere,' the Widow Cattermole said, shuffling into her spacious kitchen and pointing at a large pot over the fire. John and Smythe needed no second invitation and were soon seated by the fire, stuffing broth-soaked bread into their mouths hungrily.

'Your hospitality is appreciated,' John said, half his stew already devoured. 'We have had a trying day.'

'I'm sure,' said the old woman.

'We were told that you may have had... a disturbance here last night. We came to investigate.'

'Investigate, eh?' the old woman chuckled. 'And did they send you? I've told them 'undred times, there's nowt they can do to me. I'm an old woman, and I've got nowt left to give, and none left to give it to. I keep meself to meself, and if that i'n't enough for 'em, they know what they can do.'

She folded her arms and nodded to signify her final word had been said.

John and Smythe exchanged looks. John cleared his throat. 'Actually, Mrs. Cattermole, we have come from London. We are here to find out what's been happening in the north... we are here to help.' Trusting the woman was a risk, but John reasoned that she did not seem best disposed towards the Knights Iscariot, and she was but an old woman, living alone on an isolated farm. Even if she wished to give them away, it would take an hour or more for her to reach help, and she posed no threat to them alone.

'London, eh?' she said thoughtfully. 'Took your time.'

'Yes, we've rather heard that once or twice already,' Smythe intervened.

'Well, you're 'ere now, I s'pose,' she said. 'I 'spect you've seen the goings-on in t' village?'

'We have,' John said. 'It concerns us greatly.'

'Right it should! Used to be nowt but good folk round 'ere, or so you'd think. But they changed soon enough when their own necks were on the block. Oh aye, Commondale is a village o' traitors, and it's not the only one. Bloody disgrace!'

'Mrs. Cattermole, we do not wish to drag you into these affairs and endanger you unnecessarily. We have reason to believe that you have information vital to our investigation.'

'Oh?' The old woman looked suspicious.

'We spoke with one Mrs. Galtress, at the post office,' John said.

'Agnes? She were in a bad way when last we spoke. How is she?'

'Faring little better, I'm afraid. She was... not entirely the full shilling.'

'No, she wouldn't be. Them bloody "knights" took both her bairns when it all started, before it calmed down and they took over the running o' the place, an' she never got over that. How could she? Her 'usband is a sly one—bloody coward n'all. As good as turned over his own daughter to them monsters; barely fifteen she were.'

'You said "before it calmed down"?' John asked.

'Oh aye. Heard tell of elections and fancy talk elsewhere, but not 'ere. They come in from the moors one day, monsters, killin' anyone who stood up—my old man amongst them—and taking the wee ones away to who-knows-where. We've seen bad times 'ere, Mr. Hardwick—we've all lost someone—which is why it beggars belief that them villagers turn on their own kind to save their own skins. Makes me sick. Only mercy is that I'll be dead soon, so I won't have to suffer their cowardice much longer.'

'It is just such traitorous behaviour that has brought us to you, Mrs. Cattermole. Two of our people went missing last night, and we believe that Mr. Galtress was involved in their abduction. He was... unavailable, and so we spoke with his wife. She pointed us to you.'

'Aye, sounds well. Explains a few things an' all.'

'Such as?' John asked, eager to get to the point.

'Summat set the dog off last night. 'Ee's an old sod, so it takes a lot t' get 'im riled. Saw some lanterns over yon, by the barn. Too far for me t' walk nowadays, and I learned long ago t' keep me nose out when queer folk is abroad. Like I said, I keep meself to meself. That's why I'm still 'ere.'

'What time was this?'

'Can't rightly be sure. Well past midnight in any case. I bolted me door and went back abed. No point worrying about the likes o' them. If they come, they come. If they leave me be, I'll see out another day. Makes no mind to me in any case.'

'We would very much like to inspect the barn tonight.'

'Be my guest. You'll forgive me if I don't come along. Me legs aren't what they used t' be.'

'Of course. Mrs. Cattermole, do you have horses?'

'No, not no more. But I got a saddle you can borrow. Saw you riding bareback like a gypsy. Thought to meself you might have got into a spot o' bother, had to make off quick, like.'

'Very astute,' quipped Smythe. 'Perhaps you missed your vocation, madam.'

'There's two types o' people in the north these days, Mr. Smythe—them 's pays attention, an' them who's dead.'

Smythe slurped the last of his broth, and rolled his eyes surreptitiously at John.

'Well, Mrs. Cattermole,' John said, 'we will take up no more of your time. If we may take a saddle, we would be for ever grateful. Is there anything else you can think of that might help us in our search?'

The woman thought for a moment, and then said, 'Ar. Don't expect t'see your friends in one piece. If the knights caught 'em, they'd have been dead by dawn.'

John stood outside the barn, struggling to light a cigarette with trembling hands.

'Sir Arthur Furnival was the best Majestic I've ever met,' John said, taking a long draw on his cigarette but feeling no comfort from it. 'They... bled him dry.'

'Perhaps...' Smythe's voice cracked; he cleared his throat and tried again. 'Perhaps it wasn't the knights. Perhaps the Riftborn finally caught up with him. You know what Cherleten always says about the Nightwatch? About how they have one foot in the afterlife, always waiting for their ghosts to catch up with them?'

'It was no ghost who did that,' John said. 'And where is Lillian?'

Smythe had no answer. John could only think of Mrs. Cattermole's harsh words. *Don't expect t'see your friends in one piece.*

John looked across the dark fields, stained bruise-purple by the faint glimmer of liquid fire in the night sky. Shadows moved in swirling patterns across moors and fields; and then John realised that something really was moving, further down the hill. Tiny points of light danced about, appearing to flicker as they passed between ink-black trees. Perhaps a dozen lights, less than a mile away—men, carrying lanterns and torches. Were they searching for him and Smythe? Or for something else?

John felt his nerves settle immediately. His face grew hot as anger took hold of him.

'There,' he said to Smythe, pointing down the hill and across the field.

'The mob?' Smythe asked.

'Come on. We have some unfinished business with the men of Commondale.'

'John, I...'

'We still hang traitors, don't we?'

With that, John started down the hill with nothing more in his mind than violent revenge.

The sight of the first slaughtered cow had barely thrown John off his stride; he was numb to the activities of the Knights Iscariot now, and full of rage. The second, however, gave him pause. Its throat had been torn out as if by a wild animal, and its blood had turned the rough grass thereabout into foul-smelling sludge. The third made him stop, as did the alarmed shouts that carried towards the two agents upon the freezing wind.

Ahead, through a cluster of bushes and brambles, where lanterns and torches swayed, men cried out. Some jeered, others sounded alarmed. John crept forwards, Smythe by his side, and soon it became apparent that a dozen or so men had formed a loose circle, and were in turn dashing back and forth into its centre, as if they had trapped some wild beast. Their shouts were garbled, hurried, indistinct.

'Get in there, lad…'

'No, no, not to me, bloody 'ell!'

'Bring the rope. Now—now, you fool!'

Something moved in the circle of firelight—darting and stooped, lithe and bestial. John would have believed, after the briefest glimpse of the thing in shadow, that it was a wolf, cornered and snarling. And then he heard the creature cry out.

A snarl became a high wail, which in turn became a scream of fury and hate and frustration. It was barely human, and yet all too human, all too familiar.

Lillian.

John felt Smythe snatch at his arm to restrain him, but he shrugged his partner away and raced forward, leaping over an irrigation ditch, through a hedgerow that snagged at his clothes, and into the midst of the Commondale mob.

He saw the men's leering faces, some angry, some hateful, others fearful, more than one lascivious. Galtress, tall and spindly, barked instructions while hopping about on his good leg. They circled a dead horse, its innards spilled out onto the scrub, its neck opened much like the cows'. Beside the horse was Lillian, half naked and caked in gore, fingers curved like talons, legs bent, carrying her body low to the ground, ready to strike; her face was turned upwards to the bobbing lights carried by the men, making her eyes shine bright. Violet eyes, sparkling like diamonds, and filled with hate. Her lips were turned back, revealing bloodstained teeth in a bestial snarl.

The shock of it made John pause, and two men turned to face him, overcoming their surprise quickly and lunging for him. In a trice, Smythe was by his side, barrelling his full weight into the nearest man. John ducked beneath the flailing arm of the second and delivered a brutal uppercut that felled his would-be assailant at once. The others turned. John had his pistol in hand, and discharged it into the air, causing the men to scatter to the four winds. All but one: Galtress had been so intent on directing the hunting party that he had been caught in two minds. As he turned awkwardly on his wounded leg, Lillian leapt at him and, to John's horror, caught the man's prominent Adam's apple between her teeth, tearing it out in one fluid movement. Her screams were guttural and animalistic, inflected with emptiness, sorrow and endless hunger.

By the time Galtress had ceased twitching, only Smythe and John remained to bear witness, the grotesque scene illuminated by fallen lanterns.

'By God,' Smythe said, 'she has become one of them! How is it possible?'

John had no answer. He could only look upon the ruin of his sister, who even now slurped greedily upon the blood of the postmaster, though God knew how she had not already drunk her fill from the slain beasts that littered the fields. John rubbed at his face, refusing to believe the evidence of his own eyes. Finally, he stepped forward, and picked up a lantern from the ground.

'Lillian?' His voice sounded weak to his own ears. The lantern shook in his hand. His sister did not respond.

John took another step. 'Lillian.'

The horrid wet sucking sound stopped at once, and the violet eyes flicked upwards towards John. Lillian remained crouched low, arms outstretched, supporting herself on all fours. Galtress's blood dripped from her mouth. Her body, naked but for a black cloak fastened at her breast, was slick with gore. Her hands were black from clawed earth and dried blood. She did not look human.

'John, I would step away if I were you,' Smythe warned.

'We must help her.'

'I have seen this, in Hyde. It is bloodlust—she will not know us, John, not in this state. Perhaps not ever again.'

John flushed at the thought, and anger burned at him again, and pushed him to rashness. He stepped forward more firmly, and held out a hand to Lillian.

'Lillian. Sister. It's all right. We've come for you... we've come to take you home.'

Lillian's head tilted, her expression utterly void of emotion. She regarded John like potential prey.

John was about to move closer still, when he saw the sudden flex of Lillian's limbs, the tautening of her body, and he had no time to recoil before she leapt at him with incredible speed. He dropped the lantern in his haste to protect himself; Lillian barged into him with the force of a wild animal. Even as John fell, he pushed at her desperately, the vision of Galtress with his throat being torn out foremost in his mind.

He rolled across the cold earth, Lillian's weight upon him. Fingernails scratched at the back of his neck; teeth snapped near his face. She was strong, far stronger than he remembered— her legs braced them both, and then a knee was driven into his midriff, pinning him to the floor. He looked up and saw those sparkling eyes level with his own, triumph crossing blood-smeared features.

Smythe charged into her, knocking her clear of John before she could strike. As John scrambled to his feet he saw Lillian leap up and crouch low again ready to pounce.

'I'm sorry, Lillian,' Smythe said, with such sorrow in his voice that John did not at first understand the meaning. And then he saw the gun.

Smythe's arm was outstretched, the pistol aimed at Lillian. And she knew what the gun was, or at least what it was for, for she flinched back, eyes trained upon it. John was still checking himself for wounds when he saw Lillian leap at Smythe. The gun fired, Lillian darted sideways into shadow, and then lunged once more into the circle of light cast by John's lantern. She shrieked with fury. Smythe knocked her aside, and she rolled across the ground, again crouching to all fours at once and facing her opponent. Her prey.

Smythe, hand shaking, pulled the trigger again. This time, John was already upon him, pushing his arm upwards so that the shot thundered into the night sky.

'No!' John cried.

Smythe pulled his arm away. 'She's one of them, John! She'll kill us both if she can.'

'She's my sister!'

As they argued, Lillian circled about, and was closing on Smythe. When she pounced, the surgeon was blindsided, and barely fended her off. Smythe was dragged away from John in a split second, with John racing to catch up while his fellow agent was pulled into the shadows as though he weighed nothing.

John sprinted into the darkness, grabbing Lillian by the arm and heaving her away from Smythe. Smythe crawled away, and John saw he was already searching for the gun.

Lillian struggled against John, her strength prodigious, her arms and legs flailing like a dying insect, every impact making him wince with pain. This was not the Lillian from the dojo; there was no deft movement, no subterfuge or grace. She was not a subtle knife, but a hammer, and John was the anvil.

An elbow cracked into John's injured ribs, bringing water to his eyes and driving him back. He kept hold of her wrist, but still she swung her other arm at him, her blow so powerful he dropped to his knee and was forced to let her go. Lillian's teeth snapped at John's face. In that moment, Smythe returned, cracking the butt of a pistol over Lillian's head, which served only to enrage her further. Lillian leapt shoulder-first into Smythe, knocking him down, pummelling him with her fists. John saw Smythe grab for the pistol and raise it to Lillian's stomach, his face a grimace as he prepared to shoot.

John jumped forward and caught Lillian's wrist again, this time twisting it as Mrs. Ito had taught him at the academy. Lillian turned, momentarily under John's control, and he seized the opportunity, wrapping himself bodily around her, locking his arms and legs into position, and hoisting her to the ground with him. Even with her new-found strength, she could not escape— the manoeuvre was too well executed, his grip on her too fierce. She resisted with every ounce of her being, wailed, gnashed her teeth, but to no avail.

'Lillian!' John shouted.

John caught sight of Smythe staggering away, rubbing his face, shaking his head ruefully.

'Lillian! It's John. It's your brother.' He felt certain that this time her struggles abated, just a little.

'I... shall... kill you!' she cried. She meant it, but John did not lose heart, for it meant that she still had some sense within her, some vestige of humanity.

'No, Lillian, listen to me. You are my sister. You are my best friend. I have come for you, Lillian! I've come to take you home.'

'You're too late,' she hissed. 'I shall kill you and drain you! Just as I did *him*!'

John's heart sank. He knew she must be speaking of Sir Arthur. He remembered the shrunken features of the corpse back at the barn, the papery flesh...

'Lillian, none of that matters. Please, I beg you, let us help you.'

'You can't!' she cried, and with a mighty effort, unbelievably, wrenched herself free. She skidded to a halt when Smythe stepped in front of her, pistol aimed at her head. Her shoulders heaved as she panted with exhaustion, and she turned her back to Smythe and faced John.

'Tell Smythe to do it,' she said, coldly. 'I am Lillian no more. I might as well be dead.'

Smythe cocked the pistol, but John shook his head at the surgeon. He stepped towards his sister and, with no fear, placed a hand upon her bloodstained cheek.

'No, sister,' he whispered. 'I once told you that, one day, even you would be unable to stand alone. And on that day...'

'You would stand with me,' she finished. She looked down as John pressed an object into her hand. A large silver locket that had once been a watch. A locket that contained portraits of their parents.

Tears streamed down Lillian's cheeks, making pale tracks in the blood.

'Whatever they've done to you, we shall make it right. Together, we are stronger than the Knights Iscariot. Let me take you home; if there is terror to face, we shall face it together. If there is revenge to be had, I shall help you exact it.'

She finally fell into John's arms. 'I have no home, brother, and never shall again.'

'This is unexpected; most unexpected.'

The Artist stepped away from the canvas, set down his brushes, and took up his lamp, shining it close to the glistening oils to better see what he had wrought. It was always this way— he painted the future in a frenzy, barely stopping to look at his work, his hands guided by some unseen force. He often said that he might as well be blind.

He had placed the finishing touches upon a golden crown, which glistened in the light of the red sky. The scene he had painted beyond the crown, however, was most interesting.

Satisfied, he stepped away from the painting, and took a moment to admire his reflection in the full-length mirror that he kept next to his easel. He was handsome, and knew it. From his Chinese father he had inherited a smooth complexion and lean body; from his English mother, imposing height. He had angular, aquiline features, and eyes black as coals. His dark hair hung loose about his shoulders, framing the dragon tattoo that twisted around his naked torso. He smiled at his reflection, and then took up his cane and rapped on the floor of the attic studio.

He heard footsteps at once, answering his summons and clomping through the warren of his opium den, the House of Zhengming. An affectation, that name; the 'House of the Dead', the exact spelling bastardised so that his English patrons could pronounce it. Once, it had been a warning to his enemies when he had first arrived after his ill-fated sojourn in Burma. His first task had been to subjugate the Chinese crime bosses of the East End. Now it was merely a fitting tribute, for who else but Tsun Pen, the Artist, had such mastery over the lives of others?

There came a rap at the door, and it opened immediately. The Artist's most trusted servant, Hu, entered, bowing low to await his master's instruction.

'It would seem, Hu, that Lord de Montfort is braver than any of us expected. He has had the courage of his convictions, and the repercussions will be far reaching indeed.'

Hu inclined his head. He was a man of few words, but that did not matter. The Artist waved a hand at the painting, and smiled. The meaning was doubtless lost on Hu, but in terms of both the clarity of the premonition and the artistry of the painting, it was a triumph.

'It could be said that I influenced him—unintentionally, of course. De Montfort is cleverer than I perhaps gave him credit for, and he has somehow masked his true purpose from me. He has upset the apple cart, as the English say, that much is certain. I would wager that he will return to us before long, for his masters shall want his head for this. Were he not a vampire, I would have foreseen this and capitalised earlier… for now, I shall just have to make do.

'As soon as this paint is dry, see that this is delivered to Lord Hardwick. It will cost him three times the normal price. Make sure he understands that there has never been a portent of greater significance, nor of greater urgency.'

Hu bowed again. The Artist waved him away, and he hurried backwards out of the room, closing the door as he left.

The Artist turned again to the painting and smiled. His place was not to judge, nor to intervene in earthly matters. His place was to use his gift as his conscience—or lack of it—dictated. His place was to provide information, and to make money. No more, and no less.

He took a deep breath, pleased with his day's work, and turned back to his reflection. He admired once more the chiselled features, and the sleek torso that, in the reflection, was curiously free of tattoos. He smiled at his reflection, and the man in the mirror merely nodded, knowingly, and turned back to his own studio, in the mirror-world.

SIXTEEN

Sir Toby Fitzwilliam stepped though the screen that separated Lillian's hospital quarters from the rest of the large, empty ward, and placed a hand on Lord Hardwick's shoulder.

'How is she, old friend?' he asked.

Hardwick said nothing; he sat motionless in his chair and stared at his sleeping daughter. To Sir Toby's eyes, Lillian looked as though she were dead. Her skin was pale and hard, free of the suppleness and colour of life. Her dark-brown hair made a ghastly contrast against her pallid features. Her lips and fingernails were grey-blue, her eyelids dark, and her breathing so shallow that she would doubtless pass for a corpse in any mortuary in the land.

It was Cherleten who answered, stepping from the shadows. Sir Toby had not realised he had been there.

'We have performed every test that we know,' he said.

'And?' Sir Toby had no patience for Cherleten's obstructiveness at the best of times.

'It is as I suspected. The process is… irreversible.'

Sir Toby sucked the air through his teeth, his eyes upon Hardwick, who held his peace.

'If they made it so, why can it not be unmade?'

'It is not a disease, to be transmitted through infection,'

Cherleten explained. 'If it were, the Knights Iscariot would be no threat to us. She is transformed, fully. She might as well have been born this way.'

'And so their threat to the world is revealed,' Hardwick said, absently.

'Quite,' Cherleten agreed. 'They threaten to do this to the prince, and reveal the results to the world. Can you imagine?' There was an edge of gleefulness to his tone that riled Sir Toby at once.

'This is not some scandal to be whispered of at the card table,' Sir Toby chided.

'Of course not. But it rather puts us on the back foot, does it not?'

'What becomes of Agent Hardwick?'

'She will be sedated until we are sure we can control her. And then we will begin her rehabilitation. If such a thing is possible.'

Lillian had not spent long awake since returning to the club two days prior. She had not submitted peacefully to testing, and had been gripped by fits of rage and uncontrollable bloodlust, which had only been sated with massive blood transfusions. She drifted from lucidity to madness with alarming speed, as though possessed by two intellects, and had already injured an orderly, two nurses and Agent Smythe during her episodes. Now she was confined to a room in Cherleten's secret domain, sealed beneath St. Katharine Docks, with several tons of water overhead to flood the facility in case of a security breach. Lillian represented the most severe threat to security since Apollo Lycea had constructed the armoury's secret headquarters.

'What will this "rehabilitation" entail?' Sir Toby asked.

Cherleten smiled mirthlessly; for once, Sir Toby did not think the peer relished what was to come.

'Training. She will spend time with alienists. And, of course, the Nightwatch will have her for a time, to ensure that she is not... compromised.'

'The Nightwatch?' Sir Toby spluttered. 'Has she not endured enough?'

'I fear, Sir Toby, this is only the start of Agent Hardwick's troubles.'

Marcus Hardwick stood abruptly, and stared at each man in turn, worry etched upon his face. He looked for a moment as though he might speak candidly, but then his features took on their more customary hardness. 'Gentlemen, I am sure my daughter is in safe hands, and thus I am afraid I must leave. I have unavoidable commitments at the palace; I have kept Her Majesty waiting long enough already.'

'Lord Har— Marcus, I am sure the Queen will understand a little tardiness at this most difficult time,' Sir Toby said. He knew Hardwick was not late for the appointment, so why he would quit his vigil now was a mystery.

'Then you do not know the Queen,' replied Hardwick. 'Where her own children are concerned, there are no allowances.'

'You will return tonight?' Cherleten asked, showing uncharacteristic concern. 'She will wake in a few hours, and we shall need your permission to—'

'You have it. Do what you must. I am afraid I shall not return tonight, nor for perhaps a week hence. The work I am conducting has suffered long enough due to this complication.'

'Complication? Marcus, have you—' Sir Toby began

'Do not presume to lecture me on this matter,' Hardwick interrupted. 'You know as well as I do the importance of this project. The fate of the very world rests upon its success. Cherleten's sequestering of Tesla has already caused a great delay—there can be no more upsets if we are to weather the coming storm.'

Sir Toby nodded. The Hardwick obsession with duty was often admirable, sometimes unfathomable. They walked together through the dark hospital ward to the door, whereupon Hardwick stopped, and took something from his breast pocket.

'Toby, would you see that my daughter gets this,' he said, quietly. It was a small sealed envelope that bore the Hardwick seal.

'Of course, Marcus.'

Hardwick looked for a moment as though he might say more, but instead he nodded curtly and took his leave.

'You know,' Cherleten said when Sir Toby returned to Lillian's bedside, 'Agent Smythe tells me that the girl asked to die in Yorkshire. Her brother spared her, naturally, although I don't believe he fully comprehended the situation.'

'What do you mean?'

'I mean that from the point of view of national security, not to mention the well-being of the girl herself, pulling the trigger would have been the best solution all round. A convenience for the Crown, and a mercy for Agent Hardwick.'

Sir Toby slumped into the chair that had been vacated by Lord Hardwick, and squeezed his lined face with his hand.

'Lord Cherleten,' he said when at last he looked up, 'you and I rarely see eye to eye, and I confess that the Order is often healthier for our differing views. But I warn you—never say that out loud again. Not to me, not to anyone. Do I make myself clear?'

'Perfectly,' said Cherleten, a thin smile playing fleetingly upon his lips. 'I shall give you a moment alone. The guards are outside, should you need them.'

Sir Toby listened to the sound of Cherleten's footsteps recede through the ward and into the corridor beyond. When he was sure that Cherleten was gone, he placed Lord Hardwick's letter on the table beside Lillian's bed, and took her hand in his. It was ice-cold, and hard.

'My dear girl,' he whispered. 'I swore to your mother I would keep you safe, and yet here you are. How can I ever forgive myself? Because I knew... I am sorry, my girl. I knew.'

Sir Toby bowed his head, and remained there motionless, taking up the vigil abandoned by Lillian's father. He understood a little of Marcus's sense of duty; for after all, no matter how much he gave to the Hardwick family, he always felt that his debt to them would never be repaid.

* * *

John paced about the waiting room, his growing agitation exacerbated by the departure of his father with barely a word. It had been hours since the doctors had last attended Lillian, and John had been kept in the dark ever since.

He tried once more to enter via the stairs that led deeper into the armoury basements, and was met for the second time that afternoon by two guards, whose expressionless faces and imposing stature suggested they had not been picked for the role for their reasoning abilities. He held up his hand in a placating gesture and returned to his seat in the waiting room.

The escape from Yorkshire had not been easy. The agents had been hounded every step of the way. They had bribed, cajoled or bullied cabbies and goods drivers to cover fifty miles of enemy territory before commandeering a canal barge and taking a slow journey to Lincolnshire, where finally they were able to catch a train. With Lillian prone to alternate fits of rage or trance-like melancholy, progress had been wearying. They had fought men who opposed them, and run from the accursed vampires more than once. And yet John knew they had been *allowed* to leave. The Knights Iscariot could have killed them many times over, but chose not to. They wanted Lillian to return to London, and John was the means of her delivery—he was certain that was the only reason de Montfort had not honoured his promise to kill John should he return to the north. No, John knew the only reason he was alive and home again because this was where the Knights Iscariot wanted Lillian to be. She was their message, their example to the world. De Montfort fancied himself a prophet, and he now had the means to create disciples, born of his own blood. Born into murder.

'Lieutenant Hardwick? Lord Cherleten will see you now.' A servant had appeared at the stairhead. The young man was dressed like a club servant, in tailored suit and black tie, even though the armoury facility was certainly nothing like a gentlemen's club. The man escorted John down the stairs, past the guards, and into a long, whitewashed corridor, walking straight-backed like a waiter escorting a diner to supper.

The armoury facility was far larger than the basements beneath St. James's Square and Pall Mall. A large network of corridors divided up a labyrinth of laboratories, workshops, storerooms and operating theatres. John had heard tell of another level below these, which extended into an old catacomb pre-dating the Great Fire, and of large boathouses that could send men out onto the Thames by means of massive sluice gates. He had passed these off as fancies, but could never be sure. Cherleten was always one for the ostentatious display of power and prestige.

John met the man himself outside a ward in the hospital wing; a ward in which there was at present but one patient.

'We have done everything we can, and I am afraid the transformation is irreversible,' Cherleten said, without preamble. 'She has been told already, naturally, and has taken it surprisingly well.'

John felt his world began to fall apart. All of his training at the academy had taught him to make his face a mask, and he did that now, instinctively. His little sister… Cherleten was now telling him that she was replaced by a monster, perhaps for ever. And because Cherleten was a man of the Order through and through, he expected certain conduct from John. He expected a cool head. He expected acceptance. Acceptance!

'There is much more to ascertain before she is allowed beyond this ward… She has retained some semblance of her own personality, and may be close to her old self once the trauma has passed. We shall have to keep her secure down here. A month at least, perhaps longer; you understand—'

'May I see her now?' John said.

Cherleten hardly batted an eyelid at the interruption. 'She is not best prepared for visitors. She has had a trying time. More trying than you could possibly imagine.'

'I must see her.'

'Hmm. The alienists should be finished with her by now… I

can make an exception for you, I suppose. It may do her good to see a friendly face. Or it may drive her into one of her fits. It shall be interesting nonetheless, don't you agree?'

John stared at Cherleten icily. Even now, all the man could think about were his experiments.

'I see you share your father's lack of humour,' Cherleten sighed. His devilish smile quickly returned as he extended an arm towards the wards. 'This way. *Ibi cubavit lamia.*'

Lillian sat upright in bed, looking uninterested as a doctor withdrew a needle from her arm. She turned as her brother and Lord Cherleten entered; John found the way she looked at him unsettling. She did not behold him with great recognition or fondness. Indeed, John was put in mind of his cat, Chuzzlewit, when he espied a sparrow outside the flat window—the knowledge that he could not reach the bird did not stop the cat contemplating how tasty it would be.

John paused momentarily, and then resumed his advance towards his sister. One of Cherleten's alienists—a mind doctor— scratched away in a pocketbook, no doubt assessing Lillian's mental condition. As John drew near, he felt a tingling sensation at the back of his head, and the cold creep rushing over his skull that signified the intrusive presence of a Majestic. He noticed that in the shadows around the edge of the ostensibly empty ward, curtains had been pulled around rails. Behind the curtains, something moved, and breathed raggedly. The Nightwatch. Too socially distasteful to be left in open view, even down here, they had been concealed behind the curtain, probing Lillian's mind, and John's too, for signs of psychical weakness. John shuddered at the thought of the wasted, shaven-headed form sitting behind the curtain, electrodes attached to its scalp, its breathing assisted by valves and billows, while etherium regulators steadily pumped the psychic opiate into its body.

It. John chastised himself for thinking of the wretch in such a fashion. He was not sure what he found worse: the process that transformed young men and women into living difference engines, or the fact that they often volunteered for the part.

'Dear brother, so good of you to visit,' said Lillian. Her voice was mirthless but a thin smile played upon her colourless lips. 'You are my only visitor, you know, besides… these.' She waved a hand dismissively to indicate the attendants, and John fancied she included Cherleten in her gesture.

'Not entirely true, dear sis,' John said. He swallowed the feeling of reticence and apprehension, buried it deep, and stepped confidently towards Lillian, taking her hand in his. He almost did not react when he felt her ice-cold skin. Almost.

'I hope you are not about to tell me that Father sat dutifully by my bedside,' she said. 'For I would find it hard to believe.'

'As a matter of fact, he was here for a while,' John said, flushing as he thought of their father abandoning Lillian in her darkest hour. 'But it was Sir Toby I meant.'

Lillian looked surprised.

'It's true,' John continued. 'He sat with you for the longest time, when no one else was allowed admission. He only left but recently due to a summons to Number 10.'

She appeared to consider this, and then said, 'Did you know Father left me a letter?'

'I… yes, I had heard.' John knew he would have to find some way to defend their father in the coming exchange, though his heart was not in it. He resolved to do his best to change the subject as soon as possible instead.

'He wrote that he was very sorry about my condition, but he could delay no longer, for his great work must take precedence in this most trying of times. Finally he has entrusted me with some snippet of information. He believes he has the means to our salvation—not mine, obviously, but the world's. Apparently Mr. Tesla is an even more vital player in this little game than I had first thought. Do you know what he's talking about, John?'

'Agent Hardwick,' Cherleten intervened, 'might I remind you

that the contents of that letter represent more than an exchange between father and daughter. They contain secrets of Apollo Lycea that are known by fewer than a dozen people in the world, and are not to be divulged openly.'

John was relieved—he had heard a little about his father's plans purely by keeping his ear to the ground in the right places. He was certain he knew more than he ought, and did not want to get into a guessing game with Lillian.

Lillian smiled at Cherleten; it was not a friendly smile. At last, she turned to John again.

'Our father goes to explain himself to the Queen. Is there any news of the prince?'

'None,' John said. 'The Knights Iscariot have made no demands as yet. We have no idea if they will make good on their threat to—'

Cherleten coughed. 'That is enough for now, Lieutenant. No need to tire your poor sister out with all of this talk of business.'

'He means I cannot be trusted,' Lillian said. 'I am one of them now, John. Although I'm not sure they'll knight a woman. What do you think?'

'I am sure you do not really wish to find out,' John replied. Then he added, gently, 'You will never be one of them.'

'Oh, I don't know, brother,' she said. 'Lord Cherleten has already told me that I am slowly rotting, and that my humanity is slipping away by the hour.'

John shot an angry look at Cherleten.

'That is not what I said... not precisely,' Cherleten said.

'My flesh is necrotising, because I am dead. Have I not understood correctly?'

'In a manner,' said Cherleten, as much to John as to Lillian. 'You are not dead, strictly speaking. The fluid that flows through your veins is unlike human blood. It is pinkish, it is cold, and it does not nourish the flesh. As a consequence, your flesh will begin to lose pliability and colour, and may slowly come to... decompose.' He looked awkward as he said it. 'We can treat it though, have no fear. You do not have to look anything less than your old self, if you wish it. But more than that, you must understand that you are undergoing a transformation—a very long transformation—which may or may not ever reach its final stages.'

'What on earth do you mean?' John asked, his throat going very dry.

'He means, brother,' Lillian interjected, 'that the Knights Iscariot are not human; that at the end of their very long lives, they become something ugly and monstrous—something that no living soul has ever seen, but that we are assured is terrible indeed. And if I have truly become one of their "purebloods"... then that fate awaits me, one day.'

'That day is a very long way off, Agent Hardwick,' said Cherleten. 'Before then, there is much more we need to do. We have caught you in time—with the help of my doctors and my Nightwatch, you will remain your own woman. You may experience a... loss of empathy, and some physiological changes, but I believe we can keep you on the side of the angels.'

'I do not understand,' said John. 'Are you saying that Lillian may lose control of herself because... because of what they did to her?'

'He is saying that I may have already lost control,' Lillian said. 'That if it were not for this facility, I would be relaying my location to Lord de Montfort even now, and perhaps have killed everyone here while I waited for him to take me away.'

'That is not quite what I said, Agent Hardwick,' Cherleten scolded. 'I merely referred to your loss of memory, and wondered if you might have let... someone... in, during that time.'

'Memory loss?' John asked.

'Your sister remembers nothing after the death of Sir Arthur, save for waking up on a canal barge in your company. We do not know how much the enemy may have gleaned from her unconscious thoughts during that time.'

'I know only that I owe you a great debt, brother,' Lillian said. 'You and Smythe saved me, perhaps from myself. But I tell you this: if I really am to recover, I will use my new-found strength to return to Commondale and exact my revenge.'

'Revenge?' John asked.

'Yes. It is a village of traitors. I remember taking refuge in the post office, but the postmaster was hiding in his cellar. He crept out while we slept and knocked me unconscious, then turned us over to the enemy. He will be the first to feel my wrath.'

'Galtress?'

'Was that his name? I forget.'

'Lillian… he is dead.'

'Dead? John, have you denied me my rightful vengeance?' Her tone was inappropriately playful.

John remembered Lillian's savagery on the edge of the moors; he remembered her eagerness to kill, and the terrible manner in which she had done it. After everything he had seen in his short career as an agent of the Crown, Galtress's demise stayed with him more vividly than anything else. He wanted to tell Lillian a lie, to do her a kindness, but he hesitated a moment too long, his eyes downcast to his shuffling feet.

'So, I killed him,' she sighed. 'A pity; I would have liked to confront him with my wits about me. But, it is as well—I should rather not return to that godforsaken place.'

She did not bat an eyelid. If anything, her eyes glimmered brighter for a moment, and the corners of her pale lips were upturned. She seemed pleased with herself, but quickly—deliberately—hid her glee. She assumed instead an uninterested posture.

'Lillian, I—'

'Lieutenant,' Cherleten interrupted, 'I must ask you to bring your visit to a close. Our patient needs time to recover from her ordeal.'

John nodded. He felt sick.

'A kiss, for your sister,' Lillian said, her voice taking on a strange, musical lilt.

John felt some unkind emotion rise within him. Not revulsion, he hoped, but something akin to it. The longer he stood in

Lillian's presence, the less he felt that he had brought anything of his sister back from Yorkshire. Dutifully, however, he stooped to kiss her cheek. And she whispered in his ear, so quietly that he almost felt her voice rather than heard it.

'Help me, John. I cannot abide it here.' It sounded heartfelt. Her mask slipped, almost imperceptibly.

'Lillian... I shall return as soon as they allow it. You will not be alone.'

Her face became impassive, but her eyes moistened. John knew in that moment that his sister was herself still, somewhere within this marble-white form.

'I... I cannot feel,' she whispered.

John saw in Lillian's face confusion and helplessness. It instilled in him such anguish that he could barely keep from shaking.

SEVENTEEN

The vase smashed against the tiled wall, sending fragments of glass tinkling across the floor of the hospital ward. Beauchamp Smythe stepped back to what he thought was a safe distance. Lord Cherleten stood firm.

'Three days!' Lillian shouted. 'Have you not ascertained all you need by now? Or am I to remain a prisoner here for ever?'

Lillian had become more prone to fits of rage as time had progressed—in fact, she gave in to them willingly, for it was the only way she could feel anything at all. Anger, it seemed, was a powerful force. Since John's visit she had been alone on the ward, examined hourly by Cherleten's endless army of medical personnel. She had tried to leave several times, and had been greeted by barred doors, behind which stood armed guards. In the rare moments she was alone and not sedated, it was all she could do not to take her own life. She spent those moments ignoring the books that Cherleten brought for her, and instead hugged her knees, rocking back and forth in the darkness, praying that de Montfort could not hear her thoughts; praying that the Knights Iscariot would not come for her and make her a bride for their lifeless, Nameless King.

'You are not a prisoner, my dear, you are a patient.' Cherleten's voice was steady, even though the nurses quailed at Lillian's anger. When had he started to call her 'my dear' rather than 'Agent Hardwick'? That irked her more than her confinement.

'Your only patient,' Lillian said. 'And one who is kept under guard.'

'For your protection, not ours.'

Lillian looked to Smythe, whose face belied Cherleten's assertions. 'And why is Agent Smythe really here?' Lillian asked. 'He purports to be my visitor and brings me flowers, and yet he carries his surgical bag.'

Smythe's eyes moved to the flowers that were now strewn across the floor. He looked rueful. Lillian almost felt sorry for him.

'We thought you might like to see a friendly face,' Cherleten said, maintaining the charade. 'And I confess that Agent Smythe's singular expertise may be useful in the coming days and weeks.'

'By "singular expertise", you do of course mean his knowledge of cadavers.'

'I would not put it so indelicately.'

'Naturally.' Lillian held Cherleten's gaze with an impudence she had never previously dared. She had nothing to lose any more. 'And will you have Agent Smythe prod and poke and slice at me, like the rest of your lackeys?'

'In a manner, although I think Agent Smythe's treatment will be of far greater benefit to you. And it is not as though you truly feel discomfort, is it, my dear?'

Lillian scowled. 'Only from the indignity. If I am to take up residence here, might I at least have my clothes?' She looked down at her linen hospital gown disapprovingly.

'It has already been arranged. There are not very many tests remaining, and then we can assess your… situation.'

Lillian thought about this for a moment, and then turned to Smythe.

'I will brook no more delays. Agent Smythe, if you have tests or treatments, then you will kindly administer them at once.'

'I…' Smythe glanced at Cherleten, who nodded assent. 'Of course, Lillian.' He reddened at the use of her Christian name.

Lillian sighed and looked again at Cherleten.

'Lord Cherleten, may we have some privacy? I really am tired of all this.' She waved a hand at the staff.

In the room at present, there were three nurses, a junior physician, an alienist, and the Nightwatch. The wasted Majestics were hidden from view; from all but Lillian. Their psychic emanations prevented most people from noticing they were there—one tended to look past them, or ignore them altogether. Lillian had had training to see through the Majestics' tricks. Smythe had received that training too, though he pretended not to notice the presence of the two unsettling youths in the shadowed corner of the room. But it was not training that revealed the presence of the Nightwatch to Lillian. The previous day she had begun to experience strange visual phenomena. They began with coronas of violet light flashing before her eyes, and at first she had complained of the sensation to the doctors, who exacerbated the situation by shining lights into her eyes. Eventually, the sensation became more muted, and Lillian saw that she was not only able to see well enough in darkness—a talent that had manifested itself immediately after her transformation—but could also see strange coronas and ghost-like manifestations around the people who visited her bedside. They collected like cobwebs around certain people; skeletal blue-white phantoms or orange-hued balls of light that followed doctors and nurses hungrily. Around the Nightwatch was an incandescent dull amber glow, which flickered outwards periodically, twisting into plumes of indigo smoke, from which leering faces and flashing eyes flickered occasionally, so rapidly that Lillian thought she had imagined them. It was only after two days of observing these phenomena secretly, saying nothing about what she saw, that she came to realise that the stench of the Riftborn hung around the Nightwatch at all times. She wondered if these were the 'transmissions' that Tesla had spoken of, and whether, if Sir Arthur had lived still, she would have seen the same manifestations around him.

What was worse, and what made her wonder if she were simply going mad, was that a faint amber glow shone around her. She saw it when she looked into the mirror, pulsing about her head. She would have assumed it was some insight into the unique nature of the vampire, but for Lord Cherleten. She saw it upon him, too, and she knew not why. But to speak of it to him or anyone else would only prompt more tests and delay her release. She held on to hope that she would be discharged eventually, no matter how unlikely that seemed at present.

Now, however, Cherleten relented. He had a nurse unlock a private examination room, allowing Lillian and Smythe to enter alone. Lillian noted with some dismay that Smythe looked the unhappiest of all about the arrangement.

Beauchamp Smythe's hands trembled as he laid out his medical apparatus.

'I hope you are not planning to operate on me with such unsteady hands.'

'I... it's just that...'

'It is just that I am no longer the Lillian Hardwick you know. You have seen me kill in most unsavoury ways, and were even tempted yourself to end my life.'

'Your memory...' Smythe stuttered.

'It is returning, slowly, in fragments. I am having trouble piecing those fragments back together, but I remember your willingness to shoot me well enough.'

'I—'

'Do not worry, Beauchamp,' Lillian said, gently. 'I do not hold it against you. I might have pulled the trigger sooner— you know me.'

'Not entirely,' he said, avoiding her gaze.

'Have you spoken to John?' Lillian said, changing tack.

'Yes.'

'Did he say anything about me? Did he send any message?'

'I am not supposed to speak of matters outside with you, Lillian. I am sorry.'

'Beauchamp, please.' Lillian hopped down from the gurney. As she stepped towards Smythe, he turned his back to the wall and edged away, nervously. She was a head shorter than Smythe, and slight of frame, but even before her transformation she had been more dangerous than he, certainly in Mrs. Ito's dojo. 'For pity's sake, I have no intention of hurting you, Beauchamp. We have known each other for a long time. Have I not suffered enough without losing my friends also?'

He beheld her for a moment, and then sighed, the tension draining from his shoulders. He looked ashamed.

'I am your friend, Lillian,' he said. 'No matter what. I wish you really knew that.'

Lillian reached deep inside herself, to recall what it was like to elicit warmth from another person. With every day that passed she found it harder to empathise, or even to speak to another human being without mocking at them. She hoped it was down to the company she was forced to keep, but she did not think that was the whole cause. Now, she took Smythe's hand in hers, trying desperately not to show her dismay when he recoiled from her freezing touch. She concentrated on softening her features, so that the hard mask she had come to recognise as her own face might take on something of its old aspect. Finally, she spoke, as softly as she could, aware that her voice sounded more unlike her own by the day.

'Beauchamp, I fear that Lord Cherleten seeks to keep me here for a very long time. I have seen my brother but once, and Sir Toby briefly, and no other friendly face but for yours. Even if I was so altered that I sought to betray you, my family, and my country, I would be unable to. The Nightwatch have erected a prison around my thoughts just as Lord Cherleten puts one around my body. I just wish to know that my family are well, that the Order endures, and that the monsters who inflicted this… this blasphemy upon me are to be punished. Please,

Beauchamp, would you leave me here without hope, alone but for His Lordship's lickspittles?'

Smythe looked conflicted. She knew it was unfair to make him feel so, but she could not find it within herself to care, not truly. Eventually, Smythe seemed to resolve his inner struggle.

'I would not,' he said, in a hushed tone. 'But I must be brief, for Lord Cherleten cannot know I am speaking with you of any matter beyond your medical examination. Please, take a seat, and I shall talk while I work.'

Lillian obeyed, and Smythe busied himself, his hands finding their steel again. He took samples of the pale fluid that passed for Lillian's blood these days, scraped tiny slivers of skin from her forearm, wincing as he did so even though Lillian felt not a thing, and finally, almost reverently, he took a lock of her hair. All of these things were placed into small glass phials, then filled with a brownish liquid.

As he worked, he spoke quietly. The prince was still missing, and there was no word from the Knights Iscariot. No messages had so far reached the north, and even Pickering's fledgling resistance had gone quiet. Lord Hardwick had surfaced from his secret project only that morning, carrying a dire message to the palace. As a result, the Order was preparing for the worst; the Queen would leave London that very day, for a secret destination. As for John, he remained at the Apollonian, stationed there by their father so as to be out of harm's way, for it was widely believed that the Knights Iscariot now had even greater reason to further their vendetta against him. Lillian smiled when Smythe told her that John had already been reprimanded twice in a short space of time for trying to harangue his way into the armoury's subterranean facility.

Smythe took a roll of instruments from his case, along with a phial of yellowish solution. The roll contained numerous scalpels, lancets and coils of wire, and Lillian shifted uncomfortably despite herself.

'I have had a good many samples taken from me these

past days,' she said. 'But it seems you are about to make a subcutaneous injection.'

'Most astute, Lillian. Let me explain. Lord Cherleten has most crudely alluded to the decomposition of your flesh over time, but he paints only the direst picture of your situation. In truth, it will take months before any signs of necrosis will be noticeable, by which time we will have it well under control.'

'How... comforting.'

'I have here a concoction of my own devising. It is primarily a preservative—mostly formaldehyde, truth be told—but it also contains not only bleaching agents to keep the skin looking flawless, but also several new innovations created by the Order's best medical Intuitionists. For want of a better term, an elixir to encourage the skin's healing process even when blood is... ahem... lacking.'

The mention of blood brought stabbing pangs of hunger, and Lillian felt sick at the thought, and betrayed by her own body at such a revolting instinct. She knew all too well that the degeneration of her flesh would be slowed by imbibing blood, but that the degeneration of her mind would only be hastened by it. The 'curse of the vampire', Cherleten had called it.

'You wish to... embalm me alive?' Lillian could not keep the dismay from her voice; this was one indignity that she could endure with neither smile nor scowl.

'I... I am sorry Lillian. Today we only wish to get you accustomed to the idea. We do not have to administer the chemicals if you do not wish it. But eventually...'

'Eventually I will need it, and increasingly often.'

Smythe nodded. An awkward silence passed between them.

'If it is not strictly necessary, I would rather not. Not today. I do not think I can face it.'

'Of course. It is a lot to get used to, on top of... everything else.'

'What else is in the bag?' Lillian sniffed, with apprehension.

'I, um, that is...'

'Please, Beauchamp, spit it out.'

'Very well. I was asked, while I was here, to fit you for a wig.'

'My... my hair?'

'Not for some time,' Smythe said hastily. 'It is just a precaution, and better to prepare you for the eventuality now, Lord Cherleten said.'

Lillian thought she should feel more sorrow than she did, but somehow she resisted any temptation to cry. In fact, she admitted to herself, there was no temptation at all. The longer Smythe talked, the more inured she became to any feeling whatsoever. Except for the hunger; that remained very real.

'Can that wait for another day, also?'

'Of course. It will not be necessary for a while.'

'How long?'

'Months, at least. Perhaps as long as a year.'

Lillian took a deep breath. That did not seem a terribly long time at all. 'Anything else?'

'Ah, yes. But this is good, I think, if a little uncomfortable at first.' Smythe produced a small silver case and opened it up so that Lillian could see within. It contained two eyes; or, at least, two pieces of thin, coloured glass designed to look like eyes. 'You wear these over your eyes. You will be able to see through them perfectly well, I assure you. And it will, um, disguise the... you know.'

'You mean I shall be able to pass for human without frightening small children in the street.'

'Not just children,' Smythe joked, but the weak laugh died on his lips when his eyes met Lillian's. 'I am sorry. If you will allow me?'

Lillian looked at the lenses warily, and finally acquiesced, allowing Smythe to lean in to insert the strange lenses over her eyes. So close to him—inappropriately so, were he not a medical man—she could smell the nervousness on him, and the blood pumping through his veins. She bit her lip to quell the urge to tear out Smythe's throat.

As she had suspected, she felt nothing. When Smythe was done, she blinked madly. It felt like he had thrown sand in her eyes.

'You'll soon get used to them,' Smythe said, stepping back to admire his handiwork. 'Here.' He took a small mirror from his bag, and handed it to Lillian.

The sight of hazel eyes, a close match for her old self, brought a lump to her throat. For that moment of feeling alone, she was grateful to Beauchamp Smythe.

'I… do not know what to say,' she said at last.

'If you are happy, then you need say nothing. If you are displeased, then tell me what I may do to make amends. I am, as always, your servant.'

Was Smythe still sweet on her? Was such a thing possible? More likely he was merely being the perfect gentleman and consummate professional. A few weeks ago, Lillian would either have dismissed him bluntly, or encouraged him cruelly, depending upon her mood. Now she did not want to do either.

'Beauchamp… something troubles me.'

'I imagine a great many things trouble you, Lillian. But is it anything I can help with?'

'It is about your help, as it happens. All of this…' She waved a hand across the medical supplies that Smythe had brought with him. 'These things could not have been prepared in just two or three days, even with the help of Intuitionists. The tests that Lord Cherleten has conducted so far cannot have borne fruit yet. And so… how is it that you come to know so much about my condition, and how to treat it?'

'Ah,' Smythe said, averting his eyes from Lillian's.

'How long has the Order been preparing for this? Did they know about the Iscariot Sanction?'

'Good lord, no,' Smythe said. 'Lillian, this really is not my place to say. The Order is built upon secrets on top of secrets. We all play our part in the great game, without ever holding all the cards. Lord Cherleten comes deuced close, though.'

'That was not an answer.'

'Just this once, it is all the answer I can give you. You will have to ask Lord Cherleten for the rest.'

'I will,' Lillian said, determination and frustration washing over her in equal measure.

Smythe began to pack away his things. 'Best not dilly dally much longer,' he said. 'I'm sure Cherleten is already suspicious. Just… try not to land me in it, will you?'

Lillian thought about that for a second, then nodded. 'Of course not.' Then, although she resented herself for it immediately, she brushed her fingers against Smythe's cheek, and whispered to him. 'You are a dear friend. Please… visit again.'

Smythe did not recoil this time, and she knew then that his feelings for her still burned strong, and were overcoming his fear and misgivings. She needed that, not only because she craved some contact with the outside world—some weak link in Cherleten's chain of secrecy—but also because she needed to feel like a human being. At least a little. At least for now.

Smythe took her hand and kissed it. 'I shall return as soon as I can, and as often as I can. And I shall give your regards to John. He won't rest until they let him come back to see you, you know. He's proving quite the squeaky wheel back at the club.'

'A dog with a bone.' Lillian smiled. 'He won't give it up. Bless his heart for it.'

Smythe held her gaze for a moment longer, before clearing his throat and opening the door, making a show of it for the doctors back in the ward.

'And if those lenses give you any trouble at all, tell one of the nurses at once and I'll get them remade. Farewell, Lillian.'

She followed Smythe out of the examination room, where Cherleten was waiting. By his side was a nurse, holding a neatly folded stack of clothes. One of Lillian's own uniforms, with a pair of boots, cleaned and polished, on top.

'My dear, please forgive me,' said Cherleten, with uncharacteristic humbleness. 'I have allowed my pursuit of scientific endeavour to blind me. Your frustration earlier was not unwarranted, and for as long as you remain here I would not have you feel like a prisoner. Please, take the examination room as a dressing room for the time being, and I shall have an orderly make one of the other rooms available for you.'

The nurse handed the clothes to Lillian, who was so surprised at the gesture she said nothing.

'When you are ready,' Cherleten said, 'I would have words with you in private. I am making that room in the corner my office. Meet me there at your convenience.' He indicated one of the locked rooms nearest the main doors.

Lillian gave a small curtsy. She felt foolish at once, but Cherleten did not react. It was the proper form of thanks when done a kindness by a peer of the realm, after all. Lillian went back into the room to change; a simple act that felt like the most important thing in the world.

Cherleten was different somehow. He sat behind a desk in the windowless office, which was sparse and clinical, having been, until recently, a disused private room in the ward, Lillian surmised. He offered her a seat, which she refused—she had spent far too long prostrate recently. She likewise turned down a glass of brandy. She had eaten no food nor taken any drink but small amounts of water in three days. She felt none the worse for it, and the smell of the brandy overwhelmed her even from two yards away.

'I expect Smythe's news came as a shock to you?' Cherleten said, once he had made himself comfortable and poured his drink.

Lillian tensed. Had he overheard? She said nothing.

'It is a lot to absorb in such a short space of time,' he continued. 'The transformation you are going through is... unprecedented. If what de Montfort told you is true, then the repercussions for us all are grave indeed.'

She relaxed a little; Cherleten knew that Smythe would confront her with wigs, glass eyes and formaldehyde, and it seemed he meant no more than that.

'Lord Cherleten, it seems I am a living experiment, first for them, and now for you. Might I ask what you hope to discover with all these tests?'

Cherleten swilled his brandy around the glass, and put it down on the desk without taking a drink. 'De Montfort explained some of the vampires' nature to you, did he not?'

'He did. It was barbaric.'

'They come from ancient times. Everything was barbaric then. These days we are taught that men evolve; perhaps the vampires have evolved too, albeit much more slowly. For what good is evolution through natural selection when one can live for a thousand years? And that is really the crux of the matter, Agent Hardwick. For the vampire, procreation is difficult. They despise the very process, for it means debasing themselves with "lesser creatures"—humans. I can see from your face that this subject repulses you, so I shall put it in as fine a way as I can. The vampires have half-breed servants, some of whom, like de Montfort, even rise to prominence due to quirks of their blood. But even those of the old lines, of the Blood Royal, are not truly pure. They masquerade as such, and are certainly powerful, but they are degenerates, slowly becoming more grotesque with each new birthing. Weaker, less able to walk amongst men without evoking fear and revulsion. You must understand that the curse of Judas Iscariot cannot be transmitted like some disease spread in a brothel. It is passed through the generations, a taint passed from father to son—or sometimes daughter—by birth. The Iscariot Sanction, if it truly does what de Montfort claims, creates new purebloods from the line of kings. It distils the very essence of Judas and bestows it upon another. If de Montfort can create a new vampire of such power by taking just one human life… well, he could transform as many of the populace as he wished, and slaughter the rest.'

'I still do not understand how I can be a "pureblood",' Lillian said. 'If de Montfort is not of the Blood Royal, then surely he could not make me so.'

'Even now, under such immense trials, your enquiring mind does you credit, Agent Hardwick. Where, indeed, did de Montfort acquire the Blood Royal for the transformation? You said he transfused his own blood into you, which means he must have imbibed the Blood Royal first. But that is dangerous for one of our kind—unpalatable, at best. Legend has it that the blood of the elders is so powerful, a single cupful can cure disease and heal grievous wounds… or strike one dead on the spot. There are manuscripts locked away in the vaults of the Vatican itself, supposedly written by those who witnessed Judas Iscariot's ascension—or destruction, if you like—and those fables would make your toes curl. There are probably three or four people in the world who have read those suppressed tomes, and I am one of them.'

'You have entered the Vatican's vaults?' Lillian was almost impressed. Such a thing was unheard of, and the more fervent esoteric groups of London spoke of the vaults in tones of reverence and awe. Indeed, Pope Leo XIII had made Rome almost free of the Riftborn taint, supposedly through means inherited from the occult lore locked within those very vaults. Lore that he was, allegedly, unwilling to share.

'A lifetime ago, when I was striving to understand my own nature.' Lillian frowned, as Cherleten continued. 'You see, my dear, there is a reason that the Order is so well versed in vampire lore. Why we know how to preserve your flesh and make you look human.' He pinched his hands to his eyes, and removed the lenses that covered each of them, and when he looked again at her, his eyes glittered violet in the dim light of the office.

Lillian stepped back. She could not comprehend what he had shown her.

'No, I am not one of them, nor could I ever be,' he said, answering a question that she had not asked.

'Then… what are you?'

'The Knights Iscariot would call me an abomination. Do not worry, my dear, I am no interloper—Sir Toby knows, and has since the beginning. Smythe is one of a select few medical personnel who is trusted to attend me. I am not sure about your father... perhaps that's why he dislikes me.'

'De Montfort... you know him?'

'Good lord, no. Understand, all of Apollo Lycea's knowledge of the vampires comes through study—primarily of me. We have not treated with them, and nor would we, had they not forced our hand. We had thought their activities restricted to the most remote parts of Britain, and with the Riftborn posing the greater threat, we rather mistakenly let the vampires grow too bold. It was only when your brother uncovered de Montfort's plans in Hyde that we realised just how bold.

'What I mean to say is that I have never returned to the race that sired me, nor ever wished to. If they knew me—knew my true nature—they would kill me, without question, for I represent an abomination in their eyes. You see, my mother was the concubine of one of the Blood Royal—an inbred, imbecilic creature, half-vampire, half-human, kept in chains in some crumbling ruin in France. My father, while still a young man, came across this wretch while on the Grand Tour. He was lucky he found the lair during daylight hours, by all accounts, for the vampires within were sleeping. He took the woman away, and made her a servant in his household. As time went on, my father grew old and fat, and more than a little mad. The concubine, on the other hand, aged but slowly, and despite her... condition... came to be more attractive to the aging Lord Cherleten. Eventually, as was so often the way in those times, he had his way with the woman during a night of drunken excess, and the product of that coupling was... me.'

Cherleten held out a case, and Lillian took a cigarette from it without thinking. Etiquette be damned.

'So, you are... human? For the most part?' Lillian asked, lighting her cigarette and drawing on it eagerly. The sensation was not unpleasant, though very different from how it had felt in her former life.

'The taint of the vampire is strong. By day I find myself

lethargic, by night I am invigorated. I can see things with these eyes that other men cannot—I know you see them too, although that can be our little secret for now. And yet, for all the advantages of my birth, I rot. I age more slowly than a normal man, but age I do. I have lived for almost a hundred years, and for half of that time I have relied on unguents, arsenic powder, and the attentions of the finest physicians in the land to stop my body falling apart. The Awakening was a blessing for me, I can tell you, for only through the endeavours of the Intuitionists has my condition been made bearable.'

'This… this will happen to me?' Lillian asked, feeling somewhat selfish at the question.

'That depends on whether or not the Iscariot Sanction is as potent as de Montfort claimed. If you are a highborn vampire now, then your flesh will necrotise, but you will also undergo other physical transformations over the years. And you will grow stronger too. If you are lucky, you might even glean some of those Majestic skills as evinced by the likes of de Montfort.'

'Lucky?' Lillian thought of Arthur. He had never seemed particularly blessed by his so-called gifts.

'It does not come to us all,' Cherleten explained. 'A pity, for the ability to control the vampires' servants would be rather useful, don't you think?'

'You said there would be… other transformations?'

'Yes. The more immediate ones, whether you are of the Blood Royal or of both human and vampire parentage, like me— are rather unpleasant, I am afraid. You have already started to be inured to physical pain; eventually you shall feel none whatsoever. That in itself can have a strange effect on the mind— the loss of physical sensation almost always accompanies a loss of empathy. For one such as I, who has never truly known the finer feelings of the human species… it is hard to comprehend. I imagine it will cause you some distress, until you lose the ability to feel even that, of course.'

'Go on,' Lillian said.

'I am afraid, my dear, that your hair shall fall out, and then your teeth.'

'My teeth?' Lillian was aghast.

'They are an inefficient means of extracting blood. Highborns of great age invariably develop interesting new mechanisms for feeding, although they have rarely been seen, and certainly never studied. Think of it much like a child shedding its milk teeth and growing a stronger set.'

'I do not want to think of it at all,' Lillian said, stubbing out her cigarette. She did think of it, though.

'I'm am afraid you must. When it happens, we shall of course provide you with a set of false teeth, like mine.' He tapped his front teeth proudly. 'You'd never tell the difference. But for the purposes of feeding, well...'

'Feeding? Is there no other way? I mean, must I...'

'My dear, you have never stopped. I am sorry to break this to you so indelicately, but while you have been sleeping we have been transfusing you with blood. It is the only reason you are not flying about trying to kill my staff.'

Lillian gripped the desk, for fear she might faint.

'I would rather die than drink blood,' she said.

'And die you would; but your body will not allow it. If you do not feed, you will lose yourself in a frenzy until your thirst is sated. Go long enough without blood, and you would become one of those pale-skinned hunters you despise so much—halfway between highborn and the mindless ghouls that follow them. It is a fate that awaits us all, if the proper precautions are not taken.'

Lillian held her head. Her brain had started to pound in her skull.

'Eventually, you will learn to control your thirst. We shall provide you with needles, much like a Majestic might use etherium. Or you could do what the Knights Iscariot do, although it is a little... crude.'

'What is it?'

'They use a feeding tube. I rather fear you may have seen

one first hand. It attaches inside their mouths by means of small metal clamps, and the other end is affixed to the vein of their victim. The vampire—or a servant, more usually—pumps the blood directly through the tube, into their master's throat. A human can be completely drained in minutes—the capacity of the vampire to consume blood is really quite extraordinary...'

She thought of the vampire woman on the royal train, who had used such a device to so rapidly drain the prince's valet of blood before her very eyes.

'I am going to be sick,' she said.

'I am afraid that is quite impossible. There is nothing inside you, you see. You have not eaten—although there is nothing stopping you from doing so if you desire. Only, you are losing the capacity to enjoy food and drink, and hunger for nothing but blood. And blood is absorbed by the vampire physiognomy so completely as to be miraculous. It invigorates and nourishes, until it is used up, and dissolves to nothingness. When that happens, we grow weak, and must feed again. The younger the vampire, the more frequently they must sate this hunger. Hence we have transfused you daily, although the frequency will lessen soon enough.'

'Must it be human blood?'

'No, not for the purposes of mere sustenance. But human blood, for reasons unknown to us, is the only kind that truly sates the hunger, and imbues us with our vitality. I suppose we must be related species after all, for Smythe calls our blood "compatible".'

'And you? You drink... blood.'

'I have, and may do again, as necessity dictates, although I must stress that there is no need for either of us to kill for it. With the imbibing of blood comes the greatest pleasure a vampire can experience—the *only* true pleasure. But it is a base and primitive sensation, one that we can rise above, should we desire. What separates me—and, I hope, you—from the Knights Iscariot is that very desire; the wish to embrace our human nature, rather than our inhuman one. The wish to live in society, and not in the shadows.'

'But de Montfort seeks to bring the Knights Iscariot out of the shadows, to create his own society.'

'And he will fail, because there is no world in which human and vampire can exist peacefully. The Knights Iscariot themselves might say it is the wolf lying down with the lamb. I myself think it is the wolf and the lion, for both species are bloodthirsty, and would kill the other given the chance.'

'One is far stronger than the other,' Lillian said.

'And the other is more numerous, and just as cunning. But answer me this, Agent Hardwick—which are you?'

'Wolf or lion? Or human or vampire?'

Cherleten only smiled.

'I barely understand my own mind,' she said, deciding that honesty was the best policy. 'I hate de Montfort. I hold on to that hate as I hold on to my own self. But do I feel kinship with my fellow man? In just a short space of time, I feel I have lost all ties to my former life. I remember my mother and father, my brother... I feel loyalty to them still. But do I love them? I do not think I can love any more, Lord Cherleten. And even that terrible, desolate realisation stirs nothing within me.'

'Loyalty is a fine start,' said Cherleten. 'It has kept me in the light, and from the darkness, though I have often trod a fine line, I confess, and a solitary one, too. I am not a good man, Agent Hardwick, but I am a loyal one. You will find, as I have, that our kind is predisposed towards meanness of spirit and even downright cruelty, but we are not incapable of free thought. The Knights Iscariot *choose* murder, chaos, and treason, just as I choose to oppose it.

'I can offer you scant reassurance right now. But I tell you this: if hate is the only thing we can feel, and I believe you are right, at least for now, then you should well hold it tight. It is your talisman. You are still Lillian Hardwick; but you are defined now by what you are not, rather than by what you are.'

'But you have been defined by what you are. Had you not been born the heir to a fortune... what would Lord Cherleten be then?

Cherleten appeared amused at Lillian's audacity. 'That is a

question, isn't it? One that we need never know the answer to.'

Lillian thought of the pallid, bestial monsters, stooped and clawed, that fed on the flesh of the deceased. Beneath Cherleten's mask of rank and title and gentility, beneath the arsenic powder and formaldehyde, the red-haired wig, the teeth made of ivory... was he fending off degeneracy of the most heinous kind?

'Are you still loyal to the Order, Agent Hardwick?' Cherleten asked.

'I am. Or, at least, I would rather be, than the alternative.'

'That is good enough. For now.'

'Good enough for what?'

'To begin your training. You must learn to use your new abilities to your advantage. Your heightened senses, your strength and speed.'

'I do not feel stronger,' Lillian said.

'But you are, relatively speaking. Your muscles do not feel fatigue like a human's, and therefore you can perform feats beyond your normal endurance. To push too hard, however, is to do yourself an injury, although even that will heal rapidly enough. A gunshot or blade in a vital area will put you down, and hurt like bally-ho, but you will recover in time from most wounds. Just try not to get shot in the head or decapitated. Even those wretched ghouls can't come back from that.

'You have not had the opportunity to put yourself to any test as yet, but believe me, you will be surprised. Though you are not physically faster than you were, your reactions will make you appear so. You can see danger coming almost before it happens, and avoid it accordingly.'

'I have seen the monsters dash out of the way of a bullet,' Lillian mused.

'Because they saw and heard your finger tighten on the trigger, and began to move even before your shot fired. You will do this too, with time and training.'

'How much time will I need? How much longer must I spend here?'

'It has been decreed that, for as long as Prince Leopold is in the hands of the enemy, we cannot take any unnecessary risks.'

Lillian narrowed her eyes. 'You mean, by releasing me, you may be unleashing a traitor into your midst.'

'I did not say that.'

'You did not have to, Lord Cherleten. And who issued this decree? You?'

'If you must know, it was your father.'

Anger grew inside Lillian again. It was good to feel something, she realised, even if it was rage.

'Even now, he shepherds the Queen to safety,' Cherleten went on. 'We cannot know if the Knights Iscariot view the breakdown of negotiations as our fault—and therefore a declaration of war—or whether they planned the prince's kidnap from the start. Either way, I doubt very much there will be an end to this matter any time soon. And in that time, you must remain here, although I am sure we can open up more of the facility for your use, so that you are not so confined. Trust me, my dear, I—'

A low rumbling noise gave Cherleten pause. The electrical light hanging from the ceiling flickered, its chain jangling as it swayed gently. Outside the office, footsteps thudded.

'Forgive me, Agent Hardwick, I must attend to this,' Cherleten said, standing.

Before he had even reached the door, a great, thudding boom sounded from somewhere above their heads, deafeningly loud. The room shook violently. One of the nurses on the ward screamed. Plaster dust fell from the ceiling. The light flickered twice more, and then went out, leaving only a paraffin lamp burning upon the desk.

Cherleten flung open the office door, and Lillian followed him out into the ward, which had been plunged into near-darkness. Staff raced for the doors in panic, while three guards supervised their evacuation.

'You,' shouted Cherleten to the nearest guard. 'Get them out of here!' He indicated the Nightwatch, one male, one female, strapped to their invalid chairs and attached to strange, etheric machinery. They were too valuable to risk in the event of the armoury being compromised. Lillian wondered if the same could be said of her. Her question was quickly answered.

'You two,' Cherleten said to the remaining guards, 'lock the doors behind us. No one comes in or out without my order, do you understand?' He turned at once to Lillian. 'I am sorry, Agent Hardwick. I trust you shall be comfortable until I return.'

'You cannot leave me here!' Lillian snapped. 'What is happening?'

'I do not know, but I mean to find out. Have no fear, this facility has never been compromised, nor do I imagine it shall be now.'

EIGHTEEN

De Montfort stood for the longest time with his forehead pressed against the cold stone, his hands before him, fingertips tracing the outline of ancient, weathered carvings. He breathed deeply, filling his nostrils with the smell of mildew and saltwater.

'My lord? That is the last of it.' The human serf shifted uneasily. De Montfort did not deign to look at him.

An uneasy silence passed for a while, until finally Lucien de Montfort pushed himself away from the stone and opened his eyes. He held out a hand, and an attendant passed him his hat, gloves and cane. As he donned them, he at last turned to the serf. The man was grubby-faced and nervous. De Montfort preferred to use only imbeciles for tasks of such secrecy, but in this instance the duty was far too important to risk any failure. He had to rely instead on old-fashioned terror to persuade the humans to serve him, and this man—Mosby—was certainly terrified.

'I expect this shipment to be at my estate by morning,' he said.

The man nodded with exaggerated enthusiasm. 'It will, my lord, you can trust me.'

'I am a man of my word, Mr. Mosby. Your wife will be waiting for you when the shipment is delivered.'

'Thank you, sir. Bless you, sir.'

'Go,' de Montfort said, turning back to face the stone, waving a dismissive hand at the man. He heard his cousins hiss as they parted for Mosby, and Mosby's fearful murmuring as he hurried from the graveyard.

'Brave Ezekiel, first among the cadre,' de Montfort said, and at once a black-clad hunter moved silently to his side, awaiting his command. De Montfort placed a hand upon the hunter's shoulder. 'I would entrust this task to none other, Ezekiel. See to it that Mosby arrives at Montfort Hall unmolested. With the blood that he carries, the Artist's predictions will surely come to pass, and nothing must jeopardise that.'

The hunter bowed, a low croak emitting from the back of its throat.

'Oh,' de Montfort added, 'and you may take Mosby as payment. But he has done us a great service, so make it quick.'

The hunter's eyes flashed, and it slipped away, gliding through tendrils of low-hanging mist, with four of de Montfort's ghouls trailing behind it. Before long, the heavily laden wagon was clattering away down the narrow cliff-side lane, its monstrous escort alongside it, leaving de Montfort with his last three hunters, standing sentinel amongst the crumbling headstones as waves crashed far beneath them.

De Montfort delayed pulling on his second glove, instead reaching out to touch the stone once more. Almost as if responding to his presence, a chorus of muffled, agonised cries came from deep within the crypt.

'O, I see the crescent promise of my spirit hath not set. Ancient founts of inspiration well thro' all my fancy yet.' De Montfort smiled to himself. He looked to his loyal hunters and said, 'Entombed within these walls are those who would call themselves gods. And yet all that they are, all that they ever were, I have taken from them with science. They have nothing; they will die a slow death, in a tomb fit for a Nazarene. And with the blood of the ancients, the blood gifted to them by Judas Iscariot himself, we shall replace them. We shall not waste this gift as they did. We shall become gods worthy of the name. I could not have done this without you, my brothers. For your loyalty, my first decree as king shall be to raise you up, to restore to you that which was taken at birth by a cruel father. Soon your voices shall be heard, your will shall have meaning, and your vengeance shall be granted!'

De Montfort's voice carried upon the wind, raising against the waves that thundered far below the craggy hilltop upon which he had entombed his enemies. No, not enemies—aloof, capricious *wampyr*, impossibly ancient, who had not even been aware of his existence until he had come for them, one by one. With such a quantity of highborn blood at his disposal, his plan was almost at its fruition, but for a few more experiments. Only then could he challenge the Nameless King.

His brothers, the hunters, chattered in their guttural clicks and croaks. De Montfort was uncertain whether he could truly lift the curse of their blood, but he would try, as he had promised. He would be as good as his word, for what was a gentleman without honour? He thought of Mosby's wife, already dead at Montfort Hall. He had said she would be waiting for him, and so she would, albeit in a casket.

'Come, ready the carriage,' de Montfort said, pulling on his gloves and leaving the wails of the elders to fade behind him. 'We have a long way yet to go.'

Lillian paced the length of the dark ward for the umpteenth time. At least she had her clothes, and no longer felt the cold. It would have been a rum business if she had been her old, warm-blooded self, stuck in an empty hospital ward with only a nightgown for comfort. She checked her thoughts and laughed ruefully at the darkness. It was not in her nature, then or now, to play the optimist.

She wondered what to do with herself. There had been not a sound since the rumble, which she felt sure had been either an explosion or an earthquake. There was only one way out of the ward, and that was through the locked and barred doors, and past the armed guards on the other side. It seemed delusory at best to start reading or attending to needlework while a battle perhaps raged above her head. A battle so close that she feared for John. And so she resumed her pacing, feeling that at least she would be prepared to answer the call to action should such a call come.

She stopped at the sound of two muffled cracks, almost certainly gunshots. .38s, if she were any judge. They had come from beyond the main doors, though at what distance she could not tell, for the doors were reinforced and sounds from without were always indistinct.

Lillian spun on her heel and moved swiftly and silently towards the door. She had long ago learned to move with great stealth even in boots, though now she surprised herself with her almost feline grace.

As she pressed her back against the wall next to the door, hiding in the deepest shadows, there came a soft click, and the door swung inwards. No light flooded into the ward; there was but pitch darkness in the corridor beyond, and utter silence. Some sixth sense took hold of Lillian, warning her not to call out. She felt sure that it was not the guards come to check on her. The prickling at the back of her neck told her that the armoury was indeed compromised, despite Cherleten's assertions.

A thin man entered, clad in black much like the agents of Apollo Lycea. The gleam of his bald, white head, however, with its map of blue tributary veins, betrayed his nature. The hunter sniffed the air, and stepped fully into the ward, noiselessly, its motions fluid. Lillian did not hesitate.

She flew from her hiding place, right hand outstretched like a talon, aiming for the creature's throat. It was instinctive, and she yielded to that instinct. The creature was quick, and flinched away at the last moment, so that Lillian's fingernails rent only shallow trails in its neck.

An arm, hard as iron, folded around Lillian's neck, and wrenched her with great force towards the door. She jolted her head back into the creature's face, and as its grip slackened she drove her left elbow after it, smashing into its nose. The creature released her, but did not so much as make a sound to show its discomfort, which enraged Lillian still further. She spun and grabbed its arm, avoiding a clumsy strike as she twisted and wrenched it around, controlling her opponent's momentum as she had learned in the dojo. She heard a satisfying crack as its shoulder dislocated, and she slammed it head-first into the wall. She had been utterly focused on her enemy, but now her ears pricked as a low, avian trill echoed through the otherwise silent facility. Only then did she look into the dark corridor.

At least six pairs of violet eyes gleamed in the darkness, moving closer.

Lillian threw the slumped form of the hunter down and slammed the doors shut, throwing herself against them. But they burst it open and Lillian was tossed bodily across the tiles, the skittering of claws behind her.

She was carried away upon a tide of pallid flesh, bony fingers digging into her, claws scraping at her cold skin. She struggled, but there were too many, their hold upon her too strong. She was pulled upwards and spun around in the darkness, head wrenched back to look into the ward behind her. From the shadows at the door, the form of the hunter she had fought coalesced like an apparition stalking from fog, sliding from a black heap upon the floor until it assumed its full height, a wet popping sound accompanying the jerk of its arm as it clicked it back into position. Its eyes opened, and gleamed with malevolence.

Six ghouls, half-naked, malformed things, now carried Lillian aloft like pallbearers. The hunter came forward until its ugly face was inches from her own. It could have been one of the very creatures she had encountered upon the moors, one of the creatures that supervised the slaying of Arthur.

Even if she had not rearranged its features during the struggle it would have been impossible to tell.

'You... come... with us,' it whispered, the words coming laboriously, as a rasp deep within its throat, stilted and clicking.

She tried once more to struggle, to free her arms and lash out, but the more she struggled the more the ghouls tightened their grip. In the end, she could only resort to spitting in the hunter's face, and even then it did not so much as blink.

At that moment Lillian became dimly aware of another presence in the corridor; she heard it—smelt it—before she saw it. The hunter felt it too, and began to turn even as Lillian heard the click of a trigger, the revolution of a pistol chamber. She flinched as the report of the gun echoed around the ward; then she was dropped unceremoniously into the tangled midst of the ghouls as the hunter's skull opened up.

Another shot winged one of the monsters, and the ghouls scurried for the shadows, their courage failing now that their overseer was no longer directing them.

Lord Cherleten hoisted Lillian to her feet and pressed a gun into her hand.

'More will come,' he said, through ragged breaths. 'Clear this area first. Leave none alive.'

Lillian needed no further invitation. Her keen eyes alerted her to every movement in the darkness, searching for the tell-tale signs of a dull amber glow around the heads of the ghouls as they scrabbled behind beds and clawed their way up onto the vaulted ceilings. The creatures could react faster than a human, Cherleten had said, but they were not dealing with humans here. The pistols compensated for the enemies' numbers, and the ward quickly became a killing ground.

Only when the last creature had fallen did Cherleten place a hand on Lillian's shoulder.

'Agent Hardwick,' he wheezed, 'we are undone.'

She saw at once that he clutched his stomach, and a pinkish ooze seeped from a grievous wound. His wig had slipped, and his right trouser leg was ragged, as if it had been savaged by a pack of hounds.

'You are hurt,' Lillian said, as Cherleten leaned on her.

'I will heal, which is more than I can say for this country. Or this world.'

'What—'

'Help me to the examination room; over there, quickly.'

Lillian did as she was bid, and only when Cherleten was finally heaved into a chair and began to rifle through boxes of medicines and chemicals did he explain itself.

'They have killed the Queen,' he said. His face was more ashen than usual, his expression one of utter defeat. 'They have detonated an etheric bomb, Agent Hardwick. The destruction is... beyond reason. The Queen is dead: countless others with her.'

'John?'

'I do not know. There were two bombs, one near Whitehall, and one here. They know about this place. They know where you are.'

'I have to get to the club,' Lillian said.

'You will not get near it. Did you hear me? It was an etheric bomb. The veil is thinned, the rifts are opening all over London. By God, I cannot describe what I have seen out there. It is the end.'

'Pull yourself together!' Lillian snapped. 'Where are the weapons? What can I arm myself with? I must fight.'

'I suppose you must, not that it will do any good. We are all going to die, my dear; even the immortals amongst us.' He fished in his pocket for a set of keys, and picked through them to find one in particular, which he detached from the ring. 'Take this. Follow the corridor to the end, turn right, then right again, and go up the stairs ahead of you. You will find an unmarked door, and in it is a weapons locker, where we store our latest acquisitions. Take the Tesla pistols, and whatever else you need. There is etherium ammunition for the Riftborn, but there are too many to fight. Far, far too many...'

'I am going to the club. I am going to find my brother. Will you come?'

'I...' Cherleten looked down at the floor, and then said, quietly, 'There is no point, Agent Hardwick.'

Lillian considered him for a moment in silence. What had he seen that had changed this cock-sure, near-immortal old blatherskite into a broken and wretched figure? She guessed she would soon find out.

'Very well, Lord Cherleten. Stay here, and lock the doors behind me. Perhaps I shall see you in the next life.'

She stepped back into the dark ward, littered with the bodies of the vampires, and made her way out along the dark corridor beyond. If Lord Cherleten spoke again, she did not hear him.

John staggered to his feet with no small effort, dust and broken glass falling from him as he steadied himself. He barely comprehended at first why there was a gale blowing into the club's normally cosy smoking room, but as he blinked brick-dust from his eyes and shook his head to clear it of the muzzy sensation, he understood all too well.

He faced out towards the window that overlooked Pall Mall, only there was no window any longer, and no wall either. With the explosion, a great rent had been opened up in the side of the building, exposing crumbling brick and burning timbers. An unnaturally fierce wind swept into the building, almost knocking John from his feet, and he braced himself against it, shielding his eyes with his hand. All he could see was fire and smoke; the venerable old clubhouses across the road were ablaze, mirroring the burning sky above them. He heard screams.

Father.

Lord Hardwick had left only moments earlier as part of the Queen's escort, taking the road from St. James's Palace. He could not have avoided the blast. John turned to flee the room, pausing as he noticed for the first time the bodies lying about him, the bodies of friends and colleagues. The sight made him check his progress for a moment, to ensure he was armed. Feeling his pistol still at his breast, he swore a silent oath to avenge those who had fallen to a coward's bomb—after he had found his father.

John stumbled along a corridor littered with rubble, portraits by English masters lying in tatters on the floor, crystal chandeliers reduced to a million glittering fragments. At the end of the corridor John saw over the balcony to the great hall, now half-buried beneath rubble. Agents, clubmen and servants groaned in pain, or helped the fallen, or lay dead.

'John!'

John turned to see Beauchamp Smythe emerging from the library, with Sir Toby leaning heavily upon him. John quickly took up a position on the other side of the old judge, and helped him to a nearby chair.

'Do not worry about me, agents,' groaned Sir Toby. 'There are far more important matters.'

'My father...' John said.

'Yes, and the Queen. And Nikola Tesla... and your sister.'

'Lillian?' John's head swam; he still did not understand what was happening.

'John,' said Sir Toby gravely, 'listen to me very carefully. The Knights Iscariot seek to unleash anarchy upon us. They have detonated an etheric bomb, the effects of which are entirely unpredictable. Our responsibility first and foremost is to the Crown—we must protect the Queen. But your father's work with Tesla... that is of near-equal import. Without Tesla, there may be no way back from this catastrophe.'

'What... I do not understand.'

'An etheric bomb, Agent Hardwick. It has the power to tear the fabric of reality, as well as destroy half of London. What it could do to the Majestics in this city...'

'And Lillian?' John was trying hard to remain focused.

'She is the very reason for the attack,' said Sir Toby. 'They will weaken us, and then use your sister to show the world what they can do. She cannot fall into their hands.'

'Where is Tesla?' John asked.

'Underground, in the armoury,' said Sir Toby. 'If the bomb has not compromised the basements, then he should be safe.'

'But if it has…'

Sir Toby only nodded. Blood ran down his forehead. His hands shook, but the steel in his eyes remained.

John took heart from that, and turned to Smythe. 'There are not very many of us active, Smythe. Are you hurt?'

'No, though lord knows how or why,' Smythe replied.

'Then may I ask you to find Tesla while I look for my father?'

'Of course.'

'And when you find our Serbian friend, ask him where he keeps those fancy pistols of his. I have a feeling we may need them.'

NINETEEN

The air itself screamed hot and angry.

The Riftborn tore through the streets outside St. Katharine Docks, bestial and monstrous, their keening howls sending terrified citizens into fits of madness. Incorporeal claws ripped through human flesh; honeyed whispers from a realm beyond the real echoed in the heads of simple folk, driving them to acts of cowardice, or rage, or barbarism against themselves and others of a kind undreamt of for a thousand years.

Lillian had only ever half-seen the creatures before, as well as any man or woman could, and only after careful and taxing training. The Riftborn were not real—they were denizens of another universe, tearing violently through the veil, only truly existing when they shattered the sanity of the beholder, and revealed themselves through madness. These days, everyone was a little mad, or else touched by strange phenomena, and so the demons ran riot. Sometimes they appeared as man-sized, gangrel creatures, with a form that rippled as though made of quicksilver, reflecting the fire in the sky. Yet, in viewing them from another angle one might suddenly behold them as towering, many-limbed beasts of pulsating flesh, standing taller than St. Paul's and at the same time occupying no more space than a mouse. Other times they were hollow, little more than holes in reality that fluttered like flags in a breeze, and through which the very pits of hell could be seen. When confronted by the multitudinous complexity of the Riftborns' existence, most men went mad.

Lillian was not, of course, a man. And no more was she human.

Through violet eyes—dead eyes—she saw the Riftborn for what they were. No, not what they were, but what they *should* be. Gibbering beasts, fairytale horrors with bodies made in the mockery of men, long-limbed, filthily rutting in streets that blazed with liquid fire wherever they trod. Their flesh was translucent, and the blood in their veins coursed red and purple, glittering like a million stars pushed into an arterial space. Great yellow eyes flashed with fiery brilliance; horned heads turned upwards as the monsters called to the skies, where dark, flapping beasts spiralled like ragged gulls in the flaming air.

Above them a high-pitched whining sound intensified, screaming fever-pitch in Lillian's ears. And it emanated from the shadow; great tendrils, taller and fatter than any structure ever seen on any skyline in the world writhed and clawed from beyond the veil. The sound was maddening. Lillian could see it all around—men and women tearing at their own eyes and ears, their faces bloodied masks, their fingernails echoing the scratching inside their heads as the tendrils plucked at the edge of the atmosphere.

Lillian saw the shadowy tendrils pulsate with energy. She knew at once that the humans around her could not see the thing as she could. Her vampire eyes brought focus; she saw it as it was meant to be seen, and yet she did not go mad. Or perhaps, she reasoned, she had merely persuaded herself that she was sane, as all lunatics must be wont to do.

As she gazed upon the chaos, she felt her skin tingle as if with a static charge, and looked about herself at once, her newly enhanced senses thrown into focus. The Riftborn had seen her; truly seen her. The demon stood stock-still as its warped brethren continued their wave of murder. It stared at her with blazing, saucer-like eyes, and she stared back at it and, despite herself, smiled her most wicked, barbed smile.

'What is the matter, demon? Have you never seen a dead woman with a gun before?'

The beast roared, drawing itself to a dizzying height and a miniscule bullet of fire all at the same time, igniting the ground beneath its floating, ever-changing form. Its flesh blazed hot, transforming into a skin of lava, and then it swept towards Lillian, its rage so powerful, so all-encompassing, that even Lillian felt it inhabiting her, rising within her to such heights that it became elation.

'Thank you for that,' she whispered, giving herself over to the feeling entirely for just a moment, before raising the pistol with preternatural speed, and pulling the trigger.

As Tesla had described, the electrical charge within the weapon coursed through the little etheric cartridge, evaporating the brownish liquid in a heartbeat, and projecting a bolt of blue lightning outwards from the barrel with incredible force. Lillian felt the exhilaration wash over her as the demon was enveloped in tendrils of arcing electricity. She felt its pain; she felt its utter joy at feeling such pain, elation that it was dying. She was sure her human self could never have understood such conflicting emotions, but her vampire self drank it in as hungrily as blood. The creature lashed out in its death throes, and Lillian danced away from its flailing tendrils. In the creature's final second it was reduced to a pile of blackened slag and steaming rock, which in turn popped out of existence in a fizzing bubble of heat, leaving nothing but shimmering air and the smell of brimstone. A wave of emptiness and despair exploded from the point of its banishment, followed by an absolute joy as, somewhere in some other time and place, the creature was reborn. Lillian felt these things—knowledge and energy and raw emotion from the Rift—crash against her like a cold wave crashing against a yacht.

Even as she shuddered with the pleasure of the kill, she felt other eyes upon her. Hungry, demonic eyes. She felt tears on her cheek. She heard herself laughing giddily as the creatures advanced. She realised she had already reloaded the Tesla pistol, ready for the next attack.

If Lillian were truly dead, then why did she feel so alive?

John put his hands to his ears to stop the scratching sound that almost deafened him, but it did not cease. The sound—the sensation—was inside his head, like long fingernails scraping across a writing-slate. Madness was all around him; people wailed and screamed, from injuries sustained in the blast, and from those they had inflicted upon themselves. Venerable old clubmen frolicked naked in the streets, running through flames and setting upon each other with knives and bare hands, or disfiguring themselves while screeching in unintelligible languages. Starry rifts hung shimmering in the air, denizens of another world seeping through, invisible beyond the mind's eye, but horrifying to those who dared concentrate upon them. The fire in the sky burned brighter and hotter than ever before, great streaks of lavender cloud roiling beneath a blast-furnace of liquid fire.

Ahead, John glimpsed the royal carriage half-buried beneath debris, burning with unnatural flame. It shifted in and out of focus; sometimes he could see his father's body, broken and burned, lying amongst the corpses of liveried footmen. In another instant, the scene of death and destruction was obscured by a dark shadow, as swaddling as a London particular. The shadow projected into the sky, to dizzying heights, sometimes invisible, at other times taking the form of a cyclopean, many-tentacled beast, redolent with insanity and malevolence. Like a rainbow, the phenomenon was at once near and far; John thought he was within the belly of the beast, and then in the next instant it seemed very far away.

Somehow, through the deafening noise that was, in part, created by his own involuntary screams, he knew the source of the shadowy thing. It had come from the carriage.

John did not know how he had reached the upended royal coach, or when, but he found himself digging through the rubble. His father was dead, his face already ashen, lips blue. Beside him was Kate Fox, the noted medium, the progenitor of the Awakening and all the terrors that had followed it. Her face was contorted in such an expression of horror that it was terrible to behold. Her head was spun right around, facing backwards—facing the sky. Shadows leaked from her, drifting upwards like smoke. The shadow on the sky had come from her. John knew, though he could not explain how he knew, that the Fox woman had been holding back this terrible thing alone since her sister had died. John had been too young to be aware of it at the time, but the story of the famous Fox sisters was taught to every new recruit at the academy. Margaret Fox had been assassinated in New York by a group of conspirators claiming affiliation with the Latter Day Saints. Her death had unleashed psychic devastation across America, causing half of Manhattan to fall into the sea. Kate Fox had fled to England, becoming a political exile. With her as a bargaining tool, the government had restored British interests in the recently formed Confederate States. The Knights Iscariot, in slaying Kate Fox, had unleashed something more terrible upon the world than they could have dreamt of. If ever Lord Hardwick had needed to succeed in his great plan, the escape plan John had once heard him speaking of, it was now. But Lord Hardwick was dead.

John fell to his knees and wept. His father—tyrant, and would-be saviour—was gone. A few yards from Marcus Hardwick's body, protruding from a mound of bricks and ashes like a sapling from dirt, was a hand, festooned with jewelled rings.

Queen Victoria was dead.

Kate Fox, Lord Marcus Hardwick and the Queen. All claimed by the vampires' bomb. And with their deaths, John felt a desolation such that he had never felt in all the years since the Riftborn had first made ingress into the world. He felt the death of hope.

He knelt within that terrible shadow, with that wailing in his ears, in his head, for how long he could not say. Someone, far away, was shouting his name, and he could not answer, so complete was his numbness.

'John! For heaven's sake get away from there!'

A hand grabbed John's shoulder, and eventually he felt himself being dragged away from the body of his father. John realised he was kicking and screaming in resistance, until at last a hand slapped him hard across the face. He saw Smythe standing over him, and he stared at the surgeon dumbly.

John watched, childlike and passive, as Smythe rolled up the sleeve of his jacket and administered an injection into the vein at the crook of his left elbow. John was puzzled at first, and then felt a cold tingling sensation sweep over him, travelling up his arm and through his body with remarkable speed, until his brain felt it might freeze in his head. He gasped for air, and then came to his senses at last, though his head swam.

'What...' he stuttered.

'Had to think on my feet, old fellow, with a bit of help from the Serbian. Morphine, mundane etherium—a few other things it's best not to think about. You'll feel wretched in the morning; we all shall. If we see the morning.'

Smythe helped John up. The voices in his head became whispers of unfulfilled promises. The scratching in his skull lessened to a distant itch.

'Mundane etherium?' John asked. It had never had any effect on a normal human, as far as he knew. Its source was a closely guarded secret, although the rumours of its origins were ghastly to say the least. Ghastly enough to make him baulk at the thought of having it inside him.

Smythe shrugged. 'Worth a try. It seems to work, too.'

John looked about, and his heart sank. The streets were in chaos. Now that he was able to focus, John saw... things... slip in and out of reality, occupying spaces that they should not. The Riftborn cavorted through the streets, creatures of shadow and fire, driving men to commit foul atrocities in their name, or flaying the weak themselves with scissor-like claws. The shadow was present too, though now it came only sometimes into view, when John looked upon it askance. It avoided his scrutiny, but it was always there, in his mind's eye. John shuddered. His eyes alighted once more upon the sundered carriage, and he stepped backwards, stumbling weakly as Smythe helped to steady him.

'We have to get out of here,' Smythe said. 'The drug will protect us, but I don't know for how long. They feed off fear and madness. Look to your training, John. Don't let your grief make you weak. Close your mind, and hold on to something stronger.'

'Hold on to what?' John said. He was consumed by grief, and felt very weak indeed.

'Anger,' Smythe said. 'Here, take this.' He handed John a Tesla pistol, and a brown leather belt stuffed with etherium capsules. 'There's not much of this stuff, so use it wisely. Now, are you ready?'

'I am,' John said, surprising himself with the determination in his voice, although he had never felt more timid.

'St. Katharine Docks?'

John only nodded, and climbed down the mound of debris that had become his father's grave.

The ground beneath Lillian's feet began to tremble. Great chunks of masonry fell to earth, smashing into the pavements of Smithfield, crushing many who had been driven to inhuman revelry in the streets by the madness of the cyclopean shadow. A sound like thunder came from the south, accompanied by the crash of waves as though the ocean itself were lapping at London's door. Lillian wondered if things could get any worse.

The Riftborn turned from her, flowed around her like water, as though she were anathema to them. It was human souls they craved. She moved quickly through the ruins of her city, jumping over chasms as they opened in the earth. The sky was redder, brighter than ever before. She looked ahead, to the west, to her destination. She had to shield her eyes from the roiling elements; those same senses that allowed her to tell human from vampire, and to see the Riftborn for what they were, now pained her as she tried to get her bearings. The sky was both dark and bright to her inhuman eyes, dazzling in its horror. Squawking, flapping night-terrors danced amidst the flames above the Tower of London on leathery wings, paying balletic tribute to the clawed shadow that seemed to tear upwards from the heart of the City like a kraken, leaving desolation in its wake.

Ahead of her, watching her laboured progress through the hellish streets, were three dark figures. She knew them for what they were. Even had the faint corona of amber light not shone from them, their violet eyes glimmered like stars as they fixed her with malevolent intent.

Come with us.

It was a whisper, it sounded somewhere deep in her head. In her blood.

Lillian ejected the unused etheric cartridge from her pistol, and cranked the generator handle.

The central figure remained stock-still, but the two that flanked it swept forward. They were single-minded in their approach, moving swiftly, low to the ground, like hunting hounds. Lillian stopped dead; she would only have time for one shot with the Tesla pistol, but it was not the only weapon she had taken from the stores.

They arrived almost simultaneously. Lillian was still until the last possible moment, for the creatures were as capable as she of dodging bullets. Only when they were almost upon her did she throw herself sideways, beneath the grasping, clawed hands of the first hunter, and away from the second. She slid across the broken ground, her jodhpurs tearing, but she managed to spin around to face her attackers, who were already converging upon her. Now they were together, lined up for the shot. She pulled the trigger.

As the blue light flared from the pistol, and the air fizzed hot and bright, the first hunter leapt away, shielding its eyes from the blinding flash. The second, its view impaired by its fellow, was struck with the full force of the lightning. A gargled, inhuman scream carried over the sound of crackling energy, and the creature's charred, twitching form was thrown backwards, falling into a chasm that had split the road in twain. The first hunter recovered and pounced before Lillian had gotten to her feet, while she was still fumbling at her belt for another weapon. She felt hands close around her arms for but a moment, and then was thrown bodily towards the yawning crevasse. She hit the cobblestones hard, and with dismay saw the Tesla pistol slide into the dark abyss.

From the corner of her eye, Lillian saw the ragged, crow-black form of the hunter leap towards her. Her hand gripped the hilt of the large knife she had procured, and she paused as though injured, masking the blade. She felt the change in the air as the hunter drew near, smelled its deathly odour. It landed lightly, silently, beside her, and rough, clawed hands grabbed at her. A gargling, avian click came from its throat, was answered in kind by the third hunter, who had maintained its aloof distance.

The creature's arms, sinewy and strong, lifted her up as though she weighed nothing, and in that instant Lillian swept the knife outwards, towards its throat. It was a large blade, a Bowie knife from the Confederate States, and its gleaming edge flashed towards the target. The hunter's reactions were startlingly quick, and it flinched back, although the knife must have been longer than it expected, for the tip of the blade still cut a furrow in its pale, wasted flesh. Pink blood oozed thickly from the wound. The vampire did not falter, but clawed at her wrist in an attempt to rip the knife from her hand. Lillian was ready, her own strength formidable, her academy combat training telling. She parried its flailing claws and it lunged forwards, but Lillian sidestepped nimbly, slashing across its ribs. Strike, parry, riposte; the hunter's attacks were lightning-fast, but it was savage, its style crude. Lillian doubted it had ever fought an opponent who was not only its rival in strength and speed, but also clinical and well drilled.

The hunter was strong. Perhaps, as Cherleten had intimated, it had lived for an extraordinarily long time, and grown more powerful with age. In any case, when its blows did land, they jarred Lillian to the bone. A clubbing right hand had her seeing stars, but again she recovered and spun about on her heel, throwing the hunter off-balance and sending it flailing. This time, she drove straight with the knife, thrusting it between the hunter's shoulder blades. It thrashed and spun so wildly that the knife was wrenched from Lillian's grasp. It reached futilely for the handle, but it was buried too deep.

Lillian rushed at the creature and pushed it with all her might towards the yawning precipice that ran across Upper East Smithfield, and was already now breaching the formidable brown-brick walls of the Royal Mint.

The hunter did not fall. It teetered upon the brink, balancing precariously with supernatural grace, and then turned, grabbing Lillian by the hair and pulling her with it.

For a moment Lillian felt weightless, hanging in space, gazing down into an abyss. Below them, the crack in the earth seemed to extend impossibly far, into a black void punctuated by starlight. But those points of light were not stars; they were eyes. Riftborn, in their thousands, climbing upwards from the bowels of the earth, from Hell itself.

Lillian reached out in desperation, her hand finding purchase upon a cobblestone, her body slamming hard into the ground. She cried out as the hunter's weight yanked her hair so hard she thought her neck might break. She felt the claws scrabble at her jacket as it pulled itself up. The guttural cry of its leader rose in pitch and volume. It was angry; its fellow-creature was risking the life of their prize. Lillian understood, and even as she felt the hard fingernails digging into her back, she knew that she was not expendable, that these creatures had been sent to kidnap her. The thing scrabbling at her, hanging from her as a dead weight, was trying to save itself at her expense, and that clearly was not part of the plan. So the hunters were not, after all, mindless fiends, but could fear for their lives. She could use that.

She was losing purchase on the cobblestones. The creature's arm was around her throat now as it climbed, pushing down on her as it dragged itself up. And then a shadow stood over them both: the third hunter. It grabbed Lillian's hand, lifting her out of the pit with the other hunter still holding onto her. With its other hand, the lead hunter swatted aside its subordinate, causing it to relinquish its grip on Lillian. Lillian snatched the hilt of the Bowie knife, which slid from the vampire's back as it fell screaming into the abyss.

Lillian struck at her rescuer before the monster had time to restrain her. The blade bit into necrotic flesh, between the ribs. The hunter snarled and twisted away with such force that the blade snapped, leaving Lillian holding the hilt. She threw it down, ducking forwards to avoid flailing claws, drawing a .22 pistol from her boot-holster in one fluid motion.

She fired twice without aiming, hitting only shadows. The hunter fled, its wound not slowing it one jot. Lillian felt her heart beating hard for the first time since her transformation.

'Lillian!'

She looked up to see a horse, and upon it her brother, and Smythe. They had pulled up on the other side of another great crack in the road, and even now demonic eyes turned to behold them hungrily.

'Do not let that creature escape!' she shouted.

'Leave it, Lillian, we have to—'

She saw the shadowy figure of the hunter leap a great height through the breached wall of the Royal Mint, and at once gave chase. Her brother would help her or not as he saw fit, but the hunter represented her best chance of tracking down de Montfort, of taking the fight to the enemy, of revenge.

She smiled to herself as she heard the whinny of the horse, and the sound of hooves upon cobblestones as John tried to find another way around. If she were any judge, he would help her regardless of his own agenda, as he always had.

She followed the hunter through the elegant courtyard of the Royal Mint, now awash with blood and filled with panicked screams, and out into the next street. Its footfalls were almost silent, but it moved with unerring speed and unwavering energy. Lillian pursued as fast as she could, surprised that her limbs still did not tire. As she passed through the gate she was forced to dodge aside as a manhole cover exploded upwards from the road ahead upon a jet of incandescent flame. As she turned, she stumbled headlong into a mob of wretched lunatics. A man with jagged shards of glass protruding from his face yanked violently at Lillian's hair; an old woman, an eye hanging from its socket and pendulous breasts exposed, cackled maniacally as she swung a plank of charred wood with glee. Behind them, the press of the mob came on like a tide, invisible Riftborn cavorting amidst their number.

Lillian tore herself away from scrabbling hands, resisting the urge to fire into the crowd that kept her from her target. An elbow to the throat of the nearest assailant bought her breathing space. Lillian spun the old woman about and shoved her back into the crowd, where she set about her comrades with the wooden plank enthusiastically.

The vampire was far ahead now, cutting through a narrow alleyway on to Minories. Lillian lost the hunter somewhere in the growing shadows. She listened for the sound of distant footsteps, but the assault of the Riftborn upon her senses was unrelenting. And then she remembered what the hunters themselves did. She stopped, back to the wall of the dark alley, and sniffed the air.

Her mind sorted the scents upon the breeze faster than she could believe. Sulphur and smoke, the tang of blood, the stale odour of sweat, mould and urine, igniting gas jets... and dead flesh. The faint smell of a long-cold corpse and mortuary chemicals drifted upon the wind, and Lillian knew the hunt was on once more. She trusted to her senses to guide her, and followed her nose.

She caught sight of the shadowy figure again, darting through the churchyard of Holy Trinity Church, through a crowd of wailing petitioners who clamoured for God's mercy. She gained on the hunter, saw it tear around the corner of Minories and Aldgate. She afforded herself a smile as she heard at last the clattering of hooves behind her, and picked up the scent of John's horse upon the air. She did not slow, instead raising her pistol in readiness for the shot, rounding the corner in search of her prey. She saw it, back to the wall, eyes sparkling at her from the darkness. She aimed.

Something struck her hard across the head. She fired the pistol instinctively but hit nothing, and the gun was wrenched from her hand. Claws dug into her shoulders, her legs, her arms. They came from above, naked and scuttling dead things, following the wordless bidding of the hunter. She knew at once that the stench had not been the lone hunter, but a pack of ghouls that had lain in wait for her. She had trusted too fully in the heightened senses that were entirely new to her.

There were too many, their strength too great—Lillian found herself being carried away. Then she heard hoofbeats from somewhere behind her. Shouts, and a gunshot. Several pairs of clawed hands released her. She heard scrabbling on flagstones as the monsters peeled away to face the new threat.

John shouted, but he seemed so very far away.

Another gunshot. A flash of brilliant light and energy that could only be a Tesla pistol. Screams.

Lillian lurched as the creatures dropped her, but was lifted again at once. She heard her brother's voice, loud and ragged.

'Lillian! I'm coming. Don't stop fighting!'

John did not see the hunter, crouching low in the shadows. It burst forth through the crowd of flesh-eaters, marble-white face hanging in darkness for just a moment, before crashing into John with such force that he was swept away from Lillian, out of sight.

There was another flash; more screams. In her daze, she

thought she heard Smythe's voice. Strong arms gripped her once more, sinewy, dead arms. Lillian realised she was being carried downwards—down steep flights of stairs beneath Aldgate Station, into lightless tunnels where warm air hung pregnant with thick, stale smoke. She heard voices calling to her, deep inside her mind.

As Lillian's eyes closed, she wondered if she were going home. She wondered where that was.

TWENTY

SCARROWFALL, YORKSHIRE

John looked about futilely. The room was dark, save for a crack of silver moonlight that shone through a narrow, high window above him, dimly illuminating the far wall. He was lying on a cold floor. The smell of moist earth and stagnant water filled his nostrils.

He crawled up onto his knees and a chain rattled at his right ankle. He tested it gingerly—he was manacled to the wall, and the iron clasp dug painfully into his leg. John shivered; his jacket and shoes had been taken, and wherever he was being held was freezing cold.

He did not remember much after the vampires had attacked him in the alley beside Aldgate Station. He had seen Lillian being carried away; he remembered Smythe fighting his way clear from the savage press of ghouls. He had shouted instructions to his fellow agent, which he only hoped had been heeded, if indeed Smythe had survived the attack—his salvation rested upon it, for no one but Smythe would even know where to look for him. Beyond that, John was not sure; he seemed to recall a train journey, sleeping on a hard floor among a pile of slumbering, pale-skinned monsters; salt spray upon his face during a journey by boat...

He could not be certain if these were dreams or memories. His head throbbed, and he touched the back of his skull, withdrawing his fingers when he felt his matted hair, and a flash of pain brought stars before his eyes.

John took a deep breath. He needed to think clearly if he was to escape this cell—and escape he would. He patted his hands across the creases of his trousers, wincing as he touched bruises that he had not realised were there. Eventually he felt the thin lumps of concealed picks and pins, and began to roll up his trouser leg to get at them.

Something moved in the darkness. A soft rustling at first, then a slow, heavy dragging sound of hard skin or leather rasping across rough stone. There came the wet slap of hands and feet, followed by a scrape of claws that set John's teeth on edge.

He froze and listened as some creature sniffed the air, dreadfully near. John turned slowly, trying not to make any sound, nor even breathe. From the darkest corner of the room, a low, throaty growl rose in pitch, and two beady, violet eyes flashed bright.

Lillian woke upon a soft mattress, staring up at a white satin canopy. A cool breeze blew through a nearby window, causing several dozen tall candles to flicker, and shadows to dance across lavender-painted walls. The clarity with which she saw every detail of the room was uncanny; the strength in her limbs was prodigious. She did not feel the cold from the open window. She was not the old Lillian Hardwick; Lillian Hardwick was dead.

She rubbed her eyes. The lenses were gone. It felt strangely discomfiting that her mask of humanity had been taken from her.

Lillian swung her legs over the end of the bed, only then realising that she was dressed in a long gown of silk and lace.

The thought that someone had changed her clothes repulsed her. As she stood, she saw a chaise beneath the window, upon which was arranged a set of clothes, including an elegant, loose-fitting dress with almost Regency styling. Lillian scowled; it was the type of frock her mother often asked her to wear for parties, but which she almost always refused.

'But it would suit you so well.'

Lillian started, spinning to confront the voice, which she recognised at once. De Montfort stepped from the shadows by the door. He must have been standing there the whole time, but Lillian had not noticed him, for all her heightened senses.

'Where am I?' Lillian asked.

'Never have I met a young woman so forthright,' de Montfort said, his features blank.

'Answer me,' she demanded. De Montfort was a fool if he had come to face her alone.

He smiled the small, polite, infuriating smile, which she now knew he used to hide his ill intent. 'I told you that you would come to us eventually. You are home.'

'I did not come to you. I was abducted.'

'A minor detail. Events were set in motion somewhat faster than I had anticipated. I had to act. I had to save you.'

'Save me?' Lillian laughed in disbelief. 'Even now you think you have done me a service?'

'Especially now,' he said. 'The Riftborn have broken through the veil in unprecedented numbers. London falls, one soul at a time. When they finish devouring the weak, they will turn to greater sport—and our kind represent a threat too great to ignore for ever. Alone in London you would certainly have perished eventually. As I said, I had to act.'

Lillian blinked at de Montfort in disbelief. She surprised herself by not lashing out at him, wondering if her restraint was born of a lack of emotion within herself, or from the Majestic's insidious influence. 'The bombs were your doing,' she said at last. It was accusation, question and explanation all in one.

'Not just mine. In a way, they were *our* doing.'

'What? How dare y—'

'Oh, do not be censorious. My experiment went better than anyone could have dreamt. The Iscariot Sanction worked like a charm, and our plans had to be brought forward. I had not expected the King to support the attack on London so wholeheartedly, but once he learned that you had already found a way back there, and that you were indeed one of us, he decided it was time for action. The Queen is dead, long live the King, and so on.'

Lillian slapped de Montfort hard across the face. His smirk remained. She tried to slap him again, but this time he caught her arm and twisted it hard.

'That is quite enough of that. Do not think for a moment that I have come here without due insurance.'

Lillian relaxed her arm, and eyed de Montfort with growing suspicion. 'Insurance?'

'I am afraid one of my hunters rather disobeyed orders, and brought your brother along with you.'

'John? Where is he?'

'Calm yourself, dear girl. His situation is precarious, though I can help him… presuming, that is, that I can rely on your cooperation.'

'What have you done with him?' Lillian asked through gritted teeth.

'Me? Why, nothing. I have long since forgiven your foolhardy brother for his transgressions against me, for I am not the sort to hold a grudge. But his sort are not exactly welcome at Scarrowfall, and so he has been consigned to the dungeon for the time being, while those of the Blood Royal decide what is to be done with him.'

'I suppose there is something I must do to secure John's release?'

'Only hear me out. Once you have done so, I trust that you will act according to your conscience. And I am confident you will find our causes better aligned than you may presently imagine.'

Lillian scoffed, but nodded acquiescence regardless. De Montfort's smile grew into a parody of warmth.

'Then, madam, I shall leave you to dress and then we shall talk. I will have a maid come to attend you in… shall we say, twenty minutes?'

'If it please you,' Lillian said, in mock servitude.

'Very good,' said de Montfort, opening the bedroom door a fraction. 'Oh, and I am sure I need not say it, but just so that there is no misunderstanding—you will find that your quarters, although comfortable, are most secure, and that Scarrowfall is very remote. I trust you will not feel the need to verify either assertion.'

Lillian glared at the odious creature as he bowed, slipped through the door and closed it behind him. She heard a key turn in the lock.

She set about disobeying de Montfort at once. Lillian moved to the door, and heard muffled footsteps moving away. A shadow passed the crack of light beneath the door; a guard, she assumed. She went next to the window, throwing open the curtains to find iron bars set deep into the frame. Lillian squinted into the darkness, and saw a rugged coastline stretching out before her, upon which Scarrowfall sat precariously close to the edge. Moonlight gleamed off a rough, inky black sea. Beyond that she could see little—she was on perhaps a third floor, but her view was obscured by parapets and buttresses of aged stone, giving her prison the appearance of an abbey or castle rather than the country pile she had expected.

She shook the bars out of frustration, but they were solid and did not so much as rattle. Lillian took a deep breath and tried to compose herself, to ask herself what John would do. Or, indeed, what John was doing right at that moment.

Lillian closed her eyes, and exhaled slowly. What John would do, she felt sure, was dress for dinner and reveal some cunning plan later. If only she had such a plan.

* * *

John worked the small metal tools within the manacle lock, his hands shaking as much from tiredness as from fear. He wished he was as deft as Lillian when it came to lockpicking. John felt the thing in the shadows watching him; he smelt its foul breath and heard its shuffling paces upon the cellar floor.

The mechanism clicked, and John took heart, redoubling his efforts. If the creature were to pounce, he doubted he would stand much of a chance unarmed and weakened as he was, but he would rather die fighting than chained to the wall. Why it had not attacked already was beyond him.

Another click; he was getting closer to freedom. But then he stopped.

He heard a different sound, from further off in the darkness. A groan at first, and then a low moan. It was not one of the creatures—or, at least, he did not think so. Indeed, it sounded like a woman.

Lillian? Had they brought her here too?

The thought lent urgency to his hands, and he began again in earnest, forgetting the numbness in his fingers for a moment and twisting the pins within the lock's mechanism. The woman's pained murmurs grew louder, more fearful. Even before the final click of the lock, the scraping of clawed feet on stone became frenetic, and louder.

The manacle fell from John's ankle, and instinctively he threw himself back towards the wall as the creature burst from the shadows. Glittering eyes announced a pale form, yellowed claws illuminated by faint moonlight as they reached for their prey. The hands stopped inches from John's face, grasping frantically. Chains rattled; the creature grunted.

John knew at once that the ghoul was chained just as he had been. He pressed himself against the wall, out of the creature's reach. It could have attacked him at any time. Perhaps it was starving, or weak. Perhaps it had been commanded to leave him be unless he tried to escape. Regardless, now it was awake, and hungry.

John felt his way around the edge of the cell, which was much larger than he had first thought. The creature tracked his every move, until he had gone far beyond its reach and it had faded away into the darkness again, its eyes becoming violet pinpricks of light. Its growls quietened to a low, frustrated clicking sound.

As John moved away from the creature, praying that he did not stray unwittingly into the reach of another, he heard again the cry of the woman. It did not sound like Lillian, but he continued regardless, for if there were any others down in these foul depths he would help them if he could.

He had not moved much further when he saw cracks of faint yellow light some distance ahead, almost certainly outlining a door. John paused and collected himself, listening carefully to gain his bearings. He heard a sob from somewhere ahead and to his left.

'Hello? Who's there?' John ventured. He heard the chink of chains from the far end of the room from where he'd come. The ghoul? John tried to pinpoint the crying again, but infuriatingly it stopped at the sound of the chains.

'I... is there... someone there?' The voice was weak, nervous. It was a woman, young by the sounds of it. Uncultured, judging by the hint of an accent, and frightened.

'Yes. Are you hurt?'

'My... baby,' she said, and grunted with pain. John realised that the woman must be pregnant.

'Try to stay calm; I will come to you,' he said.

'Hurry... please.'

John abandoned the wall reluctantly, having gained an idea of the woman's position, and moved forwards stealthily and slowly, hands out.

He touched flesh. He recoiled, as did the figure, but with a frightened gasp that revealed it as the woman he sought.

'Shh,' John whispered. 'My name is John; I'm here to help you.'

He reached out again, this time feeling a bare foot, ice-cold and clammy, with a manacle about it. He moved along the floor, being careful as he went, until he thought he could make out the outline of the woman by the faint light.

'How did you escape?' she asked through ragged breaths.

'I have my ways,' John said, being careful not to divulge too much intelligence in case the woman was there to trick him. 'What is your name?' he asked.

'H... Hetty,' she said. 'Please, help me.'

'What can I do?'

'The baby is coming, I can feel it,' she said. 'I don't want to die down here.' Her small hand gripped John's, and squeezed it tight.

Chains rattled, and the bobbing violet eyes of the ghoul drew nearer. A low growl rumbled in the creature's throat. John swore he heard lips smacking.

The woman squeezed John's hand harder, and let out such a scream that John flinched.

'Try to hold still,' he hissed, and set about picking the lock of her manacle, willing his tired hands to stop shaking.

Hetty cried out again, trying in vain to stifle her moans. The creature strained against its shackles, snarling like a mistreated dog. John's wrists and fingers ached with the repetitive action of lockpicking. The woman's cries would surely draw the wrong kind of attention.

The door was flung open. Light spilled into the room, and for a moment John was half blinded. He forced himself to stand, but even as he tensed ready for a fight he felt hands upon him. Two men restrained him; large, thuggish brutes with podgy faces and dull eyes. Not vampires, but docile serfs. The figure that entered behind them, however, was very much one of the Knights Iscariot. A tall, slender figure, with a long black coat, fitted at the waist and flowing past the knee, giving the impression that it glided into the room rather than walked. Its head was bald, face gleaming white. Scars spread out from its mouth and branched around its face, in places pierced by golden rings. One ear was missing, leaving a horrid, puckered crater in the side of its head. The creature cocked its head to one side, studying

John as he struggled against the lumbering oafs, whose strength was prodigious. It turned its violet eyes to the woman, and hissed, at which two more creatures entered the chamber. These were female vampires, thin and bald, and immodestly dressed. Their scarred flesh was also pierced, their scalps adorned with hooks and barbs, with jewels and chains hanging from them. They moved at once towards Hetty, who John saw for the first time was a slip of girl, much younger than Lillian, with wasted, hollow features and a swollen belly. The creatures whispered to each other, 'She is ready'; 'Yes, take her. Take her!'

John roared at them to leave the girl alone, and for his efforts was lifted from his feet by a blow from the tall vampire. He felt a clawed hand upon his chin, forcing his head up to watch as Hetty was lifted by the two pale women, hoisted into the air as though she weighed nothing, and carried off into the torch-lit passage beyond the open door. Before he knew what was happening, John was being dragged back into the depths of the cell, which he now saw was littered with bones around the chained ghoul's deadly radius. He was too winded still to protest, and could only moan despairingly as he was once more fastened into manacles. This time John's jailers patted him down roughly, finding one more lockpick concealed within the lining of John's trousers at the hem, tearing it out with a knife. John gritted his teeth as the blade bit his flesh, and warm blood ran down to his bare feet.

As his guards left the dungeon cell, John took a mental picture of the room, of the corridor beyond, and of the vampire overseer. He committed every detail to memory, so that he could begin to plan his escape.

And then the girl's screaming began. It was a long time in ending.

Lillian looked around the great dining room, which was every bit as opulent as she expected from de Montfort, who sat at the opposite side of the great table to her. Behind the Majestic, a hunter stood tall, eyes fixed ahead like a soldier.

In each corner of the room stood a human, tired, sickly and timid. Three women and one man, all trembling and fingers touched nervously to their temples, eyes closed in concentration. Majestics.

'I am glad you decided to join me, Lillian,' de Montfort said. 'May I call you Lillian?'

Lillian shrugged.

'May I offer you sustenance? Blood—harvested humanely, I might add—or wine. It is up to you.'

'I am not thirsty,' Lillian said. It was a lie—the thirst had raged within her from the moment she had woken. Every time she so much as glanced at the humans in the room she had to fight down the urge to leap from her chair and attack them. The human maid whom de Montfort had sent to attend Lillian was lucky to be alive. Lillian was disgusted with herself, sickened by her own unnatural cravings. What de Montfort meant by 'humanely' was anyone's guess, although Lillian recalled Sir Valayar Shah's assertions that some young men of the north gave their blood willingly to their vampire overlords.

'Very well,' de Montfort said, sipping from his own glass. 'I will tell you now, that within these four walls, in the presence of these Majestics, we may speak freely. Elsewhere in Scarrowfall our liberty is less assured.'

'Our liberty? Are you not the favoured ambassador of the Knights Iscariot?' Lillian put the question as scathingly as she could, but she was puzzled nonetheless.

'Let us just say that not all of us who speak for the Knights Iscariot are welcome to dine at the top table. I am sure you are familiar with my position, having a similar status yourself within the Order of Apollo, no?'

His words stung, and Lillian was thankful to her half-dead flesh for once for not betraying her feelings. She maintained her composure. 'But if you find yourself at odds with your "king", why involve me? I owe you no allegiance. Far from it.'

'You owe me more than you realise, but that is not why I take you into my confidence, Lillian. Rather, I am confident that your opposition to the Nameless King shall far outweigh your enmity towards me.'

'That remains to be seen. Your "Nameless King" is not the one who did this to me. He is not the one who killed my friend.'

'Ah. I see you have not yet shed the irrational consequences of your former emotions. I would ask that you at least try to set them aside for now, for those feelings, vestigial as they are, will prove your undoing within Scarrowfall. Here, there are eyes and ears everywhere, and no one can be trusted.'

'Except for you, of course?'

'Oh, good heavens no. You should trust me least of all, for I have ambition, and an ambitious man is a dangerous man. But at least reserve your hatred for those more deserving. What I have done, I have done to secure the future of my kind. Is that so wrong?'

'You have done it at the expense of mine!' Lillian snapped, but checked herself at once.

'Ah, despite your words, I think you come to see it at last. You are one of us, not one of them. I have saved you from the ravages of time and the predations of the Riftborn. And I shall save many more now that I know the Iscariot Sanction is a success.'

'You seek to… turn all of humanity into vampires?'

'Not all—that would be unsustainable. But enough to have us step once and for all from darkness, and to carve our own place within a world that we have only tangentially influenced for centuries. The Nameless King, on the other hand, would use the Iscariot Sanction for a much darker purpose.'

'Which is?'

'He wishes to enslave humanity, to shackle every man, woman and child like animals.'

'This differs from your plan how, precisely?'

'You do me a disservice, though I confess I understand your animosity. My intention has only ever been to create a fairer world, one in which my kind can live free of the tyranny of an ancient and crumbling monarchy, and co-exist in relative peace with humans. You did not ask for this gift to be bestowed upon you, I know, and yet here you are.'

'I would not call it a gift,' Lillian said, glaring at the hideous features of the snub-nosed hunter standing behind de Montfort—features that she suspected she might one day possess.

'Not yet, but it is, believe me. I have both human and vampire parents. I was elevated beyond my humble station by happenstance; the Awakening made me both Majestic and Intuitionist—an almost unprecedented event in anyone's books, let alone the *wampyr*—and that is the only reason I sit here now. I am afforded freedoms that others of my blood are denied. My flirtation with the Blood Royal has made me strong of body, but I shall never be one of them. You, however, are. You may not think it now, but you will one day be stronger than I can ever be. You will probably outlive me, unless I can find some way to alter my own nature as I did yours. You are, physically and scientifically, a highborn.'

'But that would mean I was transfused with the Blood Royal?' Finally, Lillian thought she might glean some answers.

'Correct.'

'And yet, it was you who bestowed the Iscariot Sanction upon me. Your blood that I...' She stopped, realising that de Montfort's smile had become a smirk, and that he had raised an eyebrow in mockery of her slow-wittedness. 'So it was not your blood. Then... whose?'

'Lillian—perhaps I should have given you more time in the company of your club's scientists. Your education on this matter is frightfully deficient. Here, I shall inculcate in you some knowledge of your... condition.

'The remarkable thing about *wampyr* blood, I have found, is that it cannot be diluted, but rather carries its properties to anything it comes into contact with—human blood, for example. If, let's say for argument's sake, one of the Blood Royal were to feed on a human, its blood would, for a time, become palatable to other *wampyr*—this is how they give the gift to those like me. If, however, I were to glut myself wholly on the Blood Royal, beyond the point of mere satiation, I would effectively carry their entire essence in my veins, at some small discomfort to myself. Theoretically, through the process of transfusion, I could pass this essence on to a suitable host. Not a vampire, unfortunately, as our physiology cannot be altered for reasons that as yet elude me. But for a human...' He smiled, pleased with himself. 'And yet my experiments failed time and again, until now. You see, it is not a matter of simply exchanging blood. I had to distil his blood using all my scientific skills, to create from that accursed ichor the very essence of the *wampyr*; the spark of divine blessing that once bred a line of kings, but now breeds only madness and degeneracy. I found God in that blood. Or perhaps the Devil. In any case, I imbibed it; I took the essence within myself. Then I gave it to you.'

'So... you killed a Blood Royal for your experiment?' Lillian understood now why de Montfort had taken such precautions with his security. He had committed treason.

'Not killed, exactly. I starved him for a while, then made him drink, then opened his throat and collected his blood. Every last drop. He has not the strength to recover from his wounds, but he lives still, if it can be called living.'

'And... Sir Arthur,' Lillian asked, feeling at last a well of emotion other than anger. 'Why him? Why did you...' She could not finish.

'Why not? He set himself against us, and paid the price. But this was not mere revenge. He was nothing more than a commodity.'

'Commodity?' Lillian almost choked on the word.

'Human blood is needed to sate the fledgling hunger. Without it, the transfusion would not have taken, and you might have died. I took your blood as recompense for the vital fluid lost to me. I gave you his so that you would not die. I confess, I could have chosen one of the villagers, but what harm had they done me? They were loyal to my cause—well, to the Nameless King, but why split hairs? And perhaps it is in my nature to be a little cruel. It is in yours, too—you will have surely felt it by now.'

'You are giving me little cause to trust you,' said Lillian. 'If you would betray your own kind—'

'The Blood Royal are not my kind!' he snapped. 'Have you heard nothing I have said? They are enslavers. They are debauched tyrants. They live as though they are Dark Age kings, with harems and slaves.'

'Do you not have slaves?' She waved a hand around the room.

De Montfort's thin smile faltered for a moment.

'My hunters are not slaves. They are members of a warrior caste so ancient that their forebears saw empires rise and fall. They are bound to me—and I to them—through ties of duty and honour that you could not possibly understand.'

'And the Majestics?'

'They are paid, they are protected. Servants, if you will. But I keep no courtesans, nor debase members of my own race to attend my every whim. You shall see that side of *wampyr* society for yourself, soon enough. The Nameless King is most eager to meet you.'

'Oh?'

'You represent more than just a means to bargain power from the humans. You are to be his latest plaything, his chief concubine. A true *wampyr*, untainted by centuries of inbreeding, and capable of giving birth to a royal child without dying in the process. A prize indeed.'

Lillian scraped her chair away from the table and looked about. With all of her training, could she kill the guard and overpower de Montfort?

'No, you could not,' said de Montfort, reading her thoughts. 'There are others loyal to me standing guard outside this room. And if you were caught within Scarrowfall by the King's servants, you would suffer the fate I have described and more. He would think you part of a conspiracy to overthrow him, and make you suffer for the rest of your immortal life. If you will extend even a little trust to me, Lillian, I will set you free, and your brother, too, and end the dark curse that the Nameless King has brought upon the land.'

Lillian weighed up her options and found she had very few. She did not relinquish the idea that she could fight, regardless of the consequences, and that thought brought a flicker of... something... to de Montfort's stony features. Fear, perhaps. Or so she hoped.

Her thoughts were interrupted by a knock at the door, and a smartly dressed human servant entered. This one did not look as broken as the others Lillian had encountered; indeed, he looked as fine an under-butler as might be found in any grand country house.

'My lord, the guests are arriving. The King shall join the festivities at ten o'clock.'

De Montfort waved the man away, and only when the door was firmly closed did he speak again.

'The timing of your arrival is most propitious. Among our kind, the feast of All Hallows is a sacred one, though its celebration is anything but sombre. It begins upon the stroke of midnight, and the revelry extends for a full day, until even the *wampyr* are too tired to continue their debauchery. Tonight of all nights you will see the Nameless King for what he really is, and if ever there was an argument for helping me, I am certain it shall be made for me.'

'I still cannot see how helping you will benefit the Crown,' said Lillian. 'Why trust one devil and not the other?'

'The Crown is hardly a concern for immortals such as us,' said de Montfort. 'And less so since the death of your stone-hearted queen.'

Lillian could not contain a gasp, but knew it was a reflex, an echo of a feeling from her human life. She felt little if anything at the news, though the suddenness of it, and the repercussions such an event would surely have, left her mind reeling.

'Ah, you did not know about the Queen? That was remiss of

me; I had assumed your brother had told you. I am afraid it was Victoria's attempt to flee London that rather forced my hand—I still have some explaining to do about that, I can tell you. The most unfortunate part of the whole affair is that Kate Fox was travelling with the Queen at the time. None of us could have predicted the effect her death would have upon the Rift.'

'The Riftborn... the shadow?' Lillian said, a creeping dread taking hold of her.

'Yes. It seems she was harbouring a quite terrible secret. London could go the same way as New York now that she's dead.'

Lillian remembered the stories in the academy of Margaret Fox, and what had happened in New York. The effects of those events were still being felt six years later, and now, if Kate Fox's death had caused similar chaos, the balance of world power would undoubtedly shift again. Lillian wondered if that truly were accidental, for it seemed to play precisely into the hands of the Knights Iscariot, who alone did not fear the Riftborn.

'Oh, but we do,' said de Montfort, trespassing into Lillian's thoughts again. 'Not for the same reason that humans fear them, naturally, but we have no desire to live in a world of war and destruction. We are as much a part of this world as humans.'

'And yet your schemes have damned it. By betraying your ruler, you have killed ours, and consigned the world to Hell.' Lillian spoke coolly, and wondered if de Montfort truly could not see the damage he had done.

'Again, you speak of betrayal—and yet your own beloved monarchy is guilty of worse.'

Lillian frowned.

'I mean Prince Leopold,' de Montfort said. 'Did you really think the prince could be so easily abducted if he did not wish it? That his guards would really turn against him after a lifetime of loyal service? That the plan to treat with us aboard the royal train, passing through our strongholds, was a sensible one? No, the prince influenced his mother, and in turn his mother influenced your father, and so it all came to pass.'

'Why?' Lillian pushed her chair away now, and stood at the table, fists clenched, drawing a low, menacing click from the hunter.

'Leopold is a haemophiliac,' said de Montfort, waving a hand to dismiss Lillian's burst of anger. 'His condition cannot be cured. Except by me… specifically, by the Iscariot Sanction. To have vigour, and immortality—these things are worth more to the prince than sovereignty. Even the news of his mother's death has not swayed him from his path. Yes, I can tell by your expression that you understand at last. You were an experiment, a test subject. The Nameless King believes you to be of his own blood, gifted to me to further my experiments. As such, he believes he has total control over your mind and body, and will keep you as a curiosity, to take pride of place in his harem. He wishes to repeat the process upon Prince Leopold, creating a trueborn son who is heir to both human and vampire thrones. Leopold will be a puppet, nothing more, but he believes that together they will rule over this hellish new world of ours for all eternity. Unless, of course, we stop them.'

'We? It is you who has paved the way for this madness!'

'No!' de Montfort shouted, a flash of indignation in his eyes. 'I did what I did to secure my freedom. The Nameless King seeks to use my scientific breakthrough in order to conquer the world. This is the curse of all the greatest minds of science, is it not? We create gifts that can change the world for the better, and those in power wrest them away to wage war.'

Lillian thought for a moment of Tesla, forging weapons at Cherleten's behest. She said nothing, and only hoped she had not betrayed the Serbian or her Order with her thoughts.

'The Iscariot Sanction shall prove not to be the King's making,' de Montfort raged on, 'but his undoing. I have set a plan in motion that will destroy him.'

Lillian saw clearly that de Montfort actually believed his own lies; he had convinced himself that his goals were noble.

'And what is your plan?' she asked.

'Do you not see it? Do you really think that you were plucked out at random, from the many thousands of possible candidates to receive the greatest gift ever bestowed upon a human? No, my dear Lillian, I chose you. Prince Leopold helped to ensure that you were on that train, that you would fall into my hands. I *chose* you.'

Lillian sat back in her chair, mortified at the magnitude of the betrayal, and resentful of any part she would yet have to play. She had one more question, and even though she knew the answer, she had to ask it.

'Why? What did you choose me for?' she asked, her voice almost a whisper.

De Montfort leaned back in his chair, his smile widening.

'To kill the Nameless King. Why else?'

TWENTY-ONE

De Montfort and his hunters led Lillian from his private chambers, through wide corridors lined with grotesque portraits, down sweeping staircases and along crumbling passages. When at last they reached a large, ironbound door, through which strains of orchestral music and excited chatter drifted, de Montfort stopped.

'Remember, Lillian, the blood of the elders flows in your veins. The Nameless King cannot intrude upon your thoughts, but he believes that he can control you all the same. You will hear instructions in your mind—they will be from me, interpreting the wishes of the King so that your charade might go undiscovered. Obey me instantly, and without question, until the time is right to strike.'

'And when will that be?' Lillian asked.

'I believe that you are the expert in combat and assassination. You may choose the time and the method, as you see fit.'

'And weapons?'

'Though I am certain you will trust me once you have seen the King, I am not so certain of your allegiance right now. To arm you here would be foolish of me... I am sure you understand. Besides, if you are searched, my work shall be undone, and I cannot have that. No—you must find your own way. But remember, he is strong; stronger than any of us. That he believes he can control you utterly may give him pause, and you can use that against him. But you must either sever his head from his body, or burn him to ashes. Anything less may allow his survival, and as long as he lives, his servants will take heart. If he receives the final death, then my circle of brave knights shall do the rest.'

Lillian scoffed at that. His scarified attendants were more like the creatures of myth that 'brave knights' would quest to slay.

'And my brother?' she asked.

'John Hardwick is being held by the King's loyal serfs, in the dungeon. When the King is dead, those serfs will be of no consequence. You have my word we shall free him.'

Lillian thought on this, and nodded. She still harboured a desire to kill de Montfort too, and he doubtless knew it. But for now, she would have to play along.

De Montfort smiled his thin, sly smile, and his servants opened the door. Beyond was a long, broad corridor, draped either side in velvet curtains and tall tapestries in crimson, purple and black. Fires burned in tall iron braziers, and hundreds of candles burned in a row of massive chandeliers. At the end of the corridor, men and women—or, rather, vampires—filed from rooms and passages to enter a grand hall, from which the sound of music came, louder now; a string orchestra playing melancholic, discordant tunes. The guests wore sinister costume masks and garish, formal clothing styled after a bygone age. They swirled about in motions too fluid and graceful for mortals, their otherworldly presence and glittering eyes betraying them as monsters dressed as men. It was a picture of bourgeois decadence, as if Bosch had lived to paint a nightmarish Venetian ball.

De Montfort placed a hand on Lillian's arm.

'I warn you,' he said quietly, 'there are such sights in here as to overwhelm your sensibilities. The humans who attend the Feast of All Hallows have seen it before, or else have found themselves on the dinner menu. As for the *wampyr*... we have found, over the centuries, that only in excess can we feel anything. And no one in the world can imagine excess quite like us. Do not quail, do not flinch. They expect you to be one of us; show no fear, and steel your mind.'

Lillian nodded, although she did not think she could truly feel revulsion or fear any longer; she almost hoped to be proven wrong.

'Oh, and put this on,' de Montfort added, handing Lillian a small velvet eye-mask studded with glittering crystals.

Lillian donned it as de Montfort tied an identical one around his own head.

'Now, we are ready. Come, Lillian, it is time to meet the master of Scarrowfall.'

John dreamed of fire, as he so often did. He dreamed of the night his sister had run away across the fields and had almost died. Except in the dream she did not drown, but was attacked by a vast, fire-breathing dragon with scales of gold and red and a maw that could swallow a man whole.

John fled the dragon, but his father faced it. He returned home with Lillian in his arms, stepping through a wall of flame as though it were nothing, while the wails of the great beast echoed in the night. In the dream, Lillian died. She always died. Their father looked down at John sorrowfully, and shook his head as John reached out to Lillian's cold hand. A hand blackened by fire.

John woke to the dark cell. The low grunt of John's inhuman cellmate drifted from the shadows; it was there still, watching and waiting. Another sound joined it, from somewhere above John's head. The sound of scraping on stone. He tensed; was there another of the creatures in the cell? Was it climbing above him like a bloated spider, waiting to pounce?

'Hardwick! For pity's sake, are you there?'

The voice was a harsh whisper, and had the urgency of someone who had been trying for some time to attract the attention of another.

'Smythe?' John hissed back, craning his neck to look at the small window.

'Look, we don't have much time. I'm going to get you out of here, but you need to hold on until help comes, do you understand?'

It occurred to John that he might still be dreaming. It seemed singularly unlikely that Smythe had escaped the vampires back in London, or indeed tracked him down here. But then again, the surgeon was one of the few agents who knew where John was likely to be taken, and if the Order still functioned following the attack, Sir Toby would surely be hell-bent on revenge against the Knights Iscariot.

'There's no time, Smythe. Get me out of here now!' John replied, heedless of whether or not he was whispering to a hallucination.

'Hardwick, just hold hard. If I break you out now I risk raising the alarm. This place is swarming with guards, and worse. Every vampire in Europe is here tonight. Pickering is escorting a fleet along the coast. When the guns start firing, I'll come back for you.'

'I'm not alone down here, Smythe.'

There was a pause. When Smythe replied, it was more cautiously. 'Who's with you?'

'One of those things,' John said. 'I don't know how long I have. I don't know how long Lillian has.' It felt somehow wrong to use his sister's name as leverage against Smythe, but it was true nonetheless.

Another pause. And then, 'Hold on, someone's coming.'

John strained his ears, and thought he heard footsteps on gravel, though very far off. When that sound had passed, he spent what seemed like an eternity listening to silence, until he thought Smythe must have either left, or he'd dreamed him up.

'Hardwick?'

John breathed a sigh of relief. 'I haven't gone anywhere. How could I?'

'I cannot jeopardise the plan, but I can arm you. Do you understand?'

'I'm not an imbecile, Smythe.'

'Very well. See if you can't get loose, and then find somewhere to lie low. Don't cause a scene. We attack at dawn, and nothing must alert the Knights Iscariot to our plans.'

'Very well, but please get on with it.'

Chains rattled, and the ghoul's low growl became a more agitated snarl. John swore. Seconds later, the sound of scraping at the window-ledge overhead was swiftly followed by a dull thud on the floor. Then a second thud, slightly further away.

'Sorry, old boy, I think that last one went astray. Look now, I have to go. I've tarried too long already.'

'I understand,' John whispered back.

'Good luck, Hardwick. See you on the other side.'

Silence descended once more, but for the snarling from somewhere off to John's left, accompanied by the bobbing of those baleful eyes. John patted the floor around himself for whatever Smythe had thrown. When it was not immediately apparent, he risked moving about as far as his chains would allow, searching desperately in the darkness, alert to every soft clink of chains in case the ghoul should rush at him. Only when his ankle grew raw with the effort of straining at his manacle did John finally get a fingertip to a cloth bundle. He stretched out as far as was possible, holding his breath.

His fingers had scarcely closed around the bundle when the creature sprang from the darkness. Jaws snapped at his face; a claw swept a hair's breadth from his hand.

John rolled away, pushing himself across the flagstones as the creature strained at its bonds, its growls becoming a pained gargle as its stocks bit into its throat. It let out a shrill cry of frustration, and John heard its chains scrape as it retreated once again.

He relaxed only when he had returned to his original position, his back pressed against the rough stone wall, clutching the bundle in his arms like a baby. That thought made him remember Hetty, and the recollection stung. He had failed the girl, and he could only guess what they had done to her after they had dragged her from the cell. He thought of Lillian, and wondered if her fate would be the same. These things mattered to him more even than his own life.

With numb fingers he unwrapped the bundle. There was another package somewhere else in the darkness, but he could not risk scrabbling around after that just yet, with the beast so near. He half hoped to find a gun. Instead, his hand felt a small knife, a book of matches, and a thin strip of leather, which John unrolled to reveal a set of lockpicks. John flexed his numb fingers and sighed. He slid two picks from the leather roll, took a breath, and set to work.

Lillian was led by the arm through a vast chamber, where pairs of pale-skinned dancers whirled across a polished floor, never pausing for a moment, and never once impeding her advance towards the large dais ahead. Lillian spotted humans mixing freely with vampires; subservient, letting their blood or bowing and scraping to their monstrous lords. She had grown used to her preternatural senses now; around all the vampires was a dull amber glow, which she had almost come to ignore. This aura was more volatile and colourful around Majestics, while humans emitted no trace of such phenomena.

Even with her heightened senses, or perhaps because of them, the scene was overwhelming. The music was jarring and frantic, played by six skeletal creatures who sat within an alcove balcony, their movements rapid and jerking, their faces hidden behind black veils. Around the edges of the hall, more twisted, ancient creatures stood silent and still, watching intently, their masks not hiding their ugliness. Above them all, overlooking the floor that swarmed with dancers in their clockwork trance, was a high vaulted ceiling painted with a vision of Dante's hell, from which dozens of still-twitching naked bodies hung from long chains. Lillian saw with growing horror that the incumbent victims—human and vampire alike—groaned and writhed with what could be either pain or pleasure, or both. Drops of blood fell to the floor like rain, staining the gaily coloured costumes of the revellers. The scene was lit by flame rather than gaslight, with great fires burning within iron bowls, sickly sweet incense mingling with the smoke.

They continued through the centre of the room, de Montfort's arm in hers; Lillian felt hundreds of pairs of eyes upon her. She heard the whispers even over the screeching din of the violins: 'It is her,' 'Heresy!' 'The King's new bride...' 'So, it is true, de Montfort thinks himself a god.' Her escort revelled in the attention, nodding to the assembled courtiers shamelessly.

The dais before them housed a long table, set with finery before thirteen places. Only half of those places were taken, and Lillian fought to hide her disgust at the sight of Prince Leopold. To the prince's right sat Sir Robert Collins, his face ashen and drawn, looking as though he might be sick at any moment. To the left sat a fawning vampire maid, inhuman of aspect yet attractive compared to the other females in the immense ballroom. Standing behind the prince's chair, straight-backed, eyes front, was Colonel Ewart. If the Scot was repulsed by the scene before him, he did not show it; Lillian imagined he had long since thrown in his lot with the Knights Iscariot, and was perhaps accustomed to their ways. The maiden whispered something in the prince's ear, and laughed musically. At this, Leopold—looking vacant and sluggish—turned to look at Lillian, and raised his glass to her.

'Curtsey,' de Montfort whispered.

Lillian did as she was bid, at which the prince turned back to the vampire woman and became at once absorbed in conversation with her. Sir Robert tried his best not to so much as glance furtively in Lillian's direction.

'What now?' Lillian whispered.

'Patience,' de Montfort said through the side of his mouth.

Trumpets blared abruptly. The music stopped and the dancers froze as if they were figures in a clockwork music box, whose mechanism had wound down. A prancing, spindle-limbed creature in a costume reminiscent of a plague doctor leapt upon the stage, dancing to his own music for a moment before bowing low to the silent audience. Where the creature's skin was exposed at the hands and throat, it was dark and dry, rustling like crumpled parchment.

'My lords, ladies and gentlemen,' he said, in a rasping, throaty voice that projected magically across the hall. 'The Nameless King bids you welcome to Scarrowfall, the heart of the *wampyr* court and, as you all know, soon to be one of the great royal residences of the British Empire!'

This was met by a ripple of appreciative, yet mirthless, laughter.

'We welcome to the royal table tonight a very special guest,' the master of ceremonies went on. 'A royal prince of England is among us, signalling, we hope, the dawn of a new age of cooperation and prosperity between our two peoples. Please join me in welcoming Prince Leopold to Scarrowfall, and in extending our condolences for the recent, tragic loss of his dear mother, the Queen.' The creature adopted mock sincerity, and his performance drew further laughter and a ripple of applause from the crowd. The prince was unmoved. Sir Robert looked even more ill, appearing to shrink into his chair until he all but disappeared.

'We also have a new member of our hallowed ranks, escorted here tonight by Lord Lucien de Montfort. We extend welcome to Lillian Hardwick, who will tonight be inducted into the Nameless Sisterhood. Come, child.' The grotesque compere beckoned to Lillian.

Go to him. De Montfort's voice rang in Lillian's mind. Though she had no desire to join this mysterious sisterhood, she moved to the side of the dais and ascended a small flight of steps. As she walked past Prince Leopold, drawing a surreptitious glare from Ewart, she looked around at anything she could use to escape. To kill. On the wall behind the stage, flickering torches burned theatrically. Great claymores hung upon the walls in front of tapestries depicting Old Testament scenes of plague and destruction. She wondered if her vampire form gave her the strength to wrest them from their brackets. She saw that Ewart was armed, and presumed therefore that other armed guards would also be present among the Nameless King's attendants.

'Come, come,' said the master of ceremonies, a bony hand outstretched, strange, blackened fingers clacking long fingernails together. The creature smelled of oil and ash, and moved in unnatural, jerking motions as though its bones were fused together and it had to break them anew with each exaggerated sweep of its arms.

'Our sister is shy!' the creature proclaimed to the room. 'Or perhaps she thinks I bear her ill will, for past transgressions. There, there, Lily-white, Snow-white… I hold no grudge for crimes committed in a former life. How could any of us immortals be so petty?'

Lillian did pause now, checking her stride as she came to the grim realisation of the compère's identity. Though the voice was pained and rasping, it was unmistakeable. Had it not seemed such an impossibility, she would have guessed as soon as the scarecrow-figure took the stage.

'I see she remembers Sir Valayar Shah at last!' said the creature, clapping its hands together dramatically. 'Miss Hardwick was surely destined to become one of us; she remembers not the lives she has taken. No matter! How can I bear any malice towards this creature, for she gave me the greatest gift of all: the gift of exquisite agony, that I shall remember for all eternity.'

At this, Shah removed his mask, and even Lillian, inured as she was to horrors, checked her advance and stifled a gasp. Shah's flesh was no longer marble-white, but tobacco-brown. His rictus grin, which Lillian was certain had been carved surgically onto his features, was now more grotesque than ever, the electrical energy from the Tesla pistol having burned it back to the bone, the edges blackened like burned paper. His eyes still glittered behind the torn mask of a face.

Shah clacked his fingernails again, bringing Lillian back to her senses. She joined him at the centre of the stage quickly, taking his gnarled, dry hand, her skin crawling as his horribly long, bony fingers curled around hers, cracking as they did so. He began to bow, jerking awkwardly as though his back could hardly bend.

Curtsey.

Lillian heeded de Montfort's mental instruction, feeling like a marionette in a puppet show, next to a black-clothed Punchinello. From up on the stage, the crowd looked even more ghastly, their smiles almost as grotesque as Shah's, their forms shifting dizzyingly as glittering costumes reflected the torchlight. Smoke hung in the air above them in a fragrant miasma.

Shah raised Lillian's hand, and twirled her around as if to display a prize, before passing her over to a human servant, dismissing her as yesterday's news so that he could continue his address. Lillian was led by the hand around the back of the long table, past a group of three well-dressed vampires who looked at her with a confection of morbid fascination and haughty derision; past the arrangement of swords upon their fixed metal mounts; and was finally seated by yet another servant next to Sir Robert Collins. The comptroller of the prince's household avoided her gaze diligently. The prince smiled, a vacant expression on his face as though he had already been at the wine for some time. Lillian felt Ewart's eyes boring a hole in the back of her head.

To her right was the largest seat at the table—a great gilded throne, positioned at the centre of the top table. She felt something in the pit of her stomach, and only slowly came to recognise it as trepidation. The Nameless King would undoubtedly be seated next to her. Her audience with this mysterious creature could not be far away.

In front of Lillian's seat, she was relieved to find a large silver candelabra blocking her view of the crowd, and theirs of her. Beneath its arms, however, she saw de Montfort being led up the steps at the side of the stage, whereupon he took a place four spaces along the table to Lillian's right, and was instantly caught in the fawning pull of a hideous, wrinkled vampiress, whose teeth had been filed to points, and whose eyes shone in the candlelight. The creature tossed her head back as she laughed, revealing an ugly red brand upon a saggy, milk-white neck, and while she spoke to de Montfort, her eyes remained fixed upon Lillian, filled with malice.

The other seats at the table began to fill with strange-looking creatures that Lillian did not recognise. Throughout it all, Shah had not stopped his performance, drawing laughter and gasps from the crowd in turn, prancing back and forth along the stage like a music-hall comedian.

'Please put your hands together for Count d'Aurenga of Montelimar, and His Grace the Bishop Ferdinand of Limburg,' Shah was saying, as more of the Knights Iscariot's membership took the stage, filling the final places.

Bishop? Lillian thought, incredulous at the notion of a vampire inveigling its way into the church hierarchy in any nation. Perhaps the title was an affectation, taken through some tradition or historical technicality, much as de Montfort's position seemed to be. Or perhaps even these depraved highborns had been able to disguise their monstrous nature to live among mortals, much as Cherleten had for so long.

It appeared that the assembled lords and ladies at the top table represented some of the more important figures in vampire society, drawn from around the globe. Their exotic accents and outlandish ornamentation gave them away as foreign-born, although their pale, scarred flesh and violet eyes lent them a homogenous appearance; one that Lillian realised, with some distaste, she now shared. She wondered if the vampires had their own society, away from the artificial distinctions provided by political borders and racial incongruence. She wondered if, should she fail in her mission, whether she would meet her end, or become instead inducted into that culture, eventually forgetting all that she had been previously. There was some dark comfort in this thought, in the idea of being embraced by a new family.

De Montfort was still inside her mind. He turned to fire her a glance as she thought these things, and with it sent a psychic progression of a single word. A name: *John*.

She looked away. Her brother was locked in some stinking dungeon and whatever happened, she would see him freed; she owed him at least that much. She owed it to the ghostly vestige of her humanity. These thoughts, and others, she buried deep, hopefully deep enough to be concealed from de Montfort's mental prying.

The throne, and the seat to its right, were the only empty places remaining. Lillian noticed this only when Shah had ceased his droning, and the crowd's laughter at his show had subsided. Her concentration upon guarding her thoughts had distracted her. She looked about, catching the eye of Collins briefly, before he turned away hastily, guilt and fear writ large upon his countenance.

The momentary lull was ended by another blare of trumpets, at whose signal Valayar Shah shouted to the chamber, 'All rise for the Nameless King!' The scarecrow-man bowed low, and fair scuttled backwards to the wings of the stage, as a heavy curtain behind them lifted.

All those at the table stood, as did every seated vampire within the hall. Lillian, reluctantly, followed suit.

From the shadows behind the curtain, dozens of pairs of violet eyes shone bright, and one by one their owners stepped out into the light of the hall; it was an entourage the likes of which Lillian had never seen—a gruesome, twisted line of creatures more removed from humanity than any vampire Lillian had encountered.

The procession of the Nameless King had begun.

TWENTY-TWO

The music recommenced, an assault on the senses. To its maddening strains, the procession took to the stage, a long line of bizarre creatures, some nimble and lithe, some shuffling and feeble. Concubines, half-naked vampiresses and slender, immortal youths, their skin scarred and powder-white, violet eyes dull, heads lolling upon their chests.

Each of the entourage was in some way misshapen, pierced with jewels and barbs, their pallid flesh like pin-cushions. Some were hunched, others had missing or withered limbs. Some were mutilated with bony crests beneath the skin or necks elongated by metal rings in the manner of the tribeswomen of the Dark Continent. Lillian wondered if, like Shah, these creatures were once those very people. It was impossible to tell now, for even if they had retained any features of their race, they were long subdued beneath sickening scars.

The leaders of the troupe were the sprightliest of all, shaven-headed women, though almost androgynous, ugly and somehow seductive, dancing in sinewy motions ahead of the others, swirling great veils about their slight, scarified forms. Their bodies twisted and contorted awkwardly, and with such immodesty that Lillian found herself averting her eyes more than once. The creatures hissed, and stretched out their malformed limbs to the crowd, extending long talons from fingers and toes. Lillian noticed, with growing distaste, that all of the creatures wore collars, and threaded between them was a silver chain, held by two guards who followed the cavorting slaves. Was this to be her own fate? A cavorting slave-beast, paraded naked before the King and his sycophants like so much cattle?

More servants came behind the procession, that laggard kind of human serf that Lillian had seen before. Their close-cropped scalps with their roughly sewn scars told another story; their vampiric masters had perhaps exercised the cruellest form of control over them. These liveried servants were big and strong, breathing in heavy grunts against the leather stocks about their necks. Lillian thought that they would be little use as guards in a hall full of vampires, and equally poor as servants for all but the most desultory tasks. They were doubtless nothing more than a vulgar display of power over humanity, akin to a fine pair of spotted carriage-dogs. Lillian remembered the servants she had seen in royal residences over the past few years, their ancestors taken from the furthest edges of the Empire as slaves, and now given an illusory freedom in the service of their supposed liberators. The vampire king was not so very different from English nobility perhaps.

As the dancers took up positions on the floor in front of the great table, seated upon velvet pillows, the liveried servants stood to attention on either side of the dais. Only then did four more vampires take to the stage.

The first two were the familiar sort, and Lillian took note of them especially—hunters, faces puckered where their flesh had necrotised, or else had been cut away deliberately in some ritual mutilation. They wore severely tailored coats, which flowed almost like gowns past the waist, while their high collars barely hid the brands that marked their throats and the undersides of their jaws. The other two creatures were women, dressed a hundred years out of style. Their waists were drawn in by impossibly small corsets, their bosoms pushed up outrageously, ghastly faces painted paler still, so that they fair glowed in the subdued light of the hall, and the whole arrangement topped with improbably tall powdered wigs. They fanned themselves and paraded around like music-hall viragos—parodies of ladies, perhaps intentionally so. One peeled away from the group and took a place near to Lillian, on the right hand of the throne. She smelled of iodine and arsenic powder, and smiled as though her features were incapable of change.

Finally, the music stopped and the crowd quietened to a reverent hush. Something changed in the very air, almost imperceptibly at first, and then more noticeably. Shadows gathered around the stage, the light from the torches failing to permeate them. Despite the heat of the packed hall, the temperature dropped to an icy chill—Lillian barely felt heat or cold any longer, and so she knew it must be a severe change. She saw the breath of the human serfs, Collins and the prince fog upon the air. The darkness intensified. Lillian felt the back of her head buzz, and a pressure grow about her eyes.

It is the influence of the King, the voice in her head intoned. *Show no weakness—his chosen few are immune to these effects, but most are completely in his thrall.*

Sure enough, Lillian saw dozens of vampires rubbing at their foreheads or dabbing themselves with kerchiefs as the malign influence of the King pervaded the chamber. She found herself craning about to look at the curtain at the right-hand side of the banqueting table, waiting with bated breath for the Nameless King to make his entrance. But he did not.

Instead, a collective gasp from the dance floor caused Lillian to turn back. From her vantage point upon the wide dais, she saw in the centre of the room a great shadow stretched out like an enormous spider. The vampires scurried away from the black, smoky void, pressing back into the crowd as the form coalesced and began to fold in upon itself. Tendrils of smoke and pure darkness retracted from floor and ceiling, taking shape within the centre of the hall. From the reactions of the vampire nobility,

Lillian guessed few, if any, had witnessed this before.

It is a trick. Do not be afraid.

Lillian risked a glance at de Montfort, but his eyes were fixed ahead. She took a deep breath, trying her best to quell the discomfiting sensation in her head.

Finally, the shadows shrank and swirled further, as though a tornado of darkness were forming in the room, and reality seemed to snap back into place, violently. Onlookers ducked as a great chorus of shrieks and squawks filled the room, and from the darkness came a tide of blue-black feathers. A murder of crows, hundreds strong, erupted from the shrinking shadow. In their wake, a wave of dream-like energy crashed through the hall. Lillian felt it wash over her; her skin prickled with it, and the pressure that had steadily built within her head at last dissipated.

As Lillian blinked away the sensation, she saw that the disturbance had ended. The fires burned brightly once more; the aerial supplicants groaned their agony again, but now to the accompanying call of crows. And in the centre of the hall the Nameless King stood tall, his entrance complete.

Fear not, Lillian, came the voice again. *It is naught but illusion. With my help, you will see through it all. You will see that he can be killed, just like any one of us.*

The figure advanced. The Nameless King towered over the assembled courtiers, who stared up at him in both reverence and astonishment. He was tall and whip-thin, clad all in black. Across his shoulders was a thick mantle of crow feathers, from which a long cloak tumbled down to the floor, and was lifted as he walked by two cherubim-like vampire children. His arms were bare, ending at long, thin hands tipped with sharpened black talons. His dark flesh was marked with strange symbols, like an ancient script carved into his skin. A hood was pulled over his head, shrouding his face in darkness but for the gleaming eyes. Yet the hood could not mask the grotesque features of the King fully—his neck was unnaturally long and wrinkled with blue-tinged skin, which folded over myriad scars. His jaw was angular, jutting from the cowl to reveal a grinning mouth full of large, artificial teeth, black lips shrunken away from them. Lillian squinted at the creature, whose form seemed reluctant to become fully solid. Shadows clung to him, unwilling to relinquish the devoted embrace of their master.

All of the grotesque oddities that were present in Shah were apparent in the Nameless King too, but taken to the extreme. Taller, more severely thin, like a stick insect in a collector's case. Lillian wondered just how old Shah must be, and whether all vampires grew to such stature and ugliness.

The Nameless King moved in measured strides, his body held rigid, his motions fluid and graceful. He covered the ground to the stage too quickly; he was upon the dais before Lillian had seen him take more than two or three steps, and he brought with him his own personal darkness. The snarling, naked child-things that held the King's trailing cloak looked about furtively with sunken, violet eyes.

Shah welcomed the King to the stage, before bowing low and retreating to his place. The King looked towards Prince Leopold, and then at Lillian, holding her gaze for just a moment. His eyes were brighter than any she had seen before. She felt the blood in her veins move like a tide towards the waxing moon. She began to doubt that she could resist the power of this creature. She suddenly felt insignificant in the presence of this millennia-old immortal.

He welcomes you to his family. Acknowledge him.

Lillian bowed her head subserviently, averting her eyes from the King's, and immediately feeling the pull of his presence subside. She knew not if she had done the right thing, but he turned away from her all the same, and looked at the quietened audience. As he raised his arms, all the vampires around the table, and those around the edges of the hall, took their seats; Lillian followed suit.

'I bid you welcome to Scarrowfall, to my home, on this auspicious night,' said the King. He did not speak alone. The entourage, the horrid vampire children and lithe women, all lent their voices to his, in a jarring chorus. His own voice was almost a croak; the skittering of loose rock down a quarry bank, presaging an avalanche. Yet through unknown means the unearthly choir of voices could be heard by all within the vast chamber. 'For some of you, this is the first time you have spent this night in our presence. For some, it will be the last opportunity you have to make this pilgrimage. All of you, young and old, are welcome.

'This is the most important All Hallows in the history of our people. Most of you have heard whispers of Lord Lucien de Montfort's great experiment. You have seen for yourselves the fruits of his labours, and know that the rumours are, at least for the most part, true.' The King paused as a murmur rippled through the congregation.

'Recent events have caused great concern amongst our kind. I imagine that our kindred in the furthest corners of the globe have yet to hear of the great threat that has been unleashed upon the world. I have been asked to say some words to assuage your fears on this matter. I cannot do that. Even as we speak, the Riftborn spread through the south like a cancer, and the humans shall swiftly discover that they live on borrowed time. We shall, of course, endure, but not without cost. Nor, it seems, without change.

'In the space of a decade, a mere blink of an eye for such as us, the Iscariot Sanction has gone from myth, to theory, to heresy, to reality. It is a symbol of these changing times, of our growing power. I decree that this is not something we should fear, but neither is it something we should embrace hastily. Lord de Montfort would have us bolster our race with fresh blood; to create a veritable army of highborn *wampyr* from human stock, as God created Eve from the rib of Adam. But that is not our way. That is not how we have endured the long centuries.'

De Montfort made to stand, and thought better of it. Yet his action was enough to draw the attention of all at the banqueting table, and of the King himself, who now turned to face his Majestic servant.

'Please, Lord de Montfort. There is something that so preys upon your mind that you would consider interrupting my All Hallows address.' The King's voice was alone now, his choir paused, staring vacantly. His every word dripped malice, and strength. 'If you have something to add, I would bid you do so, for all who sit at my table are equals on this night.'

If it was possible for a cold-skinned vampire to look nervous, de Montfort did now. Lillian enjoyed watching him squirm, before he seemed finally to steel himself and get to his feet. Beneath the cowl, the Nameless King cocked his head a fraction; a movement imperceptible perhaps to a mortal, but enough to show surprise at de Montfort's audacity.

'Your Majesty, I apologise. I merely wished to point out the risks we have taken to perfect the Iscariot Sanction. Though my eagerness is perhaps born of a personal investment in the matter, I am ever your servant.' De Montfort bowed and took his seat once more. The King seemed to consider these words but briefly, and then turned back to the chamber.

'I am old.' The King's choir intoned again. 'All of you know the story, that I am so old I have forgotten my own name. It is true. I have ruled our kind since the earliest days. As far as I know I am the only one of our kind remaining who ever saw Judas Iscariot before he passed from this world. And in that time, I have led us with caution. I have built an empire in the shadows, immutable as stone. I have not reached so great an age, nor gathered such power, by embracing every foolish idea that has come our way. And yet, in this, my hand has been forced. The events in London, as regrettable as they may seem, will tear the world of the humans apart. By the time the Riftborn are finished, the humans will be crying out for a saviour. And they will look no further than Scarrowfall. They hate and fear us now, but eventually they shall have to embrace us.

'Lord de Montfort's innovations will serve us well, at least once more. But they shall serve us as a deterrent, a display of our power over the humans, rather than a crude weapon. We have ever been the knife in the darkness, rather than the mailed fist. We shall never need to issue the Iscariot Sanction, for the very threat of it shall be enough to dissuade the humans from taking up arms against us. It is without further ado, therefore, that I introduce to you the product of Lord de Montfort's scientific endeavours. A woman who was, until very recently, human, but is now of my very blood. The first pure *wampyr* to be created in more than a millennium; a *wampyr* who bears all the power of my house, but without the terrible curse that afflicts the later generations of our kind. I give to you: Lillian.'

Go to him, slowly. Be the perfect lady, for he commands it and expects it.

Lillian stood, wondering how to act the perfect lady when, according to her mother, she had never managed it before. She walked as confidently as she dared, past the glower of Colonel Ewart, past the vampire bishop, and through the tangled mass of half-naked courtesans who sat at the foot of the table. She stopped before the King, masking her disgust at the stench of death that wafted from him. He took her hand in his enormous, wizened claw, turning her like a prized slave to the crowd.

'Behold, the product of the Iscariot Sanction. Let no one among you doubt the truth of it. Let none among you label her "blasphemy", nor seek to do her harm, for after this night Lillian shall be my bride. Her purity shall secure the strength of my line for all the days to come. Our greatest glories are ahead of us; this I promise.'

The applause began, softly at first, growing like a rainstorm, until it became deafening. The cheers of the vampires were little more than nauseating screeches and clicks, their vocal utterances far beyond human. Lillian felt sick. De Montfort was right— the Nameless King would make her his bride if she did not do something about it.

Take three paces back, and stand still, de Montfort's voice rang in her head again.

The King released her hand, and she did as she was bid.

The applause died down. Lillian did her best to maintain her composure as cold, slender hands pawed at her dress and tugged at her sleeves. The vacuous, lolling concubines seemed fascinated with her, like children playing with a new doll.

'I am sure that the human delegation at my table has not gone unnoticed,' the Nameless King croaked, his thralls lending a many-faceted harmony to his words. 'I am equally certain that one amongst them requires no introduction. It is my very great pleasure to welcome Prince Leopold, to extend to him the hospitality of my house, and to secure, through him, an agreement between our two peoples that is unique in two thousand years of history.'

There was a ripple of applause. The prince stood and bowed formally, though he looked sicklier than ever, and not entirely of his own mind.

'I said that the Iscariot Sanction would be issued once more,' the King said. 'The recipient of this mighty gift shall be none other than Prince Leopold himself. With this one blessing, the prince shall not only have his ailments cured, but shall serve as the greatest possible symbol of the new unity between our people.'

The prince walked around the table and stood to attention before the King. Leopold was almost as pale as the vampires that surrounded him, and now did indeed look weak and sickly to Lillian's eyes. He was dressed in his military uniform, with medals upon his breast, though such a thin, callow youth would never have the opportunity to earn such plaudits upon a battlefield. He stood before the assembled mass of grotesque creatures in their masquerade costumes. Lillian fancied that the prince fitted in well with his new bedfellows—they all pretended they were something other than they were.

'My lords, ladies and gentlemen,' the prince said, almost as though he were talking in his sleep. 'It is a great honour and privilege to be accepted into the ranks of the Knights Iscariot, surely the most prestigious order still surviving today. It is my solemn promise to use this mighty gift wisely, to become an ambassador for both our peoples. I count the days until this blessing is bestowed—'

'Enough!'

Lillian recognised Robert Collins' voice. She did not require de Montfort's psychic command to keep her eyes front and her demeanour composed.

The Nameless King's eyes burned from within the shaded cowl, like coals reignited. They stared over Lillian's left shoulder, to where Robert Collins had been seated. A low, grumbling, croak came from the King's throat, barely audible. It was uncomfortably similar to the guttural sounds made by the ghouls.

'As adviser to Prince Leopold, and a gentleman with a place at my table, I shall overlook your lack of manners,' said the King. 'If you would have words with your master, then by all means do so. But I would advise you to choose your moment more opportunely.'

Lillian still did not turn to look at Collins, but she could sense him shift uncomfortably; she could smell the fear on him, putrid and raw. He did not retake his seat.

'Your… Majesty,' Collins said to the King, his voice quavering, 'I have held my peace long enough. My prince—Leopold—I must advise against this course of action. You cannot do this.'

Confusion crossed the prince's features for a moment, and was replaced swiftly by the vacant stare. Was he drugged? Hypnotised?

Lillian heard footsteps behind her. There were gasps from the crowd, and salacious giggles too. This time Lillian did turn, for she was certain that there were no eyes on her now. Everyone stared instead at Collins, who was even now shrugging off Ewart's heavy hand and walking around the table with some trepidation. The man looked pleadingly at Prince Leopold, though his eyes betrayed how futile he knew his actions to be.

'Sit down, Collins, there's a good fellow,' the prince said.

'I humbly beg your pardon, Your Highness,' Collins replied, slowly approaching the prince, 'but I cannot. I am your servant, and you may do with me as you will, but I shall not hold my tongue. It would be the ultimate betrayal of my duties if I allowed this... this madness... to go any further.'

'Oh, don't hide your true feelings on our account, Sir Robert,' Valayar Shah intoned from the sidelines, a jest that was met by a ripple of cautious laughter from the audience.

Collins ignored Shah's interruption. 'My prince, I beg you. The Knights Iscariot have taken too heavy a price. They have killed your mother; they have opened the Rift!'

'What is done is done,' said Leopold, with a dreamy wave of his hand. 'We find the world in grave danger, and it needs a saviour. I wanted the gift for selfish reasons, but now I see it is more important than me; my fate is inconsequential in the grander scheme. The Knights Iscariot shall save everyone from the ravages of the Riftborn: don't you see that, Collins? Sit down now—you are embarrassing us in front of our host.'

'You will not be a saviour, my prince,' Collins said, quietly. Lillian groaned inwardly; she sensed that Collins had now pursued his pleas beyond the point of no return. 'You will be a puppet. And these monsters shall pull your strings.'

The Nameless King moved so fast that Lillian could not follow him, for all her keen senses. He was a flurry of shadow and crow-black feathers, and appeared to not so much rush at Collins, but to coalesce next to him from thin air.

A long, painfully thin arm took Collins by the throat and hoisted him off the ground as though he weighed nothing. The Nameless King's cowl fell back, revealing a thin, drawn face, wizened with age, blue-black in colour, and covered in horrendous scars in swirling patterns, pierced a hundred times with tiny rings of gold. The flesh of the cheeks and nose was eaten away by rot; the eyes blazed within sunken sockets; the ears were large and misshapen, with the fangs of some great beast pushed through the lobes. The King's large wooden teeth chattered momentarily as if in anticipation of the feast that was surely to come. The head jerked upwards, revealing a long, avian neck, which began to ripple and bulge. Though Lillian's feelings had been numbed from her own transformation, what she now witnessed filled her with a cold horror, for it was proof at last of the vampires' utterly monstrous nature, and her own grim future.

The King's mouth yawned open, impossibly wide, and his entire upper body seemed to grow as the cavernous mouth stretched further, until he was a grotesque mass of pulsating flesh beneath rippling black feathers. The false teeth fell onto the floor. The creature's jaw split in twain, craning outwards, and from each corner of the petal-like maw that was once his face, four great fangs slowly extended, aimed directly at the terrified man that stared at them in dumb horror.

Collins screamed, high and mad, the sound gargling in a half-crushed throat. Every vampire in the hall smiled and hissed in glee. Prince Leopold's expression remained blank. The Nameless King dug his talons into his victim's neck, so that blood flowed in a great torrent. Collins bled into the hideous maw, before the King drew him close, and thrust him headfirst into the hideous, yawning gullet, like an Indian python swallowing a deer. The great fangs clamped at last around Collins' shoulders, and the Nameless King took the wretch in an embrace that drained every drop of blood from him in an instant.

No, Lillian. Not now! It is too—

De Montfort had sensed Lillian's thoughts, but his mental warning went unheeded. Lillian had seen enough, and seized her chance. She leapt up onto the table and launched herself at Ewart. To his credit, he almost reacted in time, but her vampire speed was too much for any mortal, and as she flung him backwards through the curtain behind him, he was missing his revolver, which was now in Lillian's hand.

Even as the Nameless King discarded Collins' withered husk upon the dais, Lillian's first bullet struck his bulging throat. The second hit his shadow, which parted in swirling patterns as the bullet passed through it. The third nicked Prince Leopold in the shoulder, tearing off an epaulette and drawing a girlish cry from the addled royal.

Before Lillian could fire a fourth time, she was hoisted from her feet. The grotesque features of the King, now whole again, faced her. One massive hand was about her throat, another closed around her pistol. The gasps and cries of the vast crowd of vampires reached her ears. To stop now would be to accept death, or perhaps a fate worse than death. Her only option—her time-honoured tactic—was to attack beyond the point of reason.

Calm, Lillian. He thinks he has you under control.

The King was too strong, but he had not fully restrained her. For a second, Lillian went limp and compliant, and only when the Nameless King paused to inspect his rebellious bride did she strike. She lashed out with her foot, catching him so hard in the jaw that for a moment she saw it split apart again into two mandibles, before snapping shut. She twisted behind herself, wrenching a torch from a sconce with all her might, and thrust the flames towards her assailant.

The King screeched as the flames touched his face, and dropped Lillian upon the dais. The gun landed by her chair. Guards rushed towards her from all directions.

Lillian trusted her instincts. She spun away from the first guard, an oafish human, and stooped to pick up the gun. The second guard, a vampire with an iron-hard grip, placed a hand upon her, and she quickly fired the gun upwards through the creature's chin. As the guard fell, she tugged a curved blade from its belt and used it to slash backwards at yet another human serf who rushed headlong at her. The other highborns around the table rose to attack her, de Montfort with them, encouraging them, as he made a charade of being distraught at the actions of his blasphemous creation. The King had not retreated, but instead began to gather himself as guards filed into the space behind the great table.

The curtain behind Lillian billowed, and Ewart leapt from the wings, knife in hand. Lillian had almost been taken unawares, but her response was so fast she surprised herself. She deflected Ewart's charge, sending him flying into the nearest vampire guard, and used the distraction to leap up onto the table, and propel herself to the sword brackets behind the stage. She dropped the curved dagger, and instead grasped the hilt of a great claymore, tearing it from its iron cradle, and dropping to the ground nimbly. As one, the guards checked their advance. The King roared something unintelligible in a language Lillian had never heard.

Lillian summoned her wickedest smile.

The sword was old, an antique, more ornament than effective weapon. Fully five feet long and too heavy for a human to wield comfortably, nonetheless it was deadly in Lillian's hands. She swept it in a flurry, each great stroke forcing the guards back or tearing into them, sending them flying over the table or staggering through the curtain. Lord Cherleten had once said that vampires were not a great deal stronger than men, that they were only able to ignore fatigue and pain, but Lillian was not so sure this was true. She realised with each sword-stroke that she was certainly stronger than the fledgling vampire guards; her highborn blood accounted for something. She doubted she could match the King himself, but she forced her way inexorably towards him regardless, the claymore hacking off the limbs of human and hunter alike in her merciless fury. With each incapacitated foe, the King's shouts grew weaker, his choir diminished.

More vampires were climbing onto the stage, clearly hoping to win their King's favour by stopping his assailant. Lillian swept the sword about her, faster and harder, creating a dizzying arc of flashing steel. She climbed again upon the table, and moved relentlessly along it, dashing in the brains of any who strayed too close. The King stood now at the head of the table, having gathered himself, his eyes burning into Lillian with fury and disdain.

He is ordering them to take you alive, de Montfort's voice said in her head.

That thought drove Lillian on.

With a wide sweep of the blade from left to right, she forced back her assailants, and charged headlong at the Nameless King, who now roared in his black tongue. He was a giant, but such details had never held Lillian back before.

She launched herself from the end of the table, over the heads of two vampire servants who rushed to protect their master, and swung the blade down towards the Nameless King's head, even as he cursed her.

Yes! De Montfort sensed triumph, and his glee echoed in Lillian's head.

The blade passed into the black mist that clung to the King's form, and cleaved onwards like there was nothing to resist it. The shadows coalesced into undulating tendrils of purest darkness, split in twain by the ancient claymore, only to be sucked back into one mass of concentrated night in its wake.

There was nothing beneath the blade. Lillian hit the ground awkwardly; the blade struck the dais so hard the wooden boards splintered and the sword embedded itself in the thick timbers beneath. The smoke dissipated and, three feet away from where he should have been, stood the Nameless King. The croaking in his throat became a foul gargle. At first Lillian thought she had struck him after all, but she realised that the noise was not a death-rattle but a laugh.

Lillian had often been affronted by laughter from those who thought they had power over her. Many were noble lords and ladies, who felt superior due to their station. For the most part, she had turned the other cheek, and simmered at the humiliation. Others were rogues, spies and ne'er-do-wells, who thought it amusing to be confronted by a woman. Most of those she had killed, or at least wiped the smiles from their thuggish faces. She decided now that the Nameless King would fall into the latter group.

She felt the change in the air about her as a dozen pairs of strong hands swept towards her. She had but one last opportunity. In a fluid motion, Lillian whipped Ewart's pistol from her dress, and stepped forward two paces. She fired the gun until it was empty, and threw the revolver into the swirling shadows, screaming with rage.

She felt de Montfort's dismay. She sensed he was already retreating, preparing to disavow himself of this failed conspiracy.

The Nameless King emerged once more from the inveigling supernatural shroud, his gargoyle features poking from the shadow, a taloned hand closing around her throat. Thick, pinkish blood trickled from his mouth. He spat the bullet into Lillian's face and hoisted her from her feet.

She tried to strike the Nameless King with a fist, but he knocked her hand aside, and held her out at arm's length. Such was his sheer size that she could not reach him even to kick him. He lowered her roughly to the ground, maintaining his grip upon her neck, as two vampire guards rushed to flank her, securing her arms, curved swords drawn, points aimed firmly at Lillian's temples. The Nameless King laughed again.

Still restraining her with a long, skeletal arm, he turned and waved away the onlookers from the dais, who reluctantly went back to their places in the hall. Lillian struggled, but she knew she was defeated. More guards took to the stage, others were dragged away, limbs missing or throats slit. Lillian took some solace in the damage she had inflicted.

'It appears we have an assassin in our midst,' the King said. 'This wench has broken the code that has held our people together for two millennia. A code that has seen the Knights Iscariot thrive where other shadow societies have fractured. We kill not our own!'

Some in the crowd repeated this phrase solemnly.

'Many of you warned that a product of the Iscariot Sanction could not be trusted, and it seems that you were right. I, your king, am not infallible after all.'

Hush descended upon the hall.

'Now, girl, if you wish to live, you will give up your secrets to me,' the Nameless King said, and leaned in, staring hard at Lillian with his bright, sunken eyes.

Lillian waited for instruction from de Montfort, but heard nothing. Indeed, she could not sense his presence at all; it felt as though a fug had lifted from her mind, a niggling voice in her head that was finally silent.

The King recoiled, and straightened. 'This creature is not of my blood!' he announced.

A great commotion rippled through the hall—shock, disgust and outrage.

The Nameless King scraped a long claw down Lillian's cheek, and dipped his fingertip in the pinkish fluid that emerged. He sucked the pale blood from his finger, and his shrunken face contorted into a snarl.

'Heresy! Treason!' he roared, and his sudden loss of composure was answered in kind by the assembled vampires. 'She is made of the blood of the elders. Viscount Blesington, if I am not mistaken. And where is he? My most loyal cousin, one of the oldest of the Inner Circle. He would not betray his king, not in a thousand lifetimes. He has been murdered—murdered to bring this blasphemy into the world!'

Masked ladies screeched and wailed. Twisted lords bellowed outrage. Behind the Nameless King, Lillian saw Valayar Shah gesturing theatrically, stirring up the crowd like an agitator at a riot. Prince Leopold sat nearby, in a pile of severed limbs and a great pool of blood, looking as though his world had capsized.

'Lord De Montfort has created an abomination that neither of us can control.' The King turned to Lillian. 'I have a mind to let you kill him, for I sense that you would like to, very much. But de Montfort's crime is no matter for such games. He has committed the ultimate atrocity against his own blood, and for that he will suffer the greatest agony before his time on this earth is spent.' He looked again at the crowd. 'Where is he? Bring Lord de Montfort forth, that he may pay the price for his treachery.'

Scores of vampires began to look at one another, and a great clamour rose up. But de Montfort was gone, and his hunters with him.

'Search the castle!' the King proclaimed. 'Leave no stone unturned. I want de Montfort alive to answer for his crimes.'

Courtiers, guards and servants alike filed from the hall, some laughing giddily in anticipation of the chase. Hunters scurried up the stone walls, climbing spider-like onto narrow balconies above.

'I had not expected de Montfort to be so audacious,' the King said to Lillian. 'You were a fool to trust him. Even had you succeeded, there are enough loyal followers in my court to avenge me. His plan was foolish, and you will both die for it; very publicly, and very painfully.'

'You should do it now,' Lillian said, good sense lost to her hatred of the King and all of his kind. 'For if I am given half a chance, I shall finish what I started.'

'You dare...' the King began, and then chuckled, though the laugh sounded more like a fit of consumption. He ran a sharp talon across Lillian's jaw, and pulled her chin upwards to look at him. 'I admire your spirit, girl. There may be a place in my household for you yet, though I should think the court Majestics shall have to subdue you a little first. You will learn to obey your king, if you wish to live.'

Lillian was about to defy him once more, but a hue and cry from one of the balconies cut her short.

'Enemies sighted! We are under attack!' a voice screeched. The King wheeled about; the vampires who had remained in the hall, indecisive, now began to push their way towards the great doors, realising perhaps that this All Hallows was not to be the great celebration they had expected.

'Who dares attack Scarrowfall?' the King rasped. 'De Montfort?'

'Humans, sire!' the voice called back. 'They come by sea.'

'So, de Montfort has shown his true colours,' the King said, more quietly.

Valayar Shah, who alone among the nobles had stayed beside the King, stepped forward and said, 'Your Majesty, Lord de Montfort would not stoop so low.'

'Then what are they doing here?' asked the Nameless King.

'Seeking revenge,' Lillian said, her words dripping malice.

The King glared at her. 'I offered them peace,' he said. 'They have chosen war. These walls shall hold, and England will find itself beset from enemies within and without. And they can expect no aid from their former allies. The major powers of Europe are indebted to me now.'

'Not any more,' Lillian said. 'When the Knights Iscariot opened the Rift, they poisoned the world. I doubt even the most opportunistic monarch will stand with you now. I may die here, I may even die as one of you. But it shall give me great satisfaction to know that I shan't die alone.'

'You—' the King began, but at that moment the entire castle shook, and great noise like a peal of thunder crashed all around. Masonry fell from the vaulted ceiling of the great hall. One of the acrobatic entertainers fell crashing to the marble floor in a bloody heap as his chains became dislodged.

'What were you saying about your walls?' Lillian scoffed.

The King paused for but a moment, and looked as though his patience was gone. He drew back a clawed hand, and Lillian prepared herself for the end.

Instead, she heard a hiss, and sensed the blades positioned either side of her relax as something attracted the guards' attention. The King flailed, and as he spun away from Lillian she saw the hilt of a dagger protruding from the crow-feather mantle at the nape of his neck.

'I spoke truth, Majesty,' Valayar Shah said, drawing a second blade. 'De Montfort would not stoop so low, but I would. His cause is just, and he has shown us the way. But it is I, Valayar Shah, who shall end your reign.'

The guards stepped towards Shah, sheer confusion slowing them.

Another shell rocked the castle; naval guns were pounding the walls, if Lillian was not mistaken.

By the time the guards had reached Shah, he had already slashed the King across the throat, causing the Nameless King to strike out in a wild flurry. For a second, Lillian thought

Shah's blade had been true, and that the King would die. Yet he gathered his strength and composure to him visibly, and the King's great hands closed around the eastern prince's head. Valayar Shah's head came away from his shoulders in the King's hands. In that very moment, the banqueting table was smashed asunder by falling masonry. Lillian was already on her feet. She extended both arms and tore the throats from the two guards. The King spun around, clutching at the dagger in his back. He was apparently dimly aware of Lillian's advance, summoning about himself his shadow-cloak, though not quickly enough.

Lillian had secreted one weapon from her captors, hidden it for such a time as this. She drove her knee into the back of the King as the garrotte from her silver locket bit deep into his puckered gizzard, where Shah's blade had struck.

She pulled as hard as she could, feeling the garrotte strike bone. The King weakened. She let the wire retract into the locket and released her grip, dashing back to the slain guards and taking up a scimitar. While his head was attached to his shoulders, she did not think he could die.

The King's head tipped back, revealing a gaping wound; his face contorted once again into a grotesque maw, with great fangs clacking uncontrollably, like the mandibles of some gigantic insect.

Lillian closed both hands around the grip of the sword, and delivered a two-handed stroke to the King's neck. Blood, now deep red from the feast Collins had provided, gushed upwards. The King's body hit the dais; his grotesque head rolled away and came to a rest beside the terrified, huddled form of Prince Leopold.

TWENTY-THREE

John pulled once more on the chains, and the guard breathed his last, rolling onto the flagstones, eyes bulging.

John slumped to the ground, exhausted. Blood ran from the claw-marks across his body. He gulped ragged breaths into his lungs and tried to steady his shaking hands. In the passageway outside his former cell, two human guards lay dead—one strangled, the other with a knife protruding from beneath his ribs. A vampire also lay motionless, skin blackened from the electric rays of the Tesla pistol, which John now took up in his trembling hands and cranked another charge into. It had been a gift indeed from Smythe, and John had had to fight hard for it, for the gun had landed within reach of his cellmate, the ravenous ghoul. He looked at his left arm and winced at the depth of the gash. He shuddered to think what infection those noisome claws carried; but that was of small concern now.

John tore off a strip of his ragged shirt and made a tourniquet for his arm. He tried on both the guards' shoes, and took the pair that fitted best, before donning one of their tatty, over-large coats. Lastly, he gathered his weapons, tucked a stolen revolver into his belt, and set off along the passage.

John stole past five doors, all solid, studded with iron, with vision-slits at head-height. There was nothing but pitch darkness behind each one, though at one he heard a low sobbing. His stomach knotted as he thought of Hetty, and he almost went back to find a key to the door, when he saw a brief flash of violet eyes in the darkness. Regardless of whether the vampire was the source of the crying, or a feral guardian like the one in John's own cell, he could not risk another fight.

He crept onwards. The end of the corridor terminated at a junction, at which a torch blazed in a rusted sconce. No other guards had been attracted by his battle, but that did not mean more were not on their way.

As John skulked in the shadows, his condition making him more cautious than was customary, he heard the distant report of heavy guns, muffled by the castle's thick walls, and followed almost immediately by a deafening explosion. The ground shook and John crouched low—the incredible sound had prompted shouts, slamming doors and heavy footfalls that seemed to come from all directions. He had almost determined to dash through the tunnels when he was forced to check his advance; a vampire swept past the end of the corridor, oblivious to John's presence, moving swiftly down the left passage.

Another explosion, and every cell revealed its occupants, moaning, screaming, or roaring in bestial fury. Pale hands, some tipped with long, yellow claws, forced their way through the vision slits, raking the smoky air of the passage beyond. John stepped away from them. He knew there might be innocents within some of those cells, but he could not help them. John thought of Hetty; he thought of Cottam's wife, Maud, and of the assertion that 'No one 's goes to Scarrowfall ever comes back.' He hoped he would have the chance to return, though he knew in his heart it was unlikely. The bombardment had begun; the soldiers would be here soon.

John had little time. He had to find Lillian, and the prince. He marched forward and took the torch from its bracket. Steeling himself, he took the left turn, and followed in the wake of the vampire he had seen, hoping to find a way out of the accursed dungeon.

* * *

Lillian swung the scimitar in a graceful arc, slicing through the neck of a screeching vampiress that flew at her from a side passage. The blade was beginning to dull, and the woman's head was severed from its neck only by virtue of Lillian's sheer strength. Lillian's arms ached—there had still been several loyal supporters of the Nameless King in the hall, and they had tried to avenge their fallen monarch.

Lillian felt a tug on her left arm, and heard a piteous cry, like a child's. She looked down at Prince Leopold, whom she had dragged through the hall by his hair.

'Stop your snivelling!' she snapped, 'Be thankful I didn't take your head while I was about it.'

The prince was a broken man. Lillian cared not. She took the hilt of the stiletto dagger that stuck out of her thigh, and pulled it out with no more than a grunt and wince. In truth it hurt little, but the blade must have torn through muscle, for her leg buckled beneath her when she put weight upon it.

She threw the prince roughly to the floor and cut away the lower portion of her dress with the knife, to improve her mobility. Leopold averted his eyes instinctively.

'There's no point playing the gentleman now, Your Royal Highness,' Lillian scoffed. 'That ship has sailed.'

'My mother shall hear of this,' he squawked. And then lucidity dawned in his eyes for a moment, before he wailed again, 'Mother! Mother!'

Lillian made to grab Leopold once more by the hair and drag him towards the great doors of the hall, but another explosion against the castle walls caused the ballroom to shake, and huge lumps of stone to fall from the high ceiling. Lillian pushed the prince out of the path of a tumbling gargoyle, and almost wrenched his arm from his socket dragging him back towards the dais as the lintel above the doors was shaken from its niche and crashed to earth, bringing half the wall with it.

Lillian wove her way through the falling debris and screaming bodies of the slaves that now plummeted from the ceiling. The prince's tarrying almost got them both crushed several times, and with each passing second Lillian regretted not tearing out his throat earlier. Something within her still clung to the idea of redemption; she knew that it was the thought of John. If he still lived, and she prayed he did, he would never forgive her for succumbing to her rage and killing Leopold before the prince could face trial for his crimes.

Behind the heavy curtains at the rear of the stage were further rooms, now in darkness, which Lillian felt sure must lead somewhere. She heard distant gunfire—either troops were entering Scarrowfall, or the guards were firing upon would-be invaders. Like as not she would be shot as an enemy of either side, given her condition.

She was about to opt for the left-most room, when she heard the frantic scurrying of claws from the hall behind her, and the hideous, high-pitched trilling of ghouls. She turned to see them in their dozens, scurrying down the walls from the balconies, gleaming eyes fixed upon her. One of them pounced catlike to the floor and at once began to feast upon a fallen slave. The remaining creatures advanced cautiously. Lillian knew not whether they came for her or for the prince, or were simply acting on instinct, having lost their masters.

She acted quickly, racing to the massive braziers that flanked the stage, pushing at them with all her might while the prince sobbed, 'My God, we are to die!' over and over to no one in particular. The first toppled reluctantly, spilling blazing coals across the floor, which flared brightly, sending a handful of ghouls retreating in ape-like bounds.

Lillian raced to the other side of the stage, aware that even her body would only endure so much. She had lost half a yard of pace, and now the ghouls reached her, lashing at her with jagged claws, snapping with elongated, pointed teeth. She slashed one across the throat, threw a second from the dais where it rolled into the spreading flames, and barely managed to grapple a third as it leapt upon her. She redirected its strength, tripping it as Mrs. Ito had taught her, but it clung to her ferociously, so bestial in its ungainly fury that the eastern arts were ineffective. Lillian readjusted her balance, and instead threw herself and the ghoul bodily into the brazier's heavy iron supports. It toppled as she crashed to the ground, rolling the creature from her just in time to avoid the slashing claws of two more.

The brazier fell backwards towards the heavy curtains, contents spilling across the wooden stage. Flames licked up the drapes almost at once. The lacquered wooden platform hissed as the coals met it.

Lillian forced herself to her feet, lashing out blindly. She fumbled for the sword that she had dropped in the scuffle and hacked left and right desperately—she had come so far, been through so much. To be killed by these base creatures would be an insult.

Even as the exertion began to tell, and her sword arm started to disobey her almost wilfully, the ghouls faltered, their eyes reflecting red and orange flame, noses sniffing at the smoky air. One by one they stopped their assault, and then backed away, whimpering. Lillian risked a glance over her shoulder, and saw what they saw: the heavy stage-curtains were fully ablaze. The ancient timbers overhead had caught fire also. The stage upon which she stood was burning.

Scarrowfall was ablaze.

Lillian cursed. Her plan had been born of desperation—now she would perhaps die in a fire rather than by the hands of the ghouls. The ignominy of such a fate was just as wretched.

Turning her back on the wretched beasts, which even now retreated from the billowing smoke, she ran to where the prince crouched, head tucked under his arms. Lillian grabbed him by the collar and dragged him with her, plunging both of them through a small gap in the curtains, flames licking at her, smoke stinging her eyes.

* * *

The human guards, armed with rifles, raced past John's hiding place towards the sound of distant gunfire.

John emerged from the scullery once the coast was clear, looking for an exit from the vast kitchen in which he had found himself. He moved stealthily, picking up a carving knife from a table as he went, testing the heft of it in his left hand while gripping the Tesla pistol in his right.

Whatever was happening in Scarrowfall, no one seemed to have any time for him. The few servants John had encountered had looked the other way; the guards had all been so preoccupied with the battle outside that they had been easily evaded so far.

John stepped from the kitchen into a dark hallway, crowded with debris and filled with smoke, which swirled as it was sucked out through open door. A cold waft of air gave John hope—he had found a way outside, though he knew not whether the best course of action was to find Smythe and join the assault proper, or to venture deeper into the castle to search for Lillian.

He paused, crouching beneath a stairway as he heard footsteps treading upon it. Two sets, moving swiftly. John chanced a look at the figures as they reached the foot of the stair. He froze.

John would have recognised the silhouette of Lucien de Montfort anywhere, even without the customary swagger. Beside him was a tall, bald-headed hunter in a flowing black coat, carrying a banded wooden chest. John could not make out what de Montfort was saying, but the vampire lord strode confidently from the castle into the night air, beckoning on his monstrous servant.

The decision was made. Though John wanted nothing more than to find Lillian and rescue Prince Leopold, the prospect of doing either in a burning building while the real villain escaped justice was not one John could accept.

He followed the shadowy pair as close as he dared. Beyond the door was a small yard surrounded by a low wall. Beyond that, what looked like an ancient graveyard stretched along the edge of a rocky cliff-top, as far as the eye could see in the first weak light of dawn. John watched de Montfort and his servant moving quickly down a narrow, winding path between jagged monuments and ancient tombs. The wind whipped more fiercely; John had not been aware that Scarrowfall was so precariously close to the edge of a high cliff, and yet he heard the sound of crashing waves so near that they almost drowned out the booming report of the naval guns.

John dashed to the wall, crouching behind it. For the first time, he looked up at the castle that had been his prison. Scarrowfall was an ancient, rambling construction of tall hexagonal towers and tumbledown ramparts. Half-timbered galleries shored up against curtain walls of thick stone; conical spires thrust towards the blood-red sky. Smoke poured from windows and arrow-slits, obscuring the tallest towers. Men—or perhaps vampires—scurried around the battlements, carrying guns, barking commands that were carried away from John's ears on the wind. He left them to their battle, remaining in cover as much as he could so as not to be noticed. It hardly seemed likely that anyone in Scarrowfall would pay much heed to a lone prisoner now, but it was better to be safe than sorry.

Once he picked up the path that de Montfort had trod, John saw the extent of the vampires' domain, which stretched for miles towards crooked perimeter walls, and thence on to the vast moors. Across acres of fields and gardens, hundreds of shadowy forms fled the castle with preternatural swiftness. John heard fighting amongst them—pistols cracked, sabres rattled. Officers shouted sharp commands, while inhuman screeches signalled the feasting of vampires upon human soldiers. John had no true plan; he followed de Montfort with a single-mindedness worthy of his headstrong sister, guilt growing within him that he was helping neither Lillian nor his comrades by leaving Scarrowfall. And yet his sense of duty, his desire for vengeance for the ruination of his country, of Apollo Lycea and, above all, the murder of his father, burned hotly in his breast.

Onwards he went, falling behind the two vampires despite his best efforts at stealth and swiftness. The sound of guns became more distant; the cliff curved obtusely around towards the rising sun, so that John was soon able to look back on the black shape of Scarrowfall, flames now licking the great walls, dense smoke filling the air.

The forest of gravestones thinned, giving way to wild thickets of gorse and bramble. John saw ahead a boundary wall, and a large iron gate near the cliff's edge, beside which de Montfort now stopped, gazing across the cove towards the castle. John circled as wide as he could, reaching the wall further inland and creeping along it, keeping in the shadows even though he was quite sure the vampires could see perfectly well in darkness. It made him feel better nevertheless. As he drew nearer, he heard the snorting of horses beyond the gate—a carriage. Was de Montfort stealing away like a thief in the night?

De Montfort was speaking to the hunter, who stood straight and tall like an enormous statue. He gesticulated towards the castle, and John crept closer to eavesdrop.

'Do not be down-hearted, Ezekiel,' de Montfort was saying. 'It is a shame about the prince, though it is of little consequence. After all, what kingdom will the humans have to rule when all is said and done? Though even the Artist could not have foreseen such destruction, it is merely a symbol of rebirth. The old order will be cleansed, and the new shall rise from its ashes. By the time we have finished, there will not be a cabal of elders left who do not pay fealty to us, and give their very life-blood to the cause of progress. Know that your freedom is assured, and that none shall ever suffer as you have. The new seat of kings shall be Montfort Hall. The next time our people celebrate All Hallows, you shall sit by my right hand, and the feasting table shall be filled with new highborns, created from stock of our choosing. We have taken a bold step here, my old friend. We have rejected degeneracy, and embraced the future!'

The hunter made some low, keening sound.

'There, there, Ezekiel. There is nothing good that can come without first paying a price. It is apt that when I visited the

Artist, he recited to me lines from Tennyson's "Locksley Hall". Mayhap he was referring to the end of Scarrowfall. How does it go, now? "Comes a vapour from the margin, blackening over heath and holt; Cramming all the blast before it, in its breast a thunderbolt. Let it fall on Locksley Hall, with rain or hail, or fire or snow—"'

'"For the mighty wind arises, roaring seaward, and I go."'

De Montfort and the hunter spun around as one, as John finished the line for them, stepping from the shadows.

Before John could blink, the hunter had dropped the wooden chest and was within arm's reach, but the vampire had not paid full attention to the weapon in John's hand. The Tesla pistol discharged with a blinding flash of light; the range was so close that John smelt his own hair singeing along with the vampire's dead flesh.

The creature's scream was deafening. It collapsed to the ground in a charred heap, its long black coat in flames as flickers of blue lightning danced across its body.

John had no time to savour his triumph. A fist clubbed him in his cracked ribs so hard he was lifted from his feet. He landed, crumpled and winded, in a tangle of thorny brambles that conspired to keep him from his feet. De Montfort stood above him, the vampire's mask of calm replaced by a bestial snarl.

'Wretch! Muck-snipe! Hairless ape! Ezekiel was the first among my followers; the most gifted and the most promising of all my subjects. You would kill him without a thought, and in doing so remove all hope for his kind? Truly you prove why humans are to be despised.'

The Tesla pistol was lost in the thorns, and John gasped for breath, trying desperately to think of a plan. He felt cold hands upon his throat, lifting him effortlessly from the undergrowth, hard fingers tightening like steel bands. He saw stars. His legs kicked thin air.

'We started this dance in Hyde,' de Montfort said. 'I should have made certain to kill you then. I shall not repeat the mistake.'

John felt himself being carried away; the crimson sky swirled above him, and he searched deep within for some escape, some tactic, or weapon.

With every ounce of resourcefulness he had left, John grabbed the kitchen knife from his belt. He had no time to think; he certainly could not aim his thrust. Instead, he plunged the knife forwards with all of his strength, and felt the blade pierce hard flesh.

The pressure around John's throat was relinquished at once, and he fell to the ground. His head lolled over the edge of the cliff, and for a moment his discombobulation caused him to think he was falling. Everything spun, the rocks below lunged up at him invitingly. With a hoarse gasp, he rolled away from the precipice as fast as he could.

De Montfort was already rising, plucking the knife from between his ribs, growling like a cornered wolf. His eyes gleamed in the growing light, though he squinted against the sliver of sunlight that cut through the flaming sky. John remembered the speculation that sunlight might weaken the vampires, or certainly hurt their eyes. The shadows all about grew thinner by the second; John forced himself to his feet, knowing that de Montfort was at as much of a disadvantage as was possible.

The vampire looked at the knife in disbelief, glared again at John, and advanced.

'That is twice you have cut me,' de Montfort said. 'Let us see how you like it.'

John had nowhere to go—the stone wall blocked his escape on one side, and the precipice on the other. He kept the sun—and the cliff's edge—at his back. He put up a pleading hand, and allowed his pain and tiredness to show, knowing that his vulnerability would encourage the popinjay. Only when the vampire came within striking distance did John pull a snub-nosed pistol from his pocket, firing it before it was even fully levelled. The first bullet struck de Montfort's knee, the second his belly.

De Montfort stumbled forwards, his leg buckling beneath him.

A lesser man would have crumpled, but John reminded himself that this was no man he faced. John pulled the trigger a third time, but de Montfort was already on his feet, and deflected the pistol with a swipe of his hand. He took a swing at John with the knife; even though he was squinting against the rising sun, he still found his mark. John could not parry the blow, and there was nowhere to escape to. He felt the blade cut into his face beneath the eye, slice into cheek and gum, crack into his jawbone. John cried out in abject pain. De Montfort snarled in triumph.

John's agony was so great he could not keep his feet. He crawled on his belly, sensing de Montfort standing over him, and rolled onto his back to face his enemy. De Montfort stooped, the knife aimed at John's throat. The vampire was a silhouette against the sun now, a black shadow of death.

The sun was at his back; the precipice was right behind him...

Digging deep into all of his reserves of fortitude, John kicked out at de Montfort's wounded knee, and fired every bullet he had. All but one flew wide. That one struck de Montfort a glancing blow upon the head, spinning him around. John pushed himself upwards, and delivered a shove into the vampire's back. It was feeble, but it was enough.

De Montfort's shiny shoes slipped upon the rocks, and he pirouetted almost gracefully as he fell from the cliff-top, down towards jagged rocks and foaming sea.

John flopped down upon the edge of the cliff, his body ablaze with agony, muscles numb from exertion. He reached to the chest that the hunter had carried, and clicked open its latch. Within was a king's ransom in gold. John laughed bitterly. Whatever else de Montfort was, he could add thief to the list.

John stared out across the cove as more gunboats arrived, flying the Union Jack. He fancied he would just sit until someone came to find him. He had nothing left to offer Queen and country this day.

'So, brother, you have denied me my revenge.'

John closed his eyes at the sound of Lillian's voice. He did not know whether to be thankful, or whether to curse her timing. A moment's respite was all he wanted.

He turned, astonished to see her dragging Prince Leopold along behind her.

'De Montfort was mine to kill,' she said.

'I think we both had enough cause,' John replied. 'Besides, it was him or me. And as your timing was so bad, I'm rather afraid it had to be him.'

She nodded, and turned to the prince. 'There you go, Your Royal Highness,' she said. 'John has avenged your mother. You should be glad.'

John staggered to his feet, Lillian offering a hand to help him. He looked at her most sternly.

'Do not forget our father so lightly,' he chided.

'What of him?' Lillian asked, and John realised then that she had not heard.

'Oh, dear sister, forgive me. I mistook your ignorance of the matter for coldness.'

'Tell me, John.'

'Father is... he is dead, Lillian. He died in the attack on London, at the Queen's side.'

'I do not believe it,' Lillian said.

'I saw him myself. He is gone. Dear Lillian, I am sorry. When I said I had cause to kill de Montfort, that is what I meant, for he was the engineer of our family's misfortune.'

Lillian bowed her head for a moment. When she looked up, her demeanour had changed. She looked cruel, reptilian almost.

'He was not alone,' she said, her voice like ice.

The next instant, she had thrown Leopold to his knees, and had her garrotte about the prince's throat.

'This is your doing, you pathetic coward,' she cried. 'Your selfishness, your treachery. You gave de Montfort all he needed to destroy the Empire... the world! You do not deserve to live.'

The prince wept. John grabbed his sister's arm.

'Lillian, think what you do! This is a prince of England.'

'He did it intentionally,' she snarled. 'He stood beside the Nameless King, and pledged his allegiance to the Knights Iscariot. It was all a plot, John. A plot that has robbed us of our queen. Of our father.'

John could not take it in. All he knew was that his sister had slipped once more into the guise of callous killer, and in her new form that frightened him more than ever.

'Whatever he has done, he shall answer for it, but not here, not to us!' John said.

'He will live out his days under house arrest,' she snapped, 'or at worst in an asylum. A prince of the realm will not be hanged, not for any crime. Is that justice? He was complicit, brother. Should he not pay the same penalty as de Montfort? A price that you yourself meted out.'

Her words stung, for John had himself abandoned his mission for the chance of revenge. He had not thought it wrong to kill a vampire. But here was Prince Leopold, a human being, threatened by a vampire no less. A vampire who was John's sister, who had earned his loyalty a hundred times over.

He touched her arm again, more gently.

'And I was wrong to do it,' he said. 'I cannot take that back, but I can stop you from making the same mistake. You know that killing Leopold will not be forgiven. It would make you an outcast.'

'I am already an outcast!' she cried. 'Look at me, John.'

'I see my sister!' he shouted back. 'You have been mistreated beyond my imagining, I know that. But you are still the girl I grew up with. I would not have you live the life of a fugitive, or be incarcerated in Cherleten's laboratory. I would have you restored to your station in the Order, to return to your people. I told you that there would come a day when even you cannot stand alone. This is that day, Lily, and I stand with you, as I promised I would. There are those who will look upon you with suspicion, but I am not one of them. Our mother will not be one of them. Do not let her lose a daughter as well as a husband.'

Lillian faltered. John did not know if she was still capable of tears, but she looked for a moment as though she might shed them. Instead, she blinked away her sadness, and put away the garrotte, placing the locket around her neck once more.

'We need to find Smythe,' she said.

'Smythe? But—'

'No arguments, brother. If we do not get you stitched up soon, the ladies of London shall gawp at you even more than they will at me.'

John wanted to smile, but could not. He did not protest when Lillian bade him lean on her, nor when she grabbed the wailing prince by his hair. Together, the three strange companions staggered to the gate, and to de Montfort's carriage, leaving the chest of gold on the cliff's edge.

EXTRACT FROM THE *GAZETTE*
7TH NOVEMBER 1879

In what is believed to be an unprecedented move on the part of the royal family, the heir to the throne, Prince Edward, has deferred his coronation until such time as the state of national emergency has passed. Speaking at an address to the House of Lords yesterday, the prince said: 'What England needs—what the world needs—at this difficult time, is continuity and stability. There is none to whom I would entrust the stewardship of the Crown's fortunes than my father. I hope, my lords, that I may count on you all to wish King Albert a successful reign, for his success will mean victory for us all against the rising tide of darkness.'

EXTRACT FROM THE *ILLUSTRATED LONDON NEWS*
10TH NOVEMBER 1879

WHAT IS THE SHADOW ON THE SKY?

In the wake of the devastation that saw Her Majesty the Queen murdered in a dynamite attack, a plague of madness terrorises London, and a strange phenomenon hangs in the sky about the city. The Prime Minister yesterday called the shadow, 'An as yet unclassified psychical manifestation, linked almost certainly to the death of Catherine Fox, the Queen's royal adviser.' Though he would be pressed no further, leading Majestics and psychical researchers alike have expressed grave concern about what this means, for similar ruptures in the fabric of the world were felt upon the death of her sister Margaret, which spelt the end of the fledgling 'United States'.

The violent tearing of the 'veil', and the resulting deaths of so many Majestics upon the streets has seen entire districts, from Rotherhithe to Dagenham, fall into the Thames, widening the river to almost four miles at its most extreme point. This tragedy only echoes the great catastrophe that befell New York City in '73.

Already, the outpouring of Riftborn across London, visible to even the most unimaginative citizen for the first time since these troubles began, has caused untold suffering. Many loathsome creatures have not yet been banished whence they came, and are said now to stalk the streets and alleys of the notorious *via dolorosas*.

Assistant Commissioner Labalmondière of Scotland Yard yesterday warned citizens to avoid travelling alone, and to stay in their homes after dark until the 'incursion is contained'.

On the great shadow, however, there is little official information. Your correspondent has heard from many who were present at the fateful Awakening seven years ago, who swear that Catherine Fox was several times seen with a 'spirit familiar' draped around her shoulders, that took the form of smoky tendrils. This has led some psychical experts to postulate on the nature of the familiar—was Kate Fox possessed by some Riftborn devil? Was she indeed holding shut the very gates of Hell? And if so, what does this mean for our future now that she is no longer with us? Already, those of means have begun to flee the city, even braving the embattled north of England in a bid to escape the reach of the great black claw.

The newly appointed security adviser to the Crown, Sir Toby Fitzwilliam, has today informed the gathered press that every effort is being taken to bring resolution to this crisis. Majestics are being employed by his agency to dilute the malign influence of the shadow. Until the situation is under control, however, citizens are advised to avoid looking directly at the shadow for prolonged periods. If symptoms of nervous prostration or strong, unnatural urges arise, sufferers must report at once to the alienists of their nearest hospital for their own safety.

TWENTY-FOUR

Wednesday, 12th November 1879
GRAVENEY, NEAR FAVERSHAM, KENT

It had not snowed in the south so early in the year for a long time, but a thick white blanket now greeted Lord Hardwick's funeral procession to All Saints. Marcus Hardwick had been born in the small village of Graveney, the son of a clergyman of moderate means. He had come a long way. His wife had insisted on holding the funeral at her husband's childhood church out of necessity as much as adherence to his wishes. Were it left to Sir Toby Fitzwilliam, Lord Hardwick would have received a state funeral in London. Given that the streets of the capital still played host to a war between men and demons, that was impossible. Only in rural environs, away from the influence of the Rift, did any semblance of peace persist, though it was tenuous, often reliant upon the frail sanity of the populace to hold an incursion at bay.

Lillian had submitted herself voluntarily to Cherleten's custody upon returning to London, and John had not seen her until now. Sir Toby had lobbied for Lillian's reinstatement as a full agent immediately following her father's burial, and Lillian told her brother that she had been treated well.

John and the other pallbearers set down his father's coffin, and he joined Lillian and their mother at the graveside, where they stood in silence while the vicar conducted the service. Lillian had done her best to look like her old self, but there was no mistaking the deathly pallor, the complexion made flawless by potent creams and powders, and the scent of perfume that masked an underlying scent of chemical preservatives. John was one of the few who understood the physical trials of maintaining a human appearance in her condition, and he felt sick for her. He nudged his hand towards her, and felt some comfort when she took it, though he felt the icy coldness of her slender fingers even through his gloves.

'You're growing a beard,' Lillian whispered to him, through a half-smile. 'I'm not sure it suits you.'

He said nothing, but touched at his cheek instinctively, feeling the ridges of his stitches through his emerging beard. The cold made the scar ache dreadfully.

John looked about at what little family the Hardwicks had left, gathered in the snow-covered churchyard. Most in attendance were from the Order, or officers from his father's old regiment. Sir Toby and Lord Cherleten stood on opposite sides of the grave. With Sir Toby was William James, an American scientist and philosopher of some international merit, who had made his name theorising upon the nature of the Rift and its relationship to Majestics. Lord Hardwick had met with him several times. Next to Cherleten stood a man John did not recognise, but whom he had been told was John Keely, the noted engineer who had been so lauded by Tesla.

Lord Hardwick's colleagues in Parliament were mostly absent, locked away in emergency talks in London with the newly crowned King Albert. The King had sent his condolences with his son, Prince Edward, who had temporarily forfeited the Crown. Pressure from certain elite peers—and, of course, Apollo Lycea—had been enough to persuade the other members of the royal family not to cause a fuss. The people, it was said, needed Albert to 'steady the ship'. Marcus Hardwick had filled a position in government that had been created solely for him. As Minister for Defence, he had been promoted amongst the people as the solution to the danger posed by the Riftborn; a saviour. There had been much placed upon his shoulders. His death and his failure were intertwined, and no new minister had yet been named. John rued the lack of loyalty to a man who had given his all for his country; but these were politicians, inconstant allies at the best of times.

The vicar finished speaking, and frosty earth was thrown upon the coffin. The church bell tolled thrice, and one by one the mourners drifted away. High-ranking dignitaries, agents of the Crown and distant cousins alike shook John's hand, gave their condolences to Dora Hardwick, and tried not to gawp at her children, before making their way down the hill to the local inn, where the wake was being held.

As John watched the mourners depart, he noticed Sir Toby engaged in conversation with Prince Edward; the two men looked periodically at him—or perhaps at Lillian—several times, before the prince took his leave. Sir Toby was joined by Keely, James and Cherleten, and looked over at the three Hardwicks. John knew that look; the men were giving John's family some space to grieve, but they expected an audience. Something was amiss.

Dora Hardwick saw it too. She glared at Sir Toby from beneath her veil, and sniffed away a tear. The past weeks had been hard on her.

It was Sir Toby who approached them at last, bowing, and taking Mrs. Hardwick's hands in hers.

'Dora, you have my deepest condolences,' he said. 'I have made arrangements with the innkeeper at the Horseshoes—you and your guests will want for nothing. The Apollonian will settle the bill, naturally.'

'You are too kind, Toby,' she said, 'but all I want is to be left alone with my children. Can that be arranged too?' Her voice was hard. Sir Toby looked remorseful.

'Alas, dear lady, I must trespass upon their time this afternoon, for duty waits for nothing in these dark times.'

'You sound like him,' Dora said, nodding towards the grave. 'It was duty that took him from me—would you have it do the same to my children?'

'I… Dora, if I could exchange places with Lord Hardwick, I would do so in a heartbeat.'

'He would not have had it so!' Dora snapped. 'You were his only friend, Toby. He did not save your life so that you could wish it away. You men are all alike, with your duty and honour. And you have made my daughter like you too. Shame on you, Toby Fitzwilliam, to come here and—'

She stopped when Lillian placed a hand firmly on her shoulder.

'Mother,' she whispered, 'do not fret on our account. The worst is surely behind us, and Father would want us to continue the fight—not for us, but for everyone.'

Dora leaned against Lillian. John stepped up and placed an arm around both of them, realising in a dizzying rush that he was now the eldest Hardwick man; that he was responsible for what was left of their family.

'Will you have need of us terribly long, Sir Toby?' John asked. 'I must insist that we spend some time with our mother before returning to London.'

'I will have you back home in time for dinner,' Sir Toby said. He looked at Dora and added, 'I promise.'

John saw his mother tense. 'Mother, there is nothing to worry about. We have friends staying at the inn, do we not? Make use of the hospitality rather than return to an empty house. We shall come and collect you presently.'

Dora Hardwick sighed resignedly, and kissed both her children on the cheek. If she felt any revulsion towards her daughter's ice-cold skin, or even fully understood what had become of Lillian, she did not show it. John thought his mother was the strongest woman he had ever known; he realised only now that Lillian was not so very unlike her.

John watched her walk through the churchyard with utmost dignity. Then he turned to Sir Toby. 'Now, forgive my bluntness, Sir Toby, but what is so important that it must interrupt my father's funeral?'

'Believe me, Agent Hardwick, every word is true,' Lord Cherleten said.

Lillian looked at the assembled men incredulously. Her brother, who looked somewhat less surprised than she, warmed his hands near a crackling fire, which had been made up in the grand committee room of Faversham's guildhall—Sir Toby had requisitioned perhaps the finest quarters possible for the Order's excursion to the old market town. Club servants had been sent ahead to make everything as homely as could be on such a wintry day. The formality of Apollo Lycea's proceedings was, however, stifling as always.

She had listened to a tale as rambling as it was unbelievable. Her father's trip to the Confederate States of America had apparently ended in him chasing down a fugitive in Alaska, who had ultimately eluded him. That fugitive, Lord Cherleten had stated matter-of-factly, had come from another universe; a world like our own, beyond the veil. The fugitive had been none other than the *doppelgänger*—the very double—of William James himself, displaced between worlds.

'And these… fugitives, or travellers, or whoever they are,' Lillian said, 'pass through the "veil" like demons through the Rift?'

'Exactly so,' said Cherleten. 'We believe—in fact, we know with utmost certainty—that the universe from which the Riftborn come is just one in an infinite number of universes. When our scientists—Dr. James here foremost amongst them—discovered this, we thought for the longest time that the Rift was merely the closest universe to ours, a place veridical to our reality. But that, it appears, is not so.'

'Indeed not,' said James. 'It is the most violent plane in

proximity to our own, and bears similar laws of etheric resonance, certainly, but the *closest* is, I believe, the mirror-world. A world so like our own, but for a few quirks of historical fact, that its denizens are almost our exact doubles in form and deed. And because of its proximity, it is relatively safe to travel to, if only we could perfect the process.'

'Perfect it? So you have already tried?' Lillian could barely hide the derision in her voice. She had listened to these insane theories for almost two hours already, and her patience grew thin.

'Several times, over the course of two years,' he replied, ignoring her tone.

'Agent Hardwick,' Sir Toby interjected, 'this is a lot to digest in a single sitting, but I expect nothing but professionalism from my agents. Given everything you yourself have been through these past few weeks, I would assume a little more open-mindedness on your part.'

It was unlike Sir Toby to scold her; that in itself made her pay heed.

'It's true, sis,' John said, not turning away from the fire. 'I… overheard a few things I oughtn't have, some months ago. Father admitted as much when I asked him, but swore me to secrecy. This was his "great work", he said.' John sounded rueful.

Lillian thought of the letter her father had written her while she was in a hospital bed beneath St. Katharine Docks, and which she still carried with her. He had spoken of his so-called great work there too. She took a deep breath—even now, even in her condition, the thought of that letter still brought feelings of sadness and bitterness into her heart. She savoured them.

'I apologise, sir,' she said to Sir Toby. 'Please… go on.'

'There is a man in the mirror-world,' Sir Toby said, sloshing his brandy gently around the glass and staring thoughtfully into the liquid. 'That he has the qualities, skills and experience to complete your father's work is beyond doubt. His circumstances make him ripe for defection to our cause; it would take work, but we believe he would join us willingly. Additionally, we believe that, should he be thrust onto the public stage in our world, the general populace would take heart. His very presence would restore hope.'

'Why would it? Who is this man?' Lillian asked.

Sir Toby gave her the queerest look, half-sad, she thought. Then he said, gravely, 'In their world he is called Brigadier Sir Marcus Hardwick.'

Lillian stared at Sir Toby, open-mouthed.

'Our father... lives?' Lillian knew the answer before she had asked the question, and felt very stupid. Sir Toby looked at her not unkindly.

'No. And yet...' Sir Toby hesitated. 'Your father's double is exactly that; almost everything that happened to him before the Awakening also happened to the man we knew. The Awakening never occurred in the mirror-world, and thus events took a rather less esoteric turn. There is but one notable difference in his life, as far as our spies can tell, and it is that difference that we shall use. Exploit, if you will.'

'Which is?'

'You, Agent Hardwick. In their world, Lillian Hardwick did not survive the bout of pneumonia she suffered in childhood. Sir Marcus Hardwick was a changed man thereafter, never fully recovering from the loss of his daughter. It is the promise of a reunion with you that may well tip the scales in our favour.'

There was silence. Lillian looked at her brother, who had turned almost as pale as she.

'You wish me to... cross over. To visit this mirror-world?' Lillian asked at last.

Sir Toby nodded. 'It will be difficult at first, but our people have managed very short visits already. Dr. Keely believes that he may soon develop the means for longer trips to their side, with the help of Mr. Tesla.'

'How long?'

'Oh, weeks perhaps, even—'

'No,' Lillian interrupted. 'I mean, how long have we been

sending people to this other... universe?'

'Ah,' Sir Toby said.

'If I may, Sir Toby?' Dr. James interjected. 'Agent Hardwick, you stand upon the cusp of something far greater than any one of us. We few here represent a goodly portion of the inner circle of Apollo Lycea, the epicentre of the world's secrets. Secrets so powerful they would destroy nations, cause untold panic, cause—or, indeed, end—wars. Knowledge of the mirror-world is restricted to perhaps twenty people. We would keep it that way.

'You ask how long we have been able to travel between worlds? The answer is not long at all. In fact, until my own double appeared in Alaska, we were not sure it was possible to pass through rifts for anything longer than a few minutes. Even then it proved... hazardous, to say the least. We had observed the other world through those self-same rifts, but it was my doppelgänger's journey here that proved the breakthrough we needed. Using the readings we took while he was in our world, we managed to improve our apparatus exponentially. Now we can cross back and forth for a limited time, rather than make mere opportunistic reaches into the dark. Of course, we need Mr. Tesla to improve our equipment, and Lord Cherleten to provide the services of the Nightwatch. That is to say—'

'Etherium,' John said. Everyone turned to him. Lillian frowned. 'Or rather, mundane etherium. The rumours are true, aren't they?'

James faded, his enthusiasm checked by an evidently unwelcome question.

Cherleten smiled thinly. 'Yes. In the mirror-world, psychic phenomena are virtually unknown. The scientific applications of compounds from their world are staggering; they render demons inert, and offer some small respite to our Majestics.'

'By compounds, he means people. We've been snatching people from this mirror-world. That's the main reason we've braved the hazards, I suppose.' Lillian felt John's moral objections keenly—it was not like him to speak out of turn. He was different, somehow. He seemed older; more assured. Less subservient to the leaders of the Order. Lillian liked this new John.

'It is a rather unsavoury, but necessary, operation,' Sir Toby said. 'We go to great pains to take only those few souls who will not be missed. The destitute, the criminal, the insane. When a window of opportunity rises, we lure them to our universe, and conduct our procedures—humanely, of course.'

'What is mundane etherium? What are you saying?' Lillian asked.

'It is a distillation of fluid from the pineal gland,' Cherleten answered, with no hint of the remorse and gravity shown by Sir Toby. 'In our Majestics, that fluid is etherium, one of the most powerful drugs in the world. From the mirror-people, the fluid has astonishing properties, and is able to nullify anomalous rift activity.'

'You... take people from the other world, and extract fluid from their brains?'

'It sounds awfully crass when you put it like that,' said Cherleten. 'But yes, in essence.'

'And yet we judge the vampires so harshly for their blood-drinking and murder!' Lillian said. 'This... other... Marcus Hardwick would surely not defect eagerly to a world where such cruelty is propagated in the name of the Crown. If so, what kind of man is he?'

'The same kind of man as your father,' said Cherleten. 'Lord Hardwick pioneered these techniques. You will no doubt find that his double is not so very different when the safety of the world depends upon him. Or when faced with the apparent resurrection of his daughter—a daughter who, I might add, cannot die. In this world, he will never have to suffer the pain of outliving you again. Our intelligence shows that this alone will be enticement enough.'

'And our mother?' John asked. 'Is there a double of her? Will the brigadier leave her readily?'

'Dead,' said Cherleten. 'Death by misadventure—there are rumours that she never recovered from the loss of her daughter and killed herself.'

'Delicacy, Cherleten!' Sir Toby snapped, doubtless seeing the dark cloud that had spread over John's expression. Cherleten only shrugged.

'And John? Does he have a double, too?' Lillian asked. John's eyes cast downwards at this.

'He does,' Sir Toby said gently, taking the reins from Cherleten. 'We would have asked Lieutenant Hardwick to take part in this mission more directly, to pose as his own self, so to speak, but for two complications. Firstly, the lieutenant's recent scar is almost impossible to conceal, even for our finest doctors. Secondly, in the mirror-world, father and son are somewhat... estranged.'

'How so?' Lillian asked.

'It seems that, following the death of his sister, the other John Hardwick's life took a very different turn from ours. He became a lonesome boy, a dreamer, a poet, by all accounts. We believe the good lieutenant here is the son the brigadier wishes to have. We shall have to tread carefully, but it is another bargaining tool at our disposal.'

Lillian wondered whether John would have been sent in her stead were it not for such complications. It would certainly be a safer option than sending her—a vampire—on such an important assignment. She did not voice her concerns.

'There is something rather... unbecoming... about this,' John said.

'Oh, I agree,' said Cherleten, with his customary ghoulishness so far removed from the piteous figure he had become during the London attacks. 'But it is a necessary evil. Their world is not in danger from the very demons of hell, while ours is on the precipice of destruction. If you have the opportunity to visit the mirror-world, and I daresay you shall, you will notice that the great cities of London and New York are intact, and have not slid into the bloody sea! Ask yourself, Lieutenant: if this was not the Hardwick family we were discussing, would you hesitate?'

John glowered. 'And in the mirror-world, are there no agencies like ours? Agencies who would not take kindly to the defection of their people, or the infiltration of their world?'

Cherleten smiled deviously. 'That's the rub, isn't it? Of course there are, Lieutenant, which is why we are handling matters rather than trusting to the army or the government. Have no doubt—if we are discovered, there will be war between our worlds.'

'I rather think our father would approve of that,' John grumbled.

'And you, Agent Hardwick,' Cherleten addressed Lillian now. 'You are well disposed to logic rather than sentimentality, are you not? What say you?'

Lillian did not appreciate another reminder that she was for ever changed, though it was true. She felt little of John's anger or sadness. If anything, she only felt incredulous at the whole affair. It seemed to her more likely that the opening of the Rift had driven Sir Toby and Lord Cherleten stark raving mad, as it had done to so many folk on the streets of London. She thought on this and more, before finally making her decision.

'I say I rather want to see this mirror-world for myself. And if it is real—if our father exists there—then I shall endeavour to do my duty to the utmost of my ability.'

Sir Toby looked grave. Cherleten beamed, and strode over to Lillian, placing a hand on her shoulder.

'Now you are your father's daughter!' he exclaimed. 'Sir Toby, I think we have our recruits.'

Sir Toby nodded grimly. He did not seem happy about the situation at all; but then, he rarely seemed happy in Lillian's recollection.

'For the foreseeable future,' Sir Toby said, 'you must forget about the vampires, and the Riftborn. By the time our work is complete, you will travel beyond the veil into the mirror-world. Once there, you must find Brigadier Sir Marcus Hardwick, and bring him back. We shall proclaim his recovery as a miracle, a genuine work of God set to restore hope and defeat the dark threat that even now overwhelms us. You shall speak of this plan to no one, not even your dear mother. Even in private, you shall refer to this assignment only as Project Lazarus, am I understood? For that is what you about to do—you are about to bring a man back from the dead. The people need a leader, a saviour, and though the dangers ahead are undeniable, they shall have one.'

'When do we begin?' Lillian asked coolly.

'Go to your mother and spend time in the embrace of family. There will be little enough time for that when the assignment starts. But I shall have you report to Lord Cherleten on Friday morning. Both of you.' He looked at John. 'You have a part to play also, Lieutenant Hardwick.'

'Do not look perturbed, agents,' Cherleten said with a chuckle. 'The battle to save our world begins here.'

Lillian scanned her father's letter yet again, willing herself to feel something—anything. It seemed to her that reading those lines, written from the heart as they were, while standing in her old childhood home, should do the trick. Yet her heart was cold, and the fire that crackled in the grate offered no warmth.

'There's a young gentleman here to see you.' Dora Hardwick smiled for the first time in many a day, and from that expression Lillian guessed her mother approved of the mysterious caller.

'What?' Lillian said, placing the letter on the mantelpiece hurriedly.

'I'll show him in.'

Without further explanation, and with no time for protest, Dora left the cosy drawing room of their Faversham cottage, and a few moments later the unusually humble figure of Beauchamp Smythe entered, stooping beneath the low doorframe.

Lillian stood with her back to the fireplace, trying hard to remember the coaching John had given her over the past day— to be more genial, to smile pleasantly, to understand that people were trying to empathise, and she should repay the kindness. It was getting harder to understand the human feeling that had often eluded her even before her transformation. With Smythe, especially, whom she had always found so tiresome, she prepared herself for an act worthy of the stage.

'Agent Smythe, so good of you to call,' she said.

'Please, Li— Miss Hardwick, might you call me Beauchamp today? Or at least Mr. Smythe? This is not a business call.'

'Of course, Mr. Smythe. Won't you sit down?'

'Actually I... I prefer to stand.'

Lillian could see that Smythe was agitated. Given the circumstances, it might have been for any number of reasons. She remained standing as Smythe shifted uncomfortably.

'Might I send for some tea?'

'Yes... no. No, thank you,' he said. And then added hurriedly, 'Unless you want tea?' Even as he said it, he reddened. 'No, of course you don't, I was not thinking, I mean...'

'Mr. Smythe?'

'Yes?'

'What can I do for you?'

Smythe took a breath, visibly collecting himself. 'Miss Hardwick—Lillian,' he added firmly, 'I called first of all to offer my sincere condolences. We have not seen overmuch of each other since your father—since Lord Hardwick... passed away. I fear that we have both been preoccupied with business at the club, and I do not want you to think ill of me as... as a friend.'

'I do not think of you... so,' Lillian said, inwardly wincing as she narrowly avoided making a cruel jest at Smythe's expense. Her wicked streak, as John had reminded her only that day, had not died with the rest of her emotions.

'Good, good,' Smythe blustered, ignoring any veiled slight. 'Is it warm in here?'

'I would not know.'

'No, of course. I've rather put my foot in it again, haven't I?'

Lillian said nothing, but smiled what she hoped was a forgiving and encouraging smile.

'Lillian,' he blurted, 'I know the timing is rotten, I really do, but with all that is to come I think there won't be much opportunity for us to talk like this. I must say something.'

'Mr. Smythe—'

'No, please Lillian, hear me out. I know we haven't always seen eye to eye, but damn it, you must know how I feel about you. And until your... accident I did not know if you returned those feelings or not. I still don't, but I cannot leave it unsaid any longer.'

Lillian was not sure how she would have reacted to the imminent proposition even before her 'accident', but she was certain her disposition towards it now was unfavourable. She was surprised at the fluttering sensation in the pit of her stomach, the tightening of her forehead, the dryness of mouth. And she realised Smythe was still talking, but she was not thinking of him at all, but of another.

'—And so, Lillian, dear Lillian, even after everything, know that my feelings have not changed. I love you. I do not care what change has befallen you, or what changes may yet come—and by God I understand them more than most. I would step out with you, Lillian, and care for you for as long as—'

'As long as you live?' Lillian said. She felt *something* stir within, certainly: bitterness, regret, loathing, of herself as well as her circumstances. She did not want to be cruel, but it was habitual. 'And how long, pray, would that be, Mr. Smythe? Would you grow old and wizened by my side, whilst using your potions to keep me young and beautiful? Would you feed me with your own blood, making me stronger as you grow feeble and wrinkled? Or would you first die in the field like... like...'

She could not finish. She felt moisture upon her cheek, though she had not thought it possible any longer. She was consumed by the abrupt recrudescence of emotion. Her thoughts were not of Smythe's proposal, but rather of one man. The memory of her lost love—and the manner of that loss—came upon her suddenly, and powerfully.

'Like Sir Arthur Furnival,' Smythe said quietly, almost reading her mind. He looked crestfallen.

'We live dangerous lives, Mr. Smythe,' she said, sniffing away the tears and hardening herself. 'I buried my father yesterday. I lost a dear friend in Sir Arthur. My next assignment, as you have clearly heard, will take up all of my time for goodness knows how long. And my "condition", as everyone insists on calling it, makes it hard for me to even entertain thoughts of any… romantic entanglement. I fear, Beauchamp, that your affection for me is wholly misplaced. If I ever gave you encouragement in this matter, I apologise unreservedly. If circumstances were different, who could say what might have happened? But things are what they are—I do not love you, and do not believe myself capable of love. I am naught but death, Mr. Smythe. That is the fact of the matter.'

'Lillian… I cannot feign magnanimity. I wish I were a stronger fellow, but I do not know how I can live knowing…' He stopped, flushing.

'You will have to, Beauchamp, as I have to. The Order needs us both. I need you, but as a friend and a surgeon, not as a husband. The world is on the brink of ending—there is more at stake than our individual happiness.'

'Then it seems we shall be miserable apart, rather than happy together. Though I hope—I dearly do—that you will not be unhappy for ever. I am truly sorry to have caused you any distress.'

'On the contrary, Mr. Smythe, you have made me feel something far beyond anger or hate, for the first time since the Iscariot Sanction. For that, I thank you.'

Smythe considered that. 'One day, Lillian, perhaps I shall make you feel something other than sadness. Though it pains me to part in this way, know that I will always be your friend. Always.'

Smythe stepped forward and took Lillian's hand, squeezing it tight. She offered him a smile, and he leaned forward presumptuously and kissed her lightly on the cheek, recoiling perhaps a little too quickly as the coldness of her skin and the smell of chemical compounds reminded him exactly what she was. He tried not to let the discomfort show, but Lillian hoped the realisation would help him to accept the rebuttal more easily.

With one last, weak smile, Smythe backed out of the room,

and a moment later Lillian heard the front door close, and saw from the window Beauchamp Smythe trudging down the garden path in the thick snow. She turned back to the letter on the mantelpiece, and read yet again her father's heartfelt missive.

Thinking you lost to pneumonia was the greatest test of my life. I did everything in my power to save you, but I could not. In the end the means of your salvation were the same as the cause of your condition. You were too headstrong and determined, too bull-headed to listen to me or your mother or your brother, and far too stubborn to die. Your mother has, many times over the years, told me that you are very much your father's daughter, and that your similarities to me would be the death of you. Perhaps they will be. Perhaps they already are.

I could not save you when you were a little girl, Lillian. You saved yourself. I could not save you this time either, when you were put into harm's way by the greatest evil we have ever known. For all my power, I must live with the fact that I have twice failed my little girl when she needed me the most. I can only hope, then, that you understand what I must now do.

I failed you, Lily, but I will not fail this world. I swear it. You may not understand, not yet, but I go now to complete my great work. I shall again be the absent father that you have grown to resent, and, by God, how I regret what I have become in your eyes. How I regret all the things that I was too stubborn and too cowardly to say to you. But this time, with the help of Mr. Tesla, whom you brought safely to London, I shall create the engine of our salvation. The Hardwick Gate shall be my legacy to the world and, I hope, the means of our reconciliation.

With eternal fondness,
Your Father

EPILOGUE

Nine months later: 22nd August 1880

AFGHANISTAN, THE MIRROR-WORLD

The trek from the camp had been more arduous than Brigadier Sir Marcus Hardwick had expected, but the message had been clear. He could not be late. He had been lucky to avoid any awkward confrontations with his own sentries, although now, four miles from the British camp near Kandahar, it was hill-bandits he would have to be more wary of.

He clambered over the detritus of a thousand years, over uneven scrub and massive stones that had once formed great Indo-Greek temples to Buddha. Now they were nothing but ruins, sundered long ago in one of many long-forgotten wars.

The brigadier stumbled over the rocky ground. He had found his way at first by moonlight, for in enemy country he could not risk a lantern. After much toil across difficult ground, with a chill wind against him, the object of his covert hike finally came into view as the sun began to rise. The brigadier squinted against the glowing rind of light that crested the hill ahead. Broken stairs of sandstone led up a steep hill, atop which a great black archway loomed against the yellowing sky. The walls about the arch were long-toppled by the conquerors of what was once called 'Alexandria', and now only headless statues stood witness to this long-abandoned holy site.

The brigadier did not think of himself as old, but neither was he a young man, and he felt age upon him acutely as he rested an arm against the rough stone, his breathing ragged and his limbs burning. It had been many a year since he had had to march double-time across rough terrain, and four miles was enough for him. He would have to work hard in the months to come if he were to endure the toil of his mission, both physical and mental. He did not relish the walk back, but he would have to be in his tent before the morning roll-call, or even he would have to answer questions he would rather went unasked.

'Turn around.' The girl's voice was light, but firm. English, well-spoken. He knew it at once, and obeyed.

'You came,' he said, and felt rather stupid for it.

'Of course. This matter is too important to entrust to another. I had to do this in person.'

'Thank you,' the brigadier said, the words sticking in his throat.

'I do not have much time,' the woman said. 'Everything is set. The battle will begin a week from now, if all goes according to plan. You must steel yourself, for the losses will be heavy.'

'I have made my peace with that,' the brigadier said.

'Good. During the battle you will be wounded—a shot to the leg should suffice, as long as there is plenty of blood to go around. Do not put yourself in needless danger, you understand?'

'Of course, I shall take care of it myself.'

'Timing is everything. When you are returned to the camp, our agents will be on hand to explain away your sudden demise. A ruptured artery, shock, fever, that sort of thing. The details are written in this book, in the standard code.'

A small, leather-bound notebook was passed over his shoulder. He took it, brushing cold fingers as he did so. He flipped through the pages to find row upon row of neat, Burmese characters.

Satisfied, he placed it in his breast pocket.

'The exchange will be made that very night,' the woman went on. 'Our people will get you aboard a ship to London, and once there you will meet our... broker. He will ensure you are hidden, and that you cross safely to our side.'

'I still don't understand why I have to return to England,' the brigadier protested.

'The journey is not safe on our side. That is one of the reasons that we need you. John and I.'

Sir Marcus Hardwick trembled. 'And... Dora.'

'In time. But she is well. You will see her, soon enough. Now, I must warn you—this broker is not to be trusted. He calls himself the Artist, though his real name is Tsun Pen. If there were any other option, we would take it, but our list of allies is thin. You will meet him at his business premises on the Isle of Dogs, and await further instructions. Under no circumstances give him your name.'

'No, of course. Lazarus.'

'Indeed. From the moment your death is certified, you will be only Lazarus, until you reach us safely. I wish you Godspeed on your journey... Father.'

'Please, let me see you,' the brigadier said.

There was silence for a moment, and then: 'Turn around.'

He obeyed. There, standing in the great archway, with the sun blood red behind her, was Lillian. His darling Lily, now a grown woman. She wore a severe, high-collared black dress, a hat with a veil, and stood beneath a small black parasol. Her face gleamed pale white even from beneath the veil, and when she pulled it away Sir Marcus was taken aback by her beauty. There was no mistaking his own flesh and blood; this was the daughter he had lost, now returned to him through a miracle. The God he had renounced long ago had not forsaken him.

He reached out to touch her face, but she took his hand away, gently, and smiled at him.

'There is not much time, Father, for either of us. Are you

confident you can complete this mission?'

'I am. Nothing will stand in the way, my dear, sweet girl.'

'Then you must go and prepare for the battle. I shall return to my people, and we will meet again on the other side.'

Sir Marcus at once began the descent from the hilltop ruins. A low droning sound struck up behind him, increasing in pitch and intensity. Before he had even reached the bottom of the slope, the sound had become a shrill whistle. He heard a great crackle and fizz of electrical power, the light from which stripped away the long shadows in front of him, and then the noise stopped, the light was gone, and all was still.

Marcus Hardwick took one last look over his shoulder at the dark archway. The woman was gone. When next he saw her, he would be embarking upon the greatest work of his life.

ACKNOWLEDGEMENTS

Thanks go out to my harshest critics and most valuable alpha readers: my lovely wife Alison, my agent Jamie Cowen, and my good friend Mat Ward. This book is better for your input.

An extra thanks to Vadim Kadyrov, a Russian translator who was kind enough to help me with my linguistic pursuits. Social media can be a wonderful thing!

Oh, and for those dear readers who are wondering what happened to the Captain John Hardwick in our own universe. Fear not.

John Hardwick shall return...

ABOUT THE AUTHOR

Mark A. Latham is a writer, editor, history nerd, frustrated grunge singer and amateur baker from Staffordshire, UK. A recent immigrant to rural Nottinghamshire, he lives in a very old house (sadly not haunted), and is still regarded in the village as a foreigner.

Formerly the editor of Games Workshop's *White Dwarf* magazine, Mark dabbled in tabletop games design before becoming a full-time author of strange, fantastical and macabre tales, mostly set in the nineteenth century, a period for which his obsession knows no bounds. He is the author of *The Lazarus Gate*, published by Titan Books.

Follow Mark on Twitter: @aLostVictorian